Altered Creatures Epic Fantasy Adventures
Book 2 of the Thorik Dain Series

Sacrifice of Ericc

Historical Date 4.0650.0410
(4th Age, 650th Year, 4th Month, 10th Day)

Copyright © 2009 by Anthony G. Wedgeworth

Published by Anthony G. Wedgeworth

Artwork by Frederick L. Wedgeworth

ISBN: 978-0-9859159-3-3

Library of Congress Control Number: 2009900346

**Altered Creatures Epic Fantasy Adventures
Historical Date 4.0650.0410
Thorik Dain Series
Book 2, Revision 1.2
Sacrifice of Ericc**
www.AlteredCreatures.com

Printed in the United States of America

No thrashers or Chuttlebeast were harmed in the making of this book.

Dedication:

For everyone, young and old,
who still finds time to read a book
in an age of electronic communications

Acknowledgments:

Everyone who took the time to read my manuscript and help me
work out the details and issues. These include JoAnn Cegon,
Alexander Wedgeworth, Tami Wedgeworth, Jonathan O'Brien,
Pat Mulhern, Josh Crawford, Fred Waiss,
freelance journalist Lyle Ernst,
and my dear friend and business mentor Dennis Shurson.

**Altered Creatures Epic Adventures
continues with the following books:**

**Nums of Shoreview Series
(Pre-teen, Ages 7 to 12)**
Stolen Orb
Unfair Trade
Slave Trade
Baka's Curse
Haunted Secrets
Rodent Buttes

**Thorik Dain Series
(Young Adult and Adult)**
Fate of Thorik
Sacrifice of Ericc
Essence of Gluic
Rise of Rummon
Prey of Ambrosius
Plea of Avanda

Sacrifice of Ericc

by

Anthony G. Wedgeworth

Prologue

Thorik's Log: April 9th of the 650th year.

After months of being stranded on an island after our boat crashed, we have been rescued by a captain of a seaworthy vessel. And yet I sit here on my seventeenth birthday filled with remorse over the death of my friend Ambrosius. But with the captain's commitment to help find Ericc, I plan to tell Ambrosius' heir of his father's fate in an effort to prevent the boy from succumbing to the same end. The prophecy of his sacrifice on June 21st must be avoided, for he is the last E'rudite who can stand up against Darkmere.

Chapter 1

The Prophecy

"Your survival leads to my death," Lord Bredgin said as he cautiously approached Ericc. "I am here to reverse this dilemma and pen a new future in your stead."

Colors faded to gray shadows as the young lord muted the spectrum of light to his liking of shades of black. Light and darkness carried great power, which affected all living things. Light provided life as well as heat when focused intensely. Dark provided coolness, and if used properly it wielded death.

Ericc shuffled his feet backward, staying just outside of the grayness which loomed around Lord Bredgin. "Who are you?" Ericc demanded as his foot felt the icy cold of the impending shadow. Refusing to turn and run, the teenage boy defied the stranger's threats while keeping a safe distance.

"I am the one foretold to fall from the strike of your blade." A shadowy sphere extended from Bredgin's body, as his presence muted light and colors several yards in every direction. Flowers wilted and clay pots cracked as he followed Ericc down the street in the center of town, in the middle of the day. People who failed to heed the ominous warning screamed from the pain given once they fell within his vicinity.

Southwind locals ran from the cloud of darkness, after witnessing the life-sucking effect on those who had accidentally strayed into its path.

Ericc refused to turn his back to the young bald man, for it was best to keep him within his sights. "I have no quarrel with you. Why would I strike you down, aside from defending myself from your hostile actions?"

"It's not a matter of why. It's a matter of when, which haunts my days. Ever since I was a child, my father has been training me to prevent you from ending my life. For years I have searched for you in an effort to end this curse against me. Today is the day I have long awaited to change the future."

Ericc turned down an alley to protect the residents from the man's wrath, as the young lord left the main street to follow.

The red brick walls turned black and the mortar cracked and crumbled as Bredgin smoothly entered the back alley. Screams from the far side of the walls could be heard as the darkness penetrated the interior of the buildings.

"Why are you doing this?" Ericc asked as he listened to the painful cries for help. "How can you possibly convict me of a crime I have yet to even consider performing?"

"Don't play this game with me," Bredgin shouted. "You have the powers of the E'rudite. You are the son of the eldest twin, of the brothers of war." He followed Ericc out of the alley and into a stable. "You are the one talked about by the oracles. Two paths lay before you, one reveals your murder of me, and the other involves your sacrifice at Surod. I have chosen the latter one."

Darkness rushed from Lord Bredgin toward Ericc in an attack to incapacitate him.

Ericc jumped out of the way, rolling into one of the animal stalls for safety.

The animals howled in pain as their bodies took the full load of the absence of light. More than just darkness, it drained the living flesh and dried up their bones while consuming all warmth from their body.

Ericc watched as the tan hay on the floor took on a sour gray. Pushing his back up against the far corner, he watched the darkness increase with each loud step of his attacker. Wooden floorboards seem to age decades before his eyes, and ropes lost their strength, dropping tools and a lantern onto the floor. The sound was even distant as the darkness subdued all aspects in its evasive assault.

Lord Bredgin reached the stall and prepared his final attack on his trapped victim, only to find the stall empty with no options for Ericc's escape. And yet he had done just that.

Furious, Lord Bredgin yelled with rage, extending his grayness over two city blocks, without care of whom or what he decimated.

Chapter 2
High Seas

The fury of the storm brought pain to all in its wake and would continue to do so until its own demise. No army could attack it, no fortress could defend against it, and no creature could outrun it. It was the lord of all storms with an unforgiving hand of pain and death. It reached out to smite all in its path.

Waves struck the side of a ship, forcing it to lean steeply, as thunder roared from flashes of lightning striking the water nearby. It was a sturdy caravel vessel, but it was too far out to sea to make port and too slow to outrun the giant swells.

A crew of over twenty members fought to save the ship, Sinecure. Sails had been tied down and goods had been stored. But this was not accomplished at the competency of the ship-hands, for they were still green to the ways of the water.

It was the fiery captain who commanded critical life-saving orders. The Sinecure, its crew, and its passengers were all dependent on his abilities as he played a deadly game against the storm and sea.

It wasn't the first time he had saved these passengers. Stranded on one of the small Palm Islands for months, they were fortunate that he had spotted them. Then again, if the ship were hit any harder on the starboard side, their rescue may turn out to be their undoing. The captain had to turn the ship's bow into the waves before they capsized.

Avanda flung open the door and ran out onto the deck. The young lady's hair whipped at her face as the wind drove the rain hard against her. "Ralph? Ralph?" she continued to yell, as the busy crew ignored her.

"Ralph?" The captain asked as he fought to steer the ship. "Who's Ralph?"

Thorik Dain stood near the captain, carrying out his orders and relaying them to his crew. "Avanda's lizard that she found on the island."

"Damn be it for the Fesh, get her below before she's washed overboard," the captain ordered.

Thorik left the captain's side and made his way down the steps to the main deck. He waited for a flash of lightning to see where she had gone. But when it struck, she was no longer where he had last seen her. Instead she was on the Sinecure's bow, reaching for the pole which hung over the front of the ship.

The thunderstorm released its worst at them. Lighting struck the water near enough to the ship to hear it at the same time it was seen, vibrating the ship with its mighty force.

Avanda climbed out onto the ship's bowsprit as the waves lashed out and pounding rain drove hard into her back. As if holding onto the ship's front pole wasn't hard enough, her legs kept getting wrapped up in the lowered forestay sails. One wrong move, tall wave, or strong gust of wind could easily knock her off the horizontal pole and send her to a watery grave. In spite of the severe danger, she continued to climb toward the end.

Ralph had climbed out onto the bowsprit. It was normally a safe location for him, out from under the crew's feet as he so often basked in the sun's warmth. It was now the most dangerous place the lizard could be as he clung for his life.

Defensive instincts kicked in, causing Ralph to spit out a gob of saliva onto the pole between him and Avanda. Even with the pole saturated with water, the deadly acid in the lizard's spit began to sizzle away, eating through the wood.

"Avanda, come back!" Thorik yelled as he reached the front of the ship.

"Not without Ralph." She yelled back over the noise of the howling wind and crashing waves.

Thorik reached out and grabbed her ankle. "He's not worth your life."

She attempted to scoot farther out, as her legs wrapped around the bowsprit. Laying her stomach on the pole, she pulled with her hands and pushed with her feet. "I took him from his island, so I'm responsible for him now."

Thorik pulled her back toward him. "He's only a lizard!"

"He's part of our family!"

In the pitch black of night, the captain turned the wheel hard, viewing what he could when lightning allowed. It was a small window of time to determine what was playing out. How far he had turned the ship and where was the next swell rising?

Both questions were answered as lighting struck the crest of a towering wave as it approached. Illuminating the wave from within, it was clear that they would not survive.

Avanda and Thorik saw the wave light up as well, just as the bowsprit broke off right in front of Avanda. The lizard's acid attack on the pole had chewed its way through, and now it swung wildly in the air, hanging from the lines that connected it to the fore mast.

Ralph clung tightly as the pole spun out of control, dangling over the water.

The ship began its climb up the swell, leaning back as the bow lifted into the air.

The bowsprit swung backward, nearly swatting Thorik and Avanda off the ship. Ralph leaped off the bowsprit and onto Avanda's head, just as Thorik pulled her back onto the ship's forecastle deck. Tumbling to the fore mast, they both watched the wave prepare to bear down on them.

"Hold on!" the captain shouted to his crew, knowing full well that the ship had little chance against such a wave.

Ralph scurried into one of Avanda's pouches while Thorik held onto her with one arm and a secured rope with the other.

Always on the offensive, Avanda grabbed for her purse of magic. Pulling out a handful of small crystals, she broke free from Thorik and dove for the deck's railing, throwing them overboard and shouting words to activate her spell.

The crystals hit the water and instantly turned it to ice. Spreading fast, a magical iceberg grew beneath it, lifting the ship.

Water crashed from above as the top of the wave struck the ship. But instead of going through the wave and drowning, the ice had lifted them up and over.

Avanda jumped away from the railing and back into Thorik's arms. "It worked this time!" she yelled.

The swell broke off chunks of the iceberg and turned them into flying debris, hurling them back toward the ship. Large ice fragments pelted the men on deck, knocking several off.

One large shard pierced the hull and crashed into the upper deck's bulkhead. Water spilled in from the wave as the crew tried to board it up and bail out the water.

"I'm not sure your magic made things any better." Thorik held her tight, protecting her from the storm's wrath.

But it had helped. The iceberg had grown large enough to allow them to ride out the storm. Nevertheless, they were unable to steer the vessel and were now completely at the mercy of the waves.

Chapter 3
Southwind

Thorik's Log: April 15th of the 650th year.

In spite of our needed ship repairs, we traveled up the Stained River and docked at Rava'Kor, where Captain Mensley has heard word of Ericc's capture. I leave my Runestones and logs of our trip here on the ship, for this may be my last opportunity to see them. The risk I take to find Ericc leads me into the city as well as into its prison.

Thorik sat by himself looking into his mug of ale feeling sorry for himself. Months earlier he had watched his friend's death, whose last images of suffering were etched into Thorik's memories forever. "Save my son," was Ambrosius' last request before Thorik had condemned him to his final demise.

Thorik's short Polenum body and soft facial features were hidden by the shadows of the pub. The evening sun was setting and only a few lanterns had been lit. Humans roamed the broken down structure while cats chased rodents in and out of openings in the walls.

The city of Rava'Kor had been destroyed by a series of major storms, including the latest one that nearly took the life of everyone on Captain Mensley's ship. Most buildings lay flat, or at best leaned to one side. The pub stayed standing due to pure luck, although it looked as if it could collapse at any time. Flying debris had punctured holes in the structure and hot humid air of the surrounding tropical forest saturated everything. Even Thorik's mug was clammy to the touch.

Calls from tropical birds and monkeys could be heard in the distance, while local insects and frogs had ventured into the broken city to make their presence known. The city had evolved within the forest over a period of many years. However the hot and humid climate and thick vegetation still remained in control of these parts.

The city reminded Thorik of himself; tired and depressed. He took another sip of the drink he had been nursing for over an hour.

"Thorik!" Avanda shouted as she noticed him through an opening in the wall, close to where he sat. The youthful Num sprinted around the outside of the pub before entering through an area that once held a large window. Her long straight hair was dirty but still showed hints of flowery colors.

Three thick lines of darker skin interlaced around her neck and wrists. A similar pattern coiled up from the top of her feet, around her ankles and up her calves before the three lines separated and continued their spiral up her legs.

All Polenums had these dark lines, except for her friend and former teacher, Thorik. The markings changed slightly as the Polenums grew older, becoming more detailed or bold, or flourishing in length and pattern.

This was the case of Avanda. She had matured quickly since they had left their hometown of Farbank. Her markings had grown in length on her legs and two dark paths had extended from her neck and tightly twisted their way down her front to surround her navel.

Soft sensitive skin lay in the dark lines and patches, causing her to shiver when traced. Coined as soul-markings, it was believed that these lines touched their inner soul because of their tender nature.

Avanda had also matured physically; her height had increased and her body had begun to fill out. It was obvious she was crossing the bridge from child to woman.

She walked past the humans in the pub as they looked down to her; some with disgust while others with catcalls and rude comments.

Bouncing up to the table, Avanda peered into Thorik's half full mug and scrunched up her nose at the smell. "I don't think you should be drinking that."

Obviously uncomfortable about seeing her, Thorik watched as three military guards entered the pub. "Avanda, you shouldn't be in here. You need to get back to the group quickly." His eyes never looked directly at her.

"I've been looking all over for you. They've finally fixed the ship." Taking a piece of bread from his plate, she sniffed it and took a bite. Setting her purse of magic onto his table, she pulled out a few items to show him. "Do you want to see what I did? I was able to enchant this mirror. It now reflects the true you. Want to try it?"

"Not now. Maybe later."

"And I also remembered Sharcodi's magical phrase to activate this string of beads." Without even a pause, she changed the subject. "I don't think Captain Mensley appreciates how hard it is to learn magic all by myself. You'd think he would've been more grateful that I saved his ship."

"Great, hurry back and I'll see you when… Just get moving." Nervous inflections could be detected in his voice as his hands tightened into fists.

"I still don't understand why we had to come all the way up the river for repairs, when the bay's port cities looked a whole lot more fun to explore."

Thorik kept his eyes on the guards as they sat down at a table near the main doors. The barkeep had their drinks ready in an effort to hold true to their daily routine in spite of the storm's destruction.

"Don't question the captain. We…He knows what he's doing." At least Thorik hoped the captain did. Thorik was about to embark on a dangerous venture based on Captain Mensley's plan. If the captain was wrong, it could be Thorik's end.

Ripping another chunk from the small bread loaf, she ate the soft inside and tossed the crust back on the table. "Did I tell you I made a wish to the lights over Lu'Tythis Tower last night? As soon as I finished, lightning raced across the sky. It must have heard me."

"More likely a distant thunderstorm."

"No, it was a clear night. It came from the center of the night lights, where the tower is."

"Captain Mensley should have never told you that folk tale. It's only a distant ancient structure."

"No, it's more than that. It answered me. You'll see."

"I'm looking forward to it. But for now, hurry back to the docks." Nervous, he took a sip of his liquid courage. He was on edge and was not in the mood to talk.

"What's gotten into you?" She was one to continue to pry until she got her answer.

Thorik's voice was now fast and agitated as he stood up to address her. "It's going to get dangerous in here very soon. Go back to Gluic and Brimmelle, now! Gluic can explain to you why."

Avanda grabbed her purse and whipped her head around to see the oncoming danger. "Where? What's going to happen?" Her voice caught a few ears and then eyes.

"Avanda! Get out of here!" His voice was loud enough to wake the man sleeping at the bar before he took a drink and put his head back down. The other patrons turned as they watched the loud Num try to control himself.

Thorik slowly sat back into his chair, while Avanda crossed her arms. It wasn't like him to yell at her, and she didn't appreciate it, especially in public.

Most of the customers went back about their own business. A few of the men at the bar, however, kept their attention on the two short Nums.

"Hey, little girl. That guy bothering you?" one of the men said. "I'll take care of you and make sure no one hurts you." Eyelids at half-mast, the drunken man gave off a creepy smile while gazing at her.

Thorik watched as all three of the men, who had turned around from the bar, were eyeing her. This was no place for a young teenage girl, regardless if they were human or Num.

Thorik needed to prevent any conflicts. "Sorry to bother you. We'll keep it down." Avanda had been his student for many years and he felt very protective of her. He desperately wanted to avoid conflict.

The widest of the three men continued to smile at Avanda. "Sure is pretty. How'd ya like to sit on my lap and share a drink with us?"

The tallest one grinned at the thought. "Maybe you could do a little dance up on the bar for us, seeing that you have our attention." The three laughed at the idea as one of them began clearing off a section of bar for her.

Turning to face the men head on, she glared at the drunks as they continued toying with her and laughing among themselves.

Trying to prevent any issues, Thorik slowly reached over and grabbed the back of Avanda's shirt to prevent her from charging them. "Don't do it," he said softly.

Still a little annoyed about Thorik ordering her to leave, she needed to make a point. "I can take care of myself." Pulling out of Thorik's reach, she stepped toward the small group of men teasing her.

"Avanda, don't," Thorik ordered without shouting.

She didn't listen. Walking the last few steps, she looked up at the hairy and dirty drunks. All of them stood at least a few heads taller than her. Swaying and belching from the alcohol, they waited for her to respond to their invitation.

"Do you have something you'd like to say to me?" she challenged.

The three men laughed at her boldness. "Yes," the thin man said as he pushed his grimy and untrimmed blond hair out of his face. "I've heard that Num females have the softest skin of any species." His buddies laughed out of support without knowing where he was taking the conversation. "So, seeing that we don't see too many Nums, I thought you could show us if it were true." He finished and provided a tooth-missing smile as his eyes glazed over from intoxication.

"Avanda," Thorik said softly as he stood up to walk over to her.

She was a girl in a young woman's body, coming of age and knowing just enough to be dangerous. She didn't like these men and quickly responded before Thorik could arrive. "If you want to feel something soft, try reaching between your own legs."

Avanda had overheard her Uncle Wess say the sarcastic remark to one of his brothers. It had been followed with a round of laughter by all. However, she did not receive the same response as he once did.

The blond recipient of this barb stopped smiling. His friends became silent as they waited for his response. Tension immediately elevated as all of the patrons now waited for a reaction. Even the seated guards turned to see what would unfold.

"I'd rather feel what's between yours." He then lunged at her, grabbing her by the shoulders.

Avanda screamed as the other two men helped by holding her still while their friend stood in front of her. She had prepared for a verbal battle but never would have expected it to become physical. No one had ever physically assaulted her for speaking her mind. But this wasn't her home village of Farbank and they played by different rules here.

The guards looked at the drunks and turned away, avoiding any view of their doings.

Brushing his long oily hair out of his face again the thin man gave off an evil smile. He stood over her and cupped his palm behind her head as she looked up at him. "First I want to see how soft your lips are. I'll work down from there." He held her head tight as he leaned down to kiss her.

"Stop!" Thorik yelled from behind the men. His battle-axe was held up and over his shoulder, ready to be swung. "Let go of her before you feel the blade of my axe."

A head shorter than the men meant very little as the sharp weapon prepared to swing and take someone's life. The men stopped and one of them stepped toward the battle-ready Num.

Swinging the axe, it grazed the man's leather vest, triggering the realization that Thorik was serious.

Placing the battle-axe back into swinging position, Thorik stepped forward. "Let go of her!"

They conceded as they all turned to face Thorik while spreading out to surround him.

Stepping up from the table, the guards had decided to get involved, until the thin drunk waved them back. "I'll take care of this. Sit down and enjoy your drinks." And to the surprise of Thorik, they did just that.

"Avanda, get out of here," Thorik yelled as he watched them slowly complete the circle around him.

Instead, Avanda reached for a red and gold purse within her cloak and pulled out a string of red beads. She chanted a few words before dropping the beads onto the ground.

Incredibly, her spell had worked and a rainstorm of fireballs fell from the ceiling hitting the three men. The illusion was weak and those not intoxicated from ale could tell it was a hoax. Fortunately, the three men could not.

The men covered their heads as they screamed, for they believed their clothes and flesh were on fire. They bolted out of the pub in an effort to put out the flames in the local river.

Thorik lowered his axe and returned his attention back to his young student. "Why do you have to do that?"

"I don't like being bullied," she answered as she picked up her string of red beads.

Thorik put his weapon in its holder on his back. "One of these times you're going to wish you had just let it go and ignored the situation."

She looked at him square in the eyes. "You should take your own advice. How many times did Brimmelle try to tell you to let it go? Instead, you had to get involved with Ambrosius and next thing I know I'm on the opposite end of Terra Australis from my parents and you're sitting here feeling guilty about Ambrosius and sorry for yourself."

Thorik knew the locals had overheard the conversation, but her statement sliced deep. "I did what was needed. I had no choice," he said softly with all the intensity as he could muster.

"Grewen says we all have choices," she said sternly, looking into her former teacher's eyes. Pulling out a hexagonal stone that hung from her neck by a leather string, she continued in a soft voice, "You taught me to take responsibility for my actions. Was that all Fesh talk?"

"Watch your tongue." Thorik didn't like some of the habits she had picked up. Her use of inappropriate words and undisciplined magic were two of them.

Tracing the rune in the center of the hexagonal Runestone with her finger, she remembered the day he had given it to her before leaving Farbank. Thorik seemed so content back then, and easier to talk to. "What happened to you, Thorik?" she asked.

"What are you talking about?"

"In Farbank you kept all of us happy and we loved being around you. Now you're grumpy and distant."

"I've grown up a lot."

"You're only three years older than I am."

"Growing up has little to do with your age."

Avanda nodded her head. "I see. So now you're more mature, like Fir Brimmelle."

Thorik did not like to be compared to their spiritual leader in such a manner. The Fir was always negative and close minded, opposite of what Thorik considered himself. "You don't understand," Thorik spoke firmly. "I killed a man...a good man." He paused. "A friend," he finished softly.

"If you hadn't, Weirfortus Dam would have released its water and this city would be under Lake Luthralum." Looking around at the disastrous state of the pub and recalling the devastation of the city she continued, "Of course, that might have been an improvement."

"It's more than that. I have a lot of responsibility now."

"I'm not sure I want to grow up if it means I can't have fun anymore. I'd rather be like my Uncle Wess."

"And look what happened to him."

"But Thorik, he lived life to the fullest. He enjoyed every minute. Never did I see him pouting or sulking like you. What a waste of time. Why can't you let this go so we can move on with our lives?"

Thorik sat back down at his table and looked at the half empty mug of lukewarm ale. This was not the place, nor the time, to explain his plan to be arrested. Captain Mensley's contacts had located Ericc in the nearby prison mines, and the only way in to see him was to get thrown in himself. Not a mission he looked forward to, but a simple altercation with local officials should get him incarcerated for a few days.

"It's complicated." Thorik bit his lip after making the statement. He hated being on the receiving end of that phrase and never thought he would be on the other side of it.

"Sure it is. I'm not mature enough to understand," she said, dramatically pointing to herself. "Well, I'll let you do your grown-up soul searching while I head back to the dock. Brimmelle sent me here to let you know the ship is fixed and we can set sail in the morning." She stared at him before continuing. "And now you know. I'll see you back at the dock, unless you have time to walk me back."

"Time?" Thorik began to panic again as his eyes looked at the guards who were finishing up their drinks. His window of opportunity to address the men was quickly closing. "No, I don't have time. Head back quickly."

Turning on the balls of her feet, she crossed her arms and stomped through the pub, out the exit, and into the street.

Most of the street lamps had been broken from the storms, many of them bent over like withering plants against the thin haze hiding an unseen moon. Walls of buildings pitched to one side or another and smoke billowed from distant fires. The smell of rotten food and sewage filled the thick damp air while sounds of wild animals were heard from the nearby dense tropical forest.

Avanda turned and noticed a silhouette of a man standing at the corner smoking his pipe. Uncomfortable, she turned the other way instead.

Walking down the street she looked back to see the unknown man following her. She quickened her pace; knowing she only had a few blocks to go before reaching her group at the dock.

Turning the first corner she looked back to see the man gaining on her. Her heart raced as she realized she was in trouble.

Charging forward into the dark alley she bumped into a man standing in her way.

"Hello again, little Num," a man's voice said.

She reached for her sack of magic but was quickly nabbed from behind. Panicking, she screamed and kicked as the two men picked her up and moved her into the light of a distant street lamp.

A large rough hand covered her small mouth as they held her tight in wait for the approaching stranger who had been following her.

"About that kiss." The stranger pushed the long stringy blonde hair out of the way and over his shoulder. "I think I'll start lower this time."

Chapter 4
Assault

A vanda twisted and bucked as one drunken man held her captive and a second one stood behind her, covering her mouth and holding her head still.

Sweat ran down her neck and back as she fought for freedom. Nevertheless, the men were able to easily control the small Num.

"Take her cloak off," ordered the blonde leader as he stood before her.

One of the men grinned as he removed it. "I get her next, Lucian."

Lucian leaned down and looked into her enraged eyes. "There may not be anything left after I'm done with her." He removed her belt and tossing it to the side. His breath was thick with ale, making Avanda recoil to avoid the smell.

Her garments were saturated with sweat from the struggle in the hot humid night air.

Enjoying every reaction he could get out of her, Lucian began unbuttoning her blouse as he whispered to her. "I bet you are so soft and pure." His rough and dry index finger touched between the buttons onto her chest. "Silky," he said from his first encounter with her skin.

Avanda was helpless. Disgusted by this man who was removing her clothes, she turned her head so she could distance herself from the situation. His continued touch made her stomach churn as tears flooded her face.

Lucian watched her reactions to his touch. "Gentlemen, you'll be happy to know that she is soft. So very soft." Lifting her shirt, he exposed her navel and placed his dirty dry palm against her bare stomach.

Leaning down he placed a kiss on her belly as he moved his hands to her legs. Slowly he moved them up to her knees. "Softer than a newborn tigra," he purred as he leaned the unshaven bristles on the side of his face against her exposed body.

"And now my friends we will know the answer to our question." Lucian moved his hands on her legs to the inside of her knees.

Avanda squeezed her eyes tight, as she felt the horror of Lucian's touch.

"RELEASE HER!" a deep voice ordered from the darkness of the alley.

Stepping out into the soft hazy light, a giant Blothrud towered over the group. Veins pumping across the tight red skin on his hairless wolf-like face and across his enormous chest and arm muscles made it clear that he was ready for a fight. Blood dripped from his lip as he clinched his teeth in anger over the scene before him.

Lucian's face turned white, as though he was seeing a ghost. "Santorray? You're dead. I... I... I killed you myself," he stammered.

"Apparently not, but I've returned to repay the favor and I don't intend to fail like you did."

But Lucian was not one to be intimidated, especially in his drunken state on mind. "Blades!" he shouted at his men, who quickly placed daggers at the young Num's neck and stomach.

Lucian shielded his position behind his two men and Avanda. "Back off, Santorray. This is not your business."

"I'm making it my business."

Avanda stood still as the men's blades pushed up against her, stretching her skin.

Lucian smiled at his position. "Leave or we will kill her and blame it on you. My word against an Altered's word is no contest."

In one swift motion, the Blothrud grabbed a saber from his side and swung it in front of him with such speed that the metal blade couldn't be seen in the dim lighting. He then stepped forward, right in front of Avanda and her captors.

"Cut her!" Lucian ordered.

But the men stood motionless.

Lucian stumbled back a few steps in his inebriated state, confused as to why they weren't following his orders. "I said, cut her!"

Reaching down, Santorray removed blades from both of the men's hands and abruptly pulled her off to the side. The men collapsed where they once stood as their heads fell from their necks and rolled toward Lucian. The lightning fast strike of Santorray's saber had cleanly severed them both.

Lucian pulled his own dagger out and threw it at Avanda, hoping to distract the beast long enough to make an escape.

Jumping toward the flying weapon, the Blothrud broke its path with the spikes that grew from the back of his hand. Turning back to confront the man, Lucian had taken the opportunity to run.

Santorray's thick and hairy wolf-like legs sprang him from his position and into hot pursuit of the soon to be victim of a tragic brutal murder. Lowering his upper body, the Blothrud used the thick-skinned palms of his hand as front feet, racing on all fours.

Without a backup plan, Lucian instantly panicked. His arrogance had turned to fear once he had lost the upper hand.

It didn't take long for the Blothrud to catch up to him. But as Santorray leaped for Lucian, the man turned abruptly and barreled his way through the doors into the pub. The creature missed his prey and skidded to a halt.

Thorik had been standing near the door, arguing with the local guards, when Lucian crashed his way in. The two collided, sending them to the floor, knocking over a table and several chairs.

Noticing it was Thorik; Lucian tried to justify himself. He could only assume that the Num was a friend of the beast in pursuit. "I didn't hurt her! We didn't rape her!"

"Rape her? Avanda? What happened?" Thorik grabbed onto the man to get answers.

Lucian struggled to get free. "He'll tell you we hurt her, but we didn't."

"Only because I stopped you. You Fesh scum!" The voice came from outside the only wall still fully intact, until Santorray plowed his way in with a crushing blow from his shoulder. "Playing with helpless Nums? How about playing with me for a spell?" He flexed his already oversized muscles on his eight-foot sculptured body.

Thorik never turned around to see the ominous red creature that knocked a hole in the wall. He focused on preventing Lucian from getting up and escaping. "What did you do to Avanda?"

Thorik lost his grip of the man, who stood up to run. Jumping forward, the Num hit Lucian in the back. Falling, they both crashed through the table occupied by the local guards who were in the midst of grabbing their weapons.

"Get him off me." Lucian ordered the men.

"Let them fight it out!" roared Santorray, assuming the girl was a friend of the Num.

Two of the three guards turned to look up at Santorray, blocking his ability to stop the third guard from breaking up the fight.

"I said, let them fight!"

One of the guards raised his sword to keep the creature at a distance.

Santorray grinned, making the man's forehead and hands begin to sweat.

The second guard raised his own sword as he grabbed a whistle and blew it hard.

Santorray's grin increased in size, exposing his long upper canines all the way to the gum. "All right, if you want it to be that way." Reaching both hands forward, past their swords, the Blothrud grabbed the men by their uniforms and tossed them over his head into the air and through the wall behind him.

The last guard had just separated the two fighters as he turned to see what happened. Grabbing a chair, he crushed the wooden furniture against the Blothrud's exposed side before Santorray could lower his arms to protect himself.

Splinters flew as the chair struck hard against the beast. Nothing remained except the chair's back, which the guard still clung too. A stone statue would have moved more from the attack, as Santorray's grin never faded.

Dropping the wooden remains of the chair, the guard pulled his whistle to his lips to call for help.

A swift red fist to the mouth stopped the noise, as well as the man, before Santorray turned back to see the fight he was missing.

Thorik had fallen onto his back with Lucian above him, stabbing a broken stool leg down at the Num. Still inebriated, he missed several times as Thorik rolled out of the way. Finally he hit his target directly into Thorik's chest. A crack from the Num's ribs could be heard.

"You pathetic peasant." Lucian stood over his victim who held his arms over his chest. "You outsiders come into our province and think you are better than us!" Kicking Thorik in the side helped Lucian vent his frustration. "You don't know who you're messing with."

"No, but I do," Santorray said.

Looking up at the beast, Lucian was still breathing heavily from his brawl with Thorik. The less than sober man was cut and bleeding. Eyes darting from side to side he began to plan his escape as the enormous Altered approached. There were plenty of holes in the walls to escape from, but all were short-term victories, for he couldn't outrun a Blothrud.

But then, a venomous smile slowly crossed Lucian's face. "I hope you have this much energy after a few weeks in the mines."

"If they can catch me after killing you, they can have me."

"Unfortunately you'll have to go there on assault charges, instead of murder."

Santorray could sense something was wrong. Peering out the holes in the walls, he could see several dozen guards taking position around the pub, ready to attack from all sides. They had heard the alert whistle.

"If I'm going to the mines, I might as well make it worth my while." Santorray leaned forward and grabbed Lucian with both hands, lifting him up in the air, slapping his body against a ceiling rafter. It was difficult to know if the crack that followed was Lucian's back or the already weakened timbers holding up the roof. Again and again he used the man as a sledgehammer against the wooden beams.

Shaking from the fight, the building creaked and moaned as it struggled to remain standing. Sections of the roof were now caving in and falling to the floor.

Bleeding from his thrashing, Lucian swung the stool leg he still clung to at the beast's face, only to have it captured in the Blothrud's mouth. Santorray's teeth snapped down on the wood along with two of Lucian's fingers, cutting them both from his hand.

Shaking Lucian like a rag doll above his head, Santorray heard the military ordering the attack. He turned his attention on the group rushing in at him, dropping Lucian hard to the ground behind his back for effect.

The guards rushed at him with spears from all sides, only to stop a few yards from him. They had a tight circle around the beast.

Spitting out Lucian's fingers, Santorray growled and showed his teeth stained with Lucian's blood. He waited for the first fool who wanted to test their courage, as he slowly rotated around.

It wasn't long before a young strapping lad with a chip on his shoulder needed to prove himself to his peers. A lunge forward with his spear grazed one of Santorray's back blades. It was all the man recalled, for the beast's instinctive reflexes kicked his back leg into the man's forehead, knocking him out as well as into his peers.

A second man stepped forward, two-handed broadsword ready for attack. He wasn't a guard like the rest. He was a giant of a man, who wore armor with royal symbols on it, as he nearly stood as high as Santorray's shoulders. Blue and gold robes bore the kingdom's symbol of water, wheat and a sword.

They sized each other up as the guards stepped back to give them room. "I am Asentar, supreme knight of the Dovenar Kingdom. You are now a prisoner of the Southwind Province. Come quietly, or I shall be forced to slay you."

Santorray was intrigued. He had fought many a man and Altered, but never a Dovenar Knight. In fact, he didn't think there were any left. "My issues are not with you, sir knight. It's with a man who takes pleasure in raping children. But if you come between me and my rightful vengeance, you will become my enemy as well."

Behind Santorray, Lucian had regained consciousness. Grabbing a dagger from one of the guards, he rushed toward the Blothrud. Blood poured from his missing fingers, coating the handle with fresh liquid. With the blade in both hands, his face tightened in anger as he swung it over his head, down toward the creature's spine.

Santorray didn't see it coming as he focused on Asentar. The knight's eyes never revealed the pending attack. Not a twitch of the cheek or blink of the eye, there was no sign of Lucian's rear attack coming until he saw a blurred movement out of the corner of his right eye.

Jumping through the air, Thorik collided with Lucian, again rolling to the floor. The Num grabbed the man's wrist and pounded it against the floor, trying to break his grip on the dagger. After several failed attempts, Thorik pressed his fingers against the stubby ends of Lucian's missing fingers. The pain caused the man to release the blade as he lay on his back. Thorik grabbed the battle-axe from his back and held it over his head, ready to strike if Lucian made another move.

Asentar used this distraction to launch an attack. A step forward allowed a swift slice to Santorray's upper thigh, with an immediate return to his stomach. The blade held steady against the rough red skin of his abdomen, causing it to stretch and indent as he pushed slightly forward. Blood from the superficial cut ran down the Blothrud's leg. The knight now had the advantage. "Surrender. I do not wish to kill you, but I will if I must."

Snarling, saliva and blood dripped from Santorray's mouth. "Now you've made yourself my enemy." His dark red skin brightened as fresh blood pulsed faster through his veins. His muscles appeared to grow before their eyes as his anger grew at the man who held a sword to his belly. The quiet tension hung in the air as the guards waited for the Blothrud to attack.

Expressionless, the Dovenar Knight stood his ground, ready to do his duty. He didn't care if it was an Altered, whether it be Ov'Unday, Fesh'Unday or, like in the Blothrud's case, Del'Unday. His only desire was to follow his oath to the kingdom, even if it was a human.

The silence ended with the sounds of a legion of Faralope hooves marching up to the building. Once there, a Southwind military official stepped down from his mount, followed by the rest of his armed men. The guards parted, allowing their general to enter the area.

In full uniform and colors, the general walked stiffly over to Thorik without saying a word. A large mustache trailed down below his strong jaw. His ability to intimidate Thorik without speaking was remarkable. Stopping just shy of running into the Num, his hand snapped out like a viper and snatched the axe out of Thorik's hands before tossing it behind him onto the floor.

Thorik backed up as the wide-chested general stepped forward. Thorik had met wild bores with a more comforting demeanor than this man. His presence chilled the room with his disapproval in what he was seeing. Thorik instinctively wanted to apologize to him, even if he didn't know why.

Santorray didn't cower from the general, but his anger was subsiding. He had left Lucian a continual reminder of him, for he would never properly wield a weapon again.

Thorik felt the need to explain himself to the general. "He raped my friend, a mere child Num. He needs be locked away."

The general reached down with one hand and grabbed Lucian's hand. With one quick tug, the general lifted Lucian to his feet and then spun him around. He now had Lucian by the hand behind his back. The general lifted the hand a few times, causing Lucian pain while pushing him forward toward the Faralopes.

Following the general, Santorray and Thorik walked just outside the pub before stopping. They had given in to the inevitable; they were captured. Fighting was futile at this point as more military personnel arrived. Santorray dropped his weapon.

Sheathing his sword, the Dovenar Knight watched the proud Blothrud exit the pub. "You were wise not to challenge me, Del."

Glaring over his shoulder, Santorray exposed his teeth while watching the knight grin at the Del'Unday's fate. With a forearm strike to the outer wall, the roof finally gave way, landing on the knight and many of the guards. "You were wise not to say that too close to me," he said calmly in the night air.

As the pub collapsed, the general and Lucian reached the Faralopes. Letting go of Lucian, the general spun him around and pushed him backward. Still intoxicated with ale, he fell against the Faralope and cradled his hand with the missing fingers.

"Damn that beast! Did you see what he did to my hand?" Lucian said with obnoxious cockiness in his voice. "We were just having some fun. Santorray had no business getting involved."

Looking down over his beak of a nose at Lucian, the general grumbled. "Do you realize what you have put in jeopardy here? If the Matriarch finds out about this, she'll have our entire family put to death. You make me sick to be your father." He followed the comment with a loud and stern instruction to his second in command. "Take the Blothrud and Num to the mines. I don't need word of this getting out."

The guard looked at the general with serious eyes for confirmation of actions to be taken.

Clarification came quickly from the Lucian's father, "Make this problem disappear. It never happened."

Chapter 5
Southwind Mines

Rats scurried away from the group as they walked down the dimly lit shaft of an old mine. Thorik's head hung low as he was pushed forward. "Are you sure Avanda is all right?"

Santorray continued to lower his head to avoid the beams that supported the rock ceiling. "Yes, I'm sure. I stopped them before they injured her," he said in his usual deep voice. "If you ask me that one more time, *you'll* be the one that's injured."

A group of bad-tempered guards moved the two deeper into the mountain. Each could blame their attitudes on their inhospitable working conditions and lack of hygiene, but the reality was they simply took pleasure in causing pain to others. It was the only power they had left in their lives. Even though they weren't prisoners, quitting wasn't an option, especially after what they had witnessed on a daily basis. An ex-guard telling tales didn't live long in Southwind.

Shaking his head, Thorik thought about his mistakes. "I should have walked her back to the ship. He wouldn't have touched her if I had been there."

Santorray ducked under a low ceiling beam as they entered a long corridor with cells on both sides. "You would have been killed at the start, to get you out of the way."

"You don't know that. I would have protected her."

"Even if you had the soul of a Blothrud, you're still only a Num," Santorray said, as one of the general's personal guards unlocked their cell.

Santorray's words only added to Thorik's grief. "This was a bad idea. This is entirely my fault."

"Yes it is," the lead guard said. "And now it'a be my job to make sure ya pay for it." Laughing, he continued, "And you'll pay. Again and again."

Pushing Thorik into the cell, the guard moved out of the way for Santorray to be escorted in by several armed men. Locking the door behind them, the general's guard handed the keys over. "They're all yours, Da'Shawn. You have the general's orders. The

Blothrud losses one finger each day for his crime against Master Lucian."

Santorray tightened his fists as he stood firm in the center of the cell. "Just try." He then spit on the floor near the cell door.

The cell was dark with cold rock walls, floor and ceiling and metal bars along one side. Flickering mining lanterns provided the only light from the corridor, which ran down the center of the dank detention units. Water dripped from cracks in the ceiling, creating puddles for the local insects to swarm and breed. Scattered remains of the prior inmates filled the cell with an overwhelming odor of rotting flesh.

Clutching the bars of the door, Da'Shawn looked through them at the Blothrud. Chewing on tobacco, he allowed it to drip down his chin before finally spitting and leaving a string of brown saliva from his lower lip down the front of his soiled shirt. "Last inmate that tried ta escape made it up to da second level b'fore he was eaten by our Frudorian Dragon. Duuke's always hungry for another meal."

Looking around the prison cell floor, he continued. "Seeing that he was quickly disposed of, we took his punishment out on his cell-mate." The guard reached his short spear through the bars into the cell and poked at the remaining torso of a human body before looking at Thorik. "I'd suggest ya talk yur big friend outta make'n a mistake that you end up paying fer."

Santorray ignored the dramatic speech as he moved to the back of the cell, kicking decomposing body parts out of his way.

"We don't want any trouble. We won't talk about what happened." Thorik attempted to get on the guard's good side. "We will serve our time for disorderly conduct and be on our way."

"Your time?" Da'Shawn's dirty face exposed several cracked and missing teeth as he smiled. "Better make yourself at home, Num. you've stepped into a rat's nest when you crossed Lucian. During his bachelor's party, no less. Soon to be wed to the granddaughter of the Matriarch, he is. She runs all the business in Southwind and Lucian will be inheriting this 'ere mine once his vows are said. So he makes the rules. You ain't going nowhere."

Da'Shawn chuckled to himself as he stepped away from the cell and walked back down the corridor.

The new inmates listened to the complaints of other prisoners as the guard walked past their cells.

Santorray spit in his hands and rubbed them together before applying it to the open wound on his leg. "It would have been easier to steal something."

"What?"

"You picked a dangerous way to get in here."

Thorik was shocked at the comments. "What makes you think that I would *want* to be in here, sitting in a disgusting prison cell?"

"I can tell by your speech that you're from the north. There are only three reasons people from the north come to Southwind. Either they're here to trade, sent to the mines as slaves, or journeyed here to save someone from the mines."

"How do you know I'm not here to trade?"

"Okay, who are you here to trade with? Be careful, I know most of the trading merchants in this area."

Thorik felt exposed, as though the Blothrud could read his thoughts. "You wouldn't know him, he's new."

"Like I said, you picked a dangerous way to get in here."

"I didn't start the fight, you did."

"No, but I'm guessing you were sitting in the bar drinking up some bravery to do enough to get thrown in here. I've seen it before. It usually ends with your own death in the mines."

Frustrated, Thorik didn't like being on the defensive. "How about you? Who are you trying to get out?"

"I came back to Southwind to pay back an old debt."

"Was it worth it? Now you're just going to rot away in here."

"Yes, I've made my mark on Lucian to remind him of his actions. But no, I don't plan on rotting away. I'll be escaping from here."

Thorik recalled the guard's story. "Um, if you escape, they will take it out on me."

"Then I would suggest you escape with me."

"I can't."

"Why?"

"I can't tell you."

Santorray put his foot under one of the rotting bodies and kicked it toward the Num. "Then I guess you will become a permanent resident."

Decaying flesh flung off the pelvis and spine as is rolled up to Thorik. His stomach churned at the sight. He surely didn't want to end up like that.

Weighing his options, he considered what his next move would be. "Can you give me a few days before you escape?"

"No."

"Why not?"

"Give me a good reason why I should allow these humans to cut off a few of my fingers over the next few days. On top of that, we just accused Lucian of rape, which means we'll be lucky if they don't try to kill us before we get a chance to talk to anyone else." The Blothrud reached down, plucked a slug up from the floor, and set it in the blood running down from his cut leg. "Why are you here? Who is so important to get out of here that you're willing to be beaten and worked to death?"

Thorik sighed. "I can't tell you. I don't even know you."

"San-tor-ray is the name." The Blothrud rolled the 'r' with pride. "And yours?"

"Sec Thorik Dain of Farbank."

"Okay, Sec, who is it you're after? Who should I put my fingers and my life on the line for, by staying in here?"

"No, it's Thorik, not Sec."

"Yes, I know. So who are you looking for, Sec."

Thorik didn't have many alternatives. "This has gotten way out of control. I had planned on being thrown into here based on a verbal confrontation with some local guards. A two-night offense." Shaking his head in disbelief, he began to pace. "I never expected to have my life at risk."

Santorray was getting tired of Thorik's lack of forthcoming information. "Not my problem. I'm escaping with or without you."

"Give me a day. Just one day to see if he is even here."

"Who? Who is worth one of my fingers?"

Stopping his pacing, he walked closer to the Del'Unday. Thorik's lips tightened and his voice lowered. "Ericc Dovenar."

Perking the beast's interest, Santorray sat up slightly. "And why would you be looking for the son of Ambrosius?"

"You know him? But how?"

"Everyone knows the Dovenar family tree. It's just hard to tell the good branches from the bad ones. Are you working for Darkmere to assassinate the hidden son?"

Thorik looked shocked at the suggestion. "No, just the opposite. I've come to protect him from Darkmere."

A grand, and yet terrifying, laugh bellowed out of Santorray. "You? You can't protect yourself, let alone Ericc from the likes of Darkmere."

"I stopped Lucian from ending your life," Thorik snapped back. He began to pace again, worried about how truthful Santorray's words could be.

Still chuckling, the Blothrud fired back, "True, but I was also getting ready to fight thirty men at the time. All you had to worry about was one, a drunken one at that." Watching the Num's silhouette travel back and forth in front of the yellow lantern light was getting tiresome for the beast. "If you don't stop pacing I'm going to break your leg off and eat it for my next meal."

Thorik's face flushed partly from embarrassment and partly from frustration as he walked over to the sitting Del'Unday. "Listen, I'm not *asking* for your help." Straightening his back, he lifted his chest. "I don't *need* your help. All I'm requesting is that you give me enough time to find him before you destroy my plans. One day. Two nights, tonight and the next."

Santorray looked at the little Num standing proud with conviction. "You have one day, Sec. I expect them to come for their first finger after I've given them a hard day's work; so get it done early so the second night is not needed. Do you know what he looks like?"

"I don't have a clue."

Santorray nodded, expecting no less. "Excellent."

Chapter 6
Finding Ericc

Morning came with the light and smell of burning torches as the guards opened up the cells and paraded the prisoners down the corridor toward the main mine shaft. Thorik and Santorray fell in line behind countless others, most of whom showed signs of starvation and unhealed lash marks.

The main shaft opened up into a large round room filled with men handing out mining equipment and daily rations. Above them, a catwalk encircled the room as archers watched for signs of misbehaving.

A thousand people slowly moved into and out of the large room. A layer of grayish brown dirt covered their bodies and clothes, making them all blend together.

"This will take more than a day," Thorik mumbled, realizing the magnitude of the how hard it would be to find a young man he had never met before.

Santorray agreed. "If Ericc is here, and they know it's him, they wouldn't cage him with the rest of us. They would separate him to keep him alive and unspoiled for Darkmere's men to come for him. Someplace constantly under watch and with a private cell." The Blothrud had been in the mines before and knew of only one place that met these criteria, the infirmary. Now the question was how to get in there.

Thorik was handed a pick and a chunk of dry bread. Placing the rations near his nose to smell something other than the sweaty prisoners, he found there was no aroma to it.

The prisoner in front of Thorik turned and snatched the bread from the Num. "This one's mine."

"Hey, give that back." Thorik looked at the guard to see if he had seen the incident. After seeing the guard roll his eyes at the issue, Thorik looked back at the Blothrud. "Did you see that?"

"How did you ever survive on your own?" Taking a bite of his own tasteless bread, Santorray swallowed hard as it scratched his throat on the way down. "Trust me. It's not worth fighting for."

Listening to his own words, the Blothrud got an idea and tossed the rest of his meal to Thorik.

"Hey! Give that back!" Santorray roared at the Num before grabbing him and lifting him the air.

Shocked, Thorik tried to kick free, as he held the bread in one hand and the pick in the other.

"Swing your pick at me." Santorray said under his breath, before yelling, "I'll rip you apart!"

Thorik began to panic from the unprovoked attack. "What are you doing?"

"I'm going to make you bleed! You'll be lucky if they can stitch you back together." Santorray raked his knuckle spikes across Thorik's stomach, ripping his shirt and skin. Any deeper and Thorik could have lost his internal organs.

Dropping his items, Thorik grasped his stomach as blood poured forth.

Santorray dropped the Num on the food table in front of the guard before picking up his bread. "It was *my* bread." He growled.

Guards rushed over while archers loaded their arrows and prepared to shoot, should the Blothrud put up a fight against them. Several slaps from a short whip pushed the Blothrud back into line and away from the Num.

"Worth keeping alive?" the food server asked the higher-ranking guard, as they both looked at Thorik.

One guard assessed Thorik's cuts. "Wrap him up and send him to the infirmary. No reason to lose a good set of hands from nothing more than bleeding to death."

After rapping a filthy rag around the Nums stomach and waist, Thorik was escorted down a different branch of the mine. A smell of fresh stew could be taken in as they entered a new open area, which housed the guard's mess hall and medical area on one side and several prisoner cells on the other.

Tossing Thorik into one of the cells, the guard yelled at a man in a long white cloak discolored with red blood, who was enjoying his hot breakfast. Returning to his duties, the guard left this man in charge.

What was Santorray thinking? Thorik thought to himself. *He nearly sliced me open.*

"Hey, are you okay?" came a voice from the next cell. Unlike the prisoner's cells, these had bars on three of its four sides.

Thorik looked over to see a young man about his own age. Mahogany hair down to his eyebrows and over his ears, and a face that looked vaguely familiar. "Ericc?"

Sliding back into his cell, Ericc asked his own question. "Do I know you?"

Thorik was beaming. "It's you! I found you. Actually, you found me. But that doesn't matter right now. You're here and now I can protect you from the prophecy being fulfilled with your death."

Ericc looked at the blood soaking into the cloth around the Num's stomach. "You're going to protect me?" he said sarcastically. "Who are you? And how do you know me?"

"My name is Sec Thorik Dain of Farbank. Your father sent me."

"My father? I've been looking for him for months." Ericc stood up and leaned against the bars, hoping to see his father walk down the corridor and free him. "Where is he? Is he coming for me?"

Stress seeped into Thorik's voice as he tried to answer his question. "No, Ericc. He's not coming to save you. He asked me to."

"Why wouldn't he do it himself? Where has he been for the past eight years and what will it take for him to see his own son?" His pent-up resentment mixed with excitement of the possibility of seeing his father again. He had been abandoned by his father and sent to live with friends of the family, away from civilization. He understood the risks of appearing in public, which had nearly led to his death when he encountered Lord Bredgin.

Nevertheless, eight years was too long to go without seeing his father. Ericc had run away and ventured into the cities to experience the life he had missed. But instead of finding the dream of freedom, he quickly became hunted by those who wished to see him dead. Escaping more than one attack, he was recently caught stealing food to survive. Thrown into the mines, he was recognized as Ambrosius' son and removed from the common labor only to be held in the infirmary until Darkmere or one of his assassins arrived to take him.

"He's not coming. He can't come," Thorik said.

"Why? What's the excuse this time? Another Grand Council meeting? A disaster in Eastland that only he can repress? I've heard them all over the years. Not this time. I'm in here until he personally shows up or Darkmere comes to kill me."

"Are you in here on purpose to force your father's hand to rescue you?"

"I'm in here on a charge of trespassing. But now that they know who I am, I'm going to put an end to this, whether it is by my father standing at my side or fighting Darkmere to the death. I refuse to live in the obscurity of shadows for the rest of my life."

"It won't work. You'll be killed."

"Then so be it. At least then I'll know my father's true colors."

"No, you don't understand. He asked me to come save you from Darkmere."

"Then you'll have to tell him to come himself."

"I can't. He's dead." Thorik blurted out. He hadn't intended to tell him in such an emotionless fashion. He had planned on a more respectful way to soften the blow.

Ericc shook his head. "Not possible. Not my father. No one can kill him."

"Ericc, listen to me. Darkmere and Ambrosius fought, and on your father's dying breath he asked me to save you, to prevent you from being sacrificed."

Now it began to sink in, as Ericc's body became cold and ridged. "How do I know you're telling the truth? How did you find me?"

"I traveled with your father in hopes of preventing Darkmere from flooding the kingdom. Draq traveled with us. My understanding is that he and his family raised you."

Thorik noticed no reaction from Ericc to his words, so he continued. "After the battle, our boat crashed upon the reefs of an island and we were rescued by Captain Mensley who helped us find your whereabouts."

Ericc stared across the hall. "Where is Darkmere?" He couldn't even look at Thorik as he talked through clinched teeth.

"Last I heard he returned to Corrock to regroup, seeing that the flood was prevented. Why?"

"I'm going to kill him."

"No, you need to hide from him."

"I've been hiding my whole life. I'm going to Corrock to avenge my father's death."

"You don't understand. He wants you to come to him. He's baiting you, just like he did to your father. Once he has you, you're to be sacrificed to prevent the prophecy from coming true."

"Prophecy, what prophecy?" asked the medic in the red-stained white cloak as he walked up to the two.

Thorik and Ericc suddenly became deaf and mute.

Receiving no answer, he opened Thorik's cell. "Fine, let me see those cuts."

Chapter 7
Matriarch

On raised steps, the Matriarch sat upon her throne of fear and deceit. She had no official authority, yet even the prominent of Southwind cowered to her demands. Ruthless tactics to obtain her power continued to escalate into her elder years. The little humanity she had in her youth had all been devoured by greed.

Her throne sat high enough to ensure everyone in the chamber looked up to her. Bodyguards stood at attention while servants attended to her every need. Her three advisors mulled over maps and decrees on a nearby table as she dictated new orders to them.

Visitors were welcome, and yet the only ones she ever received were those who asked for her help. One would have to be desperate to do so, for the payment always outweighed the support she gave. This normally meant that they were indebted for the rest of their lives.

The only others that dared approach her were those whom she had summoned. To not drop everything and rush to do her bidding was a sure way to end one's life.

Lucian entered her chamber, limping in pain from his fight with Santorray and holding a bandage over his missing fingers. Lowering his eyes and head in respect, he addressed her. "Greetings, Matriarch. You called for me?"

Selecting a fruit from a servant's basket, the Matriarch waited for it to be cut and a piece eaten to ensure its safety prior to it reaching her own lips. She was in no hurry to respond to the filthy man who stood before her.

Lucian tried to stand perfectly still as he waited for her response. But the night of bingeing on alcohol still tugged and pushed at him, causing him to sway as his head pounded from his recovery. The injuries sustained from his beating didn't help any either.

"What happened to you?" she asked in a cold tone.

"Santorray has returned, my grace."

"You told me he was dead. You told me that you had killed him yourself."

"Yes, you are correct. I saw him fall. I don't understand it myself."

"What else have you failed to understand? What else have you lied to me about?"

Lucian stepped forward and dropped to his knees. "Nothing, I swear. The Blothrud must have had help, like he did last night."

"You lied to me."

"No, my grace. I witnessed his death."

"And in doing so, I have proliferated this lie of Santorray's demise. My words are now in jeopardy of being questioned." Taking a bite of her fruit, she pondered her options as she watched Lucian ask forgiveness at the first step to her throne. "Remove his tongue," she ordered a bodyguard, "so he can't tell any more lies."

Lucian screamed for mercy to anyone who would listen.

"And castrate him, his father, and any nephews. I don't want them breeding any more untrustworthy kin." She had little change in her voice. "Inform my granddaughter that her wedding is off. She shall not be married to a man of dishonor."

"I've captured Santorray," Lucian shouted as her strongmen grabbed him. "He now sits in the mines near Rava'Kor. I will travel back to the mines and finish my task, returning to you with his heart in my hands. Your words will be again pure and my debt to you will be endless."

Overpowered by her personal bodyguards, Lucian's tongue was grabbed and pulled out to be sliced off. The edge of the shiny blade began to draw blood just as the Matriarch stopped them.

"You shall bring me his head so that I know it was him."

Lucian nodded agreement, seeing that he still had a blade to his tongue.

"By doing so, you save your life, one that is at my disposal forever."

"Thank you, your grace," Lucian uttered once he was released.

"If you do not return with it, you, your father, and all your kin shall be hunted down and drained of their blood. Do I make myself clear?"

The guards pushed him back down to his knees in front of her. "Yes, Matriarch, I am at your command. Santorray's head will be cut from his body and returned to you."

Footsteps could be heard entering the chamber, behind Lucian. Asentar entered the hall with a strong confident stride. He was tall in stature, allowing him to look directly at the Matriarch without raising his head. "Greetings, Matriarch. I am Asentar, high knight of the kingdom. The Doven Province sends words of unity to Southwind," he announced.

She sat up very straight, trying to keep his eye level beneath her own. "You are the *only* knight of the kingdom, from my understanding."

"Perhaps, I have not seen any of the others since the destruction of the Grand Council. I don't know of their well-being."

"They have all fallen. You are the last of their kind."

"All the more reason that I must speak to you about the reunification of the provinces."

"Why speak with me? I am not the Prominent of Southwind."

"Even the beggars on the street know that he is but a mere puppet on strings which you govern. You are in control of this region and therefore I am petitioning you to stand with us. Reunite the Dovenar Kingdom and rebuild a unified council to stand against our enemies."

"Our enemies may not be the same. If you are referring to Darkmere, I have already settled this issue. For our support in his endeavors, he will be granting me full power over everything south of the Volney River. Your words of giving power back to the kingdom are wasted upon my ears. I have no interest in what you have to say."

Asentar took in a deep breath, raising his chest. "What tragedy has caused the words of a Dovenar Knight to not carry the attention and the authority of the King himself?"

"Since the King relinquished his powers to the Grand Council and the council was destroyed. The kingdom is broken. Peace can now only come about by joining with our enemies."

"I would submit that these efforts to appease them will be met with your disposal, once they have what they want."

The Matriarch stood up and raised her voice in a demonstration of authority. "No one can dispose of me! I decide who lives and dies. I decide whom we attack and who we are at peace with. This will never change."

"Even if you are right, you can't live forever. They will eventually attack, for they live to destroy all that do not follow them.

I have fought for peace for many years, and have learned that we must enter talks with leverage. It is not too late to regain this. We can rebuild our kingdom and still reach out to our enemies for peace. But as long as we stay fractured, our enemies will see us as vulnerable and will launch attacks upon us."

The Matriarch smiled at Asentar as she sat back down on her lavish throne. "I fully understand the capability of leverage. As we speak, the prince of your beloved kingdom prepares to complete my next transaction." Pausing to take another bite of fruit, she enjoyed watching Asentar's curiosity. "A prisoner in the Rava'Kor mines was recently identified as Ericc Dovenar. The son of Ambrosius will soon be given to Darkmere in exchange for his E'rudite powers to rebuild my old crippling body. This will double my life and my ruling days. Your kingdom will soon have no heir and it will no longer exist. I am now the power to contend with."

"I find it doubtful that the son of Ambrosius could be captured by your people."

"You question my power?"

"I question your people's ability to pull off such a task. To do so would be a tremendous feat."

"We are a more formidable force than your bureaucrats give us credit for. They have never given me the respect that I deserve."

"I will inform them of such, if you can prove to me that you have actually captured the son of the rightful king."

"Lucian," she ordered, as she turned to the cowering man. "Travel back to the mines by daybreak to show Asentar what we are capable of doing here in Southwind. Ensure that Ericc is properly handed over to Darkmere's servants when they arrive, then kill Santorray for his crime of living."

Chapter 8
Civej

Returning to his cell, after a day of stitches and herbal ointments, Thorik was frustrated with his conversation with Ericc. He had gotten nowhere with the young man. In fact, Ericc refused to even discuss the issue any further with Thorik.

Pushing Thorik forward down the corridor, the guard from the medical area began to notice that his services were needed elsewhere. Dozens of guards were being dragged away from Thorik's cell.

Da'Shawn helped escort a few guards out of the doorway, as well. "Damn you, beast!" he yelled. "Damn you all the way to Della Estovia." Limping away, he gave instructions to his men to retrieve the remaining men still unconscious inside the cell.

Thorik looked through the bars as he approached the door. Santorray was standing in the center of the cell, covered in blood, and panting hard. Stab wounds and fresh whip marks covered his body, his left hand cupping his right fist as bright red blood poured from it. They had come for payment, to remove one of his fingers.

The guard pushed Thorik into the cell before helping remove his comrades.

Stumbling forward, Thorik felt responsible for the loss of the Blothrud's finger. Even more so, seeing that he was unable to convince Ericc to escape with them. He wondered if he had the right to ask Santorray to lose another finger while attempting to persuade Ericc again.

Da'Shawn returned to the cell and slammed the door. "We'll beat you down, we will. We'll just end up taking two of them fingers tomorrow." He cursed the beast as he helped another guard down the hall.

Santorray opened his fist to reveal one of the guard's ears in his palm, surrounded by all of the Blothrud's digits. Spiking the ear at the ground, the Blothrud collapsed against the far wall from the exhaustion of the fight.

Thorik was pleased to see all of his fingers were intact. "You're okay!"

Still breathing hard and bleeding from his open wounds, Santorray shot the Num a serious look, which for the first time Thorik felt cause for alarm. Reflections from the lanterns and torches made the Blothrud's red eyes glow bright. His heated breath appeared as smoke against the cool damp air.

Suddenly Thorik felt like he was caged with a wild starving animal. He froze, waiting for the beast to leap from his spot. Listening to his own heart race, he made no sudden moves. Instead, he slowly lowered himself to pick up a slug from the floor. Slowly approaching the wounded beast, Thorik placed the slug into the blood, which dripped from its arm. Not knowing the significance, he had seen the Blothrud do this several times the prior night and hoped the gesture would be a show of good faith.

Santorray responded. Respect had been given to him and the Blothrud relaxed his facial muscles, covering his teeth. A slightly kingly nod of approval gave way for Thorik to continue the gesture several more times while the beast healed his own gashes with handfuls of his own saliva which bubbled and sizzled upon placement.

* * * * *

That second night in the cell with Santorray was worse than the first one. Hunger challenged Thorik's already tender stomach, but it was the dehydration and the bugs that were bothering him the most. He curled up in a ball on the damp floor, brushing off the flies that were trying to get at the Num's blood stained dressings covering his stomach.

"I can't sleep," Thorik moaned.

Santorray was still leaning against the wall, watching the dark corridor. "It's wise that you don't. I'm surprised we survived this long without an assassination attempt. There must be something more pressing going on than to rid themselves of our voices."

"I've got to get back to Ericc and convince him to come with us."

"I'm not sure your stomach can take another cut. You Nums have soft skin."

"There has to be another way."

"We'll have to see what presents itself."

"Any chance you could let me know prior?"

"There wasn't any time to discuss it. If the guards had seen us whispering, before the fight, they would have assumed it was a ruse."

The two large doors at the end of the corridor crashed open, echoing though the cells as a strong narrow beam of light pierced the darkness.

Thorik sat up and watched the light turn into each cell and then back down the corridor as someone shouted questions to inmates, followed by screams of pain. The process continued cell by cell advancing toward the Num and Blothrud. An ominous heavy cat growl resonated behind the yelling.

Nerves overcame pain as Thorik looked to Santorray for comfort.

Santorray's tiny thin black hairs on his head and face stood on end as he exposed his teeth and squinted his eyes to focus on the coming terror. Drool dripped from his exposed gums as his instincts prepared him for battle.

If Thorik's skin could glow from turning sheer white, it would have done so at that moment. Edging past the cell wall was the nose of a giant black panther whose mouth could swallow the Num whole. Riding the cat was a young baldheaded man with thick tattoo designs running from his forehead, behind his ears, and down past his neckline. His quarterstaff illuminated his way, changing focus and strength at the rider's will.

Flashing a sun-searing light into the face of Santorray, the rider stared at the Blothrud.

Thorik watched as a second figure emerged. A man-sized shadow walked through the bars, entering their cell. Even the intense light from the staff couldn't penetrate the figure. A cold chill ran up Thorik's back as he watched the thick dark figure of a man walk up to Santorray and reach inside the Blothrud's chest with one hand.

Santorray bucked, arched his back and swiped at the invader with his knuckle spikes, which passed through the shadowy figure without disruption. "What do you want?" the Blothrud asked, gasping for breath.

Light from the rider's staff focused tightly on the Altered's eyes, as the man answered the question with one of his own. "What do you know of Ericc Dovenar's escape?"

"I don't know what you're talking about," Santorray forced out.

The bald rider didn't like the answer. "Civej, refresh this Del's memory."

Responding to his master's orders, Civej placed his second hand up into Santorray's skull.

The Blothrud screamed in pain, swinging wildly at the dark shadow in front of him. "I don't know where he is!"

"Do you know where he would be going?"

Civej's hand created a pain a hundred fold of any headache. Every sound and bit of light seemed to scramble his brain and intensify the issue. "I haven't seen him. I don't know." His words were broken as he struggled to get them out.

"Civej, that's enough with him. See if the Num knows anything," the rider said, pointing the beam of light onto Thorik's face.

Thorik cowered back up against the prison wall, knowing full well that if Ericc had actually escaped, he would be heading for Corrock to attack Darkmere.

Civej released Santorray, whose body went limp from the torture, and stepped over to Thorik. The thick vaporish figure's feet never actually touched the ground as he floated over to him.

"I don't know any more than Santorray," Thorik exclaimed trying to prevent the same fate as his unconscious companion.

"Santorray?" Civej's master replied, turning the light back onto the Blothrud, who had collapsed on the floor. "It is you. What has become of the hero that you would end up in such a place?" he asked Santorray, knowing he couldn't reply.

Shifting the light back to Thorik, the Num could see the silhouette of Civej standing in front of him, ready to apply pain.

"Are you a friend of Santorray?" the rider asked.

Thorik quickly considered his options. *Yes or no? One of these answers may prevent them finding out where Ericc is headed.* "We have saved each other's life. I don't know if you would say he's a friend." Thorik took a deep swallow hoping he had worded the answer properly.

"You saved the life of the mighty Santorray? An Ergrauthian Elite? The only Blothrud to stand up against the immortal Ergrauth himself and live to tell about it. You saved *his* life?"

Thorik sheepishly replied, "Yes."

A subtle chuckle came from the rider of the giant panther. "Then you are truly a legend to be talked about. Unfortunately, legendary Num, today I must ensure you don't have any knowledge about Ericc's escape." Nodding his head, Civej went to work, placing one hand into Thorik's chest, grabbing his lungs and squeezing them tight.

Thorik screamed out in pain. "Please! No!" is all he could utter before his air in his lung was exhausted.

The rider's light focused thinly on the Num's eyes. "Tell me what you know about Ericc Dovenar's whereabouts. Someone must have talked to him and heard his plans."

A second shadowy hand entered Thorik's head, shooting pain in an overloading capacity. Civej accessed Thorik's thoughts, allowing his master to absorb them through the beam of light. Pulling his memories so intensely, it began to leave parts of his brain hollow and without life. It would not take long for Thorik to lose all his memories or even his life.

Thorik's childhood memories of his parents began to fade, as well as his months of being stranded on the palm islands. The extraction was painful, as though the thoughts were being burned out with a flame caused by the rider's intense light from his staff.

Thorik couldn't take it any longer. It was too excruciating. He'd tell him anything he wanted to know to stop the torture. So, he finally broke. "Ericc," His mind was becoming mush as he struggled to formulate words. "Ericc!"

The intense light quickly pulled away, followed by the removal of Civej's hands. Thorik overheard shouting about guards found dead and Ericc's escape path being discovered. One guard shouted to the man on the panther, "Lord Bredgin, he escaped through the east tower and was spotted heading north toward Swardfar."

The Num's eyes were blurry as he began to pass out. His last view, as he tumbled over to his side, was of the shadow demon being pulled into a box held by the rider, Lord Bredgin. Snapping the lid of the small box shut, the bald man tucked it away before racing away on his giant panther.

And then all went dark.

Chapter 9
Escape Plan

The morning ritual of lantern lighting commenced in the prison corridor as though nothing had occurred during the night.

Rubbing his eyes, Thorik tried to shake out the cobwebs of his slumber. "I had the worst nightmare."

"It was no nightmare," Santorray said, resting his arm on one raised knee. Pressing his back against the wall, he pulled his shoulders forward to stretch his spine.

Squinting as he sat up, Thorik was reminded of his stomach cuts. "Who was that last night? And what was that dark mass?"

"Lord Bredgin is the son of Darkmere. He rides the black cat of Shrii, and commands the dark vapors of a Wraylov."

"Darkmere's son? He's here to capture Ericc. We've got to warn him and help him escape."

"He's long gone by now. Who knows where he's headed."

"I do. In fact it's my fault that he's going there."

Santorray's eyebrows lowered. "What are you talking about?"

Getting to his feet, the Num walked over to the bars to make sure no one was coming yet. The only person in sight was the lantern lighter as he made his way down the corridor. "I told him that his father was dead, killed after his battle with Darkmere at Weirfortus. He is now on a quest to Corrock to revenge the death."

"Darkmere has killed Ambrosius?"

"Yes." Thorik stumbled for additional words of explanation before correcting himself. "No. Darkmere set him up and left him to die."

"And how would you know this?"

"I was there. I watched it happen."

"And you couldn't do anything to help him?"

Biting his lower lip, the memories flooded back through his thoughts. Unfortunately these memories had been untouched by Civej and Thorik could remember every detail of the event. "Yes, honestly I could have. But I chose not to. I chose to seal him in his tomb in an effort to save the rest of us."

"So you lied to Ericc, putting him in grave danger."

Thorik had thought this to be true, but refused to say it out loud. "It sounds so much more menacing when you say it. As though I purposely set him up."

"A warrior does not hide the truth by finding a scapegoat for his own actions."

"Ericc and I didn't have much time to talk. We were rushed. The medic showed up sooner than I had hoped."

"Spit it out, Sec. You were afraid of his reaction if you had told him the truth."

"Yes!" Thorik slapped his hands onto the bars. "I was afraid that he would hate me for what I've done. Hell, I hate me for what I've done. How could I look him straight in the eyes and tell him that I not only watched him die, but I closed the doors which prevented his escape?"

Santorray stood up and walked over toward the Num. "So, this is why you allowed yourself to be thrown into the mines? To repent for your actions on Ambrosius, you wish to save his son?"

Thorik's head hung low between his arms, his cheeks flushed with emotion. "Yes. I can't live with myself until I can save Ericc from Darkmere. He means to sacrifice the young man. I will not rest until I have prevented this from happening."

"It is a warrior's soul you have, Sec." Resting his large hand on Thorik's shoulder, he stood next to him looking out of the prison cell. "I will help you on this quest."

Thorik wiped his face clear of tears, which had pooled in his eyes. "Why? Why would you do that?"

"Three reasons. First, you risked your life to save mine, although I'm not sure Lucian's attack would have been life threatening. Second, if Ericc makes it to Corrock before you do, I can help find him. They do not allow Nums to freely walk about. And the third is a personal reason. I owe Ambrosius a favor. This seems like the perfect time to repay it."

"You knew Ambrosius?"

Patting his shoulders a few times, he sighed. "Fought alongside him in more than one battle, many years ago."

"He seemed to have fought most of his life."

"He never backed down to evil. We were proud to have him as a So'Er'Que Dooma Family member. A strong soul with the heart of a Blothrud."

Looking up at Santorray, Thorik questioned him. "So, can you help me get out of here?" It wasn't what he wanted to ask him. Ambrosius being a family member of a Del'Unday family seemed odd if he was also an Ov'Unday family member. But the idea of Santorray willing to help him was too great an opportunity to start questioning such things.

"I can, but it will be dangerous. No guarantee. We'll have to fight our way up to the main exit, past the dragon, Duuke."

"I have a better plan. Can you get us to the supply entrance?"

"Yes, but it's a ship port, with a river that has taken the best swimmer's life and fish that will eat your flesh to the bones before you reach the other side."

"Can you get us there?"

"Yes, but it is foolhardy to venture to such a dead end. I tried it myself last time I was imprisoned in these mines. There's no way to escape from there unless we are fortunate enough to have a ship waiting for us in the port."

"Santorray, can you trust me?"

Looking down into the Nums eyes he searched for his own answer. "Trust has proven to be a vindictive temptress to me. How do I know this isn't a trap?"

Lifting the side of his shirt, he exposed the slice marks from Santorray's blades. "I trusted you. Now it's your turn."

"Do not betray me, Sec."

"Just get us there."

* * * * *

Filing out of their cells, Thorik & Santorray fell in line with the other prisoners as they weaved their way toward the main room to collect rations of bread and mining tools. The Blothrud held onto his side and his demeanor was subservient. He needed the guards to lower their defenses against the eight-foot tall beast for their plan to work. The cuts from their attempt to take one of his fingers added to the ruse.

Gathering his pick, Thorik grabbed his loaf of bread as he looked at the door behind the food table. It was a thick wooden door with a small peephole window, metal hinges and lock. Glancing up at Santorray, the beast winked.

Santorray stumbled in line, grabbing his side. Falling to one knee, he rested from the fake pain as several guards came over to prod him back into line. Using the food table for support to stand back up, it tipped over causing him to fall along with the bread.

He rolled out of line, grabbing his side as he crushed the loafs of bread.

"Get up!" a guard ordered, poking him with the end of his spear, as the food server reset the empty table.

The Blothrud complied, and pushed himself back up on his powerful wolf-like legs.

Thorik helped his friend up, receiving the Blothrud's large hand on his shoulder to give him balance.

Prodded by several guards, Santorray slowly made his way back to the line. It was at this time that the server unlocked the thick wooden door to acquire more rations.

As the key unlocked the door and the door began to swing open, Santorray single handedly grabbed and tossed Thorik at the door. Flying over twenty feet through the air, Thorik was prepared to make their escape.

Hearing the commotion behind him, the server quickly darted though the doorway to shut and lock it behind him. But before he could do so, Thorik hit the door, knocking the man back a step. Reaching for the door again, he pushed it shut just as Thorik's mining pick entered the doorway and twisted, preventing the door from closing.

Santorray sprinted forward, knocking over tables and guards as he rushed the door. Arrows cut near enough to his head that he could hear the whistle of their feathers, but none pierced the skin.

Just as the guard gave a strong shoulder block against the door to keep the Num out, Santorray reached the door with his own shoulder, slamming the man against the wall.

Once they were through the doorway, Thorik turned and quickly locked the door behind them before racing after Santorray.

The short hall opened up into a large cavernous dock area. The fragmented light danced around through the river's mist, landing on the crates along the docks. A large ship was docked at one side, where a few guards and several dockhands had converged, arguing about trade taxes and various other port regulations.

Stacks of supplies, barrels of ale, and crates of tools rested in various locations, many of them blocking the appearance of the prisoners as they raced into the dock area. The smell of tropical plants filled the air as vines hung from the upper mouth of the cave entrance.

Rounding the stacked crates, over a dozen men turned from the dock near the ship, as they noticed the escapees. Additional ship crew grabbed their crossbows and aimed them at the oncoming beast.

Thorik finally caught up to his cellmate and led Santorray to the men on the dock who had weapons drawn. Moving toward the guarded ship, there was no turning back.

A robust man in the center of the guards and dockhands convinced the guards to stand their ground. "Dat beast is look'n ta take the ship fer his escape. Stay togeth'r so he can't fight us one at a time." His clothes were different than the Rava'Kor Mine men and he had a sense of authority about his demeanor. Shirtless, his large sweaty gut hung over his belt as he straightened his vest and combed his hair with a swipe of his hand.

Santorray approached the dock, with the Num next to him. He was looking for options as he counted the heads he would have to slay to escape, assuming he could do so before the other men aboard the ship launched their arrows at him. With over sixteen loaded crossbows aimed at the Blothrud, the escapee's path had come to an end.

Thorik stopped and signaled Santorray to do the same. "Can we talk truce?" he asked the fat man in the center.

The man limped forward, using a Fesh leg bone for a cane. "Stay back by the ship, me lads," he said to the Rava'Kor guards. "I'll show ya how dis is done." Walking up to the two prisoners, he scratched his backside and laughed. "Looks like we got 'ear an escape plan come to an end."

Santorray growled and showed his teeth.

Wiping his nose on his arm, the fat man continued. "Ya know, there's never been a prison I couldn't escape from." He paused and looked back at the guards before looking at his crew on his ship. The ship's name, Sinecure, could faintly be made out from the worn paint along its side. "Including this one," he shouted back to his crew.

Upon hearing his words, a large cargo net was tossed out of the ship by the sailors, landing on the guards below. Raising up from the lower deck, a twelve-foot tall Mognin reached up and yanked a rope, pulling the net tight around the guard's feet. The entire group fell to the ground, entangling themselves more as they fought for their freedom.

"Come on lad, we been waiting fur hours and ready ta be leav'n dis place."

Thorik ran past him toward the ship. "Thanks, Captain Mensley. You were right, they had no plans of letting me leave, but your escape plan worked perfectly."

"I wouldn't say that. I see a Blothrud where the boy Ericc should be stand'n."

"I'll explain once we're underway," Thorik yelled back.

Now realizing that they were safe to escape, the Blothrud walked over to one of the netted guards and ripped off a patch of cloth from his coat. "Be glad that this is all that I'm ripping off you."

Santorray began to follow Thorik up onto the ship, but was stopped by the Captain. "Captain Dare Mensley, I be, and this 'er is my ship. Where does ya think you be going, ya Altered?"

Thorik looked over his shoulder at the captain. "He's with me."

"A Del ya say? To board me ship? A Bloth to boot, I add."

Santorray prepared to push the fat man out of his way until he noticed the captain's men aiming their crossbows at him, again. He restrained himself. "You have something against the Del'Unday?"

"Of course I does, but that ain't the reason I stopped ya. I doesn't recall you paying for passage on me vessel. Perhaps a payment of that large crate over yonder would suffice." He pointed at a crate past a stack of barrels.

Santorray looked up at the captain's men. Hand to hand combat was one thing, being showered with thick arrows was another. He agreed without acknowledging it and turned toward the crate.

With the guards and dockhands tied up in the net, there was no one to stop the Del'Unday from taking what he wanted. Lifting the entire crate with one strong heave, he walked it back over to the ship and up the ramp. Glass bottles clanked and chimed as they rattled around inside.

"Easy does it, ya beast," Mensley said. "Them aren't rum bottles ya be play'n with. She be Nectar of Irr." His mouth drooled and his eyes fluttered as he spoke the name.

Releasing the net's rope to the ship-hands, Grewen greeted Thorik. "Welcome back, little man."

"You're a sight for sore eyes," Thorik replied to the giant. "Where is everyone else?"

"Below deck," Grewen replied.

"Set sail dis 'ear ship before the workers come to der senses!" the captain shouted as he untied the ropes from the docks.

Chapter 10
Reunion

Making his way down the narrow wooden stairs, Thorik was excited about seeing his family and friends. The other Nums had been waiting below deck until the captain gave them the all clear. They all stood up when they felt the ship launch into the river.

"Granna!" Thorik yelled with pleasure as he entered their room. She was the closest to the door, and his first greeting. "I wasn't sure if I was going to make it out of there without your foresight." He hugged her tight before releasing her.

Smiling and nodding her head, decorated with various feathers and leaves, Gluic replied, "Sometimes when I grab for a stone I drop a crystal." Wrinkles tightened around her mouth and eyes as she smiled, causing the soul-markings on her forehead to appear to change shape.

"Very true," Thorik said with laugh. "I do so miss your view of the world."

"Not mine, child. Yours." Pulling one of the feathers from her hair, she placed it into his.

Confused, he didn't have time to respond, for the young female Num captured his attention. She had been standing in a corner holding onto her pet lizard. "Avanda, I'm so glad to see you're unharmed. I was so worried about you."

Reaching out to hug her, Thorik was grabbed by the front of his shirt and pushed up against a wall by his uncle. "I suppose you're proud of yourself!" His face tense, Brimmelle used his body weight to keep the boy where he was. Furious at his nephew over Avanda's incident, his thick eyebrows wedged together while he yelled at Thorik. "You let her be violated!"

"No, I didn't know about it until afterward." Thorik weighed half that of his uncle and struggled to pull his back off the wall. Even though they weren't in Farbank any longer, Brimmelle was still his Fir, and rightful leader of the Nums. Thorik would never disrespect the position by taking a swing at him.

"On top of that, you didn't tell me about your idiotic plan to get in the mine. I had to find out from your grandmother."

"I knew if I had told you, you wouldn't have let me go."

"There is a good reason for that!" Fir Brimmelle yelled. "You could have been killed. And Avanda nearly was!"

Thorik's grandmother stepped up and placed a hand on her son's shoulder. "Brimmelle, the boy meant no harm."

Thorik was thankful that she intervened. She had once again come to his rescue.

Brimmelle shrugged his shoulder, pulling away from her tender hand. "Not this time, Mother. You aren't going to mediate our problems any more. I'll handle him like I should have long ago."

"You think I'm here to be a mediator and keep you from arguing?" she asked with a smirk.

"Not any more. Take Avanda back to our rooms. Thorik and I need to resolve some issues."

Astonished, yet impressed, with Brimmelle's stance against her, Gluic gave him devilish grin. "As you say, my son." Turning, she walked over to hold Avanda's hand and lead her out of the room.

Thorik's heart sunk. His grandmother had always helped him out of these types of situations in the past. Where was she going?

Gluic winked at Thorik as she left the room.

Pressed firmly against the wall, Thorik watched Avanda leave as well, lowering her head after sneaking a glance at him, before closing the door behind her.

The moment the door shut, Brimmelle pulled his nephew from the wall and tossed him across the room.

Thorik landed on their supplies, breaking glass jars and spilling open bags. Thorik's sack of Runestones emptied across the floor as he watched his uncle cross the room toward him. "I'm sorry. I had no idea Avanda was in danger."

"That's no excuse," Brimmelle demanded.

Thorik pushed the supplies out of his way as he worked himself back onto his feet. "How could I have possibly known?"

Brimmelle kneaded his hands as he brewed about the incident. "You have to think ahead and be responsible for what could happen. She was in your care. She was your responsibility."

"You're one to talk. How could you let her walk into the city unescorted to find me? This is as much your fault as it is mine."

Brimmelle's face flushed with anger, and his Num soul-marking changed to a dark red. "That is enough! I am done with this. I've traveled across these lands for you, placing my followers and myself in constant danger. For what? Your disobedience? You're blaming these issues on *me*?"

"No. We did this for the saving of Australis, and the saving of Ericc."

Standing firm with an unpleasant scowl on his face, he raised up one of his overly bushy eyebrows. "So, where is Ericc? I thought the entire reason for us not returning home this last time was for you to enter the mine and free him. Surely this new fat friend of yours, the captain, hasn't led us astray."

"Actually, he didn't. Ericc was in the mines, as he had said. I talked to him."

Looking around the room, as though he expected Ericc to suddenly appear out of thin air, he asked, "Good, but I don't see him. Tell me that you didn't fail, again."

"I didn't fail."

"Then where is he?"

"He escaped before we could break him out."

"Why would he escape without you?"

"He escaped to travel to Corrock."

"Again, you failed to recover him and fulfill Ambrosius' dying wish. You've given this a solid attempt, but as you can see, it's futile. It is time we return to Farbank."

"We can't. He plans to hunt down Darkmere. He'll be killed."

"Sounds just like his father. The one who led us from our homes in the first place. The one who led the provinces and Altereds into a civil war, which killed most of these people. We would be better off without the both of them."

"You don't understand. I have to go after him."

"No you don't. You have no debt to that man. He's not part of your village, your faith, or your family. We, on the other hand, are your family, and yet you continue to place us in danger to follow the desire of a dead man who isn't."

"But I owe him."

"Why? Why must you owe that E'rudite anything? He led us all to Weirfortus. He put himself in a position, which would cost him his life, when we all could have escaped. This is not your responsibility. It was his doing."

Thorik snapped back at his uncle. "My chest hurts every day from the memories of allowing Ambrosius to die as I stood by and watched. You have no idea what I'm going though."

"No idea? You repugnant ignorant boy. Do you not recall my saving your life during the storm that took your parents?"

Thorik was furious at the comparison. "You can't use that against me anymore. I've paid my debt to you!" His voice cracked with anger. "Besides, it's completely different, you *saved* me. You didn't sit by and allow me to die."

"No, even worse, I allowed your mother to die!" Brimmelle yelled back. It felt liberating for him to finally tell the boy of his mother's true fate, which had been bottled up inside him for years.

"What are you talking about? My mother and I were being caught in the flooded river. She was able to help me up onto a tree before she was swept away. I watched as she sank. She died saving my life."

"No, she died while I was saving your life."

"That's not true." His face flushed with emotion over the traumatic topic. "I owe her my life and would pay it back if I could."

"But you can't," Fir Brimmelle snapped back. "When I reached you and my sister in that thunderstorm, she had been washed down to an exposed boulder. A section of the hill had just given way and a large wave of debris barreled down the mountainside toward all of us. I only had time to save one of you."

Guilt overcame anger as Thorik reflected on his existence costing his mother her very own. "You made the wrong choice."

"I know." Brimmelle's teeth clenched. "She was a good woman. The only person I could ever fully trust. And *you* stole her from me."

Thorik wasn't expecting his uncle to agree with him, and yet somehow he wasn't surprised by it either.

Recalling the dreadful night, Brimmelle gazed at Thorik. "Turning my back to her, I escaped with you in my arms. I couldn't face seeing her eyes, knowing I wouldn't have time to reach out to the boulder and pull her to shore." Brimmelle's face twisted as though he had eaten a sour lemon. "Once you and I were safe, I looked back to see that she had made her way to the ledge and had crawled up on her own. Safe from the rushing river, but not from the newly raging mudslide. It swept her away before my very eyes." Bowing his head he wiped his nose. "All she needed was a few more seconds to reach safety. A few more steps. All she needed was for me to help her. But I failed her. My fear of running back down into danger killed her. My desire for our security. My fear. My selfishness."

"Why take it out on me?"

"I wouldn't have had to endure the sight of her death if you had stayed put. By following you into that valley, I saved your life, but cursed my own. Every time I look at you, I hate myself for the cowardly way I let her die."

"Then why take me on as your Sec?"

"It's my way of paying my debt to her. Being a Fir and teaching the Mountain King's words is the only thing I know. What else could I give you?"

"How about encouragement and support for what I want?"

"That's what I gave my sister. By doing so, I encouraged her to take risks and search out her dreams, costing the lives of both her and your father. My endorsement to search for greater things set them off on their quest past Spirit Peak. I was such a fool to listen to Su'l Sorat. His tales of treasure enticed all of us to forget what was important. At least until it was too late. I learned a hard lesson about trusting outsiders which I will never forget, nor will I ever fall for again."

Chapter 11
Stained River

Filth from the mines tainted the river with slimy streaks of browns and reds. Vile flesh eating fish fruitlessly attacked the sides of the ship while freshwater poisonous slugs fought the waves in a futile attempt to reach the deck.

Captain Dare Mensley's ship sailed quickly down the sewage-filled river. At times it was difficult to endure, but they had no time to dock and rest away from the water's smell. It was a chase down the river and to the bridge which linked the cities of Krual'Dor and De'Ceit. Once beyond the bridge, they were free to sail Lake Luthralum.

The captain watched the riverside road for riders. "I can smell them at our heals."

"You can't smell anything over this foul river," Santorray said.

"Okay, then. I can sense it, ya big rud. I know they haven't just let us skip away. We just need ta make it past the Krual'Dor bridge before they get there."

"We'll need a lot of luck for that to happen."

"Luck ain't good enough. We need to beat them."

"Then we need to put luck in our favor." The Blothrud grabbed a few pieces of wood chipped away from one of the crates and walked away from the captain. "One must ask the powers of life and nature for assistance or be content with failure."

"Hogwash. Nature ain't got nothin' to do with it. It's one man's mind against another," the captain yelled over to him.

"Then we are sure to sink in this ship with you at the helm."

"You ungrateful Rud." the captain replied. "Go ahead and appease your spirits of luck for all I care. Makes no difference to me."

Santorray could feel the staring eyes of the entire crew, as he sat down on the deck, in the center of the ship. Ignoring most of them, he gave the giant a growl and exposed his teeth on one side, before turning his back to him. It was a purposeful position to show dominance.

The giant Mognin, Grewen, knew full well what his posturing was intended to do, but he wouldn't give the Blothrud the satisfaction of an argument. There had been bad blood for thousands of years between the two Unday species, and the Mognin could see that the Blothrud had no plans to resolve such issues.

Removing his necklace, which held a large obsidian talisman, Santorray unbraided one of the many spherical beads along its leather path. Tapping the bead twice against the flat stone talisman, he placed the heavy sphere into the center of the cloth he had ripped from the guard's uniform. Two small sticks where snapped in half and then half again before being set onto the Southwind Province symbol that covered most of the fabric.

Wrapping the cloth around the heavy bead and the broken sticks, he opened a hanging lantern and poured a bit of oil onto the cloth before tying it off. "Vo'lar oondra beldortha," he said strongly to the newly created object. Lighting it on fire, he allowed it to burn in his palm until he repeated his odd phrase a second time before tossing it into the Stained River.

Thorik looked on curiously at the event while sitting near the Mognin who was standing on the lower deck, but was still taller than Thorik. "Grewen, Santorray does a lot of unusual ceremonial rituals. In the prison it was with slugs and blood. Why is that?"

Grewen leaned back on the hatch opening and rested his arms on the deck of the ship. The Mognin's twelve-foot tall body caused the ship to be slightly top heavy when he stood on the main deck, so he avoided it when he could. "Most Blothruds believe that all things have a life energy and when they come in contact with each other they have an eternal link."

"What does that have to do with the strange rituals?"

"The guard's cloth could be linked to the Southwind military who most likely is searching for you. I would guess that the idea of sinking it could cause the guards difficulty in crossing the river or traveling by water to catch us. Seems a bit unnecessary to burn them."

"Magic? Is he some type of Alchemist?"

Grewen chuckled. "No, it's more superstition. You should see what they do before they go into battle." The hairless brown leathery skin, which covered his body, wrinkled even tighter when he laughed and his small ears twisted from his smile.

Three large folds on the back of Grewen's neck bulged as he leaned his head back to look at the strong wind in the sail. "If we are successful in passing the bridge before they block us, he'll say it was because of his ritual, or some hex he put on them. However, if we aren't successful, he'll excuse it as some twist of fate due to our not believing, or the powers of nature not being pleased with us. There's always a way out of it for the devoutly superstitious."

Thorik always felt at ease when he was around Grewen. Calmness tended to roll off the Mognin's shoulders and covered Thorik with a sense that all would work out well, even his issues with Brimmelle.

"All hands on deck!" Captain Mensley shouted from the upper deck. "They be in pursuit!"

Fifty riders galloped along the river's dirt road in an attempt to catch up to them. Arrows were already in flight toward the ship but simply didn't have the distance.

Brimmelle and Avanda rushed up from below, searching to see the reason for the captain's commands.

"Make yourself useful Blothrud and grab an oar and 'elp us speed up this 'ear vessel."

Standing to his full eight-foot height, Santorray abruptly turned away from the captain and went below deck.

Captain Mensley couldn't believe what he was seeing. "Damn ya, Altered! We ain't out ta fire yet. Get yur red bulky arms up 'ear."

The captain's crew consisted of humans, all shapes and sizes. Some didn't look like they knew what they were doing. Others looked as though they knew, but in fact didn't have a clue.

Shaking his head in frustration, the captain watched the useless efforts by his men to speed up the ship. "Bottom of da barrel," he said in disgust. "Shoreview's finest recruits." He coughed out a laugh at his own joke before returning to the issue at hand.

The river snaked its way toward Lake Luthralum. On a straight river they would have had a chance for escape, but the Stained River gave the advantage to the riders. Forging ahead up the next bluff, the riders prepared for their attack, while the ship followed the water as it weaved its way to the lake.

Rounding the bend, Dare spotted a wooden bridge high over the water, connecting the two bluff ledges together as the river narrowed tight. Covered with the jungle's vines and moss, thick old timbers held the structure firm as several dozen Southwind archers began to take positions across it.

"Down sails," Dare commanded, "Before they tear 'em apart with arrows and fire."

The crew began lowering the sails as quickly as they could; tossing them to Grewen who stored them on the lower deck.

Loud cracks of thick timber came from below, with a pause between each. Santorray climbed the stairs from the lower deck carrying a cannon, minus its wooden base. Each step up the stairs caused boards to snap.

"What in the blazes are ya doing with me artillery?" Captain Mensley was stunned by the possibility of anyone being able to carry a cannon as well as the fact he was bringing it up at all. "We ain't got the powder to make 'em work."

Setting the cannon down, the Blothrud ignored the captain and walked over to the crate he had brought on board from the mines. Grasping the lid tightly, he ripped opened the top in a single motion, popping the nails into the air.

Waving his hands violently to stop him, Dare Mensley couldn't believe his eyes. "Get yur hands off of me nectar."

Santorray twisted around, grabbing Dare by his vest. Pulling his wolf-like snout tight to the captain's face, the Blothrud's nostrils flared in anger.

Ripping off the front of Dare's vest, he growled as he released the captain and spit on the deck between them. Turning his back on Dare, Santorray ripped the vest into several thin strips before popping open one of the bottles.

"Take me whole damn vest if ya like, but leave me drink!" He pulled off what remained of the vest and launched it at him. "And don't you go marking your territory by spit'n on my ship."

Pouring the alcohol onto the torn cloths, Santorray saturated them before sticking one into the end of a new bottle. Proceeding to do the same action again demonstrated that he was building something.

Thorik looked at the bridge down river and then realized what Santorray was doing. Running over, he began opening bottles and sticking rags into the ends.

Dare jumped forward. "Ya criminals! Ya thieves! Use the bloody rum if ya need to, but leave the Irr alone." Grabbing as many bottles out of the crate as he could hold, he made a mad dash for his cabin, protecting his assets as he limped heavy without his cane. "Crazy beast. Doesn't ya know the value of what ye be wasting?"

Thorik tore some fabric from his own clothes to add to the dwindling stack. "I think I understand. We'll light the fabric as wicks and throw them at the bridge. Right?"

Santorray nodded as he popped open bottles and soaked more cloths.

Thorik pulled several more bottles out of the crate. "So, what exactly is the cannon for?"

A devilish look sparked in the Blothrud's eyes and grin. "Backup plan."

"How do you plan to get us close enough to throw these bottles before they take us out with arrows?"

Glancing up at the approaching bridge, Santorray shook his head. "They'll be firing at us long before we get close enough."

True to his word, arrows began to fly, stabbing the deck with their sharp tips.

Reaching as far as he could from the open deck hatch, Grewen began gathering barrels and supplies. Taking them off the upper deck, he set them near his feet on the lower level, protecting them from the air assault.

Returning to the deck empty handed, Dare watched his crew duck from the missiles and successfully flee any harm. "Running for cover appears to be me crew's strength," he muttered to himself.

"Grab the wheel and ride the port side of the river," Santorray ordered Dare.

Reaching past Thorik, the captain loaded his arms with more bottles to salvage from them. "Not until ya give up on wasting me Irr."

"We're drifting the wrong way," the Blothrud growled at Dare's lack of concern that no one was at the wheel. "Don't you care about your ship?"

"It ain't my ship, it's me lazy brother's. If ya stop kill'n me Irr I can tend to her and bring it back in one piece to the indolent."

Another wave of oncoming arrows hit the ship as Santorray grabbed the lid of the crate and used it as shield to protect them.

Without any sign of appreciation, Dare limped back into the cabin, arms filled with liquor bottles.

Thorik looked back at his uncle who held onto Avanda, protecting her under the stairwell from the oncoming attack. "Brimmelle, we need you to steer the ship."

Brimmelle looked up from under the stairs at the unprotected area at the wheel. "I've never steered a ship. Get someone who has."

"I'll do it!" Avanda shouted. Escaping Brimmelle's hold, she darted out and then up the stairs to the wheel.

Brimmelle clumsily worked himself up the steep steps in an attempt to catch her.

"Where to?" Avanda shouted. "How close do we need to get to shore?"

Sparse crewmembers were still on deck as the arrows from the bridge were landing more frequently and with better aim. Injuries were now being sustained and most of the crew had fled to lower decks.

Santorray took command. "As close as you can without running aground."

Little time was left to make such adjustments before reaching the bridge. Avanda pulled hard on the wheel and quickly realized her excitement had caused a misjudgment in the effort required.

The ship pulled hard to port, nearly tipping the vessel over in doing so. Two men were flung overboard along with ropes and other supplies, which Grewen hadn't collected yet. Loud crashes of glass and metal could be heard from supplies below.

Grewen closed his eyes and moaned as objects on the lower deck came crashing into the lower half of his body.

Thorik held onto the crate, preventing himself from falling and rolling overboard along with some supplies.

Santorray gripped the deck with his wolf-like claws on his feet, while hanging onto the crate of bottles. Nearly half of them had been converted to weapons and would be needed very soon.

Brimmelle had reached the top of the stairs and stumbled toward the wheel, which Avanda clung to. Latching onto the large wooden wheel, Brimmelle made an effort to stop the ship from running into the river's bank. Spinning the wheel in the opposite direction, Brimmelle overcompensated for her first turn. Never steering a ship before, the Fir struggled to properly make up for the direction change.

"Watch out for the cannon," Grewen announced, watching it roll out of control, out of reach of his own long arms.

The cannon tumbled along the deck, just missing the Blothrud, only to be stopped by the ship changing its bearing and swaying the opposite direction.

Realizing she didn't have control over the wheel, Avanda slid out from under Fir Brimmelle's outstretched arms. Sitting back behind him, she opened the red and gold purse at her side.

Her lizard jumped out of her side pouch and ran over to the red purse to spy on what it held.

"Watch out, Ralph, you don't want to eat anything in there," she warned him.

The ship bumped hard against the shore as Fir Brimmelle grappled with the wheel to keep in under control.

Captain Dare Mensley whipped open the door and rushed out. "What ya be doing to me ship?"

Holding the crate firm to prevent it from crashing to the side, Santorray was less than impressed with the captain and crew of the Sinecure. "Saving it. Get over here and make your mark."

Rolling back, the cannon crashed into the crate, nearly taking off one of Thorik's legs. Translucent red liquid poured onto the deck from broken bottles of Irr.

"Destroying is more like it." Using his cane, Dare worked himself along the tilted deck back to the crate. "Years I've dreamt of such a bounty. Damn the moment I let a beast on me ship." Grabbing a third armful of bottles, he left his cane and hobbled back into the cabin just as Brimmelle attempted to correct the ship's direction again.

Grewen had lifted his massive body out of the deck hatch to help compensate for the deck's uneven plane. Using his enormous Mognin body, he shifted his weight from side to side to help Brimmelle keep the boat heading the right way.

Another volley of arrows pierced the deck's surface as well as into the Mognin's thick skin. The few arrows in his arms and legs had no effect on his thick tough skin as he stood on deck, grabbing the main mast for balance.

A well-aimed arrow blazed past Grewen, nicking Santorray's arm and striking the bottle he held, pouring the liquid onto a coiled rope near his feet.

"That's close enough. First blood has been spilled," Santorray barked. "Keep us in near the shore!" he yelled to Brimmelle, who was struggling to do just that.

Grabbing the lantern's flint, Santorray sparked the drenched rope. A flame quickly grew as he grabbed two bottles and leaned the saturated cloth wicks over the fire. Once on fire, the Blothrud leaned back like a javelin thrower and launched one of the bottles high into the sky. The second one was shot from his mighty arm before the first had even arrived at its destination.

Striking the side of the bridge nearest to the boat, the bottle shattered and ignited. Flaming liquid splattered across the surface of the bridge and the vegetation that grew on it. The second bottle struck within a few yards of the first one.

Retaliation in the form of flaming arrows dotted the sky. Over a dozen oil-dipped missiles were now headed for the ship. Captain Mensley had been wise enough to ensure the sails were not up, but that wouldn't stop the ship from catching fire from this bombardment.

Grewen stood up to his full height on the front half of the ship, thus causing its nose to tilt forward and the aft to raise slightly out of the water. Reaching out with his arms, he tried to make himself as big of a target as possible. In doing so, the majority of the fiery weapons struck the thick brown skin on his back. The few arrows that passed him by landed on the deck, starting the floorboards on fire.

Thorik quickly removed prepared bottles from the crate and lit them, handing them to Santorray as quickly as he could.

The Blothrud's aim was more accurate than the archers on the bridge, as he strategically ignited both ends of the bridge with fire. Once they were fully engulfed, the archers in the middle abandoned the attack and attempted to escape.

Ignoring the battle around him, Dare Mensley limped his way back to the crate, on the far side from Santorray, to gather his next armful.

Grewen plucked out a few of the arrows and easily snuffed out the flames on his hide before the next attack of flaming arrows arrived.

A wave of cold air shot from the back of the boat, toward the bridge. Avanda's attempt to activate the magical items from her purse had again gone wrong. Her endeavor sent a crystallized mass of moisture racing for the far side of the bridge. Upon impact, it suppressed the fire, created by Santorray's bottle missiles.

"Sorry!" Avanda shouted.

"Damn, ya girl! I told ya, no magic!" Captain Mensley ordered. "Does ya not remember the hole you put in the side of me ship last time?"

"I was trying to put out the fire on our deck," Avanda said. "I think I've got this figured out now."

"No! No more," the captain ordered. "I'll make ya a deal. I has a small book on how ta control magic. It be yours if ya get below deck and never again perform magic on me ship."

Eyes growing to perfectly round circles, she was ecstatic. "Deal!" She gathered her items and ran below before the captain could change his mind.

Archers quickly ran back onto the bridge, hopping over the section of slick ice on the deck, which Avanda had created.

Santorray was furious that his attack on the bridge had been hindered by a little Num. There wasn't enough time left to re-ignite the far side of the bridge, especially now that it was covered with ice. After throwing the last few bottles at the under-support of the bridge, he reached down and pulled the cannon out of the base of the crate.

Unknown to those on the ship, the ice spell, released by Avanda, was continuing to work as it froze the bridge to such a degree of cold that it began to crack and break apart. Stress from the weight of the bridge, along with the Southwind military, caused fractures as shards began to break off and fall into the river.

Another volley of flaming arrows shot straight down at the ship. This time they passed Grewen, due to the vertical angle. Flames erupted all over the ship. The Sinecure couldn't withstand a second attack of this magnitude once it emerged from the far side of the bridge.

Santorray worked his way to the port side, carrying the heavy cannon, as they traveled underneath the bridge. Finding a railing area without flames, he waited until they began to pass the main support column for the west side of the bridge.

Swinging the cannon like a club at the column, splinters flew in every direction upon impact, and yet the column held. Santorray had one last chance, as he attacked the column from the other side, with another mighty swing of the cannon.

The column shattered and the bridge dropped, but only a few feet. The other support beams groaned as they took on the extra load. Vines began to snap as they also attempted to hold the bridge in place.

Thorik noticed shards from the frozen bridge tumble down to the river, as Avanda's enchantment continued to expand and freeze more of the bridge's base. "Santorray, can you throw something at the other end of the bridge? That frozen section," he shouted, pointing upward.

"It would take something the size of this cannon to do enough damage. And it's not possible to throw it that far."

"Nothing is impossible. Let me try." Grewen had moved closer to the others. Several dozen arrows now protruded from his back, most surrounded by oily flames.

"Mognin's have the aim of a blind mole," Santorray said. "Wouldn't you prefer to hide some place until this is over?"

"Don't confuse defensive logic with hiding," the giant said. Grabbing the cannon from the Blothrud with one of his oversized Mognin hands, Grewen turned and tossed the heavy object high into the air, as though it was a toy.

The giant's aim was not nearly what the Blothrud's was, as it bounced against the vine-covered bluff before falling back down. He had missed.

"I knew it," Santorray growled.

Falling back to the river, the cannon then slammed into the base of the main support column. It was enough to jar the column, snapping it away from its icy crystallized top, which connected it to the bridge.

The entire frozen section of the bridge shattered into shards of ice, dislodging it from the top of the bluff.

Swaying back and forth, the bridge finally began to collapse once the main support beam gave way. Military personnel attempted to flee as they ran and jumped off to the sides, while the bridge moaned and cracked.

Lucian and Asentar arrived at the scene just as the bridge began to crumble. The Dovenar Knight quickly dismounted his ride to help the men off the remaining bridge, while Lucian stared bitterly down at the ship and specifically at Santorray. The beast had escaped, but Lucian would not give up the chase so easily.

Sailing out from under the bridge, the crew of the Sinecure watched as the structure above them tilted forward. It raced the ship downstream as it fell, only to splash in front of the vessel by a few yards.

"You were right, my aim is poor." Grewen grinned at the mishap gone right.

Chapter 12
Lake Luthralum

Santorray burst into the main cabin to find Dare hiding the last bottle of saved Nectar. "You fool! Saving our skin is more important than a few bottles of liquor."

"Watch what ya say about the Irr. She don't take kindly to insults." Protecting the last bottle from hearing such words, he nuzzled it between his arm and chest. "There ain't been a drink that has come near her. Ta call her liquor is like call'n ya a Fesh."

Eyes widened and lips raised on the Blothrud. "No one gets away with calling me a Fesh."

"And that's why I didn't. But now ya understand my meaning." Dare worked his way across the room to the Blothrud. "Ta violate such grace with such loathsome words is not only pure evil, but it also sours the taste of the drink."

Blothruds had an exceptional sense of smell and Santorray was already overtaxed with Dare's body odor. The man apparently didn't believe in the health benefits of cleaning himself.

"I don't care how much you praise your drink, if you jeopardize my life again for something as dry as your Irr, I'll rip you apart."

"Not dry, my Del friend." Stepping up to the fierce creature, he leaned against the beast and looked up at him from under the Blothrud's chin. "Nor sweet. Perfection can only be explained with a taste, then ya'll understand."

Popping the cork, Dare embraced the fragrance rising from the open bottle before lifting it toward Santorray's muzzle. "Inhale."

Keeping his stature straight, he couldn't help but smell the perfume of the drink as he grabbed it. Powerful enough to remove Dare's vile body odor from the air, and yet not overstated. It was a perfect blend of fruits and barley, which could be tasted by his palette before putting any in his mouth. His curiosity had been heightened.

Dare smiled as he watched the Del'Unday on his virgin voyage into ecstasy. "Go on, take a sip. That's all ya need."

Santorray looked down at the captain. "You seem awfully eager for me to drink this. Is this some type of poison?"

"Watch ya words, beast! Give her back if ya ain't gonna partake!"

Pulling the bottle higher, out of reach from Dare, he opened his mouth and poured a swig in. Swirling it around in his mouth for a bit, he sighed with relaxation. "Why the hell did you let us throw the rest of those bottles off the ship?"

"That's what I been say'n." Reaching up for the bottle, Dare felt quite justified by his actions during the battle.

"Get your own," the beast said. "This one is mine."

"Ya can't drink a whole bottle of Irr by yourself."

"And who's going to stop me? You?"

"Na, it ain't that. It's just that it ain't ever been done before. Too much of a good thing will kill ya."

"I've drunk my share before. I think I can handle one bottle."

Dare slapped the sides of his firmly stretched stomach which hung out before him. "I've been known to do me share as well. But never a whole bottle of the mistress Irr."

Hearing the celebration from within, Thorik opened the door and entered the room as Santorray gently poured the liquid across his long tongue. "Captain Mensley, the fires have been extinguished and it looks like smooth sailing ahead."

"Aye, lad." Dare Mensley opened a second bottle and raised it in the air. "We all be safe and healthy now."

Shrugging his shoulders, Thorik didn't fully agree. "Well, Brimmelle's under the weather. I don't think sailing sits well with his stomach. I helped him to his cabin and Gluic is watching over him until he feels better."

"Ya did well out there today, young Num."

"Thank you. I appreciate your help in rescuing us from the mines."

"We be needing a toast to celebrate your escape." Licking with anticipation, he placed his dry cracked lips over the outside of the glass and used his tongue as a plug inside the neck of the bottle to control the flow of the nectar.

"Enjoy, I'll leave you two to celebrate." Thorik turned to exit.

Gasping with pleasure after his first drink, Dare waved the Num back into the room. "Thorik, lad, come celebrate with us." Raising the bottle, he grabbed Thorik's hand and pushed the two together.

"I don't think my uncle would approve."

"Bloody hell, did ya not just escape from the Southwind Mines? The notorious Rava'Kor prison mines at that?"

"I did. But I-"

"But noth'n. Ya be a wanted Num now. High on the list of outlaws. You're famous to all them that hate the Matriarch and her thugs that run dem mines." Dare pushed the bottle up toward Thorik's face.

Thorik could see residual wetness and oily marks on the outside of the bottle's mouth. Dare's facial hairs collected near the end, while small pieces of food stuck on the inside of the bottle, left over from the captain's tongue.

Thorik looked up at Santorray, who was opening his mouth for another trickle of raindrops from his own bottle. The Blothrud's red eyes were at half-mast and rolled slightly back into his head.

Looking at a few floating specks in the bottle he held, Thorik questioned the safety of drinking it. "I'm not sure..."

"Drink up!" Dare demanded.

Lowering it quickly, Thorik cleaned the neck and open end of the bottle with his shirt. As dirty as his clothes were, he still felt it was cleaner than Dare's leftovers. A quick swab of the inside of the bottle's throat was an attempt to get the visual image of Dare's tongue inside the bottle out of his mind. It didn't work.

Closing his eyes, Thorik lifted the bottle to his lips and poured a sip into his mouth. His taste buds came alive with this newfound experience. The toxic liquor went immediately to his head, providing a sense of euphoria. All fears immediately vanished. Life was wonderful. Not a care in the world existed. Vanished were the negative emotions and the regrets he had relating to Brimmelle and Ambrosius, as his mind focused on his senses of taste and smell.

Dare reached for the bottle, but Thorik was too quick. He took another swig, this time twice the amount as the first time.

"Not so fast, Num. Ya be lay'n flat if yur not careful." The captain grabbed the bottle from Thorik who was attempting to wipe his mouth on his sleeve but missed and wiped his chin instead.

Santorray's glassy-eyed gaze led him over to the table in the center of the room, where he fell into one of the chairs. "This reminds me of the celebration after the Humoric victory."

"You be at that celebration, ya say?"

Santorray nodded and raised his hand. "Front line. Couldn't walk for a month afterward. But my arm allowed me to drink."

"It be me inn where ya all celebrated. Festive time it was. Even Ambrosius stored his staff that night and enjoyed the entertainment."

Thorik's ears perked up, but his eyes struggled to do the same.

Sloshing his head the wrong way, Santorray couldn't find Dare as he talked to him. "Really? I thought we celebrated in a tattered rundown rodent infested abandoned castle keep."

Falling into the chair next to Santorray, Dare's backside tooted in a low rumble. "Yep, she was one of a kind. Could hold the lot of ya and still have room fur more."

"You met Ambrosius?" Thorik asked.

Dare was in the middle of a chug on the bottle, causing him to spit some of the liquid onto his chest. While wiping it back up with his fingers and licking them off, he answered. "More than met him. He's a close friend. He trusts me with his life, he does."

Thorik took the bottle from Dare and wiped it clean with his other hand before taking a sip. "Not anymore."

"Why ya go saying that?"

The room began to spin as Thorik struggled to stand up straight. Looking at the center captain of the several he viewed, he handed the bottle back to him. "Because I killed him."

Silence added to Thorik's vertigo allowing him to focus on the spinning.

Laughter roared within seconds as Dare and Santorray couldn't contain themselves.

Dare tried to stand, but quickly fell back into his seat. "Are ya listen'n to the little Num? He says he killed the mighty Ambrosius!"

"Has he told you how he saved my life yet?" Santorray asked.

"Really?" Laughing so hard, it was difficult to get the words out. "I hope dat I don't fall on him and 'urt him before he gets a chance ta save my life too."

Shaking off the effect of the nectar only created a headache for Thorik. "It's true." For a second he forgot what he was going to say next. "I killed Ambrosius to stop a flood that would have wiped you out." Thorik tried to point at them, but was lucky to be in the general area. "So, you see. I have already saved your life once."

Laughter continued by Dare and Santorray while the captain kicked a chair over to the Num. "Have a seat, great flood stopper."

"No thank you. I'll stand." Thorik sat down, not associating his actions with his words.

Dare leaned forward to give Thorik the bottle after his own sip. "So, tell me da truth. Is me old friend Ambrosius truly gone from the earth? Darkmere has no one to stop him now?"

Without cleaning the mouth of the bottle, Thorik took a swig. "Yes, and it's my fault that Ericc is now in danger. Ambrosius was right to do whatever it took to try to kill Darkmere when he had the chance. But I stopped him. And now Ericc's days are numbered because of me."

Santorray belched. "No, it's my fault. The prophecy of Ambrosius' son taking Darkmere's son is my fault. I put Ambrosius' son into this in the first place, when he was a child. I'm the one that owes Ambrosius."

Dare removed the bottle from Thorik's grasp. "No, it be my fault. I owes him."

Thorik's body swayed as he waited for the captain to go on. "Why? What did…you do?"

"I ain't done nothin', just feeling left out of the conversation."

All three roared with laughter until Thorik fell off his chair and crawled his way to the cabin's exit. Using the door handle to lift himself to his feet, he opened the door and stumbled out.

Seeing Avanda looking over the railing, he swaggered over to her. Placing a hand on her back, she jumped and pulled away.

Thorik was surprised at the response, as he quickly retreated and lost balance, landing on the railing. "What's the matter?"

Avanda could smell the alcohol on his breath as the vapors filled the area. His words were slurred and eyes struggled to stay open and focused. It reminded her of Lucian at Rava'Kor. Her instincts kicked in; shoulders up, heart racing, and her back went tense. A flood of emotions ran through her as she struggled not to flee.

"Get away," she ordered. "Don't touch me."

Confused, Thorik reached out to touch her arm. "It's me…Thorik. I'm not going to hurt you."

Flinching away, she wiped her skin where he had touched. "You've been drinking. I told you I don't like it when you do that."

Thinking he had straightened himself up, he was actually leaning slightly backward at an odd angle. "You can't tell me what I can and can do...can't do. You don't know what I've been through."

Tightlipped, she gave two controlled nods. "Nor do you." Turning, she walked away.

"What does that mean? I don't understand."

"Remember that." She then walked through the doorway to the steps below.

Attempting to follow her, he tripped and landed hard onto his shoulder. "Remember what?" Trying to stand, he toppled over onto his other side, where he rested as the cool evening breeze felt refreshing against his face. "Nor do you!" he said loudly, repeating her words back into the air.

Grewen raised his head up from the lower deck. "Troubles, little man?" The giant leaned against the open hatch's corner and rested his arms on the deck on two sides of the hatch trim.

"No, why do you ask?"

"Avanda just came down here in tears, and you're curled up on deck, under the stairs."

"I'm sleeping out here, where I can breathe fresh air."

"I can smell you from here. Are you going to be sick?"

Attempting to stand, Thorik bumped his head under the stairs to the ship's wheel deck. "I'm fine."

"You'd be better off if you kept your distance from your two new friends."

"Santorray...Captain? Why? They're nice to me. Having a toast to our escape."

"Just keep alert around Blothruds."

"What do you have against Santorray? He reminds me of...that Blothrud that helped you escape...from the Coliseum, last year."

"That's because he is the same one."

"I knew it! He's of good nature. He helped you and then he helped me flee from the mines. We're lucky to have him."

"Seems a little too fortunate for us to have the only well-mannered Blothrud in all of Terra Australis."

Thorik had worked his way over to Grewen, fell against the giant's shoulder, and slid down to the deck. "What do you have against Santor…torray? Why are you so standish…standoffish with him?"

"Lessons learned, little man. The Del'Unday, in general, are difficult to understand. Tensions between our two species go back before the great Unday War."

Cuddling his back up against the warmth of Grewen's arm, the Num relaxed. "The Tri-Species War?"

"No, this was at a time when the Ovs and Dels first parted paths. When Hessik and Trewek ruled the lake valley. In youth, they were close allies, but everything changed when Ergrauth launched his forces past the Guardians and into our valley."

"Grab some paper and ink from my coffer. I haven't written in my log for several days," Thorik mumbled as he closed his eyes and backed up tighter against the giant's arm.

Grewen sighed as he recalled the ancient story. "The Blothrud Hessik ruled Corrock. He wished to take Ergrauth head on. A foolish notion. Corrock didn't have the resources or strength to take on such an endeavor."

Calmness embraced Grewen's face as he changed the focus of his story. "Trewek the Wise, a Mognin, ruled over Ovla'Mathyus. He was the architect of our current beliefs. He offered salvation in his city's stronghold, an impenetrable fortress with endless resources to survive."

"Unfortunately, Blothruds would rather race toward death than to walk away to safety." Grewen reached below and lifted up a covered basket of melons. Removing the cloth, he emptied its contents into his mouth, juice splattering the deck with each bite. "Many events followed that caused the friction to increase between our species and our clans. Blothruds have always blamed the Mognins for the downfall of Corrock and will continue to use it as a reason to see us suffer."

Soft snoring resonated from Thorik. It was difficult to know how much he had heard.

Wiping his face with the blanket, Grewen snapped it clean and stretched it out over the Num.

"Safe dreams, little man. You can add to your coffer of notes in the morning."

Chapter 13
Rumaldo's Port

Thorik's Log: April 21st of the 650th year.
*Captain Mensley has docked our ship in Thasque for trading, but our
travels by water will end at our next stop in the city of Rumaldo.
Ericc has escaped the Southwind mines and is headed toward
Corrock to take revenge on Darkmere. We will gather supplies and
attempt to cut him off before he reaches the Del'Unday city.*

Avanda clutched a book tight to her chest before leaving the ship
to enter the city of Rumaldo. "Thank you so much for this."

"A deal is a deal, tadpole. Ya didn't perform any more of yur
magic on me boat. Ya lived up to yur word, so I does as well."
Scratching his backside, Dare didn't like giving away one of his
collectibles when there was still potential profit to be made from
them. Nevertheless, the profit he would have acquired from its sale
would have been less than having to fix another hole in the bow of
his ship.

Captain Mensley pulled up his trousers as he moved his rolls
of fat so they wouldn't get pinched by his belt as he adjusted it to the
next notch. "Be careful with dat book lass. Them words may help ya
figure out how some of yur magical objects work, but spell casting
can become dangerous. Take er slow."

Avanda thanked him again and scurried down the ramp to the
dock as Thorik approached the captain. She had evaded Thorik the
entire trip, his questions falling on deaf ears and her eyes never
making contact. Occasional answers over her shoulder were the most
he could get out of her.

"Thank you again for helping us out," Thorik said. "It's good
to know that there are still people that help others without expecting
anything in return."

A few of the crewmembers scoffed at the comment. Preparing
the ship for a few days at dry dock, they were anxious to get the
passengers off the ship.

"Expecting anything?" the captain coughed, as though the
words hit hard against his stomach. "It's been a pleasure help'n ya all

out. But now I must be on me way to make plans to feed these 'ear jaw flappers. A crew without any grub can turn ugly." Several of the shipmates scowled at captain. "Or should I say uglier," chuckled the captain.

Shaking hands farewell, Thorik straightened his backpack and joined his party on the boat landing. Grewen and the Nums followed Santorray off the docks, and into the city of Rumaldo. Rounding the first corner, they disappeared from the captain's sight.

"Freeloaders," one of the shipmates said. "We did our bit, now where's our payment?" He was quickly joined by others who had stopped working as they gathered around the captain.

Captain Mensley picked up his large Fesh-bone cane and wielded it like a war hammer. "Get back, ya dirty Sandrats. Did ya think I dragged ya out to sea for months to rescue them just fur me kind heart?"

"You ain't got a heart."

"Exactly, coins keep me blood moving," the captain said.

"We don't see no coins from this trip."

"Ah, look closer. Did ya not see the crate of Irr we collected?"

"That ain't coin. Plus the beast tossed most of it out."

"Aye, he did. But I saved enough to sell, given ya all a full belly until we finish our job."

"When does this charter end? First you told us it was to rescue some Nums from a deserted island. You failed to mention anything about a Mog being with them. Then you added a trip to Southwind and up to the mines, where most of us already have a price on our heads. And then we take on a Blothrud who nearly destroys our ship. Now you tell us this journey isn't complete again?"

"Get off me ship if yur gunna whine! I'm lead'n ya all to a lifetime of wealth and yur complain'n about have'n to be away from yur momma for a little longer. Get off me ship or close yur trap!"

The crew grew silent as they weighed their options. Finally one spoke up. "This is the last voyage with you. No more after this."

"So be it," Captain Dare Mensley replied.

* * * * *

It wasn't long before the crew had finished their duties and made their exit from the ship to venture into town for the nightlife.

Dare stood alone on the ship, gazing over the open water, watching the waves come into port. The unique spicy smell of longtail redfish captured the harbor as several boats unloaded their daily catch.

A thin layer of low clouds defused the sunset on the humid evening. It would have been the kind of day Dare would pull out his fishing pole and fall asleep in the breeze, if it weren't for a winged beast heading his way, from the north. Its reflective scales made it difficult to see at a distance, but Dare knew exactly who it was.

The Red-Tipped Silver Dragon dove down to the ship, expanding its wings only at the last second to stop his descent.

"Draq," Dare said. "Ya never mentioned anything about a Blothrud. He destroyed me entire crate! You'll have to come up with a new payment for my time and loss of me valuable crewmen."

The dragon folded his glossy wings and perched on the railing. Slightly taller than Dare, he had the additional advantage of the railing as he looked down over his long snout. "The only things you value are the coins in your purse and the drink in your bottle. Regardless, neither are my problems. You asked for a case of Irr as your payment. I provided it. Your inability to outwit a stupid Blothrud is not surprising, although it's still not my issue."

"Think of me crew. I got noth'n for 'em. They won't help me anymore unless I can show them something of value at the end of this trip." His head sagged as he tried to look pathetic.

"Listen, you fat repulsive human, I don't care about your problems. Besides, Ambrosius knows you stocked away armfuls of your nectar after partaking some with Santorray and Thorik."

Dare's neck cocked to the side and looked directly at Draq. "What? You been spying on me? Ya no good Altered!"

"I have better things to do than watch you. Ambrosius on the other hand is watching everything."

"Really? My sources tell me he was killed in Weirfortus. Closed behind the dam walls he be, under an ocean of water. Crushed. And yet you say he's still pull'n the strings. How do ya fancy he be doing that from under that weight?"

"He managed to float his way up to the top of the reservoir, where I found him fighting off the Death Witch's grasp for his soul."

"Why didn't you save him from being trapped by the Num in the first place?"

"I was detained."

"So, how about that. The Num was right. He damn near did kill the old E'rudite. But how did ya save him from the witch?"

"Let's just say I didn't go unscathed."

"I can just see it. Ambrosius sit'n on top of the world as he looks down from Weirfortus, bark'n orders for you to carry out."

"He's not at Weirfortus, and you are not to discuss the fact that he lives with anyone."

"Then you shouldn't have told me in the first place. It's gonna cost ya to keep me quiet."

"I told you because Ambrosius knew you wouldn't do as I asked without knowing he was backing it. I have further orders for you from him and you're going to keep his existence quiet or he will make sure you can't talk to anyone. Do you recall the battle of Lirsha Mare? Are you sure you want to go through that nightmare again?"

Dare scratched his backside as he recalled the event. "That little Num killed Ambrosius as far as I know."

"I thought so."

Chapter 14
Mythical Forest Archway

Thick twisted timbers, cut from the edge of the nearby forest, outlined the shops and houses of Rumaldo. Solid architectural designs with subtle details and changes to color tones gave the city a sense of strength and prosperity without glitter and glamour.

Thorik led his group along the brick streets in search of final provisions for their trek past the Mythical Forest, across the Kiri Desert and through the O'Sid Fields. The evening light had faded and lanterns had been lit. Pubs and shops lined the main street all the way to the very north end of town where it abruptly ended, marked by two tall twisted leafless trees.

"The entrance to the Mythical Forest," Santorray said. "Not a place you want to venture from the main road."

"Yes, I know," Thorik replied. "I was captured by the Myth'Unday once."

Crossing his arms, Santorray looked down at the Num. "Not possible. No Num or human has lived to tell about it, once captured."

"That's what I've heard." Thorik smirked at the comment. "We'll need to leave first thing in the morning."

"We don't have that option," Santorray said. "The captain's side trip to the city of Thasque to sell his goods has cost us valuable time."

Thorik adjusted his pack. "It's his ship. Be thankful he came to Rumaldo to drop us off."

"He has foolishly allowed the Southwind military time to travel north. We must leave immediately to avoid being here when they arrive, if they haven't already."

Fir Brimmelle had kept quiet long enough. He didn't like the creature's attitude toward his Sec and needed to make a point of it. "Now you listen here, don't you start telling us what to do." His nose was in the air and his tone condescending. "We don't need your help, so either fall in line or leave."

The Blothrud lunged at the Fir with both hands out and ready to grab the Num. Teeth showing, he growled hard enough to make Brimmelle's knees buckle from fear, as the Num fell to the ground.

"Don't ever talk down to me, Num. I'm trying to save your pathetic life."

"Save?" The question came from a slight distance.

A large group of humans had stepped out of a pub to witness the Blothrud in their city. It was uncommon to see Ov'Unday in town and rare to see a Del'Unday.

The man near the center, who had spoken up, continued. "We would all be better off without your kind. Words of saving our people have only led to battles which caused us to suffer."

"Perhaps we should leave," Grewen said calmly.

Santorray stepped toward the group of men. "And I suppose humans had nothing to do with the battles of this land."

"Only to fight for the survival of our kind." He then pointed at Grewen. "And his kind."

"Santorray, don't waste your time." Thorik stepped out in front of him.

"Santorray?" the crowd gasped. Whispering bled through the group.

The Blothrud stood up tall and straight. He knew the stories of his past had been salted with half-truths and outright lies.

"We heard you were dead, killed in Southwind," said one man.

"I get that a lot."

"You're a murderer. You've taken part in many battles against us, killing our people and destroying our cities," said another man.

Santorray flexed his massive muscles and pounded his fist into an open palm. "Who's to say I'm not here to take out yours right now."

Thorik waved his hands in front of the Blothrud. "No, wait! Don't let them provoke you."

The first man stepped forward, waving his finger at the Blothrud. "You're as bad as Ambrosius and Darkmere. They've destroyed this kingdom."

Thorik spun around on the balls of his feet to face the man who had just spoke. "How dare you talk ill of such a great man. Ambrosius sacrificed his life to save you, your family, and your city."

"He's dead? That calls for a drink. No more bloodshed."

Thorik was aghast. "How can you say that after everything he's done for you?"

"He's never done anything to help me or my family," the man replied.

Fists tight to his side, Thorik stepped closer to the man. "Just because you don't know of what he's done for you, doesn't mean it hasn't been done."

"What has that old diplomat ever done for us, aside from launching a civil war that broke our people?"

"He prevented Darkmere from ruling and destroying your lands. He founded the Grand Council to establish peace among different cultures. He sacrificed his life to save you!" Thorik screamed, his fists now up by his sides.

The crowd stepped back from the Num. Unknown to Thorik, Santorray had stepped up behind him, ready to attack the crowd.

Thorik's face was flush with anger and his hands shook with rage. "He gave up everything for you to have the ability to sit in your pubs and drink your life away while complaining about him and others who have fought for you." Never before had he been so angry at someone he didn't even know.

Fearing the long reach of the Blothrud, the men quietly backed off and grumbled to one another, returning to their pubs for safety.

Santorray lowered his arms to his sides. "You've done well, Sec." He then walked back to the rest of the group.

Thorik stood silently, shaking with frustration. These people didn't understand how wrong they were. They didn't know the full story, yet they had already made their judgment. If they had known Ambrosius the way he had, they wouldn't believe the lies being told. The man should have been honored, not ridiculed. If Thorik hadn't condemned him to death, others might have discovered this truth.

Ambrosius had been like a father to Thorik. He had taken the Num under his wing and inspired him to be more than he thought he could be. The old E'rudite had trusted the Num to use his judgment, while guiding him when he veered off course. Ambrosius was a mentor that few fathers could aspire to become.

Grewen stepped up behind Thorik. "You have to let this go. It's been months. Ambrosius is gone. You made the right choice, but you have to move on."

Thorik turned and pounded his fist hard into Grewen's massive leg. He then hit a second time, a third, and then a blur of quick shots as he vented his frustration. His knuckles became bloody from hitting the hard thick skin of the Mognin. "I can't forget what I've done. I see it every night in my dreams and it drags me down in the days. It fills me with anger and regret."

Grewen looked down at the Num. "No, don't ever forget. You can't learn if you forget. You can't teach others if you recall only the good times. But you do need to forgive yourself, little man. Regret and anger will only compound themselves and make things worse."

Three more punches into Grewen's leg hit hard, before Thorik broke down and wrapped his arms around the giant's leg. Tears streamed down his face as he gasped for breath from his own personal pain. "I miss him so much, Grewen. So very much."

"I know. We all do." Grewen patted Thorik on the back. "But it is time to free your heart from hate, including the hate you feel for yourself. It is time to move on."

Santorray interrupted their conversation. "Moving on is exactly what we need to do right now." He was pointing down the main street while talking.

A distant group of torches and flags headed their way, behind merchants and customers who filled the street. The holders of the flags could not be seen from their position behind the locals, but the colors of the flags were distinctly Southwind as they popped up and down from their Faralope mounts.

"Lucian has caught up with us," Santorray said. "No time for supplies, we need to head out of town right now."

"Through the Mythical Forest at night? I don't like the sound of that. Can't we hide in town until they leave?" Brimmelle asked.

"Do you really think the locals will cover for us?" Santorray responded sarcastically.

"Not after the greeting you and Thorik gave," Brimmelle spit back.

"We'll be safe if we stay on the road. Hopefully Lucian isn't aware of that fact."

Thorik wiped his eyes dry and regained his composure. "Santorray's right, we need to escape immediately. Onto the River-Green road, everyone."

The four Nums led the charge out of town; quickly passing between the two large twisted trees. Under the natural arch, caused by the limbs from each tree intertwining, a sudden chill befell them. A background moan could be heard from the tree trunks and distant screams from deep in the forest could be heard.

"Are you sure it's Lucian? We could be running from nothing," Brimmelle said.

Grewen followed the Nums under the arch, but couldn't hear the odd sounds that they did. "It's a risk either way." He reached up and softly touched the limbs of the arch.

Santorray watched the group's back, standing on the edge of the city with his nose high in the air, sniffing. He inhaled the smells from Rumaldo and its citizens, before taking in a familiar smell. "It's him. He's here. I can smell his stench a mile away. We need to hurry."

But it was too late.

A horn sounded and the hooves of the Faralopes began to charge forward. Locals had provided Lucian with descriptions of the party who had just passed through.

"Grab the older Nums," Santorray yelled, racing under the arch, scooping up Gluic, who immediately became limp in his arms.

Grewen lifted Brimmelle and awkwardly ran out from under the arch onto the River-Green road, which cut directly through the center of the Mythical Forest.

Thorik and Avanda easily outran the Mognin and Blothrud, leading the charge down the road.

Lucian emerged from the crowded street to see the criminals escape. "They're heading for the forest. Quickly men, seize them!"

Forty riders tore through the city's street after the prison escapees, knocking locals out of their way. Banners high, the horn sounded again, this time with more energy.

"I want the Blothrud alive. I wish to kill him with my own blade. Kill the rest if you must, burn the forest if you have to, but do not fail me," Lucian shouted as he and the riders reached the tree arch.

Deep voices came from the two trees. "Burn us?" The ground began to rumble and the limbs swayed violently. "Threats against the Myths, do we hear?"

Fear struck all men and beast as they entered the archway. Myth'Unday whispering and shouting came from all directions as the men looked for a source. The ground bucked as roots raised up and wrapped around the Faralope's legs, tripping them and knocking off their riders. Those who could escape did so, back toward the safety of the city.

Chaos filled the archway. With Faralopes bucking and their riders in fear of what they were hearing, Lucian rode up to one of the trees and stabbed his torch into an open knothole.

The dry old wood quickly caught on fire as an earsplitting scream came forth. Fire erupted up the trunk to the arch.

Two Southwind riders lit the second tree in flames causing the same effect.

Burning bright and hot, an arch of glowing yellows and reds filled the skyline at the edge of town. The riders quickly made their way underneath and onto the River-Green road.

"Here they come," Brimmelle said, while holding onto Grewen's shoulder.

"Get off the road, they won't follow us into the forest at night," Thorik ordered.

"There's a good reason why," Santorray replied. "I'd rather fight off a legion of Southwind's finest before taking on the Myth'Unday."

Thorik considered his suggestion until he turned and saw Lucian and his men racing up to them. "We've survived it before. We'll have to take our chances on doing it a second time."

Grewen struggled to keep within hearing distance, as he lumbered along. "Thorik, we were on the outskirts of the forest at the time, and we got lucky."

"We haven't made it too far into the forest this time either," Thorik said.

A volley of arrows shot from behind, several sticking into Grewen's back. The strong legs of the Faralopes closed the gap as the men pulled out swords for the attack.

"We stay and fight," Santorray ordered.

"Then you fight alone." Leading the charge, Thorik turned to his right and disappeared into the dark forest. "Quickly, everyone, this way."

Following Thorik, Avanda jumped off the road behind him. Visibly irritated about the decision, Santorray followed him in as well.

Grewen fell behind, as the military caught up and quickly surrounded him. The giant had slowed to a comfortable walking pace and the riders had a full circle around him.

"Thorik, help!" Brimmelle screamed into the trees. "We've been captured."

Lucian cupped his hands to his mouth and shouted into the forest. "We have your friends. Either you surrender yourself and we let them go, or you hide like cowards and we take them back to the mines in your place." Panning the dark, he waited for an answer to his bluff. He had no intention of leaving without Santorray.

Protecting Brimmelle from the soldiers, Grewen continued his slow walk down the road, interrupting the circle of riders. They were forced to move with him to keep him inside.

"Hold your ground and stop the Mognin," Lucian shouted to his men.

The riders came to a complete halt, giving the giant no more path to walk.

Reaching forward, Grewen calmly separated the men and Faralopes in front of him so he could continue on his walk. "Excuse me." He attempted to peacefully step out of the enclosed ring.

The men swung their swords at his thick arms. Panicking animals made it difficult to aim, let alone stay on their mounts. Nevertheless, a few swipes made their cuts, but did not stop the Mognin from slowly breaching their barrier.

Before the riders could obtain control over the giant again, Grewen stepped off the road to join his friends.

"After him!" Lucian ordered his men, none of which responded. Instead they looked at each other. "I said, go after them. They couldn't have gone far. Get in there and drag them back out." No response. "Those that do not obey will go in front of the Matriarch, for it is her order to return these prisoners."

It was the name of the Matriarch that finally caused them to venture forth, slowly and cautiously, into the dark forest, leaving the safety of the open road.

Lucian held half of his men back. "We'll wait here, just in case the prisoners try to escape back to the road." Lucian had no plans of personally entering the deadly forest.

A rider approached Lucian and his men after passing under the burning trees arching the road. It was the Dovenar Knight.

"Asentar!" Lucian shouted to him as he slowly approached. He knew that not even Santorray could stand up against the likes of the knight. "They have taken refuge in the forest. With your skills, you can flush them out so we can capture them."

The knight said nothing until he had reached Lucian. "You idiot! You burned down the sacred entrance to the Mythical Forest, a landmark that this kingdom promised to keep intact. In return they have allowed us safe travel on the River-Green road. Not only have you jeopardized our trade route, you may have started a war with the Myth'Unday."

"It's about time we burn down this entire forest and rid ourselves of these pests. Besides, we shouldn't be tied to agreements made by those who we no longer follow. Those men died long before we were born and their ways no longer work."

"The kingdom made a commitment to the Myths to stay out of their land and only use the road for passage. Does honor mean nothing to you?"

"When it serves my purpose." Lucian stopped as he heard screams of pain from his men within the woods. "And right now my purpose is to retrieve those criminals. So, enter that forest and bring them back to me."

"I don't take orders from you. I only agreed to travel with you in hopes of finding Ericc. But if you deviate from my path to Eastland and Corrock, then we part ways. I never consented to hunting escaped criminals."

"These orders come from the Matriarch," Lucian said with authority. Just mentioning her name struck fear in Lucian's men.

"The Matriarch does not rule the Dovenar Kingdom or its knights." Asentar turned his mount around and galloped back to the city.

Chapter 15
Myth'Unday

R acing through the forest, Thorik instructed Avanda not get too far ahead of the rest. "We don't want to be separated in here."

She slowed then eventually stopped and waited as the soft moonlight coated her with a pale blue light.

Grewen slapped his heavy feet down onto the forest floor as he awkwardly ran behind the group. He was exhausted and eventually began to slow down until he heard screaming from the soldiers behind him.

The screams were not the soldier's battle cries; instead they were yells filled with fear and pain as the noises eventually died off one by one, followed by silence.

Santorray stopped and spun around, sniffing the air to see if they were still being followed by the Southwind military. Motioning for everyone to stop moving, he listened for any followers. "I don't smell or hear anything behind us."

Brimmelle struggled free from Grewen, stepped over to Santorray, and then reached up to help his mother down from the Blothrud. "Good, they must have turned back."

"Not so," Santorray replied, peering deep into the thick forest. "Nature only sits this quiet when it has something to fear. I hear nothing, not even the leaves in the trees. We are being hunted, and not by men."

Gluic smiled with great pleasure. "Oh my, what wonderful life exists here." She quickly proceeded to collect feathers and decorate her clothes and hair with the treasures from the forest floor, such a stringy moss, long red grass, and colorful mushroom tops. A bright orange feather was the final touch to her hair décor.

A soft voice came from above them. "You are not wanted here. Trespassers must be punished."

The quiet that followed added to the eerie feeling, as the group twisted their heads to look at each other for confirmation that they had heard the voice as well.

Avanda stepped closer to Thorik for protection as Brimmelle held onto his mother's hand to prevent her from wandering off.

"Stick together." Thorik looked back up into the trees for any movement. "They tend to prey on those who stray off."

Without warning, Avanda's scream rang out and echoed throughout the trees.

Thorik turned to find her gone, when only a moment earlier she had been standing next to him. No footsteps were heard, or footprints to follow, she had disappeared, dissolved into the air and shadows.

Not only had she vanished, but so had the rest of Thorik's party, as he now stood in the forest alone.

Cupping his hands near his mouth, he shouted for them. "Grewen? Avanda? Granna? Santorray?" Soft muffled voices could be heard in response, too distant to understand. "Brimmelle?" Thorik yelled in a different direction without any answer.

Shaking with fear, Thorik was deserted and assumed he would now stand trial in the forest by the Myth'Unday for the crimes of entering their dwellings.

A crack of a stick eventually broke the silence. Fallen leaves shuffled and footsteps could be heard. More than a few beings walked these woods in the dark of the night, none of which could be seen.

"Chop him up for a stew," a voice from the shadows said.

"No, I want to taste him raw," replied another.

Thorik's movements were slow, trying to determine what to do as he caught glimpses of shadows out of the corners of his eyes.

"I want his ears for my necklace," said a whisper.

Loud pounding on the ground began to shake the forest floor, kicking up leaves and twigs. The massive invisible steps moved directly toward Thorik.

"His eyes are mine," came another voice.

A second set of slightly softer footfalls moved in his direction as well, kicking small rocks as it raced forward.

Soft voices began to argue about his body parts as several smaller footsteps scurried about, running in various directions. "He's mine, leave him alone."

The two large invisible creatures stirred up dust as they approached, as though they would collide right on top of the Num.

Thorik leaped out of the way, only to feel an enormous invisible hand grab him around the waist and lift him up.

A great noise rang in Thorik's ears as the two large unseen creatures crashed, releasing him into the air, only to fall back to earth on his own.

"Don't bruise him. It makes the meat taste bad," said a voice inches from Thorik's ear.

With the wind knocked out of him, Thorik watched as sand and leaves were kicked up by the two large unseen attackers as they surrounded him. Each time one moved toward the Num, the other would do so as well.

Thorik was again grabbed and lifted into the air. He screamed for help as he struggled to escape. Having encountered the Myth'Unday once before, he hoped that his familiarity with one of their kind would carry some weight. "I am a friend of Theodore Hempton, a Myth'Unday such as yourself. I have passed his test and have been granted the approval to enter the forest."

The voices increased as the bushes and trees rustled more violently.

"My name is Sec Thorik Dain of Farbank, I'm a friend of the Myth'Unday," he shouted out to them.

All movement stopped, though he continued to float in the air in the grasp of an unseen assailant.

Whispering could be heard from the forest floor as it traveled up the tree trunks and into the foliage before vanishing completely. The voices were gone.

Thorik stayed idle, expecting his release. But nothing happened; only the whispering had retreated.

Perhaps the name of Mr. Hempton was not liked in these parts and may have made things worse.

"Sec," a deep distant voice called out.

"Yes?" he yelled back.

"Sec, can you see me?" The voice came through more clearly this time. It sounded like Santorray.

Thorik searched the woods. "No, where are you?"

"I'm holding you in my hands."

Thorik reached out and felt the invisible attacker. The hands and arms did feel like his friend, and once he started to realize this, the Blothrud began to come into focus.

Not only did Santorray come into view, but so did the rest of his party. Each num was moving around the forest without the ability to see one another. Even Grewen stood still, looking around for his companions. Gluic seemed to be the only one too busy collecting items to notice the events unfolding around them.

"Can you see them yet?" Santorray asked.

"Yes. Where did the whispering voices go?"

Santorray set the Num back on the ground. "The Myth'Unday all scampered off once you announced yourself. Perhaps you have been granted clearance."

"I don't understand what happened. Why did you attack me?"

"Grewen was going to walk right over you. I had to get you out of the way so you wouldn't be stepped on."

"You weren't affected?"

"Until I met you, I thought I was the only one to ever escape the Myth'Unday. The Great Oracle, Ovlan herself, sent me on a quest for her cause. In doing so, she granted me immunity from their games and tricks."

"How were you able to wake me from their spell? And why didn't you wake Grewen before he reached me?"

"The close voice of one you trust can break the Myth'Unday spell, allowing you can see what's real. I tried to wake the others, but apparently they do not trust me."

"It will come with time. You have to earn it."

"That is your salvation, Sec. Trust has never been my ally."

"In this case, it was critical." Thorik moved over to Avanda who continued to call out for help. Her abandonment in the forest had spooked her, but her desire to see the Myth'Unday had trumped those emotions.

Avanda watched leaves shuffle as Thorik walked up to her. Unable to see him, she called out to the approaching creature. "Hello? Show yourself. I won't hurt you."

Thorik leaned in toward her. "Avanda, it's me, Thorik. Can you see me? I'm standing directly in front of you."

Slowly Thorik materialized in front of her once she trusted his words.

Thorik could see it in her eyes that he was now visible to her.

"You're not a Myth'Unday," she said with disappointment.

"You're welcome," he responded before turning to free the rest of the group from the spell.

He quickly broke the curse on Grewen and his grandmother, but it took Gluic to break Brimmelle from his visual deficiency.

Upon doing so, they all agreed the River-Green road was still too dangerous, so they would continue to skirt the southern part of the forest.

Still frustrated, Avanda pouted as she fell in line for the trek east. "How come I couldn't see them? Last time I was in the Mythical Forest, I was able to see what they looked like."

"Innocence lost is such a tragic thing." Removing a bracelet made of weeds from her own arm, Gluic grabbed the girl's hand to help her on her way before tying it around Avanda's wrist.

Chapter 16
Orders and Weapons

After traveling through the forest for several hours, to put some distance between them and the road, Thorik gave into Brimmelle's complaining and stopped for the night at the shore of a large lake.

The clear night gave a spectacular view of the Lu'Tythis lights over the water. Wavy sheets of green and blue lights danced in a sky filled with crisp starlight, which reflected on the soft ripples along the lake's surface. A series of lightning bolts sprang forth from the center of the light presentation, and then they were gone.

"Make a wish," Thorik said to Avanda.

Avanda put her head down, paying more attention to Ralph than to Thorik. "This one is yours," she replied in a timid voice. She had avoided eye contact with him as much as possible ever since they rescued him from the Southwind mines.

"Make all the wishes you want," Santorray said, "but we need a fire tonight and that takes collecting some dry wood."

Grewen raised a hand slightly. "I'll take care of it."

Santorray nodded. "I'm going to scout ahead for a path."

"You should take someone, just in case the Myth'Unday return."

Hesitant to the idea, Santorray replied, "I'll go alone. The Myth's have nothing on me."

"Don't go too far. It's easy to get lost in here."

Santorray ignored the last statement and ventured in the opposite direction of the lake, over a small hill. He walked for a mile until he found an opening in the woods.

Stepping up on the highest point in a small glade, Santorray pulled a bead from his necklace and tapped it onto the talisman, which also hung from it. The round bead had the weight of lead and the texture of bark, as he placed it in the center of his palm.

Tightening his grip on the bead in his right fist he repeated a phrase several times. "Illume dula fara'du." By the fourth time he had said it, red light glittered from between his fingers.

Twisting his body, he pulled his arm back into position before firing the glowing bead high into the air, over the treetops. The missile of light gave off enough power to be seen from a distance, but not enough to brighten up the area. After the apex of its flight had been achieved, the light flickered out as it fell back to earth.

Crossing his arms, he stood silently, waiting impatiently.

The sounds of the tree leaves seemed loud against the backdrop of near silence. A stray chirp from a bird occasionally broke up the bland white noise.

"Where are you?" Santorray said into the night air.

Frogs croaked softly in the distance as he stood firm, peering into the night sky.

A breeze blew through the trees in front of him, and then to his left before coming back behind him to complete the full circle, and then it receded. Silence again followed.

Santorray sniffed the air, ripe with a fresh scent. "Come forth. Show yourself."

The woods did not reply.

Regardless, the Blothrud could feel himself being stalked as though he was the prey. Not a feeling he was accustomed to.

Deafening silence interrupted nature's music as the crickets cowered, frogs froze, and birds broke off their songs in mid-chorus. Absolute quiet had a way of making the night seem darker and chilled.

A sudden gust of wind raced out of the woods and rushed up to slap at the red Del'Unday's back, pushing him forward.

Rotating quickly, he swiped his knuckle blades at the object only to find nothing was there.

A second strong blast of air pushed up against his back. Twisting, he nearly made it all the way around before he was struck by a large black mass, knocking him to the ground.

Preparing to leap up, he saw a wave of distorted lights and reflections leaning over him. It arched over his body, from the ground on his right all the way to the ground on his left. The colorless mass reflected the Blothrud's faint image several times across the archway.

"Get off me!" Santorray ordered.

"I think you've forgotten your place, assassin. You work for me."

Growling at the comment, Santorray stood up as the reflective wings from the creature folded up against the sides of the dragon.

"I'd fight my way through Della Estovia before I'd ever work for you, Draq."

The Red-Tipped Silver Dragon tightened his wings and stretched his neck out to increase his height, which still only came to Santorray's shoulders. "And yet here we are, me giving orders to you."

"Relaying orders to me. You're nothing more than a carrier pigeon."

Wings sprang to his sides in anger. A natural instinct to demonstrate his size with his huge wingspan. "Don't you dare compare me to a Fesh."

"If you sneak up on me one more time, I'm going beat you down like one."

Draq stretched his neck, fanned his wings and slapped his tail about in anger.

Lowering his chin, Santorray pressed his forehead hard against Draq's and pushed downward.

Draq raised one of his large back legs to strike the Blothrud's midsection.

Grabbing the dragon's leg before it could land a severe attack, Santorray held it at bay with both hands.

They both pushed hard against each other, neither making any headway. Growling and cursing each other's name, they locked horns in a show of dominance.

"Give me my weapons and let me perform my duties," Santorray ordered.

"I don't believe you're capable of this request. Have you even found him yet?"

"Yes, now give me the damn dagger so I can kill him and get it over with."

"Not so fast, it must be done in public. Visible to many of Darkmere's allies. The dark one himself, if at all possible."

Santorray pushed the head of the dragon down by several inches. "Don't tell me how to do my task."

Draq whipped his tail under his legs and slapped the Blothrud's legs out from under him. In doing so, Santorray tossed the dragon's leg high into the air causing the dragon to land on his back.

They both crashed hard against the moss covered mound.

Calmly, the two slowly stood back up, leaving a generous distance between them.

Draq was tired of the confrontation. "Your supplies and Varacon are just beyond that thorn grove."

Santorray nodded his head in acceptance for the information. "Tell Ambrosius that Ericc will soon be dead."

"Where do you have him tied up?"

"I don't. I found him in the Rava'Kor mine. He escaped and is heading toward Corrock. I'm traveling with a group of fools who think Ambrosius asked them to save Ericc."

"Yes, Dare Mensley informed me of your meeting with the Num, Thorik, and his friends."

Santorray walked behind the thorn bush and collected his weapons and supplies. "Don't worry, I won't let any of them get in my way." Partially unsheathing the virgin dagger, Varacon, he looked at his reflection in its spiraling blade before storing. Gems were embedded into its hilt and rune markings told of its powers. "Their deaths will only add to the list that this journey has created."

"As annoying as these Fesh can be, you are not to harm them. Ambrosius provided me instructions if you were to run into them. Follow Thorik. He is clever and will lead you to Ericc and most likely Darkmere as well."

"We are heading to Corrock. I can't ensure that Bredgin or his father will be there."

"Then stab Ericc in the Del'Unday city for all to see, including Thorik. This should take care of this mess. Bring the dagger back to me with Ericc's blood and your task will be complete and your debt paid."

Chapter 17
Avanda

Flames from the campfire turned various colors and faded away as the air smelled of rotten eggs from the poorly executed magical spell. This continued for a few more seconds as Avanda flicked liquid from her fingertips while reading a passage from the book she had received from the captain. Each phrase was spoken with more authority, as the flame finally doubled in height and twisted like a tornado before returning to normal.

Grewen leaned back on his elbows and held a foot into the magical flame. Hotter than normal, he savored the therapeutic feeling between his toes and on the sole of his foot.

Brimmelle was disgusted with the giant's ugly callused foot hovering over the fire and was not shy to complain about it.

Ralph was unimpressed with the magic as he stalked insects close to Gluic who was setting out the crystals and stones she had collected on her trip. Each item had a specific place in the sand where she gently set it down. Racing around her, the lizard somehow knew not to step inside her circle of stones.

"Avanda, Ambrosius warned us about the dangers of magic," Thorik said.

She ignored him, and tried her spell again, this time with more control and longevity.

Brimmelle's thick eyebrows pulled tight as he looked at Thorik while pointing at Avanda. It was obvious he expected Thorik to resolve this growing issue.

"You heard me." Thorik was visibly irritated.

Avanda stopped and challenged his stare. "Ambrosius isn't here, is he?"

This was the first time she had challenged him with such boldness. He had to respond firmly. "Well, in his absence, I am warning you."

"Warning accepted, but not taken."

"Yes, you will." Thorik knew he was being watched by the group to see if he could handle the situation.

"Why?"

"Because it's dangerous," Thorik said with more force than planned.

Ralph felt Avanda's tension and turned toward Thorik, raising and lowering his body with his mouth wide open to intimidate him.

Avanda tucked her magical items back into her purse. "It was an accident. One time. The captain was able to fix his ship."

"Not just from that standpoint. You're too young to understand the power that you carry."

"Who says?"

"I say."

"Who are you to say what I can and can't do?"

Snatching the purse of magic from her hand, his anger began to show in his sharp voice and movement. "I'm responsible for you."

"Really? Well it didn't seem like you felt that way in Rava'Kor, while I was being touched by those drunks. Standing there, helpless. If I had understood magic better, I could have taken care of them myself. I obviously can't rely on you to be there for me."

Avanda ran out of the camp. Her hands covered her face to prevent exposing the tears from her emotions.

"Avanda, wait." Thorik hurried to follow her. But it was too late; she had escaped the campfire light, into the shadows of the trees, which hung over the lake's shoreline.

Brimmelle smirked at Thorik as the young Num left the group. "Not so easy to raise someone, is it?"

Leaving the perimeter of the camp, Thorik followed Avanda along the lake's grassy banks for several minutes until she finally stopped and leaned against a tree.

Thorik approached cautiously, as though she was a viper ready to strike. "What's with you? Why are you always mad at me? You won't even look me in the eyes anymore." He attempted to comfort her by placing his palm gently on her shoulder.

Flinching hard from his touch, her eyes filled with anger. "Don't!"

"What happened to you? Why won't you tell me?"

"I shouldn't have to tell you. You should have been there to prevent them from..." searching for a word she could speak without feeling ill, she continued, "...groping me."

"I'm sorry about what happened, but I had no idea they were outside the pub waiting for you."

"You should have. You promised."

"I promised? When?"

"After Uncle Wess left me. You promised that you wouldn't leave me alone. You'd protect me."

"That's not fair. I didn't leave you. *You* left the pub."

"That's because you wouldn't leave with me. You told me to go."

"I couldn't leave. I had to get into the mine to save Ericc."

"His safety is more important than mine?"

"No, of course not. You would have been fine if you hadn't upset Lucian in the first place."

"So, this is all my fault. Not yours, not Lucian's, but mine. I'm the one that caused all of this."

"I didn't say that."

"You didn't have to. I can tell just by the way you and Brimmelle look at me. Your disappointment in my actions that caused it to happen."

"Well, if you hadn't-"

"See, right there. You blame me for this. I deserved it because of the way I behaved, or the way I stand up for myself, or the way I live my life."

"Avanda, we're not in Farbank anymore. You can't get away with doing the same things. The way you act directly affects how strangers respond to you. They haven't grown up with you to know how good a person you really are. It's your responsibility to make a good impression on them at your first meeting."

"Have you noticed, that not once have you told me that this was Lucian's fault? I thought you loved me for who I was and would always be there for me. Not to lecture me for what I'm not."

"I care for you greatly, and I hate Lucian for what he did," Thorik said.

"You didn't care enough about me to stop their heckling in the first place."

"It wasn't that important. They didn't bother me."

"It was important to *me*. It bothered me a lot. I've never cowered down to bullies like you do. And now look at me. I can't stand to even be looked at by a man, let alone be touched." She cleared the tears from her face. "Thorik, I trusted you. I believed in you even when others didn't. You promised to take care of me, and you didn't. And then when I need you most, you blame me for what happened."

There was truth to her words. His focus on reaching Ericc had consumed him so much that he had ignored his companion's feelings. "I dropped a crystal trying to pick up a stone."

"What?"

"Nothing. It was just something Gluic was trying to tell me."

Turning his back to her, he gave her some space. His hands tight behind his back, he pondered how to settle the issue so the bickering would stop and the tension would ease. "I'm tired of being so careful of what I can say around you, afraid that it may upset you. What do we need to do to resolve this?"

"Resolve? You can't just fix this like you mend a cut. You have to listen to me."

"But I have listened to you," Thorik said. "And I still don't know how to help you move on."

Avanda shook her head in disappointment. "You heard what I said and you want my pain to go away. But you haven't listened to me and understood my feelings. I never asked you to solve my problem, only to understand how I feel about it and be there for me."

Thorik picked up a few pebbles and started skipping them one by one across the lake's surface. "I'm sorry, Avanda. You're right, I just..." One of the small rocks stopped in midair and then fell straight down to the ground, prior to leaving the shore and hitting the lake's surface.

"Ouch," a tiny female voice said from the lake's shoreline.

He didn't see anyone. "Hello?" he asked instinctively, before realizing that he might be speaking to a Myth'Unday.

"Close your eyes," Thorik said to Avanda. He spun around and jumped back to her.

"Too good to look upon me?" the voice asked. It wasn't a whisper like the faeries from before, this voice sounded more solid.

Avanda peered past Thorik in an attempt to see what he was blocking. "Thorik, what is it?"

His hand reached for her eyes, covering them only for a second before she sprung away from his touch. "Don't look at it. It will cause you great fear."

The voice closed in behind Thorik. "Are you saying I'm ugly? A face that could turn you to stone? Is that what you think of me?"

"I want to see!" Avanda yelled, pushing Thorik aside.

Thorik heard silence as he kept his eyes shut. Reaching out, he couldn't find the younger Num. "Don't look at it. Close your eyes."

Avanda had stepped away from Thorik. "She's beautiful."

"Did you think Ovlan would create something hideous for her forest?" the voice replied.

"Run, Avanda!" Thorik shouted. "Get out of here while there's still time. Get back to camp."

Avanda ignored him. "I've never seen anything like you before. You're not like that faerie I caught last year."

Thorik's words became background noise to Avanda as he continued to shout to her.

"Yes, I'm unique in all the world."

"There isn't any other of your species?"

"Only one. But my brother is deformed and grotesque. Only I carry the beauty of our species."

"I'm so glad I can see you. You're amazing."

"Yes, I am."

"I'm Avanda. What 's your name?"

"Raython the ethereal."

"Thank you for letting me see you. I can't wait to tell everyone in camp."

"I'm afraid that won't be possible. I can't let you spin tales about my beauty," Raython said. "No words could possibly do me justice. No matter how hard you tried. Even if you could, it would just cause others to seek me out to gaze upon my beauty."

"I'll only tell a few."

"No one must know."

With a large sigh and shrugging of her shoulders, Avanda accepted the criteria. "I won't tell anyone when I get back."

Raython laughed. "Honestly, how could you not let my secret out after seeing such a magnificent creature as myself. The truth is, no one could restrain themselves. That's why you can't go back."

"What? I have to go back. They're waiting for me."

"Then they will be waiting a very long time."

Avanda's shoulder's rolled back as she crossed her arms. "They'll come looking for me, and they won't let you keep me."

"You will be long gone by that time, assuming you exist at all anymore."

Avanda felt uneasy about what Raython was saying and sought to regain the upper hand. She grabbed for her purse of magic, only to find she didn't have it with her.

An evil smile crossed Raython's face. "Say goodbye to your friend." She indicated Thorik, who was still shouting at Avanda to run away while covering his own eyes.

Avanda finally took heed of his words and bolted for Thorik, grabbing his hand on her way to camp.

The escape was short lived as she was jolted backward, spinning Thorik around as he held her tight with both of his hands.

"You've looked upon my grace, you must pay the price."

Thorik held his eyes closed. "She's hideous, Avanda. You've failed her test, and now she will take you away."

"What test?"

"You saw what she wanted you to see, what you wanted to see, instead of what she really is, a repulsive ill-looking creature."

"How would you know?"

"Her brother, Mr. Hempton, told me about her, after I defeated him in his game and won our freedom."

"Theodore?" Raython shouted, scanning the forest for her brother. "Wicked is he who lies about me. He's the ugly one."

"No, it's you." Thorik opened his eyes and stared hard at Raython. He saw her as a hunched over beast of wart-covered skin, long nose, bony arms, pointed ears, and crooked teeth.

"How dare you look upon me without my permission," Raython said. "Your eyes diminish my beauty. Like footsteps across a stone floor, every step you take wears at its luster. Who gave you the right to see me?" She lunged forward at him.

Thorik lifted up a mirror, which he had taken out of Avanda's purse of magic, successfully stopping the Myth'Unday's attack. "Your brother did." Fortunately Thorik had kept the purse after he took it from Avanda back at camp. He had recalled Avanda telling him about enchanting the mirror to only reflecting the truth.

Raython looked at her reflection and screamed, seeing the same creature which Thorik had envisioned. She backed away from the sight. "What have you done to me? You evil Num. You've made me hideous."

Stepping forward, with the mirror held firmly in front of him, he worked his way closer to the Myth'Unday.

She finally released Avanda to cover her own eyes from the horror of her own reflection.

"Avanda, run back to camp. Get help while I hold her off," Thorik ordered.

Avanda eagerly ran off to alert the others of their danger and return with help.

"I had a mirror once," Raython cried from her own reflection.

"I know, your brother told me he broke it."

"Yes, that's what caused this abomination before you."

"You weren't always deformed?"

"No, not until that day. I once truly was the most beautiful life Ovlan had ever created. I admit that I let it go to my head. Especially after Theodore first gave me the mirror. I went insane with power over my own looks as I gazed at my reflection for years. The mirror and I became one in the same. And when my brother broke it, it took my looks with it."

"I'm sorry to hear that. But it sounds like he was trying to save you from yourself."

"Perhaps," she admitted. "But if only you could have seen me back then. Long silky black hair, perfect complexion, soft Num-like nose, and bright purple eyes. I was amazing."

As she spoke, Thorik envisioned her body looking like it once had. Before he knew it, she was once again beautiful and amazing to behold.

Raython grinned. "And now, my dear Num, you are mine for failing the test."

Chapter 18
The Great Oracle

Thorik hung from the branch like an icicle. The game had been lost, he had been captured, and his options were slim.

Raython danced in front of her prisoner, enjoying her victory until she heard a noise from within the woods.

A tall, thin woman emerged from the trees and approached them. Her hair was made of golden wheat interlaced with long thin green grass, flowing down to her lower back. Her dress was a mixture of leaves and moss, and her silky white skin gave off a slight glow.

Raython turned and bowed toward the woman. "Ovlan, my lord. To what do I owe this greeting?"

Ovlan's walk was more of a glide, as her feet never disturbed the leaves she stepped on, nor left a footprint in her wake. "What have you captured, my dear little Luchorpan?"

Rubbing her hands together, Raython turned her head to look back at the Num without ending her bow. "Dinner. He failed my test, he's mine to keep."

"Indeed." Ovlan's voice was soft and airy, and yet was heard as though she was whispering into the Num's ear. "My children told me of one named Thorik who they met earlier today. Is this him?"

"I caught him without their help. He's mine. He will be a tasty meal for my starving body. I get so few outsiders."

"Not this one, my love. This one is special. My children have captured several men near the River-Green road. You may select any of those for yourself."

Disappointed, Raython knew better than to argue, so she nodded in agreement and rushed off into the forest.

Ovlan then approached Thorik, and softly brushed a finger against his cheek. "I have been looking for the Polenum named Sec Thorik Dain of Farbank." Ovlan's glossy dual-ringed eyes tightened their focus on the Num's eyes. "It's good to see you again. It has been a very long time."

Thorik's confines released without warning, dropping him to the beach. Confused, he looked at the woman before him. Her body flowed like water under a flawless silky layer of nearly transparent skin. "Do I know you?"

Her smile was warm like his mother's. So much so that it made him uncomfortable.

"Have we met?" Thorik asked.

"I have met you, but you have not met me."

"I think I would recall if I had seen you at some point."

Her smile continued. "You have done what I asked of you and risked so much for me. It is my turn to repay you."

"I haven't done anything for you," Thorik said.

"Not yet. But you will."

"I don't understand."

"What is it you need from me?" Ovlan asked. "Where are you traveling?"

"I'm traveling to Corrock to save a young man from being sacrificed. Darkmere, his son Lord Bredgin and his Wraylov are hunting him. I need a way to fight them off and protect him."

"Ah, a weapon you seek. Perhaps the Spear of Rummon." She smiled with a distant look in her eyes. "Seems fitting to bring Rummon back into the land, and by you of all people."

"I was thinking more of a sword or an axe. Something I can fight with to get in and out of Corrock. A spear seems so limited. I need something that will help me out a little more."

"No, Rummon will serve you well. It's the least he can do."

"He? The spear is a he?"

"Yes, he is the one who took the life of the one your people call the Mountain King. This would be a good opportunity for him to make amends with the Polenums."

"The Mountain King? You want to give me the spear that killed the Mountain King?"

"No, of course not. I'm only going to tell you were he is. It will be up to you to retrieve him."

"No! I don't want to wield the weapon that killed the greatest Num who ever lived. If I were to find it, I would destroy it."

"I don't think you would."

"Why?"

"Because Rummon has suffered enough. He wishes to repent and help you on your journey."

"I would have to be insane to use such a weapon. Fir Brimmelle would never let me even carry it."

"Rummon agonizes the days away beneath the water carved vats of boiling water and mud. It is in the heart of Carrion Mire where he is imprisoned to the end of time unless you save him. He waits for forgiveness. He wishes to be strong again. He needs you to find him."

"I don't even know where the Carrion Mire is."

"Your companion does. Santorray will help you. But Rummon is destined to be yours."

"But we don't have time. We must catch up to Ericc before he tries to attack Darkmere. He'll be captured. He'll be sacrificed."

Ovlan gave him another gentle smile. "You may only choose one path. Do you wish to prevent him from being captured in Corrock or sacrificed in Surod? I do not foresee you being able to do both, and the latter cannot be accomplished without Rummon."

Chapter 19
Choosing a Path

"Absolutely not!" Santorray crossed his arms and spit on the ground between Thorik and himself. "We still have a chance to intercept Ericc before he reaches Corrock. Hunting down a weapon requires time we don't have to spare."

Stepping forward onto the Blothrud's saliva, Thorik rubbed his foot in the ground and accepted the challenge. "Ovlan said it was the only way to save him, so that is what we do."

Santorray flexed his muscles and let out a roar. "Dare you challenge me on this? I've risked my fingers and life for you and yet you trust a stranger who claims to be the Great Oracle over my proven judgment? How do you know it wasn't another Myth'Unday trick? I would need to see her for myself."

"You can't. She's gone."

Brimmelle stepped up to be heard. "Thorik, we've had enough of your adventures. You promised to find Ericc and then bring us back to Farbank. Mother and I can't take much more of this. I'm with the Altered on this."

Thorik looked at his group, reading their faces of doubt about Thorik's story. "It was the oracle, Ovlan. I know it. I trust my instincts on this."

"How do you know for sure?" The booming voice of the giant Mognin came as a shock to Thorik.

"Grewen, don't you, of all people, believe me?"

A compassionate grin crossed the huge face of the Mognin. "It's simply a question, not an accusation."

Thorik panned the group. "I think it's *more* than a question from the rest of you."

Walking over to her grandson, Gluic placed two black stones in his hand. "People say I see things that aren't there also. But we know better." She winked at him in approval and then thinned out the dead grass from her belt to make room for fresh foliage.

Her words didn't make him feel any better.

Grewen pulled a flaming log from the fire and began pressing it into the arch of his foot to relax his muscles. "To be honest, Thorik, we didn't see anything."

Thorik pointed at the youngest of the group. "Avanda did!"

Lowering her eyes, she shook her head. "I only saw Raython, and you turned her into a hideous creature with my magic mirror."

Gluic lifted up a thin crystal. "Ovlan's as lovely as the forest itself. I so miss her." By now, she had collected and was wearing at least one item of every plant type they had passed. Grass, flowers, leaves, and sticks were tied to a part of her body or clothes or were garnishing for her hair.

"Well, it doesn't matter what you saw," Thorik said to Avanda. "You must believe me, our only option to prevent the sacrifice is to obtain the Spear of Rummon in Carrion Mire."

Santorray shook his head. "In Carrion Mire? It's the wrong way, costing us critical time."

"I don't care."

"Do you even know where it resides?" the Blothrud asked.

"No. Ovlan said you would know."

"I do, but I refuse to tell you for your own safety."

"Santorray, if you're too afraid to travel there, then give me the heading so we can go on without you."

"Fear has nothing to do with it. Certain death I can face, for a noble cause. Risking our lives for a weapon, when we should be catching up to Ericc, is a fool's journey."

"Allow me to be foolish. Tell me where it is and you can be on your way."

"No. Even if it was truly Ovlan, her quests are usually more dangerous than they sound."

Gluic stepped behind the Blothrud. Grasping her thin long clear crystal in one hand, she reached out and touched the side of his arm.

A fraction of a second passed as she saw his thoughts with the aid of the crystal. The trail he had traveled into the mountains and the cliff wall he climbed to Carrion Mire. Seeing through his eyes she looked out from the mountaintop and assessed his location.

But before the visions ended, the pendulum swung from past to future. Santorray raised his weapon and thrust it deep into Gluic's body. She watched herself fall to the ground; the blade had struck her heart.

The moment of contact with Santorray was over and Gluic fell to the earth in much the way she had seen herself do in the vision.

"What did you do?" Brimmelle yelled at the Blothrud. His fists prepared for attack, but were ignored by Santorray's focus on Gluic.

Thorik ran to his grandmother and cradled her head in one hand. "Granna, are you hurt?"

After a few breaths of recovery, she opened her eyes. Peering at the beast that still stood over her, she lifted her crystal to display it. "I know the way. We don't need your guidance."

The Fir's fists twirled around, ready for combat. "You heard her, be gone."

Like a flash of lightning, Santorray reached down and scooped the crystal from her. "You obviously didn't see everything, old lady, otherwise you'd realize how dangerous it is."

"I've seen enough. Past. Future. The crystal carries more than you know."

Using his mighty strength, Santorray crushed the crystal into several pieces and spiked them to the ground. "Don't ever play that game with me again."

Shocked, Gluic screamed as if she had just seen her own child die. Greenery fell from her body until she regained her composure.

"Enough!" Thorik was tired of the arguing which was rushing toward physical violence. "Gluic, can you take me to this Carrion Mire?"

"Yes."

"Good. Are the rest of you coming with us?"

"If mother is going, then I will not be left behind." Fir Brimmelle helped her up.

Avanda nodded her head in agreement, as though she had an option. Thorik and Brimmelle would have never allowed her to be left behind.

"I promised I would help protect Ericc from Darkmere," Grewen said.

Thorik's group all turned to see the Blothrud's lips ride up and expose his teeth with anger.

Thorik accepted the snarl as a no. "Then we part paths here."

"I will go with you," Santorray growled.

"We can't trust him," Brimmelle said.

"Do you need him?" Gluic asked Thorik.

It was Gluic's words that concerned him the most. *What had she seen through the crystal?* Thorik thought as he turned to address the Blothrud. "Why? Why should we take you with us?"

"You'll never make it on your own."

"We've made it across this land without you."

"Not into Corrock to save Ericc and never through Carrion Mire."

"Why the sudden change? Why do you want to join us?"

"Get this straight, Sec, it's not my passion to see that you survive. Ambrosius, himself, asked you to carry out this task. I owe the man and vow to pay it off by supporting his request."

Thorik looked at his grandmother for wisdom.

Picking up the crystal shards, Gluic spoke to each of them. "Not an ending, just a fresh beginning in a new form. We will be carried to a greater purpose."

Making his decision, Thorik made clear his rules. "Guide us, Santorray. As you have said, time is critical, so we must be of haste. But understand that I lead this quest."

Santorray barked out commands, in spite of Thorik's words. "East to Swardfar. We'll gather provisions there for our trip into the mountains."

Chapter 20
Swardfar

Thorik's Log: May 2nd of the 650th year.
Ovlan suggested that I find a weapon to help me on our journey. It's
off our planned path, but who am I to question the Great Oracle?

Days had lapsed since they left the forest as Santorray led them just south of the mountain-sized humps of the Solann Ridges. Rounding Faralope Peak, the group descended toward the city of Swardfar. Greensbrook's easternmost city side-saddled the Lax River, which slowly weaved through the endless crops and pastures.

Freshly turned soil filled the air with sweet fragrances of the rich dark red earth. Surrounded by tall wildflowers, fertile fields were plowed in unnatural patterns across the valley. Warm temperatures and afternoon showers kept the southern side of the Solann Mountains in a state of accelerated growth, perfect for the farmer's crops.

It had been an uneventful week of hiking over soft hills and around the Solann Mounds, which stood like gigantic toes out of the earth. Fruit bearing trees littered the way, providing plenty to eat, even for Grewen.

Approaching the city from the north side of the river, they crossed a wide sturdy bridge. A large open area presented itself on the south side of the river as the tall Dovenar Wall curved inward toward the city. The wall bordered all of the provinces to keep out the Altered Creatures and had a similar design throughout, but used different materials in its construction based on materials available.

Guards watched from above as two Faralope-driven wagons headed out from the large gates. Supplies filled one of the wagons while the second carried several noisy children. Their parents held the reins on each.

Gold nuggets and a single pine cone were dropped into the toll man's bucket by Gluic, as the group reached the city. After pulling one nugget out to verify its authenticity, the toll man nodded to the guards above. They were approved to enter, uneasy about having a Blothrud stride into their town, but approved nonetheless.

It was not illegal for Altereds to enter Greensbrook. The wall was there to prevent an invasion by an army of them.

Santorray ignored the looks and stares. Shoulders back and firm steps forward made it clear he was not to be disturbed by the locals, including any city law officials.

In spite of that, onlookers came from every door and window to behold the massive size of the Mognin and the evil looking Blothrud. A young boy poked his head out from under his mother's arm and waved at the Unday from his second floor window.

Grewen waved back and smiled, scaring the mother who quickly shut the window shutters.

Approaching a watering hole, a young girl carrying a large basket of flowers was startled by the odd group. The outsiders quickly surrounded her.

Santorray tossed a water bucket down the well. He quickly hauled it back up with fresh water, which he drank. Lowering it from his mouth, he noticed the entire community had come out to the large courtyard to watch them.

Santorray tossed the bucket back down the well. It seemed louder this time as it splashed into the water below. The inhabitants of Swardfar were ghostly quiet, making his actions very noticeable.

Pressing the back of her legs against the well wall, the flower girl tried to break the tension by holding up her basket of goods as a gift of peace.

"I don't mind if I do." Grewen reached down with his oversized two-thumbed hand, he plucked the basket from her and pitched it into his mouth. "Thank you, I'm famished. Salt-lilacs are one of my favorite flowers."

Screaming from the sight of giant's enormous mouth crunching down on her basket, she ran from the group and raced down the street and around the corner, out of sight.

Santorray pulled the second bucket up but felt resistance when he lifted it to drink. Thorik was holding on to it.

"You've had some, let Gluic and Avanda drink," Thorik said.

The thought had not occurred to him. It had been so many years since he had to work within a group that his natural response was to only look out for himself. Fighting his instincts to rip the bucket from the Num's hands, he shoved it slightly toward Thorik. "Go ahead; I've had my fill for now."

One by one, they took their fill of water before passing it on. Grewen added a few handfuls of wheat from a nearby wagon load to satisfy his stomach's needs.

Locals hadn't spoken a word. Not a sound, aside from the shuffling of feet. The silence became eerie as they stood staring with their blank faces.

Eventually a middle-aged woman approached from the main street, led by the young girl whose flowers were eaten by Grewen. The woman had a natural attractiveness about her without any frills or glamorous accessories. Her clothes were of earth tones and mud from the fields had stained the ends of her dress.

"Welcome Travelers, I am Pawnel Fenwood. What is your business here?" she asked.

Thorik stepped forward. "I am Sec Thorik Dain of Farbank. We are just passing through. We wish to purchase provisions."

"We have none to sell you. Please be on your way."

"We don't require much. Surely you have some bread, blankets and ropes."

"We have them, but have none for you."

Santorray growled at her, showing his distaste for her lack of hospitality.

Thorik showed no signs of anger. Instead, he was curious as to the reason. "Why? Have we done something to offend you?"

"War is approaching between Darkmere and the provinces remaining loyal to the kingdom. We wish to be left out of it and will not select a side, nor support those on either side, until the victor is known. We have seen many outsiders, such as yourselves, pass through here as of late and we wish to avoid any relationships or transactions with any of you."

"You approve of whoever wins?"

"We are isolated from all others in our province and will see no support if we join their cause. It is better for us to stay distant and tend to our fields. Once it is all over, the conquering army will purchase our crops for their men. If we take sides and favor the losers, we could be destroyed."

"If Darkmere's army wins they will take more than your crops. You'll become his slaves."

"Perhaps, but he will still need us to tend the fields. Little will change for us."

A loud distant drumbeat hit hard twice before pausing, followed by a series of three beats.

The crowd screamed and ran in every direction. Total chaos had erupted from the deafening quiet, as they ran for their houses, locking the doors behind them.

Pawnel sent the young girl home before turning back to Thorik. "What have you done? Who has tracked you down to our city?"

The distant silence was broken with a crashing of wood at the far entrance. Something was destroying the southern gate.

Pawnel turned and ran toward the sound before Thorik could answer.

Santorray stretched his chest and unsheathed his sabers. Spinning them a few times in his hands, he prepared for battle. A quick cut to his leg drew blood on purpose.

"What are you doing?" Thorik asked about the wound.

"I draw my own blood to show my enemy that I do not fear his attempt to injure me."

"No," Thorik said. "You're not here to fight anyone. This is exactly what Pawnel doesn't want to happen."

"I've evaded enough conflicts for you and your plans. I'm not going to run any longer."

"Santorray, you're neither a coward nor a fool. But let's at least find out what this threat is before we take aggressive measures against it."

"Agreed," Santorray said hesitantly.

"Grewen, find some place to hide for everyone until we get back," Thorik ordered.

Grewen smiled as he looked around the open courtyard. "I'm a little big to play this game."

Thorik began running with Santorray toward the sound of destruction. "Be creative, Grewen. Come up with something."

Grewen looked at Avanda as he placed a large basket upside down on his head. "Can you still see me?" His shoulders shook as he laughed from his own joke along with Avanda.

Santorray and Thorik raced across the town, catching up to Pawnel as she entered the large southern marketplace. Viewing the south wall entrance, it exploded, ripping the mighty doors apart.

Entering the destroyed doorway, Lord Bredgin rode in on a large black panther. An intense burst of light shot out from the man's staff, as though he was looking through the walls of homes and businesses. Colors faded to a dull gray from his presence in all directions and screams could be heard from the direction of his staff's light.

Thorik, Santorray and Pawnel stood out of Bredgin's view, on the backside of the market.

Santorray growled. "Why is he here looking for us?"

Pawnel glared at Thorik. "I knew you brought us trouble."

Thorik pushed off her comment. "Or has he followed Ericc here? He may not know we're even here."

"True, but if Bredgin is looking for Ericc, he's going to rip this town apart to find the boy, whether he is here or not. So we're going to have to fight him sooner or later, and I refuse to run this time."

"There are no strangers in Swardfar aside from you," Pawnel said.

Bredgin's power over darkness and light became very clear as he entered the main street. He and everything around him was a shade of gray, no colors could be seen within twenty feet, including his own clothes or skin, as he temporarily stored his staff.

Reaching out with his left hand, he created darkness to encapsulate a surge of local guards running toward him. Absolute emptiness of light sucked the warmth out of the men as they stumbled over themselves to find their way. Cold, fear and depression rapidly set in to all in the dismal dark.

Bright light sprang from his right palm, blinding all those who would look at it. Heat from the light could be felt from a block away, except in the dead zones of darkness.

Releasing one guard from the veil of darkness, Bredgin advanced. "Where is the son of Ambrosius? Where is Ericc Dovenar?"

The man shivered from his short time in the dark, as the light from the sun now made him squint. "I don't know of such a boy."

An intense light shot forth from Bredgin's hand, hitting the guard with such force that it knocked him backward as it burned his face.

Heat blisters covered his face and neck, oozing out puss and cracking as the man reached for them. He screamed in pain as his eyeballs exploded from the heat, before he collapsed onto the dirt road.

Lord Bredgin pointed his palm at one of the taller buildings, releasing a focused light, which ripped through its wall and started the structure on fire.

"Your attempt to hide the boy will only get you all killed," Lord Bredgin yelled to the people of Swardfar. "Hand him over, now!"

Thorik thought about the challenge as he watched the destructive power of Darkmere's son. "I think I know how we can save your city."

"We refuse to get involved," Pawnel said.

"You're already involved," Thorik corrected before turning to address Santorray. "Go back to the northern courtyard entrance and make sure everyone is still in hiding until we need them."

"You expect me to hide?"

"No, I expect you to fight Lord Bredgin and prevent him from capturing Ericc, should my plans fail. Trust me on this."

With some hesitation, Santorray returned from where they came.

"Follow me," Thorik said to Pawnel as he ran into one of the local shops.

As Thorik and Pawnel burst in to the closest shop, they found two families huddled together. Terror covered their faces as they expected Thorik to be the attacking enemy.

Pawnel kept away from the window and approached them. "It will be all right. Just stay down until it's over."

"He's not after us," Thorik explained to the locals, looking panicked. "He's after Ambrosius' son, Ericc. Do you know where he is? Have you seen him?"

Frightened, the locals shook their heads no.

Meanwhile, Santorray returned to the north entrance to find the Nums vanished and Grewen stacking crates, wagons, and baskets around him to hide behind.

Grewen waved to the Blothrud. "Will this do?"

"Pathetic," Santorray announced.

"Yeah, I'm not good at this game." Grewen looked at his temporary wall. "Where's Thorik?"

"The fool is trying to get rid of Lord Bredgin on his own. We need to prepare to attack Darkmere's successor when he enters the area."

"Attack? I'll help you restrain him, but I will not take part in a murder. Especially when we can walk out those gates and avoid the conflict in the first place."

"Listen, your friend Thorik has just put his life on the line to stop this man. Odds are he's already dead. Do we not at least owe it to him to slay his killer?"

"Revenge killing? Never." Grewen said. "I don't believe Thorik would put himself in such harm on purpose. But even if he did, he knows the risks. Plotting to murder his killer will not bring him back. It only makes us killers."

"This is what's wrong with you Ovs. You want justice but you're never willing to fight for it."

"An eye for an eye?"

"Yes!"

"No!" Grewen replied. "It perpetuates the issue and gives each side more reasons to continue to advance the conflicts."

"Instead you would cower down and be subservient to every threat that rises?"

"No, but defending oneself is a far stretch from plotting murder. Have you ever tried to use your mouth to solve an issue instead of your fists?"

"I find my fists have been very effective in resolving problems," Santorray said proudly. "Talking is fine if your enemy can be trusted. But in my travels I have found many speak only to deceive you. Lord Bredgin is one of them. To bargain with him would be to reach inside a dragon's mouth on his promise not to bite down. His instinct forces him to chomp down on your arm."

"Quiet, you two." Thorik ran into the open area. "He'll be here any moment."

Grewen and Santorray looked over at the Num with surprise.

Thorik's hasty arm movements showed his concern of their hiding spaces. "Santorray, hide behind Grewen."

"Hide?"

"Yes! Or you'll ruin everything." Thorik pushed the massive Blothrud behind Grewen's wall and then behind the Mognin. "Be still, here he comes."

A deep cat growl predicated the sighting of the black panther in the courtyard. Longer than Grewen was tall, the cat ran smoothly into the area while being ridden by his master.

The pace was fast. There was passion in Lord Bredgin's face as they bolted through the area, leaving a trail of death in his gray wake. Bricks crumbled, wood aged and cracked, and plants withered and died from the immediate exposure to his presence.

The wagons and baskets that made up Grewen's wall lost their strength and tumbled down as the panther raced by, exposing the giant. Nevertheless, the rider was too focused to even notice those that he killed, let alone those he passed by.

Out through the gates, over the bridge, and down the road sped the panther and Lord Bredgin.

Santorray exited the makeshift wall. "Why did he leave? Did he find Ericc and kill him?"

"Yes and no," Thorik answered.

"No games, Sec. Out with it."

"I ran from shop to shop telling everyone that Lord Bredgin was after Ericc, and that Ericc had recently been captured in Rumaldo by Lucian," Thorik explained. "After Bredgin started gathering this story from multiple people he finally believed it and headed out to Rumaldo."

"Clever," Grewen said.

"Lucky," Santorray added.

Thorik adjusted his backpack. "We're lucky he didn't destroy more that he did. What matters is that he's gone, which is what we need to be, so let's head out toward Carrion Mire before we lose anymore daylight."

"I believe you will need some provisions." Pawnel walked up behind him.

"Yes, but I do not wish to make you my enemy by forcing you to do business."

"You could have escaped out the north gates. This was not your problem. Instead you stayed to help without causing a fight, while saving many lives. It is the least we can do for you. What do you require?"

Chapter 21
Dor'Avell Range

Dor'Avell's western range was sprinkled with small hot springs pouring from cracks in the steep mountainside. Mineral deposits stained the rocks below the flumes, painting artistic murals across a canvas a thousand feet high and tens of miles across.

Soft green hills of eastern Greensbrook clashed with the sudden cliff-face of the mountain range as though the land had suddenly broke free and lifted to a new level without any natural progression. Scattered chunks of the fractured cliff had fallen and embedded themselves into the soft soil below.

Venturing along the bottom of the natural divide, Thorik's party discovered ancient black marble walls leaning against the base of the cliff. They were from a lone building, long forgotten and damaged by several of the fallen rocks.

Santorray led them to the roofless structure, stopping several yards shy of reaching it. "We camp here for the night and climb in the morning."

Thorik set his pack on an empty statue base and began unpacking his cooking utensils. "How are we going to get beyond the cliff face?"

"Straight up."

"Not likely. It's too dangerous for Avanda. Gluic and Brimmelle don't have a chance."

"You asked me to take you to Carrion Mire. It's up there. Your poor choice for traveling companions is not my issue."

"You joined us to help save Ericc. We come as a package. It's all of us or none of us."

Growling at the comment, Santorray hated taking the long way to do anything. "I'll see if I can find an easier path."

Brimmelle was breathing hard as he finished the final hill and reached the campsite. Watching the Blothrud explore the wall for a way up, he threw his gear down. "There is no way I'm climbing up that cliff."

Santorray was nearing his breaking point. His patience with the constant complaining and issues of the Nums had been taxed. He knew if he reacted, he may not be able to stop himself from ripping someone's head off, so he grumbled to himself instead.

Finding a fallen boulder surrounded by the lush grass of the area, Gluic climbed up on top and began her daily ritual of sorting her stones and gems. Each stone would be set in the pattern one at a time after she spoke to it and listened for a response. Afterward, she would close her eyes and let nature speak to her.

Brimmelle sat down near Thorik's backpack to perform his daily reading of the Runestone Scrolls, in spite of the fact that he no longer had the actual scrolls. Thankfully he had them memorized, so he began reading them out loud.

Santorray could not stand Brimmelle's monotone reading, which often went on for an hour or more. "Quiet, I'm not in the mood for your spiritual preaching."

"The preaching you refer to are the words of the Mountain King himself. They command respect," Brimmelle replied.

Santorray scoffed. "By who?"

"By all. If it weren't for him, you wouldn't be free."

"Not likely."

"Do you not know of the Mountain King War against the Notarians? He freed your species from slavery. By winning the war he freed all species."

"Winning the war? No Num won the Sovereignty War!"

"The what?" Brimmelle questioned.

"The war where the Del'Unday rebelled against the Notarians and destroyed their civilization, freeing all slaves."

"Your facts are skewed. It was the Mountain King who freed them. A Polenum."

"Your people may have had their own leader at the time, but it was Ergrauth himself that led the war and defeated them."

"Sacrilege! How dare you disgrace the King and his actions with your false tales. Leave it to an Altered to decimate the truth for their own bidding."

"Are you calling me a liar?"

"Absolutely!"

Grewen walked over between them and said nothing, in hopes of calming the two down by simply separating them.

Santorray stepped to the side to see past the giant while addressing the Num. "Then how do you explain the fact that we won the war?"

"You didn't, we did."

"The Del'Unday ruled this land for thousands of years following the war. How do you call that a win for the Nums?"

"The Mountain King won the war by freeing the slaves. It was only after this, that the Altereds assassinated our King and our people to take over the land. We fought for your freedom only to be cowardly back-stabbed by you Altereds."

Santorray bit his lip to draw blood as he prepared to do battle.

By this point Grewen was having difficulty holding Santorray back from reaching the Fir and ripping him apart. "I think this debate is over," Grewen said.

Thorik agreed with Grewen. "Brimmelle, can you help Avanda and I collect something to eat so Santorray can concentrate on tomorrow's travels?"

"I haven't finished my readings."

Thorik helped the Fir to his feet. "Yes, I know, but Avanda and I will be down the hill collecting berries and we won't be able to hear you from up here. Please join us."

"Of course. I'm planning to read the Rune Scroll of Truth today. You should listen especially close to this."

Down the hill the three Nums went, two picking berries and wild roots while listening to the third talk with little variation in his voice for nearly an hour. As always, his memory was perfect, but he lacked the ability to keep anyone's interest.

Grewen waited for the Nums to leave to approach Santorray. "Why are you doing this?"

Santorray continued eyeing the cliff for an easier passage. "Doing what?"

"First of all, why did you save my life in the coliseum last autumn?"

"Is that an Ov's best attempt at appreciation?"

Grewen realized his clumsiness in how he approached the subject and corrected himself. "Truth be said, truth be heard, you saved my life and I am grateful."

"Accepted."

"It's not common for Blothruds to have such valor."

"Who said anything about valor? I needed your help to escape, nothing more."

Grewen nodded, feeling that it was closer to the truth than Thorik's assumption of gallantry. "I'm glad I could be of assistance."

They both stood there eyeing the cliff as Grewen continued. "Although I find it odd, that the Blothrud we run into in Woodlen ends up being the same one Thorik meets in Southwind. Your travels are quite extensive."

"I could say the same for you."

"Stop the charade, Santorray. Why are you here? Why would a Del'Unday care about helping a human boy?"

"I told you. I owe Ambrosius and wish to pay him back by saving his son."

"A very honorable story. The kind that Thorik loves to hear. But I've met too many Del'Unday to believe this is just for your own inner peace of mind."

"Think what you wish. I don't owe you any explanations."

"No, but you will owe one to Thorik if you veer from the path you have told him. He's counting on you. He relies on you, and I will not stand by and let you hurt him. I don't trust you, Santorray."

"I never asked you to," the Blothrud said before walking away.

Chapter 22
Symbols

A soft hum could be heard over the crackling of the campfire. A musical hum, light and airy with specific tones, carried over the heads of the band of adventurers as they slept through the night.

Thorik was awakened by the noise and quietly stood to search out the source. Grabbing his backpack he reached inside for a candle as he walked toward the ruins nearby.

The melody changed often as Thorik entered what was once the entrance to the black marble building. A large piece of cliff lay in the center of the first room, reminding him why they chose not to sleep inside the remaining walls built against the unstable cliff.

Flickers of another light danced against a wall, originating from the next room. Cold to the touch, the wall was smooth under his fingers as he leaned around the corner to see beyond it.

An area of the marble floor had been cleared of dust, pebbles, and weeds by the careful hands of Gluic. Tracing engraved lines on the floor with her fingers to clean out the remaining dirt, she continued to hum her tune. "Powerful, isn't it?" she said without acknowledging her grandson had arrived.

"What is this?"

Pure of cracks and damage, the engraved floor symbol designs interlaced natural vine-like lines with hexagons as it filled a circle the width of Thorik's old shack in Farbank. The designs were that of the ancient Notarians, who had created many structures across the land before the Great Mountain King War.

"The power of your Runestones apply here."

"Granna, the stones I have are sacred to our beliefs, but they have no power. In fact I'm not sure how important they really are. The more I learn about other cultures, the less it seems we really need the stones or the Mountain King's words."

"Even more do we need him right now."

"But, what if Santorray is right about Ergrauth freeing the slaves instead of the Mountain King? They did inherit the land after the war."

"True, and yet not."

"Who do I believe?"

"The Runestones."

"Why?"

"They are the wind, the water, your skin. They existed long before the Mountain King War and have much to tell us. They have the answers to everything."

"Yes, I know. The Runestone Scrolls tell us everything we need to know."

"No, not the scrolls, the stones. Your stones."

"Gluic, you're asking me to believe something that I've never heard you even talk about. You've never attended Brimmelle's readings or tried to teach me the King's words."

"His words should be said and heard. They are good words, but both of these acts are short lived. Living up to them is what is important. Your Runestones go beyond our lives and touch all things."

"Why haven't you spoke of this before?"

"There is less time now than there was before."

"Less time? What do you mean?"

"You must learn to understand the runes."

"I know what they mean. Fir Brimmelle pounds them into me every day."

Gluic walked over, reached into his backpack and pulled out the pouch of his Runestones. Grabbing one, she slapped it into his hand. "What is this?" she asked.

Thorik tried to move his hand out from under Gluic's hand so he could see the symbol, but she refused to let go. "I can't see the symbol."

"You don't need to."

"Yes I do."

"Trace it with your fingers and your mind."

Thorik pacified his grandmother's request and began moving his fingers around. Thousands of years of wear had diminished all sharp edges and nearly removed some of the ridges altogether. The symbol on the gem in the center categorized the meaning, but it was the ridges on the stone itself that defined their individuality.

Gluic tightened her grip on him by slapping her other hand below his and squeezing. "No, not so fast. Slowly. Close your eyes. Touch the pattern. Feel the stone's power."

Pausing only slightly, he slowly traced one of the raised lines on the stone. Once it came to an end, he moved on to the second one, and then to the third. "Is it the Runestone of Kindness?"

"Stop thinking what you have been taught and begin understanding what it really is."

"I don't-"

"Keep tracing," she interrupted. "Only think what the stone tells you."

He traced another line, eventually splitting into two. "How do I know which way to follow? Are there rules to observe? I'm pretty sure it's the Runestone of Kindness."

Covering his hands from above and below, she closed her eyes and waited for him to continue.

Again he tried, time after time with no results. Guessing would only upset Gluic so he refrained in doing so.

After an hour went by he began to get sleepy, relaxing his eyes, his shoulders and his mind. It was at this point that he jolted from a sensation within his palm. A flow of light, of energy, of information, he could not recall. Just a burst, a flash of something deeper than reality.

Thorik opened his eyes to see his grandmother standing at a distance, in the center of the floor circle smiling at him. His palm was very warm as the Runestone of Kindness rested in it. "What just happened?"

"More than symbols of our faith, they explain the fabric of our world."

"No, they're stones. Passed down by my father, yes, but no different than any other stone carving of the King's runes."

"Passed down from the maker for you to use, for you to understand."

"For me? How does the maker know who I am? And who is this maker?"

"Shhh, son, I have a lot to teach you in a short time. Focus on the stone. Trace the lines. Understand what it is."

"But-"

"Trace the pattern."

He did as he was told. Over and over again he tried until once again he relaxed, allowing the stone to control him. The gem in the center of the stone began to give off a slight glow.

Tingling crept into his fingers, then his palm and up his arm. Streams of energy flowed from the stone as though miniature tadpoles raced inside him, warming his body.

As the sensation reached his head he felt light of weight. His vision blurred. His hearing went deaf. Cut off from all outside disturbances, Thorik no longer thought of himself as a Polenum, but instead he was one with the air, the wind, and the sky.

Dropping the Runestone, he crashed back to earth as his legs gave way.

Gluic kneeled beside him and held his overly warm hand. "What is this stone's true nature?"

"Air."

"Ah, good. That's one of the three we need. Get up so we can find the other two."

Chapter 23
The Climb

Time had been wasted on breakfast as the morning sun climbed into the sky. Bags were now packed and it was time to venture to the Carrion Mire.

"I'm telling you Thorik, there is only one way up and that is to climb. I looked for other options and there's none to be had. So you either have your friends follow my lead up the cliff, or they can stay behind." Santorray placed a large coil of rope over each shoulder as he prepared for his ascent. "Of course, we could just forget this foolishness and head to Corrock. There may still be enough time to intercept Ericc."

Thorik pulled on his own backpack. "Why won't you at least try what we found? If it doesn't work we'll try something else."

"Sec, you are trying to revive life into a Notarian device. This can only bring us bad fortune to our journey. I will not allow the nature of luck to frown upon me by touching such a thing. I'm going to climb up to that first outcropping and secure a line for those who wish to join me. Test your theory and then start your climb. We don't want to get caught on the cliff face after dark." The Blothrud began to scale the steep rock wall. "Alone this would not be easy, but with the older ones and the Ov, it may not even be possible."

Thorik watched the agility of the Blothrud as he made quick work of the first dozen yards. "Have it your way."

Santorray grasped the small exposed notches of rocks with his feet and hands as he moved upward. Boiling water from underground springs flowed from small cracks along the way, scalding his skin when touched. Loose sections of rocks gave way and fell to the ground when bumped or grabbed. Soon, the first three hundred feet were behind him.

A thin segment peeled away from the rock face as the Blothrud pulled his body up with it. Letting go with his left hand and swinging himself to the right, the rock missed his body and tumbled down to the green grassland below, embedding itself into the lush grass and soil.

Hanging by his one arm, he swung himself back to the left just as steam blasted out from where the thin rock had once rested. The scorching humid air hit him square in the chest.

His skin instantly blistered and turned brown as he swung again to the right. But the steam left a permanent trail across his chest and shoulder. Any closer to his face and he could have lost his vision.

Thorik settled the rest of the group down.

Grewen sat cross-legged in the center of the engraved circle, which Gluic had exposed the night before. He took up most of the space, so the Nums had to sit on the Mognin's legs or in Avanda's case, on his shoulder.

Ralph stood outside the circle, lifting his body up and down as he hissed at Grewen. Opening his mouth, he took on an attack stance to take on the giant.

Grewen finally got the hint and lowered one hand to allow the lizard to run up his arm and over to Avanda. Perching on her shoulder, he hissed at Grewen in a display of dominance, while Avanda laughed at her little friend's unwavering bravado that he was as big as everyone else.

Brimmelle squirmed for the fifth time and adjusted the blanket he sat on to ensure a barrier existed between himself and the giant's leg. "This is foolishness, Thorik. How embarrassing this will be for you when nothing happens."

"I don't know that anything *will* happen, but I'm willing to give it a try."

"I don't see why we need to be part of this experiment. Seems foolish to put us at risk. Let the Altered go by himself to see first," Brimmelle said.

Gluic rested her stomach against the folds of Grewen's leg to lean over the Mognin's knee as she instructed Thorik. "Now, recall what you did last night. Listen to them. Once you hear them and feel them, place them where they belong."

Thorik tightened his backpack and held three of his Runestones out before him. Selecting the top one, he closed his eyes and felt the energy within it. The flow through his fingertips was no longer single directional. He could feel energy traveling into his arm as well as out of his own body to the stone itself.

The gem in the center of his Runestone began to give a slight glow and the stone itself became hot to the touch. Holding it as long as he could, he finally set it firmly down into one of the carved hexagonal symbols within the floor.

He quickly repeated the sequence two more times as he walked around the group. Sitting inside the circle when he released the third and final one, he held onto Grewen's foot just in case something major occurred.

Silence followed.

Brimmelle continued to sit up straight on the giant's leg. "Like I told you before, they are Runestones, not some sort of magical rocks from Avanda's purse of disaster."

Avanda perked up at the idea, grabbing her purse of magical items. "Thorik, I can help."

"No!" the entire group said in chorus. She reluctantly put it away.

Ralph spun around on her shoulder as he hissed at all of them for shouting at her, until she finally stroked the back of his head to let him know it was okay.

Thorik watched the gems in the center of the stones continue to glow and pondered his options. Eventually he closed his eyes and touched the carvings in the floor themselves to perform the same process he had done with his individual Runestones.

Gluic smiled and nodded. "Hold on tight."

Suddenly, the entire circle, on which they were seated, blasted up in the air. A column of marble, from under the engraved circle, raced toward the sky. The outer carved ridge of the circle itself was now the edge of the column's surface.

The force knocked Brimmelle backward into the center of the circle, with his head wedged under Grewen's loincloth. Avanda and Ralph shot off of Grewen's shoulder, landing on Brimmelle's stomach.

"Wheeee!" screamed Gluic as the speed and force prevented her from lifting her head to see just how high the marble column had lifted them.

The force had caught Thorik off guard as well. Slipping at the onset of the upward blast, his head and shoulders leaned over the edge of the ever-increasing tall column while his arms wrapped around Grewen's toe.

Unable to pull himself fully back onto the surface, he watched as their camp from last night shrunk into the distance. Speeding past Santorray, Thorik had no time to react as he watched the Blothrud nearly lose his footing at the sight.

Rocketing up the cliff, Grewen struggled to move his jaw to speak. "Thorik." His loud deep voice was faintly audible by even the Num's ears. "Will this stop on its own? Or will you need to do something?" he shouted over the rumbling of the column.

The thought never even occurred to the Num. Thorik pulled on the giant's toe with all of his might, in an effort to lift himself back onto the platform. But he was unsuccessful until Grewen pulled his foot in tighter. This dragged Thorik in, but wedged Brimmelle even deeper into a position he had been trying to get out of.

Thorik lay flat on his stomach and reached out to the carvings. Feeling the energy, he willed it to slow down.

Nothing happened.

"Gluic, I need your help. It won't do as I tell it to."

Gluic enjoyed the ride, resting on the crease between the giant's calf and thigh, just over Thorik's position. "I won't always be there for you. You can figure it out."

"Granna, this is not the time to learn."

"It's the best time."

He tried again to order the stone to stop. It did not.

"It won't obey me," Thorik shouted.

"Who gave you the right to order it?" she said.

They were reaching the top of the cliff at a violent speed. Thorik knew his forcing of the column to stop wouldn't work, so he compelled himself to relax and allow the stones to draw out his calmness and slow down. It was only a theory, but he had to try something different.

Reaching out his palms to touch the ridges in the platform, he thought of slowing down, but the fierce speed continued as they came into view of the cliff's plateau.

Thorik had to forget about what was going on. He had to recall a time when he was extremely calm, a time when he was at peace.

A vision finally appeared in Thorik's head. He was floating in the waters near the city of Kingsfoot. Back when they had first left Farbank. Back when life seemed so much simpler.

Thorik's arms stretched out at his sides as he and his beloved Emilen relaxed in the warm spring lake. The water tingled against his skin as it healed his cuts and battle wounds. A layer of mist coming off the lake made him feel like he was floating among the clouds.

The vision then changed to Emilen and Thorik embracing. Holding each other, they peered up at the thousand-foot tall Mountain King carving as they rested in the half-submerged tail fin of a dolphin statue. He was at peace. He was content. Pulling her in tight, he knew it would be one of the few times in his life he would feel this way. Thorik turned to kiss her.

Thorik suddenly realized they were stopped and snapped out of his daydream state. Opening his eyes, he quickly pushed himself away from Grewen's toe, which he had been cuddling. While wiping his lips, after being pressed against Grewen's skin, he noticed the giant's grin at the event.

The column had stopped adjacent with the top of the cliff, where a lifeless crust of land stood before them.

A muffled voice could be heard. The group looked about, wondering what it could be.

Thorik jumped off the monstrously tall column and onto the plateau. Still hearing the voice, he spun around. "It's not coming from out here, it's coming from the column.

Grewen helped Avanda and Gluic over to the cliff before pulling Brimmelle out from under him, by his legs. "I thought that muffled voice was you." The giant's smile was large as he uncoiled his legs, hanging them both off the column's ledge.

Brimmelle hung upside down from Grewen's grip, furiously wiping his face. "Put me down you filthy Altered."

Grewen complied and set him down in front of him.

The Fir straightened up his clothes before wiping his face again. "The smell. I'll never get it out of my nose. It's horrid."

"Watch it." Grewen warned Brimmelle of the dangerous location where he stood.

However, the Fir took it the wrong way. "No, you watch it. Don't ever touch me again." Brimmelle backed away from the giant as he talked to him, unknowingly closing in on the column's edge. "How dare you put me, the seventh Fir in my family line, into a position that makes me look like an…" His voice trailed off as he finally noticed that he was on top of a column's platform, which was now a thousand feet in the air. He had missed the entire trip.

The Fir's knees buckled and ached. Light headed, he began to sway. Nausea kicked in as he envisioned himself falling. Unbalanced, his arms began to flail erratically, tipping him over the edge.

Brimmelle fell from the column.

He tumbled several feet before the giant's outstretched hand caught him. In spite of the safe landing, Brimmelle's body went limp as if he had crashed into the camp below.

Grewen carried the shaking Fir onto the top of the cliff, toward Thorik. "Don't forget your stones, little man."

Thorik agreed, removed his backpack, and jumped back onto the column. "The risk is that by removing them, the column may go down just as fast as it came up. Or perhaps it can't move at all without the Runestones in them."

Grewen set Brimmelle down so he could get his bearings. "Or you could leave them and avoid the risk entirely."

"I've left my Runestones once before, and I vowed never to do that again." Thorik leaped back across onto the column's sturdy platform. Slowly, he placed his fingers on the edges of one of his Runestones to pull it up. Tilting the stone slightly, he was able to get his other fingers behind it and pull it out of the carved inset. The light from the gem in the center immediately went out.

Crash! The thunderous noise echoed in their ears. Thorik dove for the cliff, landing and rolling to a stop at Grewen's feet. Looking up, he could see a confused look by the giant who had his hands together in a clap of excitement. The noise had come from the giant, not the column.

"Sorry, I was pleased to see the first one come out so easily," Grewen said.

Thorik placed the Runestone in his pack, and jumped back over to grab the rest. Reaching down to take the second one, he turned to watch Grewen who had his hands tucked firmly at his sides.

The second and third Runestones came out without issue and the Num jumped back to safety as Santorray climbed up to the surface of the plateau.

Hot, sweaty and exhausted, the Blothrud pulled himself up onto the ridge and sat back to observe the rest of the party.

Brimmelle fanned himself to cool off his dizziness and regain his composure. "Let's get out of this place, away from this cliff."

Panting from the hard climb, Santorray continued to rest. "You're going to wish you were someplace as peaceful as this ledge once we enter Carrion Mire Valley."

"At least we will be down in a valley instead of up here in mountains."

Santorray pointed away from the cliff toward the passage leading between the mountains. "Around that bend is the base of the valley. There's no going back down without going through the valley."

"We'll get back down the same way we came up." Brimmelle pointed toward the column.

The column, however, had been forgotten for a few minutes and, in the meantime, had already slowly lowered itself nearly fifty feet as it continued its way back to the campsite.

Santorray grinned. "I think your luck just ran out."

Chapter 24
Carrion Mire

Terraced pools of steaming clear water created a landscape of naturally formed pyramids, some leaning against the mountainside while others stood independently. Crystallized minerals acted as dams for each step down to the next tier as water flowed over the dam walls of each level.

Colors rich in reds, greens, yellows or blues coated bases of various pools. Some were stained with syrupy red mud as it oozed its way down the terraced hillsides like a long snake of oil.

Sulfur burned the Num's sinuses and caused their eyes to tear up as they watched the boiling water vomit thick bursts of liquid from exposed holes. The area tasted of death and yet felt alive in a primitive earthly way, before any animals occupied the earth.

This was Carrion Mire, a valley without any plants or animals.

There had never been any valid reason for anyone to purposely enter the valley. And yet here they were, Thorik leading his mismatched group of oddities into the bowels of Australis.

Santorray took in a full deep breath and savored the flavor of the sulfur before releasing it. "During the third age, the Va'Del'Unday used to send their young men up here to test their courage and fortitude. Those few who returned had to show the mark of the beast to prove they had stood against her in battle."

"You never said anything about a beast." Thorik looked at the valley walls with concern.

"Would it have mattered?"

Stumbling on his response, Thorik realized that it wouldn't have. "No, but your tendency not to disclose everything you know until the last minute is less than desirable. What does the beast look like?"

"Its body is of stone and it spits boiling water. A heart pulses liquid rock through its arteries. An attack by the beast will either crush you or burn you alive."

A slight rumbling of the ground preceded a rush of water from one of the ponds, shooting a hundred feet in the air for nearly a minute before ending just as abruptly as it started. A shower of mineral water fell back to earth, some of it drifting toward the group.

The smell sickened Thorik, as he held his hand over his mouth and nose. "What would happen if they fought the beast without receiving a wound?"

Chuckling, the Blothrud pulled out a small thin carving knife. "There is no fighting the beast without her leaving her mark. The question is whether she will leave enough of you intact to survive." Cutting his palm with the blade, he tightened his fist, dripping blood into one of the pools of water.

"What are you doing?" Thorik asked.

"Let's get this over with."

"You're calling out the beast?" The Num's heart began to race. "Are you insane?"

"She knows we're here. She's waiting for us to get farther into her lair where we have no chance."

"With our back against that cliff, I think she has us at a disadvantage already. Surely we can sneak in and collect the Spear of Rummon before alerting it."

"Are you oblivious to what I've been telling you? She knows we're here. The valley and the beast are one in the same. The blood I bait her with will cause her to react and make mistakes. It's her desire to taste blood that is her downfall. Given the time to plan, she will devour us all."

Thorik looked across the valley walls for a creature to appear. "Where will she strike from?"

"She is the valley. These pools are her stomach."

"We're inside her?"

"Yes."

"How does this help me find the Spear of Rummon?"

"Did Ovlan tell you where it would lay?"

"She said he was imprisoned in the heart of Carrion Mire."

"Then it is there that you must travel while I distract her." Santorray pointed to a crack in the distant valley wall. "Run to the cave of Carrion's heart, once she attacks. I will detain her as long as I can."

The valley launched its attack on Thorik and his team. Geysers erupted from dozens of spouts, filling the air with hot steamy air. The ground shook violently and heaved up under the group's feet. Water in the nearby pools turned from clear to a dark red.

Thorik struggled to stay on his feet as the ground continued to shake, waiting for Santorray to give him the approval to run for the cave.

Without warning, the ground stopped moving as quickly as it had begun.

"Run!" Santorray yelled.

The Nums launched from their stance, running as hard as they could before the creature attacked with more force. Grewen quickly fell behind them as he heaved his heavy body forward.

The earth cracked below Santorray's feet, spraying up searing steam.

Jumping out of the way, the Blothrud fell to the ground.

The crack opened further, exposing a deep gorge with a magma river flowing through it. Vents sprayed their hot water at Santorray, pushing him toward the gorge's edge.

Unable to withstand the pounding of intense pressure and heat, the Blothrud jumped across the gorge, allowing the pressure to help him across.

The victory was short-lived, for the pools on the far side began to churn and swirl. As the gorge increased in width, the ground buckled and rolled in an effort to push him back in.

Santorray grabbed onto one of the tier walls for support, burning the flesh on his hand.

A wave of fiery water roared down the pyramid of tiers, crashing against Santorray's body, knocking him off his feet and into the gorge.

Thorik reached the cave entrance and turned to ensure the rest of his group would make it as well. He had held onto Brimmelle the entire way to keep the Fir's pace up.

Avanda followed quickly behind as she assisted Gluic. All four Nums turned and paused to catch their breath from the long dash.

Grewen lumbered along as quickly as his wide Mognin body would allow him. His heavy feet pounded the ground as he swayed his massive weight back and forth.

Carrion Mire changed its focus from Santorray to Grewen as the ground rose and a wave of earth rushing behind him. As the rolling earth caught up to Grewen, the pools began firing blazing hot water at him.

However, Grewen never lost focus. If anything, Mognins enjoyed the heat of fire and boiling water. What he avoided at all cost was jumping over open crevasses, like the one that began to open in front of him.

The new crack in the earth spanned the distance between the tiers of hot sulfur water, blocking his route to the cave.

Without missing a step, Grewen turned and stepped into a nearby water pyramid. Climbing up the terraced levels of boiling water, he was able to avoid the ground fissures.

However, Carrion Mire fought back. A thick geyser forced its way up under the Mognin, nearly knocking him off balance. The rush of water was so wide that only Grewen's legs and arms could be seen as water shot in the air and against his body.

The ground shook and buckled as geysers erupted one after another.

Stepping out of the mighty geyser's stream, Grewen managed his way down off the lowest tier of the mineral pools and into the mountain's subterranean entrance. Entering the cave, the extensive heat could still be felt from his wet clothes.

"Are you hurt?" Thorik asked.

"No, but I'm cleaner than I've ever been."

Thorik studied the valley as it reacted to its defeat with a tantrum of spraying water and cracking earth. "Where's Santorray?"

Grewen looked back. "I don't see him. I'm sure he's safe. I have the feeling that he's been here before."

"Why do you say that?"

"He has the mark of a Va'Del'Unday. He took that ancient Del'Unday test at some point in his life. I wonder if it was to prove something to someone else or to himself."

"I hope he knows enough to stay alive," Thorik said.

Grewen turned to enter the cave. "I hope he knew enough to steer us in the right direction."

The wide cave before them was filled with a myriad of stalactites and stalagmites. The dripping sound from thousands of points on the ceiling could be heard echoing deep from within.

Thorik lit a few torches and handed them out as they proceeded forward.

Hot air flowed across Thorik's face and out into the valley, as they ventured inward. He decided to head toward the origin of the heat.

Following Thorik one step at a time, the group worked their way across the enormous underground room and then down a twisting side cavern. The floor was rough with a series of holes and jagged protrusions, making their travels difficult.

Rumbling and the crushing of rocks could be heard from the cave in front of them as the heat continued to increase.

Down deeper and around another corner, the cave eventually opened up to an enormous underground river of molten rock.

Near the shoreline, a large red boulder lay in the river. Unlike most of the rocks that had fallen, this one was glowing from the inside and a low tone resonated from it.

A long crack in the ceiling opened, like a gigantic mouth, only to slam shut again. The intensity caused rocks to fall, some landing in the river, some along its banks. Each time the ceiling opened, Thorik could see the sky as well as part of Carrion Mire's valley walls.

We're under the valley floor, Thorik thought before noticing Santorray. The Blothrud had fallen into the mouth of the beast and had grabbed onto ceiling rocks to prevent his fall into the magma.

"Santorray!" Thorik shouted, pleased to see he was alive and yet fearing for his life as he precariously hung on.

The rumbling of lava as well from the boulder's low tone immediately stopped after Thorik yelled. The sudden silence of the cave made everyone freeze with caution.

Brimmelle had never seen a river of magma before, but he knew enough that its flow shouldn't be able to stop in mid-motion. "Thorik! Find the spear so we can leave this place."

"It's on the heart!" Santorray barked, as he moved to another rock for better grip. "Pull it out while I make my way down."

Large masses of lava pulled together and lifted from below, stretching up toward the shoreline, like headless snakes. Each of the fire serpents acted independently as they moved toward the group.

Unsure what Santorray meant by the 'heart', he ran past the glowing boulder to look at its other side. There, sticking out of its side, was a red metal spear.

Thorik estimated the distance from the shore to the spear and knew he couldn't reach it. Grewen was his only option to reach far enough. "Grewen, help me to grab the spear. The rest of you can start heading back out the way we came in."

Brimmelle grabbed Avanda's and his mother's hands as they made their way back up the cavern. Tremors slowed their progress as they escaped the fiery serpents. Racing around the stalagmites and stalactites, the ceiling fell, as the jaws of the cave were attempting to bite into their meal.

A sharp point scraped across Brimmelle's shoulder blade, while Gluic became penned between floor and ceiling rocks. Avanda had ducked to safety and returned to help them once the ceiling lifted back up. But there wasn't much time, for another bite from the cave was already underway. This time Avanda's arm was pinched and Brimmelle was knocked to the ground.

Lifting and dropping of the ceiling continued, as the Nums tried to prevent themselves from being crushed by the rock teeth.

As the next lifting of the ceiling occurred, Brimmelle brought the two women back into the large room with Thorik and Grewen. Fortunately for the three Nums, they hadn't made it very far up the cave before it had tried to chew on them. It had also helped that Nums were short. A human or Blothrud wouldn't have been so lucky to squeeze between the rocks.

"We can't escape that way," Brimmelle yelled to Thorik, who was dodging the striking blows of the lava snakes. "We're going to follow the cave deeper into the mountain."

The Fir led his flock of two past the shoreline and back into another cave, this one without teeth.

Grewen arrived at the shoreline and reached for the spear, but it was just too far to grasp. "I can't get to it."

Thorik dove to the ground and rolled to his feet, evading another blow from the living lava. "I recall you once saying that anything was possible."

One of the flaming liquid snakes struck Grewen from the side, sending him onto the rock floor. His clothes burst into flames as he tried to put himself out with his large hands. "I didn't say it was impossible, but I'm not going to wade my way through lava to grab it." He lifted himself back to his feet. He could withstand a quick tap from the molten rock, but any more than that would surely do him in.

Thorik jumped away from another liquid snake. "Throw me over onto the stone. I'll remove the spear and jump back so you can catch me."

"I've proven that I'm not a good aim." Grewen blocked an attack with his large forearm. He recalled his poor judgment when he threw the cannon at the bridge.

"I trust you." Thorik wanted to avoid another attack. "Hurry!"

Grewen grabbed Thorik and tossed him over onto the red glowing boulder. This time he hit his mark.

Hot, but not scorching, the boulder vibrated under Thorik's feet.

Grabbing the spear with both hands, Thorik yanked the weapon out in one mighty pull, causing a violent reaction from the cave itself.

The entire underground shook hard. Ceiling rocks broke free, lava sprayed up into the air, and chaos erupted.

Thorik lost his footing and slipped to the side of the boulder, hanging onto Carrion Mire's heart with one hand while the other clinched tightly onto the spear. He could feel the steam from the magma begin to burn his legs. He would surely roast to death if he did not quickly escape.

All of the masses of liquid rock merged together into one larger serpent as it attacked Grewen, driving him back, away from the shoreline.

Thorik was alone, slowly losing his grip on the boulder as he hung in peril. The sweat on his palm lubricated his hold, causing him to slowly lose his grip.

Thorik's hand slipped off the boulder as he fell backward toward the raging lava. His mind raced on all the things he should have done as well as the people he would miss. It was during that fleeting moment that he realized how precious his life really was to him. *I'm not ready to die*, he thought as he fell from the boulder.

"Not so fast, Sec." Santorray latched onto Thorik's arm.

Santorray had finally made his way down and landed on the heart of Carrion Mire to help Thorik with the spear.

Pulling the Num up into his arms, Santorray used his strong back legs to launch himself into the air and onto the shoreline.

The large lava serpent blocked the cave exit as it thrashed around, knocking Grewen to the ground.

Once the Mognin had collapsed from exhaustion, the flaming snake turned to attack Santorray and Thorik. Their skin wouldn't take the heat that the Mognin's could. Even a close call would burn Thorik's fair skin.

The snake hovered above them for a second as it studied its next two victims. Liquid rock dripped off its massive body like sweat, splattering fire onto the ground. Then it lurched forward to hit them dead on.

Thorik jumped one way, while Santorray leaped the other. Neither had made it out of the way far enough to avoid the heat of the creature's strike.

Covering his head to minimize the pain, Thorik waited for the flesh blistering pain. Waiting with eyes closed, he realized it must have somehow missed.

Thorik looked up to see the lava serpent frozen solid. Beyond the frozen appendage from the river, Avanda stood with her book and purse of magic. She had frozen the beast.

Standing up, Thorik realized that she had also frozen Santorray, as the Blothrud lay stiff on the ground.

Avanda shrugged her shoulders. "I'm getting better," she said to Ralph, as he peered out of her side pouch.

Grewen lifted himself back to his feet. "You did just fine, little one." Picking Santorray up, he groaned from the Blothrud's weight. "But he's going to have words with you when he thaws out."

The cracking of ice could be heard as they left the main cavern. The beast had defrosted its limb and was thrashing about in anger. Its inability to extend any farther from the magma river prevented the desired chase.

* * * * *

It was a long and arduous hike filled with waterfalls and angled passages. The cavern cooled off quickly as they distanced themselves from the heart of Carrion Mire. By following the flow of water they avoided becoming lost in the maze of underground passageways. Stopping often to rest, they made poor time. Even Brimmelle was too exhausted to complain.

The caverns led the group under the northern mountains of Carrion Mire's valley and away from the cliff that Santorray had climbed. It was the right direction, but the mountains were wide.

Torches were at a premium and they limited themselves to only one or two to be lit at a time, for they knew not how long it would take to reach the surface. Aside from burning torn fragments of their clothes on the ends of the torches, they had nothing to light for a campfire. No tree roots existed this deep under the earth. Nevertheless, they stopped to rest without a fire. Everyone was cold and miserable.

Santorray continued to shiver as he thawed out from Avanda's spell. Grasping tightly onto one of the torches, he found himself holding the fire too closely in an effort to warm himself up more rapidly, scorching his skin. Hating the cold, the Blothrud frequently gave a low growl directed at the young spell caster, and would continue to do so until he was warmer.

She ignored his snarls and posturing, which only agitated him even more.

Gluic reached into Thorik's backpack and pulled out his sack of Runestones. "Remember when we were trying to find the right stones to raise the column?"

"Yes...and one of the stones we tried ended up glowing and giving off a lot of heat." Thorik reached into his sack and pulled out several Runestones before finding the one he wanted. It didn't come into play then, but it should now.

Holding the Runestone of Belief out in front of him with both hands, he traced the worn ridges on the top and stared deeply into the crystal in the center. The sensation started. A flow of energy exited the stone into Thorik's right hand, up his arm, through his body, back out his left arm and hand before completing the circle into the stone.

The red crystal in the center began to glow as he held his thumbs on the two small blue gems near the sides. The light and heat increased and decreased as Thorik willed it to, as long as he kept his concentration focused.

Once he raised it to a temperature he no longer could hold onto, he set the Runestone down and backed away from it. To his relief, the glow and heat continued to radiate without him holding onto it, much in the way the column stayed up after he removed the stones.

Red light shined on the cave walls and warmed the group as they huddled in a circle. Every so often Thorik would lean in and rejuvenate the Runestone's intensity by holding it firm and allowing himself to be at peace with the object. This lasted an hour or so each time.

Once warmed, Thorik inspected the Spear of Rummon. The tip had layers of razor sharp points, like rows of teeth working down from the point of the shaft. Incredibly light in weight for the amount of metal teeth, the shaft was covered with tiny dragon scales. The base had a hole where a longer rod once existed to give the spear its full length. But for a Num, the extension was not needed.

It felt warm to Thorik's touch and he could feel his own heartbeat in his palms as he grasped the spear's shaft. If Rummon had killed the Mountain King, it gave off no sense of wishing to do the same to Thorik. In fact, it made the Num feel safe and secure when holding it. He hoped Ovlan was correct about him needing the weapon. He also hoped Brimmelle wouldn't find out that Rummon was the one who killed the Mountain King.

After the inspection, Thorik added loops onto his backpack to store his newfound weapon, for his hands needed to be free to climb through the caves.

Fortunately for the group, the caves eventually leveled out and they made good time through the underground passages as they followed the water, hoping it would lead them out to the surface.

After walking on and off for nearly three days, the cavern finally opened up onto the north face of the mountainside, filled with lush vegetation. They would eat well today.

Tired and dirty they walked out into the hot sun. Several trees hid the mouth of the cave as the shade helped ease the party's transition from the cool dark underground.

Grewen arms were still black from the scorch marks received by defending himself against the lava creature. Some were too deep to ever totally recover.

Burn marks and heat blisters scarred parts of Thorik's body as well, especially on his lower legs from when he held himself over the lava after grabbing the spear. He only hoped the spear was worth the effort and pain. "We made it," Thorik sighed as he blocked the sun to allow his eyes to adjust.

Santorray had fully thawed out by the time they had seen the light of the sun, but still shivered from the experience of being frozen alive by Avanda's spell. "Out of Carrion Mire, yes. But we still need to travel through the Kiri Desert and O'Sid Fields before we reach Corrock. We also need to cross River's Edge during our travels"

"River's Edge?" Thorik gasped. "No, I do not wish to see that place again. The dead continue to roam the waters. Can't we go around?"

"No other option. Eastlanders kill Unday on sight, and Ovs won't let Dels through their land. River's Edge is our only path."

Chapter 25
Crossing River's Edge

Thorik led his party down the north face of the mountains, into the southern Kiri Desert, through a large soft-hilled valley. Dry grass terrain mixed with patches of small trees, shrubs and cactus. Herds of Horned Eestoos grazed on the foliage. Eventually, the Dovenar Wall bordering the flooded River's Edge Province was finally in view.

At each campsite, Gluic had performed her healing rituals with her stones, making sure Thorik joined in and learned her techniques. Burn marks on Thorik and Grewen were still discolored, but they were less sensitive to the touch after each treatment.

As usual, Thorik logged the prior day's events before leaving camp. New species of animals and plant had been recorded along with unique terrain. Thorik didn't want to forget anything, for he had grand plans of telling his friends in Farbank about everything they had encountered. He tucked all of his notes in his scratched up wooden coffer before placing his supplies in his backpack. Or at least what was left of his backpack.

Thorik gave a slight chuckle when he gazed at the sad pieces of fabric holding his pack together, once so clean and sturdy. *We've been through a lot*, he mused.

Much of the vegetation attached to Gluic was wilting quickly as she spent time each day gardening and weeding her findings.

Pulling a handful of govi-weed out of the ground, Grewen tossed it into his large mouth as he squinted his eyes. "What's that?"

Turning to the west, the Nums could see a cloud of dust rising from the desert floor.

"Could be another herd, or a Chuttlebeast," Thorik said.

Grewen tried to determine what could be making the dust. "I've never seen Chuttles on the south side of River's Edge."

"Troop movement," Santorray said. "We need to reach the Dovenar Wall before they block our path."

Brimmelle sighed at the thought of another foot race. "Let's wait here for them to pass us by and then we can go on our way afterward.

"If we've seen them, then odds are they've already seen us," Santorray said.

"Faralopes can only run for a few hours, then they must rest for an equal period of time," Grewen informed Brimmelle. "If what we see is Lucian's army, then they are in a short race for something important. With Eastland still far to our east, my wager is on us."

"Enough talk," the Blothrud said, "Head out, now."

With a slight slope to their advantage, the group moved quickly toward the distant Dovenar Wall surrounding River's Edge. Each hill they crested provided a better view of what was heading their way. Santorray had been correct; it was the Southwind army, banners high and Lucian out in front.

Soft hills gave way to tan-colored sand dunes, slowing everyone's movement except Grewen, who quietly enjoyed the hot sand between his toes.

It wasn't long before Lucian and his thirty-four military escorts were nearly within firing range. Their steeds moved comfortably in the loose sand.

Reaching the twenty-foot tall Dovenar Wall, on the south side of the province, was both a bad and good thing for Thorik and his group. As it stood, it blocked their path until they could climb over it. But once they were on the far side, they had a better chance to escape. With Lucian and his men approaching quickly on their Faralopes, there wasn't time to plan.

Santorray and Grewen began tossing the Nums up onto the top of the wall, one by one. In spite of Brimmelle's objection, he also was tossed by Santorray.

Racing up the dune toward the Mognin and Blothrud, several Southwind servicemen removed their swords from their sheaths. Others loaded bows.

Brimmelle helped his mother down the steps on the far side of the wall as Avanda already stood at the bottom waiting for them. "Don't give me that look, young lady. Get in that water and start making your way across," Brimmelle ordered the youth.

Holding her elbows, Avanda shook her head. "I'm not getting in that water." Her memory of the attack last time in River's Edge added to prior fear of the water.

Bracing his right shoulder blade against the Dovenar Wall, Santorray squatted to extend his knee out to Grewen. "Climb up. Use me as your ladder."

The Mognin recalled how long it took him to pull his body up to the top last time he had scaled the wall. "We don't have enough time, I'll help you over," Grewen replied.

Looking at the quickly approaching attackers, he knew they didn't have luxury of time to get Grewen up and over. "You sure?"

"Yes. All I ask is that you take care of those Nums."

Santorray stepped into the Mognin's cupped hands and was lifted up high enough to climb the wall. "I'll do what I can."

"Thorik trusts you, Santorray. They are good people. Don't let him down." Grewen pushed up the Blothrud's leg to help him with his ascent.

"We can't leave without Grewen," Thorik shouted from the top of the wall. "They'll throw him into the mines."

Santorray finished his climb and stood up. Grabbing Thorik by the arm, he spun the Num around. "He's made his choice, the right choice. Hopefully it will delay them long enough to get us out of arrow range before they scale the wall." Avoiding oncoming arrows, the Blothrud scooped up Thorik and jumped off the wall into the flooded province.

The river valley was covered with water from wall to wall and small islands were sporadically exposed. Shallow near the wall, Santorray's feet drove deep into the mud beneath the water. Dropping Thorik, the beast leaned back into the water to free his legs.

Lucian's men raced to the wall and surrounded Grewen. There was nowhere to hide. It was a long walk for the Mognin in either direction, and their swords would take him down long before then. There was no stepping into the Mythical Forest for protection.

"No escape this time, Ov," Lucian said. "Tie him up. The rest of you, get up on that wall and capture his friends."

On the far side of the wall, Avanda hesitated for a moment before stepping off the final staircase riser into the water. Their last encounter with River's Edge was terrifying when undead skeletons attacked them. It had taken place far to the west in deeper waters, but the memory still struck her with fear.

Gluic jumped in, followed by Brimmelle. The muddy water was only up to their ankles, but the soft mud made them sink deeper whenever they stood still.

After pulling his legs out of the thick mud, Santorray ran north, toward the far wall, only to turn around and see the fear in the

Avanda's eyes. "Hurry up, it won't be safe here for long." As the words left his mouth, he noticed one of the first soldiers work his way up onto the wall. Pointing at the man, the Blothrud shouted, "Get out of there, now!"

Avanda saw the man gather his bearings and begin to load his first arrow. She didn't have to be told again. Launching from the bottom step and racing across the mud, she quickly passed Brimmelle.

The first arrow whistled by Brimmelle's head as he struggled to keep up with the rest. He soon caught back up to Avanda, who had stopped to dig in her purse of magic. Grabbing her by the shoulders, he pushed the girl to keep her running.

Perching on Avanda's shoulder, Ralph hissed at the Southwind soldiers and pumped his body up and down, attempting to scare them off.

Thorik held onto Gluic's hand and was nearly dragging her across the thick muck.

Another arrow landed near them, and then another. Several men had scaled the wall and were adding to the firepower. Others, including Lucian, had made it over the wall and were now in a foot race with the Nums. Neither seemed to have the advantage as they sloshed their way across the sunken field.

Nearing the center of the mile-wide province, Thorik knew the deepest point of the original river would be just ahead and they would have to swim across. But that wouldn't be an issue if they didn't even make it that far.

Brimmelle and Gluic couldn't keep up the pace and the Southwind troops quickly closed the gap.

Brimmelle stopped to catch his breath, bending over and resting his hands on his knees. His feet continued to sink in the thick mud as he stood still.

"No, don't stop." Thorik raced back to help him continue their escape. But by the time he got the Fir moving again, it was too late.

Over a dozen troops had arrived and began creating a circle around the Nums.

Santorray stopped his run and looked back to ponder his options. He could still across the river to freedom and potential to reach Ericc or he could return to fight the Southwind guards with a chance of losing everything. "I'd rather fight than run, any day." Pulling out his sabers, he cut his shoulder to draw his blood before charging at the group with the roar of a battle cry.

Additional troops arrived and created a firing line for the oncoming beast.

Lucian was not going to allow Santorray a chance to get too close. "Fire!"

Arrows flew at the beast, on target and ready to pierce the Blothrud's chest and face. Santorray fell and crashed deep into the mud just before the arrows hit. However, it was not by design, something had grabbed his legs and tripped him.

Reloading their bows, the troops watched the Blothrud violently swing his sabers at the mud. Rolling to the side he stood up, only to trip again and fall. It was as though he was fighting the mud itself.

Cautiously moving forward the archers prepared to fire if this were some type of a trick. Unfortunately they learned too late that it wasn't.

Skeletal hands reached out of the mud and grabbed the feet of the approaching archers. Surprised, they released their arrows, firing them in every direction as the men tumbled into the mud.

The group surrounding the Nums also began to feel the mud move beneath them. The Nums did as well. Fingers could be felt raking the sides of their boots. Half-fleshy faces appeared out of the mud before sinking under again.

One by one, the troops were pulled into the mud. Some fell forward, some back, and others straight down into the murky water.

Lucian made a dash back for the south wall they had climbed over. Muddy hands swiping at his feet struck several times, but never hit hard enough to trip him. He could see the water churn behind him as what looked to be several of these unseen creatures speeding after him.

Looking forward toward the wall, he could see a dozen more blocking his path. There was no way to escape, so he changed his direction in an effort to reach one of the lone islands.

The water churned on both sides of Lucian as he raced for a pocket of dry land. A grabbing of his boot caused him to fall forward into the mud, just shy of the island. A second bony hand reached out and grabbed his shirt. Rolling out of his garment, he crawled up onto the dry hard dirt and collapsed.

The Nums had their own problems. They were also being attacked and would have to save themselves, seeing that Santorray was struggling with a dozen of his own mud covered skeletons.

A semi-fleshy hand and arm reached up and grabbed Avanda's leg. She screamed and attempted to pull away.

Ralph leapt off her shoulder and onto the attacking arms. Spitting on its wrist, the arm broke away as the acid from the saliva did its work.

Avanda called out a spell from her book as she pinched a powder from her purse. In spite of her inability to focus while under siege, the spell activated and dried up the water in the area she stood. Mud, which covered the skulls and bony arms, became instantly dry, causing them to retreat for the moment.

Unfortunately the moment wasn't long, for the dry area quickly filled back in with water, rejuvenating the watery attackers with more force than before. Reaching up, several grabbed her hard, pulling her entire body under water, along with Ralph.

The Nums and the soldiers screamed as they all were being pulled into watery graves.

Santorray's sabers broke bones but the thick mud slowed his swing and minimized the damage he was able to inflict.

Grabbing his spear, Thorik thrust the weapon straight down, stabbing one of the skeletal arms holding Avanda under water. Shaking from the strike, the skeleton's arm instantly turned to ashes. A deep rumble followed the attack, and a shock wave of sound and water spread out from the spear, knocking over anyone who had been able to still stand. Thorik was the only one able to remain on his legs, supporting his balance by holding onto the spear itself.

Vibrations resonated from the weapon and through Thorik's body. A deep undertone of a heartbeat pounded against the Num's chest. Each pulsation worked deeper into his body, toward his heart until they both hit the same rhythm.

Heavy strokes of his heart flushed his skin with heated blood, causing the water around his feet to stir and boil. The dead-risen people of River's Edge sunk away from him.

The event was localized, as the rest of his group continued to struggle.

Pulling the spear from the mud and water, the dead proceeded to move in again.

"Back!" Thorik stuck the first few inches of his weapon into the water.

The enemy retreated, this time farther away.

Keeping the tip of the spear in the water, Thorik helped Avanda from the muck and up onto her feet. She was covered with mud and scratches, but her concern was with finding Ralph.

Claws tight into her leather boot, Ralph hissed at the fleeing undead, protecting his friend.

Thorik didn't understand why the skeletons were afraid of the Spear of Rummon, although at this point he didn't care as long as it continued.

Holding Avanda tight, Thorik worked his way to Brimmelle. The Fir had been on his hands and knees, trying to prevent his face from being pummeled. Miraculously, his attackers retreated the moment his Sec arrived.

Fir Brimmelle grabbed onto Thorik's arm, using it to lift himself to his feet. "What took you so long? I was nearly killed. Where's mother?"

Screams from the Southwind army continued as the Nums searched for her, but she was nowhere in sight.

Cupping his hands, Brimmelle screamed for her.

No response.

"Come on." Thorik turned and began running to save Santorray, keeping the spear's point in the water.

Brimmelle stood his ground. Searching for his mother was his top priority. However, the water near him began to churn and proceed directly toward him. Backpedaling at first, he turned to keep up with Thorik and Avanda and the safety of the spear.

The Blothrud had over a dozen of the half-flesh covered undead attacking him. Some had pulled him into the mud up to his hips; others had clung onto him as he thrashed about.

Two partial skeletons flew past Thorik, nearly hitting the Fir. Santorray was peeling them off and tossing them as fast as they advanced.

Nearing the Blothrud, Thorik drove the spear into the water. "Be Gone!"

A wave of force rammed his enemy, blowing them off Santorray and causing the attackers from under the water to disappear.

Santorray looked around in disbelief, realizing Gluic was not with them. "Only one casualty. It could have been worse. Move out."

Brimmelle was furious at the notion. "Casualty? We're not going anywhere without my mother."

"There's no way she could have survived. Skilled soldiers can't survive these things. Your decrepit old Num didn't have a chance."

"She's very resourceful," Thorik said. "Besides, we've already lost Grewen, I'm not letting go of Gluic as well."

Santorray pointed to the muddy battlefield. "There are only a few people visible above the surface, and even those are so covered with the walking dead that it's impossible to tell which one is her."

Thorik pushed through the mud back toward where the initial attack occurred, still angry about leaving members of his party behind. The rest of his group had no choice but to follow him if they wished to stay within the spear's circle of safety.

Racing to the first pile of undead, the spear did its job by making the unwanted crowd scatter into the mud. What remained was the ripped open back of a Southwind soldier. His ribs broken and his internal organs exposed.

Santorray used the gruesome sight to make his point. "Finding Gluic may not be a wise idea. You don't want your last memory of her to be something like this. We've lost one, we could have lost more."

Thorik ignored him and moved on to the next, only to find this one without a head or arms.

One group of fleshy skeletons still stood above the surface. This last one, however, stood silently in a circle.

Running to meet them head on, they turned to block and defend what stood behind them. Thorik charged forward, placing the spear in both hands ready to strike. His friends raced behind him.

As he reached his attackers, Gluic stepped out from between them.

Thorik pulled the spear quickly to the left and up in the air to avoid stabbing her in the stomach. The move cost him his balance and he tumbled into the water, splashing with the full force of his body.

The undead scattered from the near proximity of the Spear.

Tears covered Gluic's face. "So sad, their story."

Avanda jumped forward and hugged her.

Brimmelle was less than impressed. "Mother, do you realized what you put us through?

Gluic ignored him as she addressed Avanda. "So many in endless suffering. They just want to be released."

Pulling himself back to his feet, Thorik was somehow not overly surprised that she would have a group discussion with the dead. "Unfortunate as it is, we can't help them."

"I know, I told them we couldn't help them today, but that you would be back."

"I will?"

"You're not going to let them continue to suffer are you? How can you live with that?"

"I don't have the power to unravel ancient Alchemist magic."

"I know, dear. That's why I told them it wouldn't be today."

As usual, Santorray was tired of Gluic's conversation. "We must travel north with haste," he said in an attempt to get everyone moving.

Thorik turned back to the south wall, and then glanced down at his spear. "Maybe we can still save Grewen."

Archers stood on the wall waiting for the opportunity to get the Nums back in range. The chances of running through the thick mud and reaching the wall before being killed were slim to none.

Santorray scoffed at the foolish notion. "Not even a dozen Blothruds would hold up against them. They have the advantage. The high ground, arrows, and plenty of time. We have no shelter from their attacks, nor speed in our advancement."

Thorik held his weapon firm. "I don't care. I have the Spear of Rummon. It has to count for something."

"Excellent plan. Leave your family here to be killed by the skeletons while you attack," the Blothrud said sarcastically.

"I'll take them with me."

"Your weapon may scare away the undead but how will it protect them from arrows."

Thorik was becoming frustrated as he heard the logical argument. "I don't know."

"No one wants to leave one of their men in battle, but no good will come from your plan."

"I can't just allow him to be captured and tortured because of things I've done."

"He made a choice. Accept it."

"So did I with Ambrosius, and I still regret it."

Spitting in his palm, Santorray held it out to Thorik. "I'll make a pact with you, Sec. I will help you save Grewen after we find Ericc, as long as you give up on trying to save him right now and accept that he made this choice for all of us to succeed."

Thorik spit in his own palm, trying to conform to the Blothrud's ritual, and shook his large hand. "Agreed. I trust you, Santorray."

Turning, the entire party headed north across the river. Everyone clung onto Santorray as he treaded the deepest sections and Thorik kept his spear poised for any potential attacks.

Fortunately, none occurred.

Chapter 26
O'Sid Fields

Thorik's Log: June 1st of the 650th year.
We've made it past River's Edge and the dunes of the Kiri Desert,
but we have lost Grewen in doing so. My heart and prayers hope that
he stays alive until I can return to rescue him.

Spring had made its presence known as the sun warmed the southern O'Sid Fields, turning the winter's green grasslands and rolling hills into golden brown grass that crunched when stepped on. Tall trees, with long thin leaves, shaded small pieces of the open plains.

Flocks of Traccu birds perched in isolated trees, watching for field mice and other rodents. Their sky blue color made the trees appear to be bearing fruit.

Prides of Tigras and packs of Beardogs were often seen resting in the shade of the trees when they weren't hunting the local macrauachenia or other grass-feeders.

Herds of Chuttlebeasts could be seen roaming the land devouring anything dead or alive, as the small Koa birds picked ticks and other insects off their backs. Spooked easily, the herds would stir up a spiral of twisted wind and dust sometimes as high as the Lu'Tythis Tower.

With most of her decorative plants dead, Gluic began replacing them with feathers of local birds. It wasn't long before they were in her hair, shoes, and made into necklaces and bracelets.

Santorray watched from the top of a hill as a distant herd split in two, just before the group walked down into the next small valley. "Keep your eyes on the herds. Always assume Chuttles are ready to attack. They change direction without warning. Never let your guard down, they are a powerful Fesh."

Lips dry, skin burnt from the sun, and eyes sore from squinting from the glare, the Nums had little interest in the distant Chuttles. They didn't even acknowledge the advice.

Thorik walked up front with Santorray. "Santorray, I have to ask you, what exactly is the prophecy of Ambrosius' son?"

"Ambrosius' son will slay Darkmere's son if he is not sacrificed on Eve of Light."

"Yes, I know that part, but there has to be more to it."

"It was foreseen by the Dark Oracle, Deleth. Then told to his student, Darkmere, who has lived with the threat over his son all his life."

"When we were on the captain's ship, did you say you had something to do with the prophecy?"

Santorray glared down at the Num. "The Nectar of Irr affected your hearing."

"Possible. I don't recall a lot from that night," Thorik said with a laugh. "So, Darkmere has been hunting down Ericc since he was born. What a terrible life for him."

"If it was so terrible, why did Ericc leave his safe haven?"

"Valid question. But what I don't understand is why he needs to be sacrificed during a specific time and place?"

"The Eve of Light is a sacred time. It only lasts for a few moments on one day of the year, when the sun finally reaches high enough in the sky to cast light over the Shi'Pel Peaks and onto the Surod Temple."

"Again, why sacrifice Ericc? And why does it need to be at a specific temple on that day?"

"Do you know nothing about Surod?"

"No, I don't," Thorik said honestly.

"How have you Nums survived with such little knowledge?" It was a rhetorical question, which he knew Thorik would try to answer if he gave him time, so he didn't. "Surod is the birthplace of all species. The Notarians forged the first of each of our kind in that temple on that day, during that small window of time. It is a gateway to life beyond the Fesh. It is a portal to the souls we carry inside us. Without this temple, all creations by the Notarians would have been mindless beasts reacting instinctively to their environment instead of having freewill to create something more."

"Rubbish!" Brimmelle announced from behind them, displaying the soul-markings on his arm. "Nums are the only ones who have souls. Each unique. Each given by the Mountain King to give us purpose. Altereds may have ability to crudely communicate, but they don't have souls."

Santorray glanced over at Thorik. "Perhaps not everyone obtained the full level of soul and thought that was provided."

Thorik grinned before returning to the topic. "I now understand about the emotional tie to Surod for embedding souls into new species. But what does that have to do with Ericc?"

"It's an opening for souls to pass through, regardless which way they travel. When the Notarians created a new species it was void of any soul, so one would flow into it. Sacrificing someone with a soul at the Eve of Light allows the soul to pass back to the beyond, never to return."

"Isn't killing him enough?"

"No, you can kill a man's body and leave his soul amiss. You know not where it will revive itself, whose new child will be taken over with it, whose ailing body it can capture, or where it may linger and haunt. To kill someone as powerful as an E'rudite you must make sure you do it correctly."

"Ericc's not an E'rudite... is he?"

"He has the lineage, so he has the potential. The question is if he knows his powers."

Reaching the top of the hill the group stopped. The herds they had seen before had split up and now were collected into several smaller groups, which encircled the hill where the party now stood on.

Chuttlebeasts always became chaotic this time of year. Shedding of their thick wool left trails of dark brown coarse fiber across the fields, which prompted their mating season. In addition, they were getting anxious to migrate north before the summer heat swept the plains.

Aside from narrow gaps between the gatherings, Thorik's party didn't see any other options available to leave the hilltop.

"We should wait them out," Brimmelle suggested.

Santorray looked up at the sun as sweat poured down his body. "No shade, little water and the Num's sensitive skin does not bode well for your plan. It could be hours or even days before they move on."

Thorik pointed toward the largest of gaps between herds. "Chuttles can't see well. If we quietly and calmly walk in the larger openings, we could make it without them knowing we were here."

"Have you smelled one up close?"

"Yes, so let's not get too friendly."

"Agreed."

The group moved lightly down the hill into the next shallow valley. Dry grass cracked under their feet, causing them to move at an extremely slow pace to minimize the sound.

As they entered the passage between the herds, the ceaseless shifting of beasts continuously reshaped their path. Snouts blew and hooves scratched the ground when the beast started to sense something amiss.

Covering their faces with their clothing didn't stop the stench from the Chuttles, which burned the group's eyes, noses and throats. Tolerable for a short period of time, it wouldn't be long before the headaches would begin, leading to fainting. It was fortunate that they still had distance enough not to smell them up close.

Halfway through, the passage closed completely, merging the two herds into one.

The travelers stopped, signaled by Thorik who then pointed for them to return the way they came. But it wasn't more than a few steps back before their retreat was closed off as well. They were trapped.

Each member looked around for options, afraid to speak for it may alert the Chuttles. The smell was getting worse as the Chuttles closed in on them. Headaches began to affect them, followed by dizziness.

Thorik had fallen to his hands and knees as he watched Gluic pass out, followed by Brimmelle and Avanda. Santorray was down to one knee, swaying, ready to slap his upper body hard against the ground. Thorik had to try something. He had to try anything.

Jumping out of Avanda's side bag, Ralph ran up on her shoulder. Mouth wide open, he turned his body around in a circle, hissing at the Chuttles in an effort to fend them off. He was the only one not affected as he pumped his body up and down to ward off the creatures.

Taking the Spear of Rummon out, Thorik stabbed it into the ground before him. A wave of pressure rushed out in every direction, knocking over Santorray, but leaving the Chuttles standing on their strong four legs. A loud roar from the spear could be heard by the entire Chuttle gathering, as well as distant herds. A deep pounding in the ground followed.

Chuttlebeast for tens of miles around stopped in their tracks, feeling the pulsing in the ground. Instincts took over as the mating call of the female Chuttle drummed on the O'Sid Fields. The distant Chuttles charged toward the direction of origin of the sound.

The local Chuttles, on the other hand, began battling each other for the rights to what they believed was a female in heat. Massive heads knocking up against each other resounded across the landscape as hundreds of beasts exploded into a show for dominance.

Strangely enough the dirt being kicked into the air reduced the potency of the Chuttle's smell, giving Santorray and Thorik a slight reprieve from their reaction.

Ralph scurried back into Avanda's pouch as he saw Santorray approach.

Large cubic-shaped heads of the Chuttles crashed together as the seven to eight-foot tall wild beasts ran over anything in their paths. Many of the creatures fell to the ground after being knocked unconscious from such head to head strikes.

Picking up Brimmelle with one arm and throwing Avanda and Gluic over his other shoulder, Santorray fought his way across the landscape. Swinging his free arm, he pounded hard against the woolly Fesh'Unday in his way.

A full body block was needed at one point to move the tail end of a Chuttle far enough for him to force his way through. Nearly dropping his companions during the move, he avoided performing it again. Instead, he used his razor sharp bony blades across his back and elbow to inflict enough pain to make the crazed creatures steer clear.

Thorik removed the spear from the ground, but the earth continued to shake from the Chuttlebeasts in heat. At twice his height, Thorik was more likely to be stepped on than rammed. Rolling under wool-matted stomachs and between kicking legs, the Num dodged the best he could with his head spinning from the fumes. Reaching the edge of the turmoil and seeing Santorray, he dove under the last beast, only to be kicked in the head, knocking him out cold.

Chapter 27
Corrock

The Hessik and the Fount rivers merged together to form the Squalid Waters. Behind this joining of waterways stood a city of ruin as well as renewal. Damaged walls and new towers shared the same locations. A backdrop of sharp pointed mountain peaks added a feel of the land's mouth opening and preparing to devour the city.

Ancient outer walls of sturdy granite now stood with gaping holes revealing centuries of construction and destruction. No recent attempts had been made to repair any borders; defensive measures were few.

Multiple bridges crossed both the Hessik River to the south and the Fount River to the west. Some had been destroyed from past battles and never restored.

Thorik woke and looked about with weary eyes, his head still painfully aware of the Chuttlebeast's kick. "Where are we?"

"Welcome to Corrock, Sec," Santorray said.

Santorray had taken control and brought them the rest of the way to the city during Thorik's Chuttle-induced slumber. The Blothrud had kept the group of travelers far enough back from the city to prevent detection.

Thorik retained a shallow headache and a red bump on his forehead, in spite of Gluic's healing techniques. Shaking off the lingering pain, he got straight to business. "Santorray, how do you propose we get inside?"

"I'll walk in."

Thorik slowly stood up to test his legs. "How about the rest of us?"

"You're not coming with me."

Already in a bad mood from the pounding still in his head, Thorik's face flushed to match the lump above his brow. "Yes we are. This is our journey, which you joined, not the other way around. We will go in together."

The Blothrud crossed his arms. "You're going to make a very simple event into something complicated. Let me do what I need to do and I'll bring Ericc out to you, assuming he ever made it to Corrock and that he's not already dead."

"Then I guess we're going to make it complicated. I haven't come all this way to just sit back and wait for you to find out what has happened to him. What was the point of obtaining the Spear of Rummon if I'm not even going to attempt to save Ericc? Ovlan wouldn't have told us to get it if we didn't need it."

"Give me the spear if you think it's needed. Nums aren't welcome in Corrock except as slaves. You're a liability."

Thorik pulled the spear in tight. "No."

"Seems odd that a Num would cling to a weapon which killed their king."

Brimmelle scoffed at the comment. "It's more likely that an assassin's dagger held by a Blothrud killed our king." Fortunately for Thorik, Fir Brimmelle didn't take Santorray's comment seriously.

"Ovlan told me that only I was to wield him," Thorik added before Santorray could respond to the Fir's verbal jab.

"Him? It's an object. Metal, leather, skins." Santorray bent down to grab it out of Thorik's hands.

Thorik backed up, gripped the weapon firmly in both hands, pointing the spear at the Blothrud. "We're going in together to save Ericc."

Santorray instinctively grabbed the spear out of his hands before Thorik could react. "Don't ever point a weapon at me. I've killed people for less."

The moment became precarious as a low distant growl emanated from the weapon as Santorray held it to his side. Fragments of words could be heard but not understood as the spear began to glow red. Tunnel echoing sounds raced forward as though they were going to leap out of the object.

Santorray threw the spear to the ground, kicked dirt on it and stepped back with caution. "It's possessed. The spirit of Rummon still lives within it."

"And apparently doesn't like Blothruds for some reason," Thorik said.

"There's a reason. The dragon Rummon was killed during an attempt to harness some of his energy for the most powerful weapon ever seen. Apparently they captured the dragon's life force as well."

"For who?"

"Ergrauth, the mightiest Blothrud Deleth ever created. He was unstoppable with the power of Rummon at his side, equal to that of the Oracles themselves. He dominated the land, air and water. At least until the spear was stolen and hidden, only to be unearthed thousands of years later by a little Num named Sec Thorik Dain."

Thorik bent down and gently picked it back up. The ghostly voice subsided, as did the red glow. "Like I said, only I am to wield him."

"Even if that old relic has that dragon's soul, it is too old and weak to take on the entire forces of Corrock."

Changing his grip on the spear, Thorik stood with confidence. "If this was such a powerful weapon for Ergrauth, perhaps it will do the same for me."

"The heart of a Blothrud you have, Sec. But you fail to understand that you are just a Num, a Num without any soul-markings at that. What makes you think you can take on such a task?"

Soul-markings showed maturity and characteristics of Nums. To not have them, made others question Thorik's ability to be taken seriously. He sighed while straightening his shoulders. "Ambrosius once told me that I was intended to be more and achieve great things in spite of my lack of markings. I believe he meant that I have an honorable lineage and that I have abilities passed down through generations. I was meant to be more than just an average Num."

Santorray could appreciate his pride, but understood all too well the dangers inside the city. "And you will be. The average Num does not travel to Corrock to die."

Chapter 28
Bound and Chained

Thorik led the Nums into Corrock. Each Num had their hands tied with a rope that linked them to the rest of the Nums. Santorray walked in front, holding the rope, which controlled them all. It was the only way that the Nums would be allowed in the city, as slaves.

The Del'Unday species ranged from the small Rico rodents to the Blothruds themselves. Some looked like man-sized insects while others hid behind cloaks and hoods.

Corrock was built with numerous types of architecture erected over thousands of years. New construction comprised of mud blocks built on millennium old foundations and half walls of marble or granite.

Houses and shops expanded upward over the years as tenants used lighter materials such as wood to add additional floors. Rooftops pierced the skyline like jaded rocks, in visual harmony with the mountains just to their east.

Fresh Fesh meat hung in open windows of a few shops waiting for a customer to scrape off the flies and purchase. Shops of weapons and slavery shared street corners with shops of jewelry, fruit, baskets, and blacksmiths. The streets were busy with customers and merchants.

Santorray occasionally struck up conversations with merchants in an effort to find information about the son of Ambrosius. As he had predicted, they were too late. Ericc had recently been apprehended and held for justice for his father's criminal acts against Corrock.

"Your quest to find your spear has cost us our chance to prevent Ericc's capture," Santorray said to Thorik as they walked along the streets.

Shoulders drooping with the feeling of defeat, Thorik did the only thing he knew how to do; come up with a new plan. "Can you find out what prison he is in? There must be a way to free him."

Santorray chuckled. "The Del'Unday don't have prisons. We give the victims of your crime an opportunity to take vengeance upon you. If severe enough, we put you to death afterward. Why would we spend time and effort housing and feeding criminals who had little care of our well-being?"

"That seems extremely harsh."

"Not at all. If you broke into my home and killed my child, I have the right to take my anger back out on you in any way that I see fit."

"What if I only stole an item? Do you still have the right to torture or kill me?"

"Yes. You've taken your chances when you illegally entered my home. Our laws make you think twice about committing a crime."

Thorik grew slightly tense at the thought of accidentally breaking a law unknown to him. His best bet would be to keep his head down and stay close to Santorray. "So, if Ericc's not in a prison, where would he be?"

"On display for the locals to taunt and take out their anger over Ambrosius' legacy. He will be tied up in an open area until he dies or Darkmere's men come for him."

After several hours of wandering through the streets, the travelers entered the fourth district of the city. Each section of the city had all streets end in a central gathering place. The fourth district was known as the lower quadrant ever since it was partially destroyed nearly a decade ago. Depressed even more than the rest of the city, less new construction and commerce were seen as Thorik and his team walked into the center of the district.

Standing in the middle of the courtyard, Ericc had his hands bound in chains above his head. Whipped and bloody, the young man had passed out from the torture he had taken. Blood dripped down his body and pooled at his feet, but not enough yet to cause his death.

The boy was displayed for all Corrockians to take out their anger at Ericc's father. Ambrosius had single handily destroyed the fourth district eight years prior. Killing innocent Del'Unday and crushing ancient temples had outraged the locals against Ambrosius, his family, as well as the entire human race.

Thorik froze in his tracks. "Santorray, it's Ericc."

Del'Unday walking through the open area stopped to mock the human. Some would throw sticks and small rocks at the prisoner while others approached him to give him more personal pain.

Santorray waited until no one was standing on the platform where Ericc hung like a piece of Fesh meat. "Let's approach."

Thorik tugged back on the rope, which held all the Nums. "In broad daylight? With hundreds of Del'Unday in view?"

"We need to at least let him know we are here so he hangs on to life long enough for us to save him."

"Agreed."

Santorray led the way, pulling the Nums behind him. As he approached Ericc, the Blothrud inconspicuously pulled out his small virgin dagger and held it between his hand and the hair on his leg. The blade glistened with a polish never tarnished with the blood of a victim, at least until this day. Varacon's twisted blades came to a sharp point and the gems within its hilt began to glow with the anticipation of a first strike.

Walking up the steps to the chained boy in the center of the crowded courtyard, Santorray continued to modify his hold on the dagger to make sure he had a strong grip on it. Designed for a smaller hand, it never felt quite right.

The ideal location for this assassination would be in front of Darkmere at Surod. Regardless, Santorray was ready. It was time to stab Ericc in front of plenty of witnesses and in front of Thorik. It was time to end this quest and to repay his debt. It was finally at an end.

Stepping forward to Ericc, Santorray pulled the blade away from his hairy leg and quickly shoved it forward.

"Ericc!" Thorik shouted, jumping between the young man and the Blothrud.

Santorray nearly stabbed the blade into Thorik's back, before he halted the weapon.

Ericc's swollen black and blue eyes opened. His vision was blurry, but the Nums voice triggered his memory.

"Ericc, it's me Thorik from the Southwind mines. We're here to rescue you."

"Rescue? Where's Darkmere?"

Santorray pulled the weapon back into hiding, waiting for Thorik to move out of the way.

"Haven't seen him yet," Thorik answered. "We'll come back after dark and rescue you, so don't give up."

Santorray sheathed the dagger before it could be spotted. "Yes, stay alive until we return."

One of the local Blothrud guards stepped toward the platform. "Get your slaves away from the prisoner. You know better than that."

Santorray pulled back the rope to get Thorik way from Ericc, before dragging the group of them out of the open area and into a side alley.

Thorik was thrilled that Ambrosius' son had not been killed. "All we need to do is wait for dark and then we can grab him and sneak him out."

Santorray snarled. "You fool, you nearly got us caught. Your little conversation with Ericc may have drawn more attention to us than the single guard who told us to leave."

"What's the issue? We did as we were told."

"Any attention to us is not wanted. We were fortunate he didn't recognize me."

"Do you know him?" Thorik asked.

"No."

"Then why would he?"

Santorray paused before answering. "My reputation tends to precede me. If I'm noticed, our plans may be at an end."

"Fine, we'll return after dark when it isn't so obvious what we are doing."

As promised, the adventurers returned to the open courtyard after dark fell. Dozens of oil lanterns circled the platform, casting light onto their prisoner and the apparatus that his chains hung from. Against the dark of the night, Ericc looked like a glowing star for all to see.

Brimmelle folded his arms and grimaced at Thorik. "Yes, much better after dark."

Thorik nodded in agreement that conditions had not improved.

Santorray focused less on Ericc and more on the surrounding windows and alleys, which could view him. "Wait until the howl is over, and then follow my lead."

"Howl?"

A single howl could be heard from the mountain foothills outside of the city. It echoed throughout the now silent city.

Once completed, a return howl began within the city, this time made up from every resident within Corrock. From every direction, long emotional howls fired back to the mountain from where the first one originated until it slowly wound down to a few stragglers before ending.

Dead quiet followed.

Thorik waited for Santorray to explain, but received nothing. "What was that?

"Praise to Ergrauth for sparing their lives." Santorray continued watching for locals who passed by windows and doorways. "Corrock and Ovla'Mathyus agreed to stand up against the powers of Ergrauth during the Unday War. However, the Ovs refused to stand alongside the Dels of Corrock when the attacks began. The Corrockians who survived the attack are forever in debt to Ergrauth for sparing their lives."

"It's my understanding that the Ovs offered refuge to the Dels."

"And forfeit their homes, land and honor? What kind of offer is that?"

"One of survival."

"Anyone can survive. Dels must live. We must thrust ourselves into every new day with vitality and ferocity as though it may be our last, for some day it will be. We would choose to live a short life of grand excitement and triumphs over a long life of serene dullness."

"Your people chose certain death against Ergrauth's forces over certain life behind safe walls?"

"My people?"

"Corrockians."

"Sec, I am not a Corrockian."

"Oh, then what are you?"

"I'm not a Corrockian." The point was made for Thorik to drop the subject.

"I found it!" Avanda had been searching for a spell in Dare's book of magic, which could help them with the situation at hand. Digging into her red purse of magic items, she pulled out a small vial of clear liquid. Etchings of small frogs surrounded the mouth of the glass vial. "If we give Ericc some of this with the right words, we can make a temporary illusion of Ericc while freeing the real one."

Silence fell on the group as they stared at her as though she was speaking a different language.

Lifting the vial up to show the group, she removed the cork. Sticking her tongue out, she placed one drop of clear liquid on it before Thorik or Brimmelle could stop her.

Smiling at first, Avanda started choking and coughing, as she pushed the cork back on.

Thorik slapped her back. "Spit it out, it could be poison."

Brimmelle told her to relax and breathe.

Pushing them both away, Avanda caught her breath. "I'm fine. It just tastes terrible."

Reading in her small book she read the verbal piece of the spell. "Lavare'Repla'Hospes" Still choking on the taste, she tried the words again a few times. By the fourth time the words were spoken correctly as Thorik and Brimmelle began to step back from her.

Avanda's body blurred for a moment in the torchlight, before a second Avanda stepped forward out of the original's body.

Two Avandas now stood in the group and spoke at the same time; neither could be heard over the other.

"Defying the Mountain King's limits, this is." Brimmelle backed away from the replica.

"Avanda, that was dangerous. You don't know what it could have done to you or how long it will last." Thorik reached over and touched the new Avanda. She was damp and tacky to the touch.

Santorray finished his scouting of the area. "We'll have to sneak out there, give him the potion, say the words and then replace the chains from the real Ericc to the magic one."

Thorik sighed. "I'll do it. It's my responsibility."

"No, I'll do it." The new Avanda grabbed the vial out of Avanda's hand.

"Give that back!" Avanda chased her likeness into the courtyard before wrestling her to the ground.

One of them finally stood with the vial in hand, only to be pulled back down by the other.

Santorray held the other Nums back in the alley, as two Krupes and a Brandercat left their dark posts hidden from the light. Dark spiked armor completely covered the two-legged Krupes from head to toes as they walked toward Avanda and Avanda.

The Brandercat's scales faded in color and blended into the dark courtyard, making them practically invisible to the observer. The large cat body was covered with color-shifting scales, which allowed it to fade into their surroundings. It took concentration to keep their scales in tune with the light and colors, preventing them from attacking while doing so.

Seeing the Krupes approaching, both young Nums made a dash for the center of the yard. Jumping up onto the platform, one of the girls was caught by a Krupe as he held onto her leg.

Screaming, she tossed the vial up to the other Avanda, who then raced over to Ericc.

A Brandercat appeared out of nowhere, leaping at Avanda across the large platform.

Diving out of the way, Avanda rolled and jumped to her feet.

The Krupe below had the other Avanda in his clutches, with no hope for escape.

Turning around, the Brandercat smiled at the Avanda who was still on the stage, knowing he couldn't miss at this close of a range.

Avanda knew she only had one chance. It was time to act like a Del'Unday and live life to the limit as though it would be her last, for today appeared to be so. Opening her vial, she lunged at Ericc, placing the mouth of the bottle to his lips and titling back his head.

Leaping through the air, the Brandercat's dislocating jaw opened and took Avanda's entire midsection into his mouth before he landed to the side of the chained prisoner.

Avanda's body went limp in the large cat's mouth as he carried her to the edge of the platform before snapping his jaws shut and tasting the fresh Num blood. Violently crushing the prey in his mouth, the Brandercat was surprised to find a wave of water gushing out from her body as though it was only a bag of bad tasting oily water.

"Lavare'Repla'Hospes" yelled the Avanda who was captive.

Ericc had swallowed nearly the entire bottle. His body began to blur to all that watched. Shaking, his body appeared to pull itself into two. A second Ericc now stood on the platform, however without being chained up.

"Restrain him," announced the Brandercat, still trying to get the wretched taste from his mouth.

But before the Krupes moved, a third Ericc appeared, then a fourth, and a fifth. It continued until the yard was filled with Ericcs, each beginning to make their own escape plan down the many streets and alleyways.

Ralph climbed out of Avanda's side bag and leaped onto the Krupe's arm, which held her. Spitting on it, his armor began to sizzle away, while some of the lizard's acid worked its way under onto the creature's skin.

Avanda was dropped, as the Krupe swatted the lizard off his wrist.

Mass confusion erupted and continued to get worse. The Krupe turned his attention to the Ericc in front of him, plunging his sword to the boy's chest. Ericc popped like a thin sack of water, pouring its sour liquid onto the ground. It wasn't a moment later that two more Ericcs had jumped off the platform and took his place.

Thorik and Santorray raced into the crowd of Ericcs to cut free the real one, while Brimmelle and Gluic found Avanda picking up Ralph and trying not to be stepped on during the stampede.

Santorray approached the real prisoner and had a free opportunity to stab Ericc in the heat of the battle, but it could easily be missed from the public's viewing.

One slice from Santorray's saber and the chains holding Ericc up were compromised. Lifting the semi-conscious young man, Santorray led the group toward the southern gate. With hastened speed, they stormed out of the city as sirens of alert could be heard from behind. The Blothrud would uphold his original plan to stab the boy when all could see. This was not the time or place.

"Darkmere?" was all that Ericc could get out before passing out from loss of blood and starvation.

Lanterns were lit and horns blared as the city awoke to the news of Ericc's escape and his running amuck in their streets.

Chapter 29

Under Siege

Exhausted from the hours of running, Brimmelle and Gluic fell hard to the ground, spraying dirt into their face.

Brimmelle spit dirt back out into the darkness and yelled. "Far enough! We can't run any farther."

"See those torches in the distance?" Santorray pointed from where they had come. "They're tracking us and gaining on us."

Avanda sat down to rest as well. "My legs hurt and I'm thirsty. I need a break."

"I can't carry you all, so get on your feet keep start moving," Santorray growled.

"Santorray, set Ericc down and give us a few moments to drink and rest." Thorik kneeled down and handed his grandmother some water. "We'll move all the more quickly afterward."

The sliver of moon gave off just enough light for them to see general shapes. Thorik was unable see the pleasure across Gluic's face as she sipped the water, but he could hear it from her sigh of relief.

"We have no time. They are nearly upon us."

Thorik slowly got to his feet. "We have a bigger issue."

Several dozen men were on three sides of Thorik's group.

Santorray saw the figures as well. Lifting his nose, he took a deep breath. "Eastland Military." Growling, he turned and squinted to see his enemy but his eyes just couldn't focus to validate his words.

Thorik stood over the Nums on the ground to protect them. "We're trapped."

Both sabers from Santorray's belt were immediately unsheathed for an attack. "Not without a fight." He allowed blood to drip from a fresh bite of his lip.

"They have crossbows. Put your weapons away before you get us killed."

"I'll die fighting before I let them capture us."

"And how will that help any of us? We will have failed Ambrosius and lost our own lives just to slay a few of their men."

"Better to die trying then not to try at all."

Thorik moved in front of the Blothrud. "There's a time to fight and a time to back down. This is one of those times to understand we can't win. We must save ourselves for a time when we can."

Hesitating, Santorray heard the stress of additional bowstrings being pulled back and locked in place. He could only assume they were pointed at him. Even if he charged forward, he would most likely perish before he even reached the first few Eastlanders.

"I trusted you at River's Edge when we left Grewen. Trust me now. I know what I'm doing. Put your weapons away," Thorik said as an order and with compassion.

Slowly, Santorray sheathed his sabers.

They stood motionless as they waited for the men to speak.

Instead, the men made an opening for them to pass forward. They knew better than to approach a Blothrud to remove his weapons. They would wait to do so back at camp when they had more reinforcements.

Thorik helped the Nums to their feet. "Come on. They're leading us someplace."

Santorray picked up Ericc and followed the Nums. "Most likely their base camp."

"Fine mess you got us into, Thorik." Brimmelle complained. "Walking us right into our enemy's camp."

"More likely your annoying voice being overhead by scouts," Santorray said to Brimmelle.

Over the next few hills, torchlight illuminated an area with tents and wagons. Flags from Southwind and Eastland were prominently displayed throughout the camp where several hundred men prepared for the night.

In the center of the camp was a thick post to which Grewen was chained. Sitting down, he leaned against the post, his wrists and ankles bound by the same chain.

A fleeting moment of exhilaration came upon Thorik when he saw his Mognin friend. Just to know he was still alive was enough, but to have him within sight was remarkable. Nevertheless, this quickly passed as the Num realized that he also would be chained up and all of them were most likely headed for the Southwind mines.

The scouts quietly led them down the hill and into camp, while one of them rushed ahead to alert their commanders.

Stopping at the main tent, Santorray set Ericc down on his feet. The injured youth had been struggling to get down off the Blothrud for several minutes as he slowly awoke.

Standing up, the young man held onto the closest Num for support, who happened to be Brimmelle. Ericc's weakened knees wobbled and his eyes tried to focus. "Where's Darkmere?" Ericc coughed. He had no idea where he was or what events were happening around him.

Exiting from one of the larger tents was an older man, ripe with scars from many battles. His red robes covered metal armor across his chest, which bore the symbol of Eastland, the symbol of bloodshed and hatred to all Altereds. Three swords crossing blades, forming a triangle, with blood pooling in the center from each weapon. "Well done men, you've recovered Ericc," the general said to his scouts.

A second figure emerged from the tent. It was Lucian. Pushing his long blonde hair out of his face and behind his ear, he bestowed a smile of devious enjoyment as he watched Santorray stand before them. "General Hatch, these are the criminals I've been looking for, especially the Blothrud. I knew they had something to do with Ericc's escape."

"Remarkably, you were correct," the general said. "As agreed, I'll give Ericc to Asentar. Do what you wish with the others." He then turned to his commander and added an order. "Remove their weapons and tie up the Blothrud and Nums."

Santorray grabbed for his sabers with lightning speed, causing the archers to prepare to fire.

"Wait!" Lucian yelled before addressing the general. "I don't want the Matriarch cheated out of seeing Santorray's death. I will address this."

The general had little respect for Lucian, but he needed to keep the Matriarch from becoming an enemy. "Commander, keep an eye on our Southwind friends in case this gets out of control." Then the general returned to his tent.

Lucian turned to address the captives. "It's over, my friends. You've been captured and we didn't even need to use your Mognin companion for bait."

Stepping forward into the street in front of them, Lucian looked directly at the Blothrud. "Santorray, I thought I had killed you once, but I won't underestimate your resolve this time. Instead, I shall behead you in front of the Matriarch herself. Then I shall mount your head to decorate her chamber's wall to ensure you never come back to life and haunt my streets."

Raising his hand with two missing fingers, Lucian made sure Santorray could see the stubs. "Seeing that you bit off my fingers, I plan to cut up your Mognin and Num friends and feed their meat to our hungry troops who worked so hard to track you down. Only fair, wouldn't you say? Of course, what would you care? Blothruds never get along with other species."

Santorray slowly cut his own shoulder before pointed his bloody sabers at Lucian. "I'll teach you what is fair."

Over thirty men pulled back and locked their crossbows. The same amount readied their swords.

Lucian nodded his head at Santorray, trying to convince him to take a swing at him, giving the archers reason to fire their arrows. "As much as I prefer to kill you in the company of the Matriarch, I can live with your death occurring right now. So I strongly recommend you and your followers drop your weapons before my good nature is taxed, and I decide to kill you *all* right now."

"Santorray! No!" Thorik shouted. "Not now. This is not the time." Removing his spear from its holder on his back, he prepared to drop the weapon to lead his party in their surrender.

Lucian laughed at the statement. "The mighty Blothrud, Santorray, taking orders from a Num? And a small meek one without soul-markings at that."

Thorik's grip tightened instead around the spear instead of releasing it to the ground.

Santorray's hands shook as he fought off the temptation to finish the job on Lucian regardless of what would follow.

"He's baiting you. Don't give him a reason to order our deaths." Thorik tried to relax his own hands.

"Your deaths have already been ordered." Lucian continued with the grin. "You might say that I'm just playing with my food. Bringing it to a boil before I eat it."

"Hold back," Thorik ordered Santorray.

Lucian enjoyed the game and decided to continue it down a different path. Eyeing one of his men, he gave him the signal to grab the girl from the back, which he did. Avanda was pulled from the group and brought around to the front.

Avanda squirmed and bucked against the man until he finally released her in front of Lucian.

Helpless, Thorik looked on with fear and anger. Would he once again not be able to protect her? Would he be forced to watch her pain this time? "Leave her alone!"

Lucian leaned down to her height. "I never did get a chance to see just how soft your skin really was."

Reaching for her red purse, Avanda was going to take care of the man here and now.

Lucian pulled out a crooked blade from his side and slapped the flat side of it against her hand, cutting her hand near the thumb, causing her to drop the purse.

She immediately clutched the injury with her other hand and cradled it near her chest.

"Not this time, little witch. No magic to help you out." Dripping with her blood, Lucian's blade moved to her neck and pushed against her skin, before he peered toward the Blothrud. "And no one here to save you this time."

Waves of Rava'Kor memories flashed in her mind. Helpless, she would soon be violated. Not alone this time, a crowd would watch her being raped. Her arms and legs went rigid, tense from the memories. She wanted to run, or attack, or anything other than stand there and relive his repulsive touch to her body.

Ralph had climbed out of her backpack and onto her shoulder. He leaped onto Lucian's hand, biting down hard onto his wrist. His acidic saliva poured out onto the man's skin.

Lucian screamed, as he reached to grab the lizard off him. But the spines on the little creature's back poked deep into his palm.

Ralph coiled his body around Lucian's entire wrist, chewing on the flesh as the acid softened it.

Unable to get the critter off, Lucian smacked the lizard's head with the hilt of his blade, knocking it out cold.

Ralph fell to the ground, exposing a severe red ring of torn flesh around Lucian's wrist.

Lifting his leg high in the air, Lucian smashed his boot onto the lizard, crushing it into the hard ground several times. He made sure the creature was dead before wiping the bottom of his boot off with his knife.

Avanda was in shock from watching the slaying of her little friend. No longer did she wish to run. Now her only desire was to see the man pay. Her body filled with rage over her companion's death.

Lucian turned back to her and placed the knife back to Avanda's neck. Lizard flesh and blood dripped from the blade onto her chest. "For crimes against me, you are now legally my slave, to do with as I wish. And I wish to feel your soft skin, all of it, every night, until I get tired of you and sell you off to slave traders."

Reaching out with his other hand, Lucian slowly pulled her injured hand toward his face. "But until then, you will please me and fulfill my desires." Slowly, he dragged his tongue across the open wound on her hand to taste her blood.

Pulling her hand back, she slapped him hard across the face. She no longer feared the man who once haunted her dreams. In some way, he had just freed her from her internal torture.

But her slap had only heightened his desire for her, as he smiled at her tenacious spirit. "I'm glad you like it rough." Lucian slapped her back across the face, knocking her to the ground. "Because so do I." Lucian lifted his blade to stab her.

"NO!" Thorik screamed in violent rage, his fist squeezing tight around the shaft of his spear.

A roar erupted from the Spear of Rummon, launching a magical flame from its point, which engulfed Lucian's head. Fire coated the man from his neck up as he screamed in pain, dropped his dagger, and placed his hands over his eyes to protect them. But it was insufficient, his eyes had been seared and the skin on his face continued to burn.

Avanda watched as white flames stirred between his fingers as his hands also caught on fire. She witnessed the flames coil inside his mouth as he yelled for help. However, there was no help to be given or time to give it. The flame ended as fast as it had begun, leaving Lucian's face and hair charred and blackened as he gasped for breath.

As the reality of the assault took hold, the archers altered their aim now to the Num for his attack.

Thorik quickly drove his spear into the ground. A mighty shock wave emanated from the weapon, violently crashing outward, followed by a rhythmic pounding in the ground. The blast wave covered the valley. Soldiers fell, tent stakes snapped, Faralopes panicked, and campfires flared from the fanning of the flames. The shock of such unexpected force took a few moments for the Eastland army to collect themselves.

"Now, Santorray," Thorik ordered, even though the Blothrud was already pursuing his first victim in the same motion of getting back on his feet.

Lucian fell to his knees, begging Avanda for help.

"You're evil and vile." Avanda's stomach tightened as she looked at the destroyed face of the man who would rape her. Picking up his dagger, still dripping with Ralph's blood, she held it to his neck. "It's one thing to fight for your morals even if they are skewed. But you have none. The world will be better without you."

His pain was overwhelming as he looked for an end. "Then kill me. Put me out of my misery."

She looked at Ralph's dead body and pushed the blade forward, only to stop before slicing his neck. "That's too good for you. I prefer that you live to feel the pain which you inflict on others."

Lucian fell to the ground unconscious from the irrepressible suffering, as Avanda stood up with a new strength and fortitude.

A tight circle of men continued to fight Santorray with long swords and flails, leaving the archers only a periodic open shot to his head. An unfortunate miss of the Blothrud could end up hitting their own men, so no shots were fired.

Thorik pulled out his throwing daggers and attempted to stay out from under Santorray's feet and away from the swinging of his sabers. The few men that reached in to grab Thorik away from the Blothrud were met by the stinging of the Num's blade.

Brimmelle and Gluic were grabbed, but put up little resistance. They were pulled back and held at knifepoint.

Avanda grabbed for her red purse with new enthusiasm.

Pulling out her red beads she began to chant, but was bumped during the commotion of the men fighting Santorray and Thorik, dropping and losing the beads on the process. Stirred up dust quickly covered them up and they fell out of sight.

Reaching back into her purse, she removed several small bones. "Bellfin'Pec." She waved her arms about. The ground near her turned to thick mud and spread out past Gluic and her son. The expression on her face was the same surprise and disappointment that came over Brimmelle. They were caught.

All three Nums were lifted out of the mud and carried over to the Mognin. Avanda, Gluic and Brimmelle were quickly chained up to the same post as Grewen.

Fir Brimmelle's eyes searched about the camp. "What happened to Ericc?"

Gluic smiled. "He decided not to join our battle."

"I wish he had taken us with him."

Backing up to Santorray, Thorik watched as men were tossed in the air by the mighty Blothrud. Weapons, shields, and helmets shot in every direction from the battle behind him. With Rummon too far to reach, Thorik put his tiny daggers away and grabbed a fallen sword and shield. He then proceeded to hold off the men attempting to grab him and tie him up with his friends.

Santorray continued to take man after man down, but there was simply too many of them. He would exhaust his strength long before they ran out of men. He knew the odds of survival were unlikely, but at least he would go down fighting.

Fighting his way forward, Santorray carved an opening for Thorik to escape and free Grewen and the Nums. It wasn't long lived; still it was enough for the small Num to twist his way through. Unfortunately the clever moves cost him his newfound sword.

Thorik reached Grewen and the Nums. "Where's Ericc?"

His grandmother replied, "He left."

"We'll search for him as soon as I set you free."

The locks on the chains around their ankles and wrists were too large for Thorik to break with the small daggers, and his spear was lodged in the ground on the other side of the Eastland troops. He had nothing to break the locks with, so he would attempt to bend them with his dagger.

"Thorik," Brimmelle said.

"Just wait, I might be able to-" Thorik finally noticed what his uncle was alerting him to. A dozen men, with swords and arrows pointed his way, stood poised for battle.

Two high pitched horn blasts sounded, causing the men around Santorray to stop fighting and back up, while Thorik was captured and added onto the chain of prisoners.

Santorray was breathing hard from the fight. Human blood splattered across his face and chest, but he was not harmed.

General Hatch had his troops back under control. "Spears ready!" he ordered.

The circle of men, encompassing the Blothrud, were handed long spears from behind.

The general demanded synchronized movements from his troops. "Spear down."

Spears lowered to the ground with single pound.

"Spears aim."

Raising the front blade of the spears to waist level and keeping the back end of it on the ground, soldiers behind them placed their boots on the base of the weapons to ensure they didn't slide backward.

Santorray was now in a prison of two dozen spear blades. Smiling, he licked the human blood from his face to intimidate the men. He wondered how many he would take out before he fell.

"Front lines down." Hatch watched his orders performed in perfect movement as the men around the beast squatted down without moving the spears.

"Archers ready."

Standing behind the squatting men, a circle of archers lifted their crossbows in unison.

"Archers aim."

Pulling back on their strings and locking them in place, the arrows were lined up to fire.

Refusing to go down without a fight, Santorray attacked.

"Fire!"

Chapter 30
Del'Unday Army

A loud howl from the hill caught everyone's attention, as an army of Del'Unday charged into the valley. Some at a run, other riding Fesh'Undays, they descended toward the camp with murderous screams of war. The Corrockians had finally caught up to Ericc and those who helped him escape.

General Hatch immediately reassembled his troops against the Del'Unday, an enemy he had fought many times. "Fall in line. Two tier front. Archers at center and side points."

The first to attack were the Entelodont hogs, with shoulders taller than Thorik and long snouts with two large lower saber-like teeth. Jumping down onto the Eastland troops, the men lifted their spears in the air to skewer them as they landed. Spears snapped in half as the beasts hard underbellies withstood most of the blows, and yet nearly a fourth of the hogs were seriously injured from the first wave.

The crushing weight of the hogs flattened many of the men as they proceeded past the front lines. With their heads down, the hogs charged the second line of defense with their thick frontal horns.

The general gave his orders to a well-organized battalion. Archers fired, taking out the majority of the hogs before they could reach the second line.

The front line held fast against the remaining hogs and prepared for the oncoming Brandercats who blinked in and out of visibility. The Eastland men tossed handfuls of white powder in front of the battle line. Large invisible cats raced forward, running through the powder, which clung to their feet and legs, allowing the men to see them.

Eastland guards began to thrust their spears forward at the locations where the painted feet shined bright in the torchlight. Hitting their marks more often than not, the men prevented most of the Del'Unday from breaching the first line of defense.

Krupes finally crested over the hill and surveyed the scene. A single Blothrud was barking out orders to the stocky creatures coated in black metal armor. The Krupes were the foundation to the Del army, defensively tough with excellent battle skills and a strong constitution.

The general pulled his frontal defense line back into an arch to capture the Krupes in the center. Ordering his archers into new positions, he walked toward the center of the front line's arch. He knew the drill. He knew once the Del'Unday have sent their preliminary forces into battle, the leading Blothrud would be open to talking about a surrender. General Hatch had no plan on surrendering, he was winning the battle, but it was a good opportunity to size up his opponent.

Krupes lined up straight across the hill, unwilling to bend to the men's arch, as the Blothrud walked forward into it.

Taller than Santorray, this Blothrud wore decorative jewelry created from pieces of his prior victims' bodies. A few skulls clanked together on a rope over his shoulder, threaded eyeballs swung from a necklace, and rib cage and finger bones created a helmet.

"I am General Hatch from Eastland. We have the right to travel the O'Sid fields."

The Blothrud spit on the general's boot. "You have our prisoner and the criminals who helped him escape."

"We have them in custody. But they will be held in our kingdom for their crimes against our people before we consider if they are to be given to you. What be your name, beast."

"Bellfor."

For the first time, the general realized he was dealing with a seasoned veteran, a legend among the Del'Unday's. "Bellfor the Savage? Your reputation precedes you. I am surprised you're willing to come forward and offer us a chance at surrendering, even though we obviously still have the upper hand."

"I'm not offering anything. I've come to take back what is ours and punish those responsible."

Shuffling of the general's troops caught Hatch's eyes. A legion of Krupes appeared on each side of the valley. He had underestimated the number of creatures at the Blothrud's disposal.

"Do you honestly expect us to stand by and let you take our prisoners?"

"No, I expect you to die trying to stop me."

Uncharacteristic of these types of talks, a second human approached the center ring. Easily a head taller than most men, his muscles were well defined and his legs were the size of tree trunks. A long sword in one hand and a short sword in the other, he made it clear that he was not afraid of the Blothrud.

General Hatch welcomed his companion. "Sir Dovenar Knight Asentar, please meet the legendary Bellfor of Corrock we've heard so much about. I believe this was the Blothrud you were in search of."

Asentar stood solid at the general's side, sizing up the creature. "I have no bad blood with you, Bellfor. It would be wise for both of us to keep it that way. For I have come to speak with your leaders about an alliance of power to prevent Darkmere's approaching war. I implore you to prevent this fight from escalating so we can discuss our potential future."

Bellfor snarled and spit at the general.

A flash of a short sword panned in front of General Hatch, catching the Blothrud's saliva. Asentar then wiped the spit off on his boot. "You will not intimidate us."

"Then we will just kill you." Howling in the air, Bellfor signaled his army to attack. Lunging forward to rip the general's head off, he was blocked by Asentar, who quickly became engaged in a heated fight with the Blothrud.

General Hatch was confident in the knight's ability to hold off Bellfor as he returned to command his troops to ensure a victory.

The sound of a hundred Krupes running in metal armor from all sides was ominous and terrifying. Reversing the front line's arch, General Hatch now had three of his four sides protected.

The battle had begun.

More Brandercats arrived under the illusion of sporadic invisibility. Enormous terra grubs broke through the earth and pulled men underground, eating them whole. Krupes deflected the arrows and most blades with their strong black armor, while more hogs charged the lines. The Del'Unday were designed to fight wars.

Organized and disciplined, the men fought back. Close range bow attacks allowed arrows to enter Krupe helmet eye-holes and kill whatever existed inside the mass of metal. Brandercats were stabbed and Entelodont hogs were attacked from both sides. Sacrifices were made as minor victories were achieved by coordinated efforts.

The blades of Bellfor and Asentar clashed again and again. The two warriors tested each other's strength only to find Bellfor had the advantage. However, Asentar's speed and skill with the sword was dominant.

Bellfor swung his mighty flail with one hand and a multi-pointed black blade with his other. Hammering hard against his opponent, he knew that all it would take was for one of his blows to shatter a leg or arm, ending the agility of the human.

General Hatch was consumed with his troops, and failed to notice his captives.

As the battle waged on, several of the Krupes moved over to the prisoners in an effort to take them back to Corrock. Breaking the chains from the post, they pulled Thorik's group to their feet.

When pulled forward, Gluic fell to ground, knocking many of her feathers from her hair. Spreading her fingers wide on the hard earth, she smiled before being helped up by her son. "Oh my. Here we go."

"Yes, mother, here we go again."

"No, my son. They have finally arrived."

"Brimmelle dusted his mother's knees off. "Who? Who has arrived?"

The ground began to rumble, lightly at first and then a rough earth-shaking tremble.

A thousand Chuttlebeast stormed into camp, hooves beating onto the ground. The constant thumping of the Spear of Rummon had called the beasts into heat. Lust had lured several herds into the valley for a display of dominance.

Chuttles ran over men and Del'Unday alike. Brandercats were flung in the air, Krupes bounced off the cubic heads of the smelly beasts, and men were trampled. No one was safe.

A few hogs met their marks, biting hard into the Chuttlebeasts, but the numbers weren't in their favor and it wasn't long before the hogs had to run for their lives.

The Krupes pulled harder onto Thorik's chain, forcing his group to walk faster in an effort to get over the hill and out of the local anarchy.

Chuttles ran in front and behind the group as Grewen dug his heels into the ground, preventing a safe escape into the Del'Unday's hands.

Gluic fell again from the tug-of-war between Grewen and the Krupes.

Angered at the captive's resistance, one of the Krupes pulled out his spiked mace and swung it hard at Gluic's head.

Just then, a Chuttle crashed its way through the Krupes as the mace swung at the Num, causing it to miss. A blur of thick wool passed in front of the Gluic, leaving only the unattended ends to their chains. The beast had left no sign of the Krupes.

Grewen was pleased at their luck, until he himself became a victim to the rampaging herd. Hit hard in his back, by a stray Chuttlebeast, the Mognin crashed to the ground, just missing the Nums. His chains prevented the Nums from seeking safety as they attempted to help Grewen back to his feet.

Loud cracks of Chuttle heads rocked the valley as the carnage increased. Tents had started on fire while men and Altereds screamed in pain, as the Chuttlebeasts frantically struggled to find the source of the thumping.

A blade swung in front of Thorik, just missing his body. Instead, it crashed down, breaking his chains.

"Go get that damn spear so we can get out of here," Santorray said.

Thorik looked up at the Blothrud. Santorray looked like a pincushion, with arrows embedded in his shoulders and chest. Blood poured forth from the wounds, as he struggled to lift his saber again to free the next Num.

Thorik couldn't believe Santorray was still alive in such a dire state. "Are you…"

"Get going! Hurry," the Blothrud demanded.

Thorik took Santorray's order and raced down the hill toward the spear. The smell of the Chuttles was thicker in the bottom the valley, burning his eyes so bad it was difficult to see.

Jumping and rolling out of a Chuttle's charge, Thorik landed at the feet of an Eastland soldier who quickly grabbed him.

"Got'cha," was the only thing the soldier said before a Krupe's heavy mace crushed his forehead, releasing Thorik to the ground.

A quick heavy boot to Thorik's stomach kept the Num from escaping, as the Krupe lifted his mace to bury it deep into his chest.

Another Chuttle plowed over Thorik, taking the Krupe with him.

Thorik was in the heart of the mess and knew the spear was close. Diving from one place to another he finally spotted Rummon and jumped for it.

Pulling it out of the ground, he turned to find a large square wool-covered head bearing down on him. There was no time to move, as Thorik held the spear with both hands and braced for the impact.

A snarl from within the spear sprang toward the beast, hitting it in the head as though it had knocked up against another Chuttle.

Pulling hard to the side, the beast charged forward as the side of his head hit Thorik, smacking the Num hard to the ground.

Lucky to not have been hit head-on, Thorik only had the wind knocked out of him. Standing back up, the Num spotted Ericc, who looked confused as he still had trouble standing and seeing.

The Chuttlebeast, which Thorik had avoided, was now heading directly at Ambrosius' son at a full gallop.

Ericc looked over at Thorik just as the beast's head hit him. Ericc vanished instantly and reappeared next to the Num. "Where's Darkmere? They said he would come for me."

Thorik couldn't believe his eyes. He must have seen it wrong. People couldn't change locations in a blink of an eye. "We saved you from him."

Ericc struggled from his health and fell to one knee. "No, I need to go back!" he demanded before he started to collapse.

Thorik helping Ericc back to his feet, and led him back through the mayhem toward his group, with the spear out in front. A corridor opened for their escape in whichever direction he pointed the spear. The two scrambled over the hill and into the next small valley to catch up to Grewen, Santorray and the Nums.

The Mognin ripped out the last few arrows from Santorray's back, as the Blothrud screamed in pain. His own blood had coating his lower body and much of the ground.

Thorik watched the Blothrud pass out after the last arrow was removed. "Is he going to make it?"

After wrapping his upper body in cloths to stop the bleeding, Grewen picked up the nearly lifeless Blothrud and headed east, away from the camp and the chaos. "He's lost a lot of blood. Arrows penetrated deep at that close range. It's hard to say."

Chapter 31
Kiri Desert

Thorik's Log: June 6th of the 650th year.
In one fell swoop, the Spear of Rummon saved us last night from being captured by the Corrockians and the Eastlanders. It caused a herd of Chuttlebeasts to storm the battlefield. Our escape during the chaos leaves us without knowledge of who won the battle, if it was completed at all. We escaped with our lives, however Santorray is badly injured. Grewen is leading us to a safe place to heal him.

Gluic removed her hands from Santorray. His massive body was spread out on the ground, with stones placed in specific locations on his body for her to heal him. Deep wounds had been sewn up but it was far too soon to know if he would ever recover.

Ericc rested nearby; his healing from Gluic had already been performed. Water, food and rest were all he needed.

Removing one of the stones from the Blothrud's head, she handed it to Thorik. "Here's your Runestone back. Keep it safe."

"I will. I always do."

"Good." She removed one of her remaining feathers from her hair and placed it in his. "Now, did you watch what I did?"

"Yes, Granna. But I keep telling you that I don't have the ability to perform a healing."

"Me neither. I let the stones tell me what to do. You'll do fine." Reaching over, she straightened his feather.

Thorik pondered on how to interpret her last statement as he watched the Blothrud moan from the pain. Gluic had suddenly started instructing him on various techniques, which she had never expressed interest in showing him before. "Granna, what did you see in the Mythical Forest, when you held the crystal to Santorray?"

"A murder."

"Of who?"

Gluic smiled with compassion for her grandson's concern.

"You? But why? Who would murder you?" Thorik asked.

"Don't fret, Thorik. Worrying about it won't change anything."

"Santorray? He's the one, isn't he?"

"And what would it change if it was?"

"First off, you could go without healing him."

"And let him die, when we can save him? Could you really do that?"

"Yes." Thorik spoke before thinking. Removing the bright orange feather from his hair, he poked the end of it a few times at his other hand. "No, but how can you heal him knowing he will end your life?

"End my life? Dear, he's only going to murder me. I'm sure it will be for a good cause. But someone else actually ends my life."

"There's a difference?"

Gluic pinched Thorik's skin. "This flesh is only a host for our souls. I talk to people all the time that aren't restricted by these barriers."

"Yes, I know. As the Mountain King's words say, 'Our soul-markings show we have souls'."

"Not exactly, but close enough."

"I suppose you've talked to the Mountain King."

"He's very nice. Even he would tell me the intent of the words are as you said, but there is more depth to it."

"If that is true, why is it that I haven't received any? Am I without a soul?"

"No, my dear. Soul-markings display your personality, your mettle, and your idiosyncrasies. That much we can see. But they also hold truths about you and your purpose in life. Your purpose is so strong that it is holding back the rest of your traits from showing through your skin."

The thought never crossed his mind. "Is that possible?"

"Can you raise a column of marble a thousand feet in the air with your mind?"

Thorik hugged his grandmother for her constant encouragement. She always had a way of making him feel better. "Thank you, Granna."

"Don't ever doubt your value, my boy."

Grewen returned to the temporary camp with Brimmelle and Avanda. They had walked up to the top of a nearby peak to scout ahead. "Looks clear, just a stray small herd of Chuttles. Did you get the litter completed?" Grewen had broken a few branches off the tree they rested under, before heading out to scout, to allow Thorik material for the device, which would haul the Blothrud.

"Yes, and we just finished another healing of Santorray. Ericc should be ready to travel as well." Thorik woke Ericc and helped him to his feet. "We have a lot to talk about, starting with your little disappearing trick back in the Eastland camp."

The young man didn't reply as he grabbed some items to carry. He had been unappreciative and agitated ever since they rescued him.

Grewen reached down and picked up the semi-conscious Blothrud.

Santorray woke from his haze and tried to push away. "I'm fine. I'll walk."

Setting him into the litter, Grewen agreed with him. "Yes, you will, just not today."

Attempting to sit up, Santorray instantly realized he couldn't. The pain was too great and his muscles were too torn. "Watch out for Chuttles." In his own way he was trying to lead the group and give them advice. "Always assume they are ready to attack. Change direction without warning. Don't let your guard down. They are a powerful Fesh."

Grewen snapped a handful of dry grass from their roots and tossed them in his mouth. "And they stink too."

Brimmelle couldn't let the opportunity go to waste. "You're one to talk."

Grewen strapped the Blothrud in and lifted one end of the litter to drag Santorray. "What? I kind of like my smell. Musky and yet earthy."

"Unearthed is more like it. Your odor is of a plate of rotten eggs and raw fish after baking in this waterless land for a week."

"That doesn't sound so bad," Grewen said. "Now you've gone and made me hungry."

"I helped Thorik gut a giant stink beetle once, when its sack exploded all over both of us, and even that smelled better than your feet."

"Why would you cut open a stink beetle?"

"To retrieve one of Thorik's Runestones, which he irresponsibly left on the floor."

"Do you really think my feet smell?"

"I've smelled better things pulled out of a pig's rectum than you."

"What were you doing pulling things out of pig's rectum?" Grewen countered, while they headed up the next hill and continued to banter back and forth.

Meanwhile, Thorik tried to get Ericc to talk. "Your father meant a lot to me." He received no response. "He saved our lives more than once. If it wasn't for him, the entire Dovenar Kingdom would be under water."

"Don't paint him angelic. I know better," Ericc finally said.

"He was a good man."

"A good man doesn't leave his son to be raised by others."

"He had no choice."

"That's a lie. He chose to leave me. He chose to never return to see me. He chose to let me grow up without him. And now to die before I can ever see him again."

"He was protecting you."

"To what end? To live a life alone, without a father? I would have rather died alongside him than hide in a cave all my life."

"He tried to do what was best for all of us. He was responsible for the Dovenar Kingdom, as well as the rest of Australis. He's saved hundreds of thousands of lives."

"Foregoing his family in his great quests. How dare he bring me into this world if he wasn't going to be there for me. I hate him for it. His responsibility to Australis constantly put my mother and I in danger. It killed my mother, and it's his fault. Where was he? He promised to protect us."

"He couldn't possibly be there to protect you every moment." Thorik recalled his own situation with Avanda.

"Then he shouldn't have told us he would. Hidden away, I've missed out on my youth. Because of him, I'm being hunted down by the Del'Unday as well as the Kingdom you talk so righteous about. Because of him, my life is in shambles."

"Listen, you need to stop blaming your father for all of your issues. He did the best he could for you. He loved you. He would have died for your mother if he could have. You need to accept who he was and take responsibility for yourself, your own actions, and your own future."

"That's exactly what I was doing before you came along. I was waiting for Darkmere to arrive at Corrock."

"To end your life?"

"To end his."

"Revenge won't bring your father back or give you those lost years of youth."

"No, but it will end this torment once and for all. I will continue to be hunted until one of us is dead."

Thorik didn't know how to reply. Ericc's last statement was correct, even if Thorik didn't agree with the boy's plans.

The two stopped talking about the subject. Aside from general communication around evening camps, Ericc isolated himself from the rest.

Thorik attempted to strike up a conversation about Ericc's E'rudite power to shift locations in a blink of the eye, but failed each time to get the young man to talk.

Chapter 32
Unwelcome

Days had passed before the terrain changed to include sporadic sinkholes filled with lush vegetation surrounded by the desert rocks. Traveling along the southern slopes of the Ossuary Range, they frequently ran across small streams, which supplied water to the great Volney Lakes. Many of these streams were underground, only exposing themselves in these sinkholes before submerging again.

Brimmelle stopped in his tracks. "Why are we traveling east? The Dovenar Kingdom is west, as well as Farbank."

"Ro-Volney Lake is east. It is a place of safety for the Ov'Unday." Grewen adjusted his grip of the two long branches on either side of the litter as he dragged Santorray up the hill. "Salvation for our people."

Brimmelle scoffed. "Your people? Haven't we had enough of cities filled with Altereds?"

"It's good to see how open minded you've become," Grewen joked.

"This entire journey has done nothing but reinforce my belief that Altereds bring confusion and harm to this land."

"Yes, because the people of Southwind were so much more gentile," the giant mused.

"Santorray attacked one of their leaders and then they escaped from their prison. Of course they were going to come after us. I consider our meeting with them in the O'Sid fields to be a blessing in an effort to escape those Del creatures."

Santorray squirmed in his confines as he awoke from his unconsciousness. He began to panic from his inability to move due to tight straps, a feeling he was not comfortable with. "Grewen, free me at once. I can't take this any longer. I'm going crack someone's skull if I'm not unrestrained."

Brimmelle pointed at the Blothrud. "See? Look at the violence inherent in their species."

Santorray struggled to break free. "You're first, Brimmelle. When I get out of here, I'll…"

"You'll what? Show everyone that I'm right by attacking a defenseless Num half your size?"

"That's enough, you two." Thorik stood at the top of a hill as the rest approached. "Grewen, how much farther to safety?"

"We're close. Just over the next ridge and we'll be bathing our sore feet in the Ro'Volney Lake."

Reaching the next main hill opened up an oasis before them. In the center of the desert was a green-trimmed lake full of life. Small beach sand dunes occasionally rolled along the shoreline, hiding the trunks of trees and large plants, but for the most part lush tropical plants filled the outline of the lake.

Huts blended into the vegetation as Ov'Unday species went about their business. Horned Cluppers filled their ivory hollow tusks with water to bring back to the settlement, while Mognins watered fields and harvested crops.

Giant sloth-like creatures slowly roamed the village as they went about their business. Known as Gathlers, this species reminded Thorik of the elderly in their slow methodical movements.

As they approached the first Ov'Unday settlement, the short dark hair on Santorray's neck stood on end. "They will not let us pass."

"They won't let you pass, is what you mean," Brimmelle said. "After what your species has done to them."

"Brimmelle, not now," Thorik ordered.

A few Mognins and one Gathler had spotted the travelers and met them on the edge of the village. The Gathler calmly addressed Grewen as the group's leader. "Truth be said."

Grewen responded to the greeting. "Truth be heard."

"I am Coova, voice of our village."

"I am Grewen, voice of our pod."

"How is it you travel with these species?" Coova asked.

"They are my family."

"Of what family are you?"

"I am Grewen of the Ki'Ov'Unday, but my travelers are my personal family pod."

"Pod members may dine with us but they are not to pass through these lands. Only pure family can venture beyond to Trewek."

"We ask for sanctuary. All other paths are blocked by those who wish to see our companion dead."

One of the Mognins looked past Grewen at the Blothrud tied to the litter. "A death sentence on a Del'Unday is not our issue."

Grewen smiled. "No, it's the human who is in this peril. He is the son of Ambrosius."

"Ambrosius? Why would you bring his tension to our land?"

"The boy is in need of safety. His father no longer can provide it."

"To invite him in would ask for outsiders to hunt him down in our lands. Why would we risk this?"

"Because we follow the compassion of Trewek. The innocent boy needs our help."

One of the local Mognins sized up the lad. "Do you request our security?"

"I don't ask for anyone's help," Ericc answered.

"Then none will be granted," the Mognin replied.

Disappointed in Ericc's response, Thorik stepped up front. "Just because he doesn't ask for our help doesn't mean he doesn't need it."

"Truth be said. Continue," Coova said.

"Ericc is angry at his father and Darkmere. He's willing to risk his life to vent those feelings. We need time to talk to him and work through this. Time we don't have out here in the desert."

Coova's brows moved slowly down in between his eyes. "We do not wish for you to bring anger into our land. No one will house it. Without shelter, you will be no better off."

Grewen got a thought and tried a new tactic. "Ambrosius used to live on the south side of the lake, just west of Lagona Falls. He was granted residency."

Coova methodically nodded. "Truth be heard, but this is not Ambrosius."

Thorik added to Grewen's path. "Ericc lived there as well when he was a child, so he is already a resident unless it was revoked."

"Not that we know of. But we are a long way from such places and would not know of such affairs."

"But you can't assume it has been revoked," Thorik said.

"Truth be heard."

"So, he should be allowed to travel to his home."

The Mognins looked at each other before waiting for the Gathler to speak.

Coova mulled the discussion in his mind for a while before finally responding. "Truth be said."

"Excellent." Thorik gave a sigh of relief.

"But not the Blothrud," Coova added.

Thorik couldn't believe the prejudice of such passive creatures. "He is injured. To leave him out in the desert would be no less than murder."

"You may travel with him back from where you came. We did not suggest you leave him here to die," Coova said without empathy for their plight.

"But that would split us up."

"Truth be heard."

Thorik's jaw tightened at the slow emotionless Gathler. "We won't do that. He's risked his life for us. He deserves to see this through as much as us. As Grewen said earlier, we're family."

"No, you're a pod. A subgroup attached to a family member, which has not been approved by the collective group. Few non-Ov'Unday are considered to be family. A Del'Unday as a family member would be a sight to be seen."

Once again, Thorik looked to Grewen for help in getting Santorray past this barrier of prejudice.

Adjusting his hands again on the litter, Grewen suggested an option to give them some time to think about the issue. "Can we partake from the lake's venue at least until we are rested?"

"With a Blothrud walking free in among our homes and children?"

"Of course not. He would stay confined to the litter."

One of the Mognin's addressed Grewen directly. "Grewen of the Ki'Ov'Unday takes responsibility for his bindings staying taut?"

Grewen lifted his shoulders up at attention. "Truth be heard."

"Truth be said," Coova replied.

Chapter 33
Blothrud Among Ov'Undays

Springing over thirty feet in the air, a Yularian snake flipped through the air in an acrobatic sequence of moves before splashing back into the lake. The aquatic Ov'Unday species had been entertaining the travelers during their feast as locals enjoyed getting to know the Nums, as well as Ericc and Grewen.

Several of the agile winged sea snakes coiled around Gluic, as she stood up to her waist in the lake. Yularians covered her and flapped their brightly colored wings as the elder Num reached out with her arms.

Brimmelle sniffed at the food with hesitation. If it weren't for his stomach growling, he would most definitely have passed on the odd-looking fruits and vegetables. "Mother, stay away from those creatures. Who knows what they are capable of?"

Avanda cracked opened a nut to find sweet tasting berries inside. "This is amazing." She had to try a taste of everything available, while stuffing several of her favorites in her pouches for later.

Ericc bit into a sour melon, and spit it out. "I can't eat this."

Thorik handed him a stock of a local vegetable. "Try these. They have a spicy bite to them, but very enjoyable."

Tasting it, Ericc found it to be true. "Why are you doing this?"

"Doing what?" Thorik replied.

"You risked your life to warn me in the Southwind mines, and then again in Corrock. What do you owe me?"

"You, nothing. I made a promise to your father to protect you from Darkmere."

"Why?"

"Because of what happened. His death."

"If Darkmere killed my father, why do you have a debt to him?"

Thorik squirmed slightly. "Darkmere didn't actually kill your father, directly..."

"How do you kill someone indirectly?"

"Ericc, your father and I were deceived by one of his minions and baited into his trap. Once we met him in combat at Weirfortus, the dam broke and Darkmere escaped, knowing Ambrosius would do the right thing and try to hold back the waters from the dam's reservoir. In doing that, your father prevented a flood from destroying the kingdom."

"I don't understand. Holding back the water wouldn't have killed him, only letting go and being crushed by it would. But then the flood would have occurred."

"Not if the reservoir doors were shut to prevent it."

"How was he able to close them while holding back the water?"

"He wasn't." Thorik rubbed his strained eyes as her recalled the event. "I was responsible for closing the door behind him."

"You trapped him in?"

"Yes."

"You killed my father."

"No, it's not like that."

"And now you feel by protecting me it resolves your transgression."

"You don't know what happened. You weren't there."

"If I had been there, I would have helped my father out instead of letting him die so you could survive."

"Ericc! Stop it. I loved Ambrosius as though he was my own father. He believed in me. He trusted me. I would have done anything to save him. But I couldn't. It destroyed me to close those doors. When he asked me to protect you from being sacrificed, I gave my word and I mean to live up to it."

Ericc absorbed Thorik's words. "I don't know what to say." Standing up from the group, he began to walk toward the lake, but stopped and turned back for a few last statements. "Thorik, I envy you. You lived my life. My father treated you as his own son; you traveled together and fought together. He praised you and taught you, and in the end he asked you to take his life to save others. I wasn't a part of any of it, the joys, the sorrows, the victories, the failures. I have no memories of my father like you do. I missed it all."

Turning, Ericc walked out by Gluic who was now covered with Yularian snakes, all flapping so hard that she had been lifted up several feet above the water's surface.

"Feed me," bellowed Santorray from the side, still strapped to the makeshift litter.

The order went unanswered again for the fourth time, but the Blothrud was not going to lower his voice and ask nicely, regardless how hungry he was.

Before he ordered food for a fifth time, he noticed a commotion among the Ov'Unday. Something was wrong.

A strong low drum beat pounded away, stopped, and then pounded again. It was their warning drum. An announcement to take cover for some, a call to arms for others.

The Ov'Unday grabbed nets and rudimentary defensive weapons and raced for the edge of the village.

Santorray stretched his neck around to see what was happening. "They tracked us here."

Thorik looked at the first set of hills waiting to see what would come over. "Who?"

Grewen watched as well. "Whoever won the battle which we escaped from."

A mass of figures appeared at the hill's crest, as the army approached the village.

Waiting for a signal, the first line of attackers finally launched forward after a blaring howl was heard from behind them.

Racing down the hill, Brandercats and giant hogs were followed by a line of Krupes.

The Ov'Unday stood steady, wasting no energy on rushing toward them. Conserving everything they could until it was required.

The Del'Unday front line reached their victims.

Mognin's tossed out nets to capture Brandercats, while grappling with the hogs as they hit their defensive lines. In spite of their size and strength, the Mognins couldn't contain them all. Several broke through and headed for the village, intending to create disaster.

The line of Ov'Unday was now broken as many chased the Del'Unday down, and others held the captive Dels at bay.

By this point, the Krupes had a military line up ready for attack. A second howl was called out, summoning the first line of attackers to return to their posts. Those not restrained by the Ovs did just that.

Bellfor stepped forward to discuss the Ov'Unday's surrender.

Coova slowly approached the halfway point to meet the Blothrud in hopes of determining how to avoid a bloodbath.

Even from a distance, Santorray could see the talk was not going well. "Cut me free. I can stop this," he said to Thorik.

"How?" the Num asked.

"Don't ask questions, just free me."

Grewen shook his head at Thorik and Santorray. "Allow the Ov'Unday to take care of this in our own way." He then headed over to stand with his people.

The leader from the Ov'Unday returned to his council of leaders. "They want Ambrosius' son," Coova informed his council.

A Clupper shook his head. "We granted him sanctuary."

"He has resident rights. Trewek promises protection," said a Mognin.

Coova listened to their comments. "They will attack if we refuse."

"They most likely will attack after we give them what they want."

"That would be characteristic of them," Coova agreed.

"We easily outnumber them ten to one."

Looking at the huts and families that lived in them, Coova sighed. "Even at those odds, we will lose family members. Are you willing to risk losing your wife or child over this boy we don't even know?"

The discussion continued among the leaders as Santorray argued with Thorik over his own freedom.

Thorik finally gave in and pulled out a dagger to cut through the straps, but then stopped himself before doing so. "These are not your people, you told me yourself that you're not Corrockian."

"I'm not, but I have a better chance of stopping a battle than these mogs and Gathlers."

They watched as Coova returned to Bellfor and signaled there would be no deal.

A sigh of relief came from Thorik until he saw Bellfor decapitate the Gathler for refusing his offer. Coova's body fell to the ground.

The Ov'Undays gasped at the atrocity, as well did Thorik and his family pod.

It was now the responsibility of the second in command to walk up to Bellfor and answer his offer. A Clupper stepped forward on all four of its hooves. His large tusks could be used as weapons if need be.

"The offer has now changed," Bellfor told the Clupper. "The boy must accompany a dozen of your adult males. My troops crave fresh meat."

Appalled, the Clupper snorted loudly. "We will not give into your demands. Any attempt on my life or any of our people will be the end of these negotiations. You know as well as I do that your army is too small to take us on."

"We'll see about that." Bellfor raised his sword to strike, only to stop at the sight of the creature behind the Clupper. He struggled to understand what he was seeing. A Blothrud was entering the open land from the Ov'Unday side.

Thorik had cut Santorray free of his restraints without receiving permission. The Num could not stand by and see the slaughter continue. He needed to trust Santorray to resolve this.

Dealing with the severe pain of his wounds, Santorray tightened his jaw as he put on a façade of being fully healed. Strutting up to the Clupper, he patted the Ov'Unday on the back. "I'll take it from here. Go back to your people."

Hesitating, the Clupper eventually trusted Santorray and backed off, returning to the other leaders. He didn't see how it could hurt their efforts to allow the two Blothruds to talk.

Bellfor spit on the ground near Santorray's feet. "What kind of Fesh are you, a Blothrud living among the Ov'Unday?"

Stepping on the ground where the saliva landed, Santorray kicked the ground to cause dust to fly. "You question me? You will not address me until I ask you to."

Infuriated at Santorray's condescending tone, Bellfor swung his weapon hard, only to be stopped by two sabers. "How dare you talk to me in such a manner. I am Bellfor, champion of Corrock." A second swipe of his weapon was stopped as well.

Santorray blocked two more quick blows before speaking. "Does Corrock no longer follow Ergrauth?"

"Damn those who speak Ergrauth's name while standing with his enemies. Corrock will defend him to our death and after."

Santorray's defensive moves to block the relentless attacks caused his wounds to open and begin to bleed. The pain was overpowering as he fought to appear in control. "Then back down and heed my command. I am a messenger of his voice."

"You're a lying Fesh with no honor."

Ripping off the bandages from his shoulder, Santorray exposed an open wound next to a symbol branded deep into his red skin.

Bellfor was stunned at the marking, holding his sword firm against Santorray's sabers instead of placing another attack. "You are an Ergrauthian Elite? What would one of our lord's supreme defenders be doing in these parts?"

"To question me is to question Ergrauth himself."

Bellfor pulled back and listened as he eyed the mark. If it were truly an Elite, his words would demand authority. Anyone caught impersonating an Elite would be sentenced to an eternity of shame and torture in Ergrauth's city.

Santorray allowed Bellfor to get a long look at the branding on his shoulder. "I am here to take Ambrosius' son to Surod to put an end to this prophecy once and for all." He covered his wound up to stop the bleeding. "Your attack here is defying Ergrauth's wishes and my plans to carry out my mission."

Bellfor stayed silent and backed up a step. He realized the danger he put himself into by striking an Elite. It was a potential death sentence.

Santorray stepped up to Bellfor. "Listen closely. I will have the Ovs release our people, then you will return to Corrock to put your efforts into rebuilding that pathetic city into something that is grand, something we are proud to call ours, like it once was. Do you understand my orders?"

Arms at his side, Bellfor nodded. "Yes, Elite. But what shall I tell Darkmere when he arrives?"

"Tell him to meet Santorray in Surod at the Eve of Light."

Chapter 34
Family

The Del'Unday were released and the entire army marched back over the hill. It was a sight no Ov'Unday would have believed if they hadn't seen it with their own eyes.

Thorik ran over to Santorray who continued to stand in defiance in the center of the battlefield. "How did you do that? What did you say?"

Santorray's pain had taken its toll. His wounds had reopened and blood had been lost to the dirt at his feet. The Blothrud fell.

Santorray dreamed of days past as a child, when his sister and he trained to fight. Visions of later battles flowed through his mind while Darkmere and Ambrosius faded in and out of view. The series of visions crossed his thoughts until he felt himself being stabbed in his right shoulder blade.

Waking from his sleep, the Blothrud felt a sharp poking on his back. One of the local Gathler women was tapping a hammer onto a long stick with an angled fine tip to it. The tip was periodically dipping into black ink.

"Congratulations," Grewen announced to Santorray. "You're the first Del to become part of the Ro'Ov'Unday Family."

The tattoo on his shoulder blade had just been finished. The symbol of the family was now a permanent mark on Santorray's body. The decorative circle with a wavy line crossing it at the center was very similar to the one he had seen on Grewen's back. Each line was actually made up of tightly placed symbols.

Grewen helped the Blothrud up off his stomach to a sitting position. "You are now free to walk our land and help us protect it from outsiders."

Santorray looked at the audience who had watched the tattooing. The entire village had come out to participate. Tears in many of their eyes, they smiled softly at the new member.

"Grewen, what's this all about?"

"They have all come to give you a part of themselves. You will now be responsible for their lives as much as they are for yours."

One of the Mognins stepped up to Santorray. Pricking his finger, he placed it up against the fresh tattoo, pressing his blood against the red skin of the Blothrud. "I trust you with the lives of myself, my wife and my children." Moving off, he let the next Ov'Unday have his turn.

Santorray realized that the entire village was standing in line to do the same thing.

Next was a young Clupper with tears in his eyes. Leaning his face against Santorray's back, he brushed his tears against the tattoo. "Thank you for saving my father's life. I'm in your debt."

Santorray looked up at Grewen. "Are they all going to…"

"Yes."

"This could take hours."

"Usually does."

By the time the last Ov'Unday pressed her lips against the tattoo, the ink had smeared down his back as it mixed with blood, tears, and saliva. The original circle and wavy line still held strong as the smeared tail faded the farther down it went.

Santorray was emotionally drained. He had never witnessed such an outpouring of love and trust. Spending most of his life on his own had made him immune to such needs. Or at least he thought he was immune.

For the first time in a long time, he felt welcomed. Not being on edge and ready to fight was an odd feeling. So odd, he didn't know if he liked it or not. But he wouldn't have time to find out; they needed to head south.

Santorray stood and walked over to Thorik who was watching Avanda and Ericc play in the lake. "We must leave."

"Why? This place is peaceful. Avanda has finally opened Ericc up. We're safe here."

"For how long?"

"Until we decide to leave," Thorik said.

"Sec, we are placing these people in danger. Don't you think Darkmere will find us here? And when he does, he will kill everyone in his path."

"We should wait at least until the Eve of Light has passed."

"No, the Corrockians know he is here and this is the first place Darkmere will look. We need to leave before he arrives. He'll know right away that the son of Ambrosius is not among them and leave them be."

"Where could we go that is safer than here?"

"We shall retreat to the mist of the Lagona Falls. My understanding is that it's the Ov's safe haven for their afterlife."

"A grave yard?"

"No one lives there, so no one will be placed in jeopardy."

Thorik breathed in the calmness of the village. Even Brimmelle was getting comfortable on the shoreline. "Are you sure?"

"Yes."

"I'm trusting you with our lives, Santorray."

The Blothrud looked at each of Thorik's family pod members and sighed. "I know."

Chapter 35
Lagona Falls

Thorik's party left the village and followed the shoreline to the east, occasionally stopping to rest in the shade of the palm trees that grew along the sandy beaches. Passing the outskirts of Trewek, they marveled at the size of the towers and architectural grace of the massive city. Santorray had no desire to enter and convinced the group to continue south, away from the Ro'Volney Lake, to the larger Ki'Volney Lake.

Days went by with general chatter, mostly from Brimmelle and how he felt they should have stayed in the safety of the village a little longer.

As they walked along the north shores of the Ki'Volney Lake, the eastern cliffs became more apparent. Harsh mountain ranges lined the region, with the most grand being the Shi'Pel Peaks to the southeast. The highest points in all of the lands.

A wide waterfall, several times the height of the marble column they once traveled on, broke free from the mountain landscape, spilling so much water so far down that it became mist before hitting. The mist filled the valley along the cliff line and out to the lake.

Thorik appeared concerned as they proceeded to travel deeper into the misty vapors, as it continued to thicken. "Grewen, is it safe to travel past the falls?"

"Safe yes, recommended no."

"Is that because it is sacred land where you bury your dead?"

"No, Lagona Falls is where we go to die. It is where we travel our final pilgrimage to seek enlightenment and endless wisdom. It is the end of our journeys and the beginning of a higher level. We don't normally plan on coming back out."

Ericc looked skeptically at Grewen. "But we can, can't we?"

"I don't see why not. I know of some who have passed it, staying out of the eternal lands. We just need to stay along the lake shoreline."

The plants in the thick fog grew taller than normal. Thick mushrooms and moss coated wide tree trunks and colorful flowers opened up large enough to sit in. The overgrowth made it difficult to see very far.

Grewen watched as several hummingbirds licked sap running off a mound of large fungi. Breaking off a piece of the mound, he took a bite. The sap was sweet to the taste. "The good news is we won't go hungry."

It was at this time that soft music, from somewhere in the distant mist, began to sing in the Nums' ears. Elegant and enchanting, the music tugged at their gentle emotions and relaxed them.

Even Brimmelle was put at ease by the tone. "Where is that coming from?"

The Nums moved away from the beach and into the forest, light-footed as they searched for the source. Avanda held Gluic's hand to help her through the heavy foliage.

Ericc and the two Unday followed the Nums, unaware of what the little ones had heard.

"This smells of a trap," Santorray growled as he finally started hearing the music. "We should stay near the lake and continue heading south."

Nevertheless, east was the direction of the two Unday and Ericc as they tried to keep up with the Nums. Thick vines spanned the trees, acting like crude nets against the large bodies of Santorray and Grewen. Ericc and the Nums, however, had no problem walking between and under them.

"Thorik! Get back here. We need to stay by the shoreline," Santorray yelled, without getting a response.

Ericc was the next to hear the sounds, causing him to race ahead and catch up to Thorik.

Grewen eventually heard the music, stopping to listen without the noise of his heavy footfalls. "Aw, Trewek's Aria. The call to enlightenment. It's more exquisite than I had been led to believe."

Deeper and deeper they went into the forest, as the mist, plants, and vines became denser. Soon the Nums and Ericc were out of the Unday's view.

Santorray cupped his hands near his mouth to focus his voice. "Thorik? Ericc? Where are you?"

There was no response.

"Enlightenment?" Santorray snarled at Grewen. "These are the reasons your people are weak. You allow these types of places to exist without knowing anything about them."

Grewen continued to move the vines out of his path as he continued forward. "What would you suggest, an invasion into these fertile lands to wipe out all dangers?"

"Absolutely."

"Barbaric. Can't you coexist with nature? Why do you have to destroy it?"

"I'll coexist with it once I know its strengths and weaknesses."

"You talk like it's a potential enemy."

"Sometimes it can be."

Passing large mounds of fungi and through thick leafy vines, the two stopped to listen for the rest of their party.

Grewen began to hum with the tranquil sounds of Trewek's song. Swaying with the music he moved forward, deeper into the forest.

"Grewen, snap out of it," Santorray ordered.

But the Mognin's grin said it all as he relaxed his eyelids and sauntered away under the music's spell.

Santorray continued to call for the others as he followed Grewen through the forest and eventually into a clearing.

A motionless pond rested in the center of the open area, as the Nums and Ericc sat along its misty shores. Peaceful silence was only interrupted by the soft song of the local hummingbirds, which hovered over the lake and around the new guests.

"It's amazing." Avanda lifted her hand out for one of the hummingbirds to land on.

"Beyond words." Brimmelle rested against a rock, watching three birds sing inches from his face.

Gluic sat near Brimmelle as she watched his enjoyment. "It's good to see you smile." Turning, she enjoyed the song from the several birds inches from her own face.

Santorray did not share their enjoyment. "So you discovered the source of the music. Now, we need to head out."

Grewen sat down. "Why? This feels safer than anywhere else we've been."

"A little too serene for my taste," Santorray spit back.

Thorik nodded. "Yes, serene. It is a wonderful place to hide from Darkmere."

"No, this is not a place to hide. We must travel south."

Desire and issues of the world started fading from their minds. The concepts of fighting and revenge mellowed as they relaxed in the safe haven.

Ericc looked at the Blothrud. "Sit down and enjoy yourself."

"Ericc, I thought you were tired of hiding from Darkmere. And yet you sit there now and do just that."

"Hide?" Ericc questioned. "If anything, I feel free. Free to enjoy life for my first time."

"You're not free. You're hiding in a forest," Santorray argued.

"I feel like I can do anything, right now. I could remove all evil from the world with a wave of my hand."

"And yet you choose to sit there and do nothing instead."

"This is a glorious place." Ericc ignored his last statement.

Thorik looked over at his agitated friend. "Santorray, we will camp here for the night."

Santorray stood silent, watching the group enjoy the serenity of the music and smells. Each member was in their own world as they gazed at the hovering birds.

The Blothrud continued to try to get them moving, even to the extent of lifting them to their feet, only to see them sit back down again.

Frustrated at the situation, he walked out of the pond area to vent his frustrations by slamming his fist into trees, logs, and anything else in his reach. Punching a mound of fungi, a large section cracked off, exposing a body underneath.

Encapsulated in the fungi sat a Gathler, leaning against a tree with a content smile on his face. He appeared to have been enjoying the same sounds as his friends.

Several hummingbirds swarmed the Blothrud, attacking him from all angles. The Blothrud had destroyed one of their food sources.

Swatting at the birds, he ripped off more of the fungi to expose the Ov'Unday. One of his wrist spikes accidentally grazed the creature, cutting it open, causing it to bleed.

"It's still alive?"

More birds showed up to attack the Blothrud. Their strong beak poked hard at the Blothrud, trying to get at his eyes. Whispers from every direction replaced the beautiful song with threats of death. "Get out!" they shouted.

"Myth'Unday! I should have known." Santorray barked, protecting his face from them.

Ripping off the top of the fungi mound, the Gathler's brain was exposed with fungi growing from within it. Sections of the Gathler's chest were also exposed as the fungi grew inside him.

There was no way to pull the Gathler out of the mound without ripping out the fungi which appeared to be keeping him alive.

Santorray ran back to the pond to alert his friends. All of them had the same blissful expression as the Gathler he had just discovered.

Gripping Grewen on the shoulder, he shook him hard to pull him out of his distant thoughts. Looking down near his hand, Santorray noticed small outcroppings of fungi across the Ov'Unday's back. It had already begun.

Hours went by as Santorray tried to wake the crew from their trance, with no resolution. Fungi continued to grow on them as the Blothrud desperately tried to remove it, while fighting off the Myth'Unday birds.

Exhausted, night fell and his ability to see new patches of the fungi became difficult. The less effective he was at removing the fungi, the less the hummingbirds bothered him.

Santorray removed his talisman necklace and untied one of the beads in it. After tapping it against his talisman, he squeezed it tight. Waiting for it to turn a glowing red, he threw it up into the air.

The red glow rocketed into the night sky before returning to the earth and extinguishing.

Santorray lit a lantern, and continued his removal process for several hours before attempting a second bead. It was this second attempt that brought help.

The Red-Tipped Silver Dragon dove down between the trees and into the opening, scaring the Myth'Unday away. The lantern light reflected off his scales, giving him a glistening effect as he landed.

"What have you done? Were the instructions too difficult for you to understand?" Draq asked in an angry voice.

"What took you so long? You're going to put everything at risk," Santorray countered.

"Why didn't you kill him at Corrock?"

"Hold your forked tongue. We need to get them out of here before they become part of the forest." The Blothrud shined the lantern on Thorik's neck, which was now covered with fungi.

Draq looked around at the party members as they gazed into nowhere. "How could you let this happen? He entrusted you."

"Don't tell me what I already know. Help me get them out of here."

"Do it yourself."

"I can't lift them all."

"All you need is Ericc. Leave the rest."

"From what you have told me, I doubt Ambrosius would want me to abandon Thorik."

"We don't have time to ask him, do we? And yet we both know the dangers of not accomplishing our mission. Grab Ericc and finish your task. Come back for the others later, once the sacrifice is complete."

"There's a good chance that they won't be alive when I return," Santorray argued.

"There's a greater chance they won't survive at Surod!"

Santorray looked around at the faces he had come to know. Recalling the trials they had been through and the camaraderie they had shown caused him to hesitate to take such actions. He had built friendships and became part of a family unit. Even memories of nearly ripping Brimmelle apart brought a smile to his face.

"No," Santorray said. "We must save them all."

"Listen, Blothrud, you have a mission to perform. Stay focused and carry it out. Killing Ericc in front of Thorik and the Corrockians would have ended this. But now that you're this far south, sacrificing him in Surod is your best option."

"I'm not leaving without my entire team."

"Team? They aren't part of your team. If they really knew your mission, they would skin you alive. So don't get emotional about friendship and trust. They trust you only because you haven't let them know who you really are and what you're trying to do."

Santorray would have rather had a physical fight with the dragon than this verbal one.

Draq watched as the Blothrud struggled with his decision. "Would Thorik save you if he knew you were an Ergrauthian Elite? Vowed to carry out Ergrauth's every order." Draq pointed at Santorray. "Murderer of Kasa, beheader of ChoFon, and traitor of Ergrauth himself. I know your past better than most, and loyalty is not your forte."

Santorray tightened his fists as he listened to this trial by his peer.

Draq continued to drill his point. "Would they risk their lives for you if they knew you've worked for Darkmere as well as Ambrosius? Face it; you've broken every alliance you've ever had. You have no friends, no team, and no companions unless you lie to them about who you are. Once you strike Ericc down, they won't trust you anymore anyway."

Santorray took a deep breath. Draq was correct, but it was a chance that he would have to take. "We take all of them or the mission is over. It is now your decision that will determine Ericc's fate."

Draq flapped his wings hard and thrashed his tail, pounding it against the mossy ground. After letting off some steam, he finally gave in. "I will carry Ericc to the Volney Shore. No more."

"You will carry him last, after the Nums."

The two Dels stood firm, ready to lash out at each other as the tension mounted.

"This is the last time I'm coming to your aid."

"This is the first and only time I've asked for your help."

"You owe me."

"Get in line, I owe a lot of people, including these Nums."

Draq accepted this as a win for him and lifted the first Num up and out of the forest.

Santorray lifted Grewen's enormous arms over his head and began dragging the Mognin to the lake shoreline while Draq took care of the rest. The fungi quickly flaked away once they were out of the forest and into a safe location.

It wasn't until sunrise when Santorray reached the Nums at the lake. He had been lugging Grewen all night long, and he finally fell onto the beach from exhaustion.

The Nums had been lying near the shore for several hours and Draq had long since flown away. Waking up, one by one, they stretched from their marvelously refreshing dreams, ready to hit the day hard.

Grewen also awoke, as he noticed his clothes filled with moss, branches, leaves, and everything else that could be scooped up off the forest floor. As he stood up to stretch, a pile of forest debris fell from under his robe onto the beach.

"How did we get here?" Ericc asked as he sat up on his knees.

Shaking it off, the Mognin was also extremely refreshed and exhilarated. "Last thing I recall was walking through the forest."

"I never even set up camp." Thorik stretched and yawned.

Brimmelle stood up and stretched his back before walking over to Santorray. "Get up you lazy beast." He kicked sand onto the back of the Blothrud to get a reaction.

Santorray rolled over after only being asleep for a few minutes. His fatigue was obvious in his dismissal of Brimmelle's comment.

"And what do you know of our getting to this place?" Brimmelle asked bitterly.

Santorray slowly rose to his knees. "I saved your life by carrying you out of the forest and onto this beach."

"Dragged, is more like it," Grewen chuckled as he pulled another branch out of his robe.

"Oh." Brimmelle showed little appreciation. "I don't recall being in any danger in the forest."

Thorik and Ericc agreed with a nod.

"Regardless, daylight is burning, we can't sleep the day away," the Fir said as everyone collected their gear and headed south.

Exhausted, Santorray slowly worked his way to his feet and began to follow. "You're welcome," he sarcastically said to the distant group of travelers.

Chapter 36
Ambrosius' Home

Thorik's Log: June 14th of the 650th year.
We have left Lagona Falls and need to keep hidden until June 21st, when the threat of the Eve of Light sacrifice has passed. We are almost there. Just one more week.

Traveling southeast, the mist-covered terrain abruptly changed back to sunbaked Volney Lake, west of the Shi'Pel Mountains. A thin strip of short bluffs along the shores remained fresh with life. They followed this shoreline oasis for most of the day until they noticed an abandoned cliff-dwelling settlement.

Several shacks were built up against the smooth rock-faced bluffs overlooking Ki'Volney Lake. Randomly placed on the short bluff, all were the size of one-room homes without paths or ladders to get to them.

Only one of the shacks rested by the bottom of the bluff, so the group investigated it.

"I know this place." Ericc was astonished at the sight. Running up to the lowest door, he looked back at Thorik with a wide smile. "This is my home."

"Too small for Ambrosius," Santorray replied.

Thorik walked up to the door, next to Ericc. "You remember living here?"

"Vaguely. It's been eight years, but I do recall that symbol." Ericc pointed to the bluff wall near the shack. Three overlapping circles, each with a single rune within it, were etched into the rock. "My father designed that to represent my parents and myself. I remember him teaching me that all would be safe when I found this symbol."

"Apparently he was wrong," Santorray said.

Pushing the door open, a large dust covered room was revealed. The shack walls were nothing more than a façade for an enormous home carved out of the bluff itself.

The large round room domed up to the center. Thick roots from trees on the bluff working their way down the walls and into the floor. Etched out shelves provided locations for art, which now lay broken on the floor. Furniture lay askew and dormant from the attack, which once terrorized Ericc and his mother.

Several hallways exited the room, all with stairs leading up to reach the other shacks they had seen wedged onto the bluff.

"This is where I grew up." Ericc moved about as fragments of memories flashed in his head. "Mother was working in the kitchen when they attacked. I was here when the door was kicked in. They grabbed my mother and dragged her out of the house kicking and screaming. I never saw her again."

Thorik stood near Ericc and tried to envision the horror of a child's view of the crime. "What happened to you?"

"They grabbed me and tied me up. We traveled for days on Notarian roads and bridges before they took me up the mountain."

"What mountain?"

"Shi'Pel."

"Why?"

"To bring me to Surod."

"Surod?"

"Yes, it's halfway up the mountain, in the Go'ta Gorge."

Thorik turned and stormed out of the house, straight up to Santorray. "This is your idea of a safe place? Within sight of the very mountain where Darkmere plans to sacrifice Ericc?"

"Yes." The Blothrud didn't blink an eye.

Thorik didn't plan on such a casual response as the Blothrud eyed Ericc standing in the doorway watching the confrontation.

Santorray leaned over and dipped a cloth into the lake. He was tending to his wounds again which were scarring over nicely. "Thorik, Ericc can't be on the run his whole life. He'd never be able to trust anyone for fear that they would turn him over to Darkmere."

"What's his other option, confront him?"

"Exactly."

"Are you crazy? Have you ever met Darkmere? He has powers we can't even begin to understand. He can change the air into fire or poison. He can manipulate the form of his body, and alter the makeup of those he touches."

"Yes, I've met him. And yes, he is powerful."

Ericc stepped closer. "So are we. Santorray is a great fighter and Grewen has strength. Thorik, you have the Spear of Rummon and I have some powers myself."

Avanda refused to be left out. "My magic can help."

"No," Thorik and Brimmelle said in unison.

Ericc wasn't backing down. "Thorik, you may have saved me, but you are sentencing me to a lifetime of hiding. I'm going with Santorray to take care of this once and for all."

Thorik looked to Grewen for advice. "And will you be traveling with Ericc to his death?"

"I told you I would do whatever I could to protect him from this fate. It would be very hard to do that from down here when he is on the mountain."

Thorik looked around for support only to find Brimmelle on his side. Gluic's grin told him that she was waiting for him to decide his own fate. "This is wrong. You're walking into a trap," Thorik announced.

Brimmelle wrapped his arms tight across his chest. "This is the end of the line, where the Nums and the Altereds separate. It is time for us to go home. We can do no more."

Thorik panned from Fir Brimmelle to Grewen. "I have to agree with Brimmelle. I've done everything I can to save Ericc as promised. But I cannot willingly go into what I believe is a trap when we have other options." Thorik's eyes swelled with water as he looked at Grewen's face. "No matter how hard I try, I cannot save someone who does not wish to be saved. This is where our journey ends and we must part ways."

"So be it." Santorray wrapped up his chest injuries. "You will be safe traveling along the shoreline to Eastland. Blend into the crowd and get transportation to Woodlen. I've never met a Num with a heart of a Blothrud before I met you. Never lose that quality." Spitting in his hand, he held it out to Thorik who spit in his own hand and slapped the two together.

Ericc collected his items before walking over to Thorik. "You honored my father's wishes. I give you credit for that. Remember him fondly; you were the son to him which I always wanted to be."

Grewen watched the first two begin their walk toward the mountain. "Thorik."

"Grewen, no, please don't go." Thorik's heart pounded hard against his tense chest and his voice cracked from emotion. "I lost you once and it about killed me. I can't lose you again."

Grewen's smile warmed the Num's heart as it always did. "Little man, you have your own journey and life ahead of you. You must do what feels right and then live with the ramifications of those actions. This feels right to me, but it's okay that it doesn't for you."

Thorik wiped his eyes. "I'll go if you tell me to."

"I would never do such a thing. Even with these broad shoulders, I can't carry that much weight of responsibility. You know that."

"At least tell me if I'm making a mistake."

"Only time can tell that." Grewen lifted the Num up for a final hug. "It takes courage to do what you feel is right, especially when those you love don't support you."

Setting Thorik back down he waved at the group. "Goodbye, my friends. Safe journey home."

Thorik stood motionless as he watched Grewen turn and walk away, slowly catching up with the other two heading for their potential end.

"I'm going with them," Avanda finally said, running past Thorik.

But it was short lived as Thorik grabbed her, stopping her escape. "Avanda, this is not your fight. We've done our part."

"You've done yours, I haven't done mine. I'm finally starting to understand how to use my magic. I can help."

"I know you can, but it's over. We promised to save Ericc and we did just that with your help. Now it's time for us to go home. We can't spend the rest of our lives watching after him."

"He's part of our family, now. It's our responsibility to be there for him when he needs us most."

"Sometimes you have to let go of family to let them travel on their own path and do things you don't believe in."

Disappointed, Avanda stood with Thorik and watched their friends disappear over the first hill.

It was over and it was time to make plans to return to Farbank. In some way it was a relief to know they were going home. If they hurried they could be there in time for the sounds, smells and tastes of the harvest festival and all the food and contests that went along with it.

It felt good to return home after doing what they had set out to do and more so.

Thorik thought deeply about how much he missed his cottage and the people of his village, as he set up Ambrosius' old house for the night. It was nice to be inside again with shelves to stack items and chairs to sit on. He forgot how much he missed the little things.

After his chores were done, Thorik sat down and pulled out his coffer of maps and notes. "It's been a long journey," he muttered at the drawings as he reminisced before adding new notes.

June 15th of the 650th year, Ericc leaves his parents abandoned home near Lagona Falls as a free man. No longer a captive of men or beasts, he travels to confront his enemy in the temple of Surod. He leaves with Santorray and Grewen, but not me. It is time for us to return home, to Farbank, for I cannot save someone who does not wish to be saved.

As he neatly straightened up his papers and returned them back in their wooden case, Gluic walked into the house.

"It feels good to give up the fight and just rest," she said peacefully as she walked past him.

Thorik was shocked at the comment. "Granna, I'm not giving up. I saved Ericc from being captured. I did what I set out to do."

She nodded at his words as she started to dig in his sack of Runestones. "Yes, you are right. You only promised to free him, not to save him from his plight."

His shoulder's raised at the underlined sarcasm. "I can't prevent him from going to Surod at some point in his life, I can't stop Santorray and Grewen from helping him, I can't stop the Eve of Light from occurring each year, and I can't stop Darkmere from hunting him down. I'm only one Num, a small one at that, without even a soul-marking for respect."

"And that is why you do not have them."

"What?"

"Dear grandson, you show great courage when under stress. But when you have time to plan, your faith in yourself falls behind all others."

"What are you saying?"

"Would you travel up that mountain if Ambrosius where here with you?"

Thorik straightened up. "Of course. We would stand a chance with him at our side."

"So, it is only worth fighting for a good cause if you are guaranteed a victory."

"No...but it is foolish to walk into a trap even for a good cause."

"Isn't that what Ambrosius did?"

Thorik realized that she was correct. Ambrosius sacrificed himself to save many, even though he knew he was entering a trap. "I just wish I was something more than what I am. I have no powers or strength to achieve such a lofty goal."

Gluic walked back to the table and set his Runestones of Belief on the table in front of him. "Physical strength and magical powers are no match for someone who never gives up and continues to believe in himself. It is the will to succeed and a relentless drive to accomplish that which makes the difference in this world, not the birthright of power."

Thorik held the Runestone in his palm and stared at it while absorbing her words. "Granna, Ambrosius once told me that I was special and that I reminded him of the Mountain King. I guess I secretly hoped to find out that I'm a descendent of the King himself."

"If you were, would you suddenly have more belief and faith in yourself?"

"I would be prouder." He took in a deep breath and swallowed hard. "Yes, I would have more faith in myself. Tell me, Granna. Am I his heir?"

"Thorik, you are not the offspring of any nobleman or king. And your pride should come from within, regardless of such. You are Thorik Dain, the one who prevented the great flood, the one who rescued Ericc from Corrock, the one who stood up to much stronger men when they attempted to lead us, and the one whose desire to do good overshadows his own well-being. I am very proud to be your grandmother. It is about time you start being proud of who you've become. It is this conflict within you that prevents your soul-markings from showing themselves."

"But Granna, I was happy when I lived in Farbank. Why didn't the soul-markings show then?"

"You were content to pacify Brimmelle and the other villagers. You haven't been proud of yourself since your parent's deaths, which happened just before your markings were to show themselves. Ever since then you have questioned every decision you have ever made instead of doing what you know is right and being proud of yourself for doing it."

Thorik was silent as she left the table and walked to the front door, holding it for Brimmelle as he entered the home carrying firewood. Closing the door behind her, she left Thorik to do some thinking.

Brimmelle walked to the fireplace. "It's about time you came to your senses and let these humans and Altereds work out their own problems. I can't wait until we get back to the comfort of our own village."

"I'm not going back yet. I need to help Ericc get past this point in his life. No one should have to live in fear of being seen alive."

Fir Brimmelle dropped his wood hard to the floor. "Oh no you don't! We agreed to let them go. We've done our part."

"Yes, you've done your part. You need to take Gluic and Avanda back to Farbank. I must catch up with Ericc to help him."

"You? What can you possible do to help them? You'll be stomped on."

"I will do whatever it takes to succeed."

"Against Darkmere?"

"If he is there, yes."

Brimmelle walked over and grabbed his Sec by the collar with one hand while pointing harshly at Thorik's face with the other. "You listen to me. We are done with this."

Thorik took the Fir's wrist and pushed his arm away, freeing himself. "No, I'm not."

"What are you trying to prove?"

"Nothing. I believe I can make a difference, and Ericc needs me."

"If you leave, I'm done with you. You will no longer be a Sec of Farbank."

"If that is your decision, than I accept it."

"If you leave and die up on that mountain, you'll make your mother's death worth nothing. She will have sacrificed her own life for you, and you will repay her by just tossing it away. How can you disrespect her in this futile attempt?"

Thorik moved his Runestone into the exact center on the surface of his coffer, tweaking the rotation to make it perfectly align with the box's corners as he thought how to respond. "It is because she gave up her life for me that I know I must use every ounce of my being to make this world a better place and to do what I believe is right."

Brimmelle turned his back to the boy in anger, before tossing logs into the fireplace. "You're not taking Avanda, under any circumstance. I've watched her and know she has deep feelings for you, but this is not up for a debate."

Thorik knew he was done discussing it. "Agreed. But I do need to tell her that I will be leaving without her. Is she still upset from our argument earlier?"

Brimmelle brushed his hands clean from the wood bark. "I don't know, I haven't seen her."

"Wasn't she outside helping you?"

"No, I thought she was in here with you."

Thorik instantly became anxious and uncomfortable. "You don't think she went after them, do you?"

"She wouldn't dare." Brimmelle raced out the front door to confirm his doubts.

Thorik ran upstairs, only to find it empty. Leaning out one of the upper windows, he could see Brimmelle ask Gluic where Avanda was. Gluic pointed down the path where Grewen, Santorray and Ericc had traveled.

The path was empty and it would be dark soon. Their only chance to catch up with her and the others was to start fresh in the morning and hope Grewen kept a slow pace.

Brimmelle stared down the lonely path in disbelief. "Mother, when did she leave?"

"A few hours ago. Right after Ericc and the others left," Gluic said very casually. "I guess that means we'll be going after her."

"Why didn't you stop her, or tell us that she had left?" Brimmelle asked in frustration.

A devious grin grew on her face. "I'm sorry dear, but as you requested back in Southwind, I'm not going to mediate your problems anymore."

Chapter 37
Road to Go'ta Gorge

Thorik, Brimmelle and Gluic walked east along the dirt path, which ended at an ancient great road leading up the cliff, and hopefully across a plateau, through the Go'ta Gorge and up to Surod. Finely carved street stones now lay slightly askew from the ground underneath giving way. Column bases bordered both sides, some with columns still standing on them.

Thorik envisioned what it must have looked like when the road had first been built and thousands of people paraded on its grand path.

Every few hours the road expanded into a round open area, often providing stone roofs for shade and wells for water. The Nums took pleasure in both whenever it was available. However, many of these structures had fallen from battles long past, as well as some that looked more recent.

Snaking its way up the first steep cliff, the road reached the top of the plateau where the Lagona Falls fell from, and yet they had just begun their hike up into the mountains. But before crossing the plateau, they needed to rest for the night after the day's long trek. Avanda and the others were still not within their view.

Gluic cleared a section of stone road to make way for her gems, crystals, and stones she had picked up along the way. "Come out of those stuffy purses and get some fresh air." She then placed the items on the road in flowing patterns. "Enjoy and revitalize."

Thorik set down his backpack and removed his wooden coffer so he could access his flint for Brimmelle.

Camp duties had changed over time. Thorik could recall when Fir Brimmelle wouldn't lift a finger to help; now he was in charge of the fire. Gathering wood and stoking the fire somehow gave him a feeling of importance that he missed from his days in Farbank.

Brimmelle got the fire started just as Thorik returned with roots and a few small prairie gophers for dinner. "It's not much, but it will keep us going."

Brimmelle set another log on the fire. "It will do."

Thorik nodded and prepped the food for dinner. "Brimmelle, can I ask you something?"

"What is it?"

"It's about my mother."

Brimmelle's shoulders tightened, but he did not reply.

"Did you mean what you said about making the wrong choice and saving me instead of her?"

Using a thick stick, the elder Num poked at the beginnings of the fire. "Yes."

"Oh." Thorik pondered the answer. "Do you really hate me?"

"I never said I hated you."

"Then why have you treated me the way you do?"

"I've been trying to make a responsible man out of you. Someone that your mother would have been proud of me to raise in her absence."

"This isn't about me, is it?"

"What do you mean? That's what we're talking about."

"No, I think we're talking about you, your guilt, and your living up to my mother's expectation of how to raise me."

Brimmelle broke his stick and tossed it into the flames.

Thorik watched the fire coil into the air. "You've been so fearful of making decisions about me that she wouldn't have approved, that you avoided making any decisions outside of the Mountain King's words."

"The King's words are wise. All should follow them."

"True as they are, they could never provide me with the warmth or guidance I needed from a father, or in this case an uncle."

"Where is all this coming from?"

"I was just thinking about Ericc. He never had the opportunity to grow up with his father. Whereas, I grew up the past several years with you, and yet it felt like you weren't there."

"I was always there for you."

"Physically, not otherwise."

"A village Fir is busy. I didn't have time to play games with you all day."

"I never asked for that. But from time to time it would have been nice to have been praised for what I did accomplish."

"You're fortunate to have what you did. My father passed away when I was eleven. I had no father figure after that."

"Yes, I am fortunate. But that doesn't mean you couldn't have told me I did well now and then, or congratulate me after a successful hunt, or even allow me to show you the maps and notes I've taken on this journey so we can teach others about what's beyond our valley's mountains."

Fussing with the fire, Brimmelle sighed. "Fine, show me your sketchings."

"Really?"

"Yes, under one condition."

"Name it."

"You close that box of notes up and stop wasting time with them."

"Forever?"

"At least until we have safely retrieved Avanda. You need to keep your focus on her until then."

"Agreed." Thorik opened his coffer and pulled out a stack of paper from within. Notes from over a year filled the pages. Maps of their travels with journals from events brought memories back to them both, causing even Brimmelle to chuckle a few times.

It had been the first time in Thorik's life that he felt a positive bond with his uncle.

Brimmelle on the other hand recalled what he loved so much about his sister, her sense of adventure.

Time passed quickly and the mountains continued to grow as the Nums moved southeast across the plateau. The ancient road eventually crossed and then followed the thin river to the base of the gorge, before riding up the north face of the Shi'Pel Range.

The river they followed had etched the sandstone gorge out to a smooth shape. Jagged red rocks had fallen from higher elevations and had embedded themselves across the canyon floor and in the river, causing violent rapids. Solid black outcroppings looked like tumors among the various reddish hues of the surrounding soil, and the water dripping from melted snow far above them looked black in the shadows of the mountain.

The south side of the Go'ta Gorge was also the north side of the Shi'Pel Peaks, a cold, dark and lonely place, even in midday. The mighty peaks continuously shaded the road from direct sunlight, which explained why the columns that normally bordered both sides of the road had been replaced with stone vats. Empty now, Thorik assumed they had once contained oil, lighting the road up the mountain to Surod.

Glaciers melted from the high peaks in the summer heat. But instead of giving life to the valley, like it did near Farbank, the water carved out rough grooves in the mountainsides. And instead of large flowing rivers, water perspired from the rocks themselves, dripping constantly as it worked its way down into the base of the gorge.

After traveling up the mountain in the peak's shadows, an off-white building could be seen hanging onto the side of a cliff. But it was more than just a building with walls and a roof; it resembled an enormous ribcage protruding from the mountain. Each rib bone connected to the rest with a thin dark skin, like a chest of a man who had starved to death. Nearing the neckline of the structure was a light shining through a round flat crystal, nearly the width of Santorray's arm span.

Above the main building was a smaller one in the shape of a skull breaching the mountain's side. Above them, a third even smaller structure was in the appearance of a hand pointing to the sky as it held another large crystal embedded in its palm.

The entire structure reminded Thorik of the Mountain King statue, only stripped of robes and flesh and more encased into the mountain itself. The size of the body was approximately the same but it didn't give off the feeling of tranquility as the one in Kingsfoot did.

The road that lay before Thorik and his family crossed a bridge and worked its way up the mountainside before ending at the skeletal building. "This must be Surod," Thorik said to himself.

Brimmelle stopped to rest, placing his hands on his knees as he breathed the thin cold air. "We didn't make it in time to stop them before they entered. They've been captured."

"We don't know that. They may have snuck in."

"Santorray, Avanda and Ericc?" Brimmelle said. "They most likely screamed war cries as they charged the place."

"Grewen may have talked them into a plan."

"Not likely."

Thorik looked at his resources for the siege on Surod, which consisted of his uncle and his grandmother. "We don't have enough for this. We've only succeeded this far because of Grewen and Santorray."

Brimmelle's face turned red. "After all I have done to help you survive on this venture to our deaths, you don't see me as an asset? I know I don't have the omniscient attitude of Ambrosius, or the smell of a Mognin, or the uncontrollable temper of a Blothrud. But whether you know it or not, I have been constantly protecting you and our family."

"That's not what I meant." Thorik hadn't planned on starting a fight.

Brimmelle walked toward the bridge, without him.

Gluic put her hand on Thorik and smiled. "He's grown a lot since we left Farbank. I'm very proud of both of you."

It was an odd statement to come from his grandmother. "Thank you Granna. Are you well?"

"Remember, strength comes from within you, and you have a lot yet to give." She escorted him down the road, behind her son.

The stone bridge before them crossed a deep ravine, which opened up into the Go'ta Gorge. The long bridge had eroded over the years with some missing stone floor tiles. Those that remained were worn down soft and wet from the moisture given off from the melting glaciers.

Thorik stepped out onto the bridge. "Careful, it's slippery."

Nearly halfway across, Thorik noticed an odd smell getting stronger as they proceeded. Following it forward, he found the source. A large section of the bridge had been eaten away by some type of acid. "What could have done this?"

Brimmelle held his mother's hand tight as he walked across the bridge, trying not to look down over the sides. "Nothing natural. Looks like something from Avanda's purse of catastrophe."

Thorik realized his half-joking comment could be correct. "There could have been a battle here, but how long ago?"

"Not very, seeing that it's still spreading."

The acid was still dissolving the stone at the center of the bridge. Several of the keystones where gone, with only one remaining. If it continued to spread to the last keystone, the bridge would collapse; assuming it would last that long.

"We need to get off this bridge." Thorik helped his uncle and grandmother over the narrow remaining block. "Run for it."

It wasn't as simple as that. Many of the floor tiles had fallen, leaving holes in the bridge. Those that remained were uneven and difficult to run on without tripping in the shadowy darkness.

Gluic tripped, taking Brimmelle down with her.

Thorik turned back to help them, tripping himself in doing so. Rolling forward, his lower half fell into a hole where a stone tile was missing. Grasping at the slick floor around him helped very little. Thorik slid down into the hole up to his chest, with his legs dangling below the bridge.

Brimmelle helped Gluic to her feet before he noticed Thorik. Running over, he tripped and slid toward Thorik, too fast to stop in time.

Brimmelle plowed headfirst into Thorik, pushing him off the bridge, into the hole.

Thorik knew he had a choice of grabbing his uncle or allowing himself to fall. If he were to grab Brimmelle, he most likely would drag him down the opening with him, killing them both. Gluic would be on her own. He couldn't do that to her. She needed him, even if she didn't think so.

Falling backward after butting heads with his uncle, Thorik reached his hands out to grab the sides of the surrounding bridge tiles. He missed.

Brimmelle reached down and grabbed his Sec's wrist, causing his own body to pull forward into the hole until it abruptly stopped.

Gluic had grabbed onto Brimmelle's leg and anchored her own feet in the unleveled section of the bridge, which Brimmelle had tripped over.

Thorik opened his eyes and looked up at his uncle's strained face. Their hands grasped each other's wrists. It looked too far to climb, and he could see the agony on Brimmelle's face from holding onto him. "Brimmelle-"

"Shut up and grab my other hand." Reaching down with his second arm, he met Thorik's other hand by the third swing. "Now climb me."

"I can't. I don't have the strength."

"I'm not Grewen, I can't lift you. I'm not Ambrosius. I can't use E'rudite powers to just push you up here. All I am is your fat old uncle, so use me as one and climb up on my back."

"I don't have the strength. I can't."

"Yes you can."

"But-" Thorik began before being cut off by Brimmelle.

"Get yourself moving. Now!"

Thorik didn't question him again. He knew that tone, and when it was released Thorik had learned to do as he was told regardless of anything else going on, so he did. Hand over hand he struggled to climb his uncle's outstretched arms until his hands clasped around the back of the older man's neck and under his armpit.

Brimmelle strained from the pain as he cradled his neck up to give whatever support he could. Clasping his own hands together, he gave Thorik a foothold, which allowed his nephew to climb the rest of the way with much more ease.

Now with Thorik out of the way, Brimmelle had an excellent view of how high they were, causing his body to start going limp as he began passing out.

Rolling off of Brimmelle, Thorik helped his uncle out of the hole before Brimmelle fell unconscious. "Ambrosius and Grewen have nothing on you, Uncle." Lying on his back, he panted for air.

Also on his back, Brimmelle rubbed the back of his neck. "That's Fir Brimmelle."

Thorik laughed. "I'm glad you were here for me, Fir Brimmelle. Thank you."

"I've always been there for you. But it was stupid for you to have us running across this slippery bridge in the first place."

Thorik grinned at the closest thing to emotional appreciation he would ever receive out of his uncle. 'You're welcome.'

Gluic closed her eyes as her hands spread out on the stone tiles. "They say we should leave. We don't have much time."

"Agreed." Thorik stood and helped them up before they quickly walked to the far end of the bridge and onto the cliff side road.

Crossing his arms behind his back, Brimmelle stopped and turned back to the bridge. It still stood firm in spite of the warnings from both of them. "Apparently you two aren't always right about these things."

Nearly on cue, the center of the bridge began to crumble down before both ends ripped from the ravine's sides and tumbled inward, crashing into the shadowy darkness.

Brimmelle sighed at the sight, and then turned back to his family. "Not a word, Thorik. Not *one* word."

Chapter 38
Temple of Surod

The road ended in the center of the lowest rib of the main structure. Unguarded, it looked unused for many years.

Black granite filled the courtyard as well as all the walls between the off-white marble ribs. Life-sized statues lay broken on the ground and cracks in the foundation offset the once flat platform.

Thorik and his family walked cautiously up to the open entrance. Soft wind streamed out from the structure, rustling their clothes, before stopping and reversing its direction back inside the massive statue's chest.

A low thumping could be felt in the ground, like a heart beating in slow motion.

Stepping into the enormous skeletal statue, Thorik's boot crushed an object beneath it. Thousands of black beetles scattered from the area, up walls, and into cracks. The sound of their shells slapping against each other made Thorik's arms nervously tingle and shake.

The beetles had been feeding on several large, human-sized creatures, lying to one side of the first room.

Thorik reached into his backpack and pulled out his sack of Runestones. Holding the Runestone of Belief, he traced the worn ridges and thought of nothing but the Runestone. Red light illuminated from the gem in the center of the Runestone, casting shadows of the three Nums up onto the walls. The oval room of red stones bled, dripping onto the floors, pooling, and trickling down the open cracks.

They knew it was only water from the glaciers above, but it made it no less unnerving.

Similar in style of the City of Kingsfoot, the walls and ceiling had been carved into specific shapes. But instead of plants and animals, corpses littered the surface of every wall and arched ceiling.

The red light added to the effect of blood pouring from the bodies and out of the skeletal mouths.

The entrance breathed out again and then back in as the ground's heartbeat continued.

Thorik walked over to the bodies the beetles had been working on. They were half devoured Krupes with their heads sliced off and tossed across the room. "Santorray's work?"

Brimmelle scoffed. "Who else?"

The beetles began to creep back into the room from their initial fright, drawn back by the smell of the dead body. It was time for the Nums to leave the room.

Deeper into the chest they walked. Skeletal arms and legs hung off the walls and ceiling as though they were making an effort to escape the stones from where they were embedded. The sizes ranged from Mognin to Num, if not smaller.

The corridor stopped at a coiling staircase going up as well as down. The staircase wrapped around what appeared to be a giant spine, matching the size and placement for the exterior of Surod's structure. Water could be heard flowing down inside the spinal column, while torches lined the staircase.

"The heart of this place is up." Wrenching his neck to see anything up or down the well-lit stairwell, Thorik placed his Runestone back in his pack. "I would venture to say the heart is where the sacrifice would take place."

Air rushed down the stairs at them, and then returned upward.

A scream from below rang out just as Thorik had started his way up the stairs. A second scream confirmed that it was Avanda.

"Wait here, where it's safe." Reversing his course, Thorik made his way down the wide spiral staircase.

Coiling around the giant spine, he followed the staircase down several flights until it finally opened up to a basement filled with structural columns and room for storage.

Avanda screamed again for help, as Thorik ran past crates, old supplies, and cages stacked up in unorganized aisles.

"Avanda?" he called out.

"Here!" she screamed with delight at the sound of his voice. She was locked into one of the smaller cages, only half her own height. "I can't believe you came for me."

Thorik took out his tools and started working on the lock. "I would never leave you behind."

"Never?"

"Avanda, I'm sorry I wasn't there for you that night in Rava'Kor." His voice was humble and soft as he worked the lock. "The only thing I could think about was Ericc, and that was shortsighted. I was a fool not to see how important you are to me. I wasn't listening to anything you had to say that night. I just wanted you out of my way. I was wrong. I'm sorry for not being there for you."

"It wasn't your fault. I knew better. Brimmelle had told me to be back before dark but I spent longer than I had planned exploring the city. Then you tried to stop me from picking a fight, and I should have listened."

"This isn't your fault. Lucian was behind this. He is the one to blame for his actions against you." Thorik tried a different tool to pick the lock.

"But you can't always watch over me. Someday you'll let me go, like you did Ericc."

"Perhaps, perhaps not. But now I have learned to be there for you when you *are* here. I trust you and believe in you." Picking the lock, he removed it and opened the small door. Pulling her out, he lifted her to her feet and looked straight into her eyes. "You are now, and always will be, my dearest friend."

The two hugged at the reconciliation of their emotional issues. The weight from their tension dropped, freeing them to look fondly at each other once again.

"You know, you never did tell me what you wished for on the Lu'Tythis lights." Still overjoyed to find her alive, he allowed himself a moment of peace before he would remind her of the danger they were still in.

Squeezing him tight, she caused him to embrace her back just as deeply. "You just made it come true." She had fantasized about him ever since she became his student, many years ago. Her desire for him to rescue her and see her as an equal was beginning to unfold.

Smiling at the thought, he finished the hug and collected his tools, knowing they needed to get back upstairs.

"How did you find us?" she asked.

"You're the only one we've found. Where is everyone else?"

"We got split up when we were attacked. I dropped my purse of magic as I made a run for it. How did you get rid of Bredgin's panther?"

"His panther?"

"Yes, the one that has been guarding me."

"I haven't seen it."

Without warning, the crates from behind the two Nums burst forward, exposing the giant Black Panther, Shrii. Her mouth was large and her teeth were so white they nearly glowed from the lantern lights.

The Nums ran, but were quickly cut off by the cat, preventing their escape to the stairs.

Thorik pushed Avanda through the metal bars of a large cage, to protect her from the cat. He followed once she was in, but it was a tight fit for him.

Shrii pounced, claws ready to rip him into pieces.

Over halfway through, he became stuck. His backpack was too large and could not fit between the bars while being worn. But there was no time to take it off. Shrii had arrived.

The straps tightened as he pulled forward and Avanda pulled his arms toward her.

Shrii attacked, biting at the Num. Grabbing Thorik by his pack, she lifted him up to the top of the cage, knocking Avanda backward.

Thorik spread his arms and legs to prevent himself from being pulled back out of the cage.

Shrii shook her head to dislodge him. Placing one of her huge paws against the base of cage for leverage, she began pulling him out.

Thorik struggled to hold on as the straps from his pack dug deep into his skin. The cat's strength was vastly superior to his. He simply could not win this.

Avanda reached up and pulled one of Thorik's legs with no luck.

Pushing forward, Shrii then snapped her head back to rip him out of the cage.

It worked. Thorik lost his grip. His pack ripped from his body, and Thorik tumbled to the floor outside the cage.

The cage had also been impacted from the final pull, as it tipped forward toward Thorik.

Shrii shook the pack for a moment before tossing it aside, returning her attention back to the fallen Num. Swiping her paw at him, the cage finished its tip and crashed onto her front leg.

The panther shrieked from the pain and recoiled her arm, causing the cage to fall onto the Num.

Thorik had rolled into position between the approaching bars, but misjudged the angle, as it crushed his left forearm. Thorik let out a murderous scream as he felt his arm break. In addition, he was now pinned under the cage, with its weight far too heavy for the Num to budge.

Avanda had fallen forward with the cage and quickly jumped up to help him, but the weight was too much for her as well.

Shrii resumed her stalking; watching the captive Num. Nudging the cage with her nose caused great pain for Thorik as he yelled from each movement.

Placing a paw up on top of the cage, the panther prepared to leap up onto it. Its added weight would easily sever Thorik's hand from his arm.

Thorik and Avanda twisted and pulled his arm with no success. Lifting the cage was just as futile. They were out of options.

A second paw reached up as the panther prepared for the leap. Shrii's eyes focused on the helpless Num, as the cat sprang up off the ground.

As Shrii's weight began to transfer onto the cage, the bars pressed deeper into Thorik's arm, soon to snap off as if a meat cleaver were cutting off a chicken leg. Thorik's only hope was that it was a clean enough cut, that it would at least allow him to escape.

The weight of the cat never fully materialized, as the panther lifted up into the room. Clawing the air in front of it, Thorik could see two large arms wrapped around the cat. It was Grewen, standing behind Shrii, holding her tight. The panther twisted and clawed as it tried to free itself from the Mognin's bear-hug.

"Escape!" Grewen ordered, as he leaned up against the cage to tilt it enough to free him.

Thorik pulled his arm in close to protect it as he moved safely between the bars before Grewen dropped the cage. "What can we do to help?" the Num asked, pushing past his own pain.

Grewen fell to the side as he grappled with the cat, destroying various wooden crates and supplies while maintaining his hold onto Shrii. "There's no time. Run to the high chamber to stop the sacrifice before it's too late."

Avanda assisted Thorik out of the cage. "I need my magical items."

Thorik followed her comment with, "And I need my spear."

Grewen struggled to keep his control of Shrii as the two tumbled around the room, breaking everything in their chaotic path. "I can't hold her much longer. Get going!"

The two Nums fought to stay clear of the two giants as they randomly twisted and rolled around the room. Thorik tried to retrieve his spear twice before realizing that he would be flattened or ripped apart.

Grewen and Shrii rolled on the ground, as the cat tried to break free, crashing into support columns and breaking metal cages.

Upon Grewen's final order, they ran for the stairs, Thorik's broken arm tight to his stomach. "Where's Ericc and Santorray?" he asked Avanda.

"It's not good. Ericc has been captured."

"And Santorray?" Thorik asked.

She paused for a moment. "He's the one that captured Ericc."

"He wouldn't do such a thing. He gave me his word."

"He lied to you. He lied to all of us."

"No, not Santorray. I don't believe it."

"Then you'll see it for yourself," she said as they raced up the spiral staircase.

Leaping from every other step they climbed several flights before reaching the main floor where Thorik had left his grandmother and uncle. But the room was empty.

"Were did they go?" he asked himself, before seeing a few odd looking stones and gems on the steps leading up. "They went up." He retrieved the stones along the way.

Porous walls provided vent-ways for the rushing of air in and out as the Nums made their way up.

The trail of gems led up onto a level with a round loft and several doors, only one of which had additional stones near it. He collected the rest and placed them in his pocket before listening to any sounds coming from the far side of the door.

Faint voices could be heard but not comprehended.

Avanda began to slowly open the door, allowing a sickly green light to escape from the room on the other side. "Isn't that the Notarian light which affects the stone carvings?"

Thorik stopped her with a finger to his mouth before swinging the door open enough to look inside at the large open chest cavity of a room. The inside of Surod's ribs filled the walls in an abnormal oval-shaped room.

The flickering green light caused the stone walls to slowly expand and contract, as if lungs actually existed inside the massive room, pushing against the structure's ribs and body. The air rushed past the Nums and down the stairs and then returned upon each gigantic breath.

In the ceiling, on the far side of the room, was an enormous clear crystal; the same one they had seen from outside near the neckline.

In the center of the room was a shallow pool of water. Next to it, away from the entrance, sat a sacrifice altar formed in the shape of an upside-down spider lying on a solid block. Its legs reached into the air as it waited for its next victim.

A single copper vat was positioned opposite the altar. Resting on a metal base, the oils within the vat gave off the enchanting green light, causing the walls surrounding the main level to be alive with magical energy as small stone creatures entered and left the stone murals.

Several large porous stones were embedded into the floor around the perimeter, each giving off steam and causing the room to be warm and moist.

Holding his broken arm, Thorik leaned in past the door to see farther, but snapped back when he heard a voice from a side passage.

"Is everything prepared?" an older man's voice asked.

Thorik had heard that voice before but unsure where, as he poked his head in again.

"Yes, Father."

Thorik knew the voice of Lord Bredgin, making the other voice Darkmere. Knowing this, his heart raced and his breathing became heavy with fear. Without a plan, he could do nothing until an opportunity arose, so he watched and waited while wrapping up his broken forearm to minimize it's movement.

Darkmere and his son walked into the main chamber. "Bring in Ambrosius' heir."

Bredgin signaled to a Krupe guard at the far doorway, who in turn opened two large doors.

Ericc was led into the room by Santorray. The young man's wrists were tied and he wore a necklace with a large translucent brown gem in it. Brimmelle and Gluic followed Santorray; their Num hands were tied up the same as Ericc's.

The Krupe guards, armored in their standard black metal, accompanied them toward the center of the room, pushing Ericc forward with their thick spiked maces.

"Santorray," Darkmere said as a greeting.

"Darkmere." He replied with a nod.

"You have done well." Darkmere turned and visually inspected Ericc. "He has been delivered in full health, I see." It had been a long time since he had seen Santorray and had wondered if he was still fighting for his cause.

"As you requested." Santorray looked at Ericc and sneered. "However, I wish to change our terms for delivery."

"Our terms were final. Your payment will be provided. Don't get greedy."

"To Della Estovia with the payment. I want the right to sacrifice the son of Ambrosius and to end this prophecy once and for all. I wish to end the lineage of Ambrosius."

Darkmere grinned. "Terms accepted."

Chapter 39
The Sacrifice

Thorik stood in the doorway with Avanda, furious at Santorray's betrayal. It took all of Thorik's mental fortitude not to scream out his anger as he watched the events unfold.

Two Krupes grabbed Ericc and picked him up off the ground before setting him onto the altar. With the power of the green flames, the stone spider legs came alive and instinctively pulled in, holding the young man down flat on the table.

Santorray kneeled near the shallow pool and performed a ritual to prepare for the sacrifice while Darkmere and Bredgin went back into the prior room as they discussed the ceremony.

Refusing to miss out, Avanda pushed her head farther into the doorway to see what was happening, bumping Thorik's arm in the process.

Tensing from the pain, Thorik moved to give her room. "Santorray's weakness is his back. He struggles to see rear attacks until it's too late," he whispered as he unsheathed two small blades from his belt and handed one to her. "I'll take down Santorray while you free Brimmelle and Gluic. Whoever is done first can free Ericc."

She looked at the small blade. "What if one of us gets caught?"

"Then it is up to the other to free Ericc and escape."

"But-"

"This is not up for discussion." Giving her a kiss on the cheek, he winked and said, "I trust you."

The two Nums ran out of the doorway in different directions, hiding behind the large steaming rocks as they made their way to their targets.

Thorik knew he needed to attack before he was spotted, but he had failed to mention this to Avanda.

Running out from behind a rock she made her way to the elder Nums.

Spotted instantly, Santorray broke off his rituals and sat up straight.

Thorik had to strike before he could alert the others. Charging out from his hiding place, with his bad arm tucked to his side, Thorik leaped at Santorray's back, hitting his target. His blade cut deep into his shoulder blade, causing the Blothrud to arch back and howl.

Thorik's body landed hard against Santorray's back blades, slicing the Num's face and chest, before he fell to the floor. There was a reason Blothrud weren't attacked from the rear, and Thorik just found out why.

Santorray reached back and pulled the blade out, releasing a trail of blood down his back, before turning to see Thorik lying on the ground in pain. The Num's clothes were drenched with his own blood from several deep cuts.

Attempting to crawl away, Thorik was quickly stopped by Santorray. "You're not going anywhere," the Blothrud said, reaching down and lifting him by one leg.

Avanda meanwhile had cut Brimmelle and Gluic free, and had run over to release Ericc. But no matter how hard the Nums pulled, the stone spider leg constraints would not budge.

Thorik could see that it was futile for them to continue. "Run! Get out of here."

Several Krupes were already entering the room to see what the commotion was about. Time for escape was minimal.

Avanda and Brimmelle continued to pull at the legs to free Ericc, while Gluic stood silently smiling at Thorik, happy to see him still alive.

"Run!" Thorik screamed again, realizing that their window of opportunity had already passed.

Krupes now blocked every doorway, while a few entered the room to gather the Nums.

Santorray dropped Thorik near the pool before tending to his own wound.

"Why?" Thorik asked the Blothrud. "I trusted you."

Santorray pulled a bandage tight to stop his own bleeding. "I told you that trust is not my ally."

Avanda, Brimmelle and Gluic were quickly captured by the Krupes, who then stood silently at attention as they waited for their master to arrive.

Darkmere entered the room to appraise the situation. The E'rudite's white clothes and skin didn't bother the Nums as much as his solid white eyes, for no one could tell where he was looking.

"Welcome, Nums. I'm so pleased you could attend our ceremony. Nevertheless, your etiquette leaves something to be desired."

Overcoming his pain, Thorik sat up in defiance to the dark lord. "I defeated your plot in Weirfortus. I plan to do the same here."

Darkmere was amused by the strength of Num's tone. "Defeated? My dear Sec Thorik Dain of Farbank, I've been watching you for some time now. Not only was I not defeated, but *you* made it possible for me to prove that Ambrosius was a war monger when you led him to Pyrth. Then *you* killed him for me inside the Weirfortus reservoirs while saving my valuable kingdom. And now *you* have led his son, Ericc, to me just in time for the Eve of Light. I honestly don't know how to thank you enough."

Struck with grief, Thorik sat in silence, pondering his actions and response. Darkmere was correct on all accounts. What had he done? How could he have been manipulated so easily?

A chill in the air could be felt as Lord Bredgin entered the main chamber, waiting for orders from his father.

"Bring out Bryus," Darkmere ordered.

Bredgin walked over to the living stone wall and literally stepped into the mural. Walking deeper into the inch thick stone wall carving, Bredgin opened a door. Inside stood a weather-beaten old man, shivering in his ripped up rags.

Pulling Bryus out through the door, he dragged him out of the wall carvings and into the main room before tossing him against the raised stone lip surrounding the shallow pool, opposite of Thorik's position.

Bryus had been beaten. Blood dripped from his lips, while bruises covered his exposed arms and chest. Ripped and frayed clothes exposed additional injuries as he leaned over and scooped up some water to quench his severely dry throat.

"It's time for you to conduct the ritual," Darkmere said to Bryus.

Bryus looked up at the Nums and then over to the Blothrud. Standing up, the battered man looked down at Ericc's face. "You have your father's looks." His voice was warm and calm before he turned to face Darkmere. "As I've told you, I won't be a part of killing the son of Ambrosius."

Darkmere nodded to Lord Bredgin, before addressing Bryus. "I was concerned that I wouldn't be able to persuade you to change your mind, so I've invited my son here to extricate what we need from you."

Lord Bredgin opened a small box at his side, releasing a black vapor, which molded into the shadowy form of a faceless man. It was the Wraylov, Civej.

Bryus watched as the thick shadow drifted over to him. Reaching out to push it back, his hands felt only the thickening of cold air. "Keep it away!"

Civej leaned down, grabbing Bryus' head with both hands.

Bryus screamed in terror as Civej's fingers worked their way under his skull, probing for thoughts that would allow Darkmere to complete the sacrifice without him. Critical words were needed to ensure it was done correctly. It was all in Bryus' head, waiting to be extracted.

The end of Lord Bredgin's staff lit up like a star, before it focused tightly onto Bryus' forehead. "Give us the words, show us the spell!"

"NO!" Bryus screamed. His body went rigid in pain. His face started to twitch.

Civej reached deeper into his head, pulling his memories and leaving pieces of his mind dead.

Soft at first, a light began to creep through the enormous crystal in the ceiling. The sunlight had been working its way over the Shi'Pel peak, reflecting through a crystal in the outstretched hand of the structure above them, and then down into the room. The Eve of Light soon would begin.

Darkmere motioned to his son. "We don't have time for this. Take it all from him. Kill him if you must."

Lord Bredgin pushed harder with the light to access the thoughts that Civej was releasing from the man. "Pull it all. Now! Leave nothing."

Bryus' body convulsions erupted from the unthinkable pain. It was only a matter of seconds before he would be dead and Lord Bredgin would have what he needed.

The light from above increased, shining down through the giant crystal in the ceiling, warming the altar as well as Ericc.

"Lux Specere Vocare Mori," said Bredgin. "I have extracted the words needed to conduct the sacrifice."

Santorray acknowledged the phrase and repeated it to himself a few times to memorize it.

Civej pulled his hands back from the man's head and waited for Lord Bredgin's next order.

Bryus collapsed on the floor, stiff as board, except for the twitching of his left cheek and eye.

Pointing to Ericc, Lord Bredgin gave new orders to his Wraylov. "Now, find out what he knows before we kill him."

Ericc panicked. His knowledge of Ambrosius' friends and hiding places would soon be exposed. The family who had protected him for so many years would be exposed and their lives placed in danger.

Following orders, Civej floated over to Ericc and prepared to strike.

With an unexpected crash, the main doors broke free of their hinges as Grewen and Shrii tumbled into the room. The Mognin was covered with scratches and bite marks as he continued his attempt to restrain the giant panther. They had been in a relentless battle since Thorik and Avanda had left the basement, except for one free moment when Grewen collected their gear and tried to break away. It was short-lived, however, and the attempted escape cost the Mognin large cuts down his back.

Rolling to break free, Shrii pushed Grewen into one of the porous rocks, breaking it in half. Steam burst from a large crack created by the impact, filling the room with a slight haze.

Releasing the cat for a moment, Grewen tossed Thorik his backpack and Avanda's purse of magic. In doing so, he gave Shrii the upper hand as she pounced on him, knocking him onto Santorray.

Ignoring his personal pain and tucking his broken arm to his chest, Thorik leapt for the items and grabbed his spear from his backpack. In one motion he drove the spear into the floor, setting off a shock wave that knocked everyone off their feet, except Civej.

Tossing Avanda her purse, Thorik was required to free his hand from the spear, for his other was still useless.

The Wraylov quickly moved and attacked Thorik before he could regain his weapon. With full ferocity, Civej drove one hand deep into the Num's chest and the other into his skull.

Tremendous pain exploded within the Num as every part of his body convulsed from the attack. The encounter was brutal and could not be withstood for long.

Shrii attacked Santorray as well and Grewen, for she liked neither. In doing so, she caused the Blothrud and Mognin to work together to stop her assault.

As they fought, Santorray focused more on protecting the dagger Varacon instead of slaying the giant panther.

Brimmelle ordered his family to escape during the distraction, as he began to run for the main exit with them.

Avanda reached for her purse, instead of running, and began casting spells, causing Krupes to freeze in place before they could grab the Nums. This opened a momentary path for Brimmelle and Gluic to escape.

Brimmelle reached the main doorway as he noticed his mother was no longer with him. She had stopped to help Ericc. Thorik on the other hand was in the final moments of life as the young man reached out to Brimmelle for help, just as Brimmelle's sister did several years prior. But the Fir had no way to stop Civej. The creature was too powerful, and to run back into the room ensured both of their deaths. He looked upon Thorik's face as he once did his sister's before he watched her death, dreading his options.

Gluic reached the altar. "It's time," she said to Ericc.

Ericc struggled to move. "Gluic, pull this amulet off me. It's preventing me from using my powers to help."

As she tried to do so, the table's spider legs tightened, preventing her from being able to move the amulet and chain over his head.

While she continued in her attempt to pull the legs back from Ericc, the light from the crystal in the ceiling continued to increase, intensifying its light on the altar.

Avanda turned her attention to Lord Bredgin and Darkmere with a volley of fiery rain, and spells of freezing temperatures.

The illusion of fire didn't faze either of them, and light from Bredgin's hand melted her frost spell before it could reach them.

Darkmere, on the other hand, easily altered the air around Avanda into a poisonous gas, causing her to stop her spells and gasp for air.

Meanwhile, Brimmelle could not allow the memory of Thorik's death to forever haunt his days. Pushing away from the doorway, he rushed over. Reaching Thorik, he tried to push Civej off his nephew, but his hands slid right through the shadowy form.

Civej's attack could not be stopped, so instead, Fir Brimmelle positioned himself between the Wraylov and Thorik in an attempt to save his sister's child.

Civej changed victims and began his assault on Brimmelle with the same tactic he was using the Thorik. The same results occurred as Brimmelle went into seizures.

Thorik began to revive from the torture and realized that Civej was hovering over Brimmelle. His uncle had saved his life. But by doing so he jeopardized his own. Thorik couldn't allow this to happen.

Rolling to his side, and on his broken arm, Thorik yelled in pain as he grabbed the Spear of Rummon with his free hand and then used it to pierce the shadowing form.

The heat and flame of the dragon's soul extended past the metal of the spear and into the Wraylov, vaporizing it in a series of wisps as they broke free from the creature's dark center.

The blood-curdling scream from the shadowy beast resonated against everyone's body.

The darkness then faded away. Civej was no more.

Furious, Bredgin held up his staff, focusing an intense light directly at the Num.

Still holding the spear, Thorik held up his broken arm to block the light, only to find that its strength was so intense that Thorik could see right through his own flesh, allowing him to see the broken bone beneath the surface. The burning of his skin could be felt on his face and arm as the light narrowed its width and focused its energy.

Thorik turned his back to the light, only to feel the heavy pressure on his shoulders pushing him down to the ground. Twisting back around he released the Spear of Rummon to attack the attacking lord.

Rummon took flight directly at Bredgin's head. A battle cry came forth from the spear as it flew through the air.

The power of the sun paled in comparison to the light from the end of Bredgin's staff. The light hit the spear with such force that it knocked the embedded soul of the dragon unconscious. The spear fell to the floor as any other metal rod would, for its power had not been enough to take on an E'rudite.

Around the altar, an intense light from above created a cylinder of white so bright it could not be seen through.

Darkmere ensured that Avanda would perform no additional spells as she fell to the floor, gasping for air. "Santorray! It is time for the sacrifice."

On the far end of the room, Shrii broke free of Grewen again and leaped at Santorray, pinning him under her. The Blothrud had had enough. Reaching behind him, he grabbed a large chunk of rock, which had broken free during their battle, and slammed it into the cat's head. Knocked out, the panther fell onto the Blothrud.

Shocked at the failure of the spear's attack on Bredgin, Thorik didn't know how to react until he saw the light of Bredgin's staff move toward him. Diving out of the staff's focus, Thorik tucked in his broken arm, rolled to his feet, and ran into the living wall mural. Although the carvings were only inches deep, he has able to move around inside the mural, for it had its own magical depth. Once there, he dove behind a carved boulder.

Bredgin turned in pursuit, following the Num into the stone landscape. Staff in hand, he exploded the carved scenery with intense light as he quickly went deeper into the wall, searching for the Num.

Thorik backtracked and leaped out of the mural. In doing so, he ran to the copper vat of flaming oil. Slamming his body against it, he caused it to fall.

The vat tipped over and landed upside down in the pool, extinguishing the green light, which was keeping the wall mural alive.

The mural froze in mid motion as a distant cry echoed from within it. Lord Bredgin was trapped.

Darkmere was startled by the scene of his son becoming trapped in the rock wall. Releasing Avanda, the dark lord turned to the mural and touched it with flat palms. "What have you done?"

The fierce white column of light from above made it difficult for anyone within a yard of the altar to see anything.

Free from the panther, Grewen saw his opportunity and made his way over to the altar. Feeling around inside the column of light he found the altar's restraints. He quickly began snapping off the table's spider legs to free Ericc.

Santorray raced over and attacked, hitting Grewen with his entire body, knocking the Mognin backward and off his feet.

Grabbing the virgin dagger, the Blothrud rushed back to the table to finish the job while the light was still strong.

Keeping his eyes shut to protect them from the overpowering light, Ericc removed the amulet from around his neck. It had been preventing him from using his unique abilities. He was now free to show everyone what E'rudite powers he had and to take vengeance on the man who was responsible for his parent's deaths.

But without warning, Varacon, the virgin dagger, was thrust forward by Santorray, piercing the flesh for the first time. Never had it tasted blood or felt the warmth of the inside of a body. Varacon was finally alive, at the cost of another's life.

"Lux Specere Vocare Mori," Santorray shouted from within the curtain of light.

Stepping back from the column of light, Santorray's hand was now stained with blood, his dagger no longer virgin.

A momentary flash illuminated the room as the column of light took on a nearly solid form, pulsing like a heartbeat against the altar and the surrounding area.

As fast as it had begun, the pulsing ended and the column of light returned to normal, still bright within a yard of the table.

The silence that followed was almost deafening.

Santorray lifted the bloody dagger, showing Darkmere the deed had been completed.

"The prophecy has finally come to an end," Darkmere stated with a sigh of relief, hands still resting on the mural he was trying to revive to save his son. Without the aid of the Notarian flame, it was questionable if even Darkmere could perform this task.

"No!" screamed Thorik. He had failed to keep his promise to Ambrosius. He had failed to repent for sentencing Ericc's father to death. He had failed a new friend as well as himself. Ericc had been sacrificed.

Brimmelle had regained consciousness enough to see the raised bloody dagger. "Never trust an Altered," he muttered.

Then the room suddenly began to shake. Cracks appeared in the walls, widening and dropping chunks of debris to the floor. Lord Bredgin was attempting to escape the solid rock he was encased in.

Darkmere's focus on saving his son increased. Fractures raced out from his hands, as he pressed them hard against the wall. Blocks from the upper walls began to fall, and the crystal in the ceiling was knocked out of its holder, ending the column of light before it fell and crashed down in front of the altar.

Shards shattered in every direction, as the Nums jumped for cover. Santorray and Grewen turned their back to the crash, allowing the fragments to embed in their back instead of their front.

With minimal focus, Darkmere turned the crystal pieces into water before they hit him. His attention was on freeing his own son. He would deal with the Nums later.

Returning to his feet, Thorik grabbed the Spear of Rummon and headed to the altar to collect Ericc's body before the rest of the roof collapsed. But to his astonishment, Ericc's body did not lay on the altar soaked in blood from the Varacon dagger. Instead, Gluic's body lay in his place.

"What have you done?" Thorik screamed at Santorray.

"Mother?" Brimmelle screamed in horror, racing over to her.

Santorray's eyes grew wide, exposing his astonishment at the accident. The blood dripping off his dagger was that of the old Num instead of the young man. "What? This can't be!"

Ericc appeared out of nowhere, just behind Darkmere. A blade in his hand, he stabbed the thin man in the back.

Shocked, Darkmere fell forward against the wall mural. He hadn't anticipated this. However, he wouldn't submit easily.

Reaching behind him, Darkmere grabbed his attacker's hand and used his powers to burn the boy's skin. By the time the dark lord had turned to see who his attacker was, Ericc was gone.

Ericc had vanished, but he reappeared behind Darkmere again, stabbing him a second time with his blade, this time below his shoulder blade.

Expanding from the wall mural, a veil of darkness covered the area as Bredgin attempted to crumble the wall from within. In doing so, he unintentionally surrounded Darkmere and Ericc in the deep shadows as well.

Darkmere fell onto the ground from Ericc's assault as well as his son's darkness sucking his life from him. He could overcome the dark but he doubted his attacker could. Rolling onto his side, he changed the air between him and the wall into poisonous gas, hoping to prevent his assailant from escaping the dark dread.

Ericc choked from the poison and vanished again, this time appearing near the altar. Grabbing a fallen piece of ceiling block, he threw it into the dark void, hoping to hit the Dark Lord.

Momentarily suppressing his grief of Gluic's death, Thorik turned to Ericc. "We need to get out of here before the entire building comes down on us."

However, Ericc had only one thing on his mind, and that was revenge.

The shaking of the floor woke Bryus from his earlier attack. He gathered what thoughts he still had, stood up, and then stumbled about as he made his way for the exit. Several Krupes had arrived and blocked his path. A quick wave of his hand and some verbal commands set off a spell which caused every Krupe in the room to scream in pain as they attempted to cover their ears.

"Avanda, follow him while the Krupes are occupied," Thorik yelled, pulling Brimmelle off his mother. "There isn't much time, we need to flee."

"I'm not leaving mother in this unholy place."

"Save yourself and Avanda," Thorik ordered as he pushed Brimmelle from the scene before waving the giant over. "I'll get Ericc while Grewen carries Gluic."

Brimmelle looked up to make sure the Mognin was on his way before grabbing Avanda's hand and racing for the exit.

Thorik tossed his pack over a shoulder and moved to grab Ericc. But before Grewen could reach Gluic, a large section of ceiling fell onto her body, crushing it and sending rock fragments in every direction.

Several pieces hit Thorik, knocking him to the ground. By the time he regained his footing, Ericc had disappeared and Grewen was lifting the large stone off Gluic's body. To Thorik's horror, her torso had been crushed. She was beyond all hope.

The sight etched itself into Thorik's memory. She had always been there for him. Her healing ways went beyond her abilities with stones and crystals. She had given him so much and had advised him so often that he didn't know how he could go on without her.

As hard as it was, his emotional tribute to his grandmother would have to wait. More ceiling sections began to fall as Thorik waved Grewen instructions to leave his dear grandmother's body and escape while he still could.

Thorik wasn't even sure if he would have time to exit as the room crumbled apart. But he had to look one last time for Ericc. And there he was, on the far side of the room, beyond the heavy dust and falling debris, being held captive by Santorray.

"Santorray!" Thorik screamed in anger as he began to charge toward them. But his movement was stopped by a section of the wall giving way, falling on top of Ericc and the Blothrud, covering their bodies with several feet of stone blocks. They, like his grandmother, had been crushed.

Thorik knew he didn't have time to move the fallen wall even if Grewen was still in the room to help him. "I've failed", he said to himself as the other walls began to give way. "What have I done?"

Rushing to the exit, he stopped for one look back to see some signs of life from Ericc, but instead he saw more rock crumble down from above.

Reluctantly, Thorik finally raced down the stairwell, quickly catching up to his group as they returned to the first floor.

The skeletons in the walls and ceiling swayed back and forth from the collapsing building, many of them falling onto the floor.

Grewen hunched over to block the majority of the debris from falling directly onto the Nums as they ran for safety. Blocks pounded hard against his back as the building structure's entrance was beginning to cave in.

Running across the large main foyer, time was not on their side. Blocks plummeted in front of the exit, far too fast to dodge while making an escape.

Grewen pushed his way forward. Bending over, he made a safe area for the Nums to pass, while his back took the beating of his life as he held up the doorway.

Brimmelle helped Avanda under Grewen and over the fallen blocks to safety. The two Nums rushed over across the open courtyard to where Bryus stood, watching the structure collapse in upon itself.

As Thorik moved under Grewen, the doorway's keystone snapped and the structural wall fell upon Grewen's shoulders. He was trapped, and so would Thorik be if he didn't leap out to safety.

"Jump, Grewen!" Thorik tugged on the giant's arm.

Grewen's legs trembled from the weight. His back cracked as he moaned from the pain. "Get away from the building," Grewen said in a deeper than normal voice.

But Thorik refused to leave, even as the upper levels began to rain down on the courtyard outside. "No, I'm not losing you again."

Grewen knew this Num far too well to argue with him, so instead, the Mognin removed one hand from his knee long enough to swat the Num out into the courtyard, and out of danger.

Thorik rolled to a stop before looking up to see his dear friend hold the doorway open long enough to say goodbye.

Grewen released the blocks on his shoulder, allowing them to collapse on him.

"Grewen!" screamed Thorik.

As the blocks fell down on him, Grewen was propelled out of the doorway and into the courtyard. Santorray, who had slammed his own body up against the Mognin's backside, had pushed him out.

Grewen and Santorray rolled across the yard to a safe distance from the building.

Thorik rushed over to Santorray and pointed his spear to the Blothrud's head. "I don't know if I should thank you for saving Grewen or kill you betraying Granna and Ericc. Perhaps both."

Santorray brushed the dust and debris from his face as he growled. "You fool! You nearly ruined everything!"

Chapter 40
Truths Revealed

Surod imploded with a crash that echoed throughout Go'ta Gorge. The ribs of the structure were gone, as well as the upper section that had looked like a hand reaching to the sky. It was all destroyed, now nothing more than a pile of rubble.

Brimmelle held Avanda tight in disbelief of losing his mother. The shock of her death left him unable to speak as he attempted to cope. Grewen's approach to console him wasn't even noticed by the dazed Num.

Firmly controlled by his good arm, Thorik's spear was still within striking distance as he pointed it at the Blothrud's face. "What do you mean by blaming me? How did I ruin anything when it was you who deceived us?"

Santorray sat up, brushing more dust off his shoulders. "First of all, if you don't get that spear out of my face, I'm going to break it over your head."

Knowing Santorray's quick reflexes and long reach, Thorik backed up. "You killed Ericc!"

"No, he's not dead."

Thorik was stunned by the comment. "I saw you. Ericc died in your grasp as you held him for Darkmere. You've betrayed us all."

"I grabbed him to pull him away from his attack on Darkmere. To help him escape, whether he wanted to or not. But he vanished as the wall fell onto us."

"I don't believe you!"

"I don't care!" the Blothrud barked back.

"I know you killed my grandmother! That I saw with my own eyes. How could you? After everything we've been through?"

"If you hadn't shown up, this wouldn't have happened, and she would have been fine."

"Then you would have murdered Ericc. How is that less of a betrayal?"

"No one would have died if you had kept your Num nose out of it."

"You don't consider sacrificing Ericc as a death?"

"Not if I had stabbed him with this!" Santorray pulled out the once virgin dagger, still covered with Gluic's wet blood.

"Varacon," Bryus said from the back as he approached the Blothrud, stopping once as a facial twitch froze up the rest of his body. "Is it truly her?"

"Yes."

Thorik looked back and forth between Santorray and Bryus. "What's a Varacon?"

Licking his lips, Bryus' fingers wiggled in the air with the anticipation of touching the dagger. "Varacon, the virgin dagger," he said to Thorik. "You know the song. *Created for his love, hoping to never see the day, when his blade is used, life won't fade away...*" Humming the next chorus, he smiled as he waited for them to sing along.

Thorik was not in the singing mood. "My grandmother is dead and we're talking about a dagger that has its own song?"

Looking at Santorray, Bryus laughed and slapped the Blothrud on his ass. "You fooled everyone, didn't you? Even Darkmere. Pretty clever for a Blothrud, I must say."

Thorik turned the spear toward Bryus. "Who are you?"

"Bryus Grum is the name. Prominent of EverSpring. Well, former Prominent." His outstretched hand to Thorik went without being shaken.

"What do you know about Santorray's betrayal?" Thorik asked.

"Oh, yes, very clever. Nearly pulled a fast one on everyone." Bryus' words were slightly slurred and he breathed hard as he tried to get them out correctly. The attack from Civej had done more damage than he was letting on.

Thorik pushed the spear up toward Bryus. "Enough with the games!" he yelled, gripping his weapon tightly, waking the dragon's unconscious soul from the attack by Bredgin.

Hot dragon's breath slowly poured off the end of spear with a slight sulfur smell to it. A low growl came from deep within the spear. Thorik knew the creature inside had returned.

Thorik made sure he had Bryus' attention as he poked the end of the spear near the man's face. "What are you two talking about?"

Bryus Grum's eyes crossed as he looked at the end of the spear, now only inches from his nose. "By the powers of Ergrauth, I never thought I'd live to see with my own eyes such a sight. Is this the Spear of Rummon?"

Thorik held it firm and ready to strike. "Yes."

"Amazing!" Bryus was overjoyed at the Num's answer. "Tell me, where did you find it? Who had it all these years? What powers does it possess? Do tell, do tell."

Thorik was getting more upset as Bryus became more overcome with excitement. Not getting anywhere with his conversation, he turned the focus back to the Blothrud. "Santorray, I demand to know what's going on!" Thorik shouted.

Santorray stood up, holding the dagger before him. "This is Varacon."

"Oh, yes, it certainly is," Bryus said with glee, as his facial tick momentarily froze his body.

Santorray ignored Bryus' commentary and continued. "I came here to stab Ericc with it, in front of Darkmere, to ensure the dark lord saw the boy's death."

Thorik shook his head. "No, you've been working for Darkmere all this time."

"It is true that I worked for the dark lord once, a long time ago. However, I led him to believe I was still loyal to him. It was the only way I could execute my plan."

Bryus slapped his knee at the joke. "What a ruse."

Thorik found no joke in the Blothrud's words. "You were planning this the entire time."

"Yes, I was."

"That's why you stayed with us, because you knew we'd lead you to him."

"Correct." Santorray's answers where sharp off his tongue. He was not pleased about Thorik ruining his plans.

Bryus swiveled his head back and forth with excitement as he watched the volley of words being passed between them.

"You used us." Thorik's hand, which held the spear, trembled with anger.

"I did."

"Everything you told us was a lie."

"No, everything I told you was true."

"How can that be? Why would a friend of Ambrosius try to kill his son?"

"For the sake of Ericc," Santorray grumbled as he clinched his teeth.

"Killing him would save him?"

"That's correct."

Bryus clapped. "Keep going, lad. You're almost there."

Thorik's focus was so intent of Santorray, he didn't even hear the man's words. "How is Ericc's death considered to be the same as saving him?"

"I was only going to kill his body, not his soul."

"And how did you plan on accomplished this?"

Santorray lifted the dagger higher. "With Varacon, the soul snatcher."

Bryus screamed with delight that the secret was out as he danced around and mumbled the song again to himself.

Thorik looked at the bloody dagger as he pieced his thoughts together. "Your plan was to stab Ericc in front of Darkmere to make him believe that Ambrosius' son was dead and prophecy had ended. Darkmere would then stop hunting Ericc. But what kind of soul deserves to be trapped in a weapon?"

The Spear of Rummon grew hot only for a moment in Thorik's hand to remind his master of its own fate. Tempted to change hands, he quickly felt the reminder of deep pain when he moved his broken arm.

Santorray shook his head. "This was only to be a temporary exile; his soul would eventually be placed back into a new body. One that Darkmere would not see as a threat."

"How did you plan to do this?"

"I don't have that kind of power. I did my part; it would be up to…" Santorray realized he spoke more than he had planned.

"Your part?" Thorik asked. "Who are you working with? Who was to complete the second part of this mission?"

"We are friends of Ambrosius. We look out for his affairs."

Thorik demanded to know more. "Who do you refer to? Who sent you on this mission?"

Pulling back his shoulders, Santorray looked into the Num's serious eyes. "My contact is Draquol."

"Draq? He's alive?"

"Yes."

"We are friends with Draq. We traveled with him while venturing with Ambrosius. Why didn't you come forward and let me know what you were planning?"

"We couldn't trust you knowing. It was too large of a risk. Darkmere and his son have many ways of getting information out of people. Which is why you must never discuss this or write of it in your journals. No evidence must exist of his escape. Your journals in the wrong hands could be dangerous. The boy's life would be at risk if Darkmere found out."

"But by not telling me, you've killed my grandmother."

Bryus stepped in between them. "No, no. Only her body, not her soul."

Looking the blade over, the Num wondered if it could be true. Could his grandmother's soul be trapped inside the weapon? Reaching back with his good arm, he placed his spear in the loops along the side of his pack to store it. He then pulled his grandmother's broken crystals from his pocket and recited the phrase she said to him. "Not an ending, just a fresh beginning in a new form. We will be carried to a greater purpose."

The words broke Brimmelle out of his intense trance of grief. "That's what mother said about her broken crystal."

Thorik disagreed. "No, she was telling us about what she had seen for her own destiny. This dagger provides her an opportunity to move into a new body to fulfill a new purpose." After dropping the crystals back in his pocket, Thorik reach up for the dagger, as Santorray allowed him to have it. "We will take the dagger back and you will extract her, just as you had planned to do for Ericc," Thorik said to Santorray.

Santorray picked rocks out of the hair on his legs as he shook his head. "I'm not going anywhere until I find Ericc and make sure he is safe. In spite of your interference, Darkmere still thinks I killed Ericc, for he knows not who attacked him. His search for the boy should end, unless Ericc resurfaces again. So, I need to reach him before that happens."

"I thought Darkmere was dead."

Santorray looked back over his shoulder at the rubble. "It will take more than that to end an E'rudite's life. Ericc disappeared as the wall collapsed. So, he could be anywhere."

"How far can he travel like that?"

Santorray was irritated that his search was starting all over again. "Depending on how far his E'rudite abilities have progressed, he could potentially have shifted locations to anywhere he has already been. He could have returned to the home along the Ki'Volney Lake, or to Rava'Kor in Southwind. Who knows, perhaps his ability only allowed him to jump past the next mountain ridge."

"But how about Gluic?"

"I have my priorities, Thorik." Stress of failing in his own mission came through his voice. "She'll stay safe in Varacon, as long as you don't draw new blood with it again."

"Why?"

"I don't know. Just don't do it. I'm not an Alchemist!" Santorray barked.

Bryus jumped in with excitement. "But I am! I can tell you why it shouldn't draw blood, how it should be handled, how to keep her soul at ease, how to-"

Thorik interrupted the man from going on and on. "Can you tell me how to release my grandmother from this dagger so she can live among us again?"

A strong twitch held his face tight for a moment before he could speak. "Well, of course!"

"Excellent." Thorik held out the dagger toward Bryus. "Please do so," he ordered with some urgency in his voice.

"Not here." Bryus laughed. "We need to go get Vesik first."

"Who is Vesik? Another Alchemist?"

"No, no, silly Num. Vesik is a book. *The* book, for us in spell casting. Vesik is the master book of spells, created by Irluk herself."

"The Death Witch?"

"Yes. Well, no. Before she became the Death Witch. When she was young and ruled magic across our lands."

"So, you have this book?"

Bryus laughed. "No one *has* Vesik. It is of its own cognizance."

"Do you at least know where Vesik is?"

"Of course, I know where it is. I'd have to be daft to even bring up the idea if I didn't know where it was."

Thorik tucked the dagger away and turned to Santorray. "I've fulfilled my promise to Ambrosius. I've prevented Ericc's sacrifice.

In fact, no one will ever be sacrificed at Surod again. It is now time for me to take care of my own family."

"Understood, Sec," Santorray replied, his tone had lowered as his temper faded. "You truly have the heart of a Blothrud. Fight for what's right and you'll do just fine."

"Are you sure you won't come with us?"

"No. I need to find out if Bredgin survived the collapse before I return to the valleys below."

Thorik nodded, before spitting in his hand and holding it out to Santorray. "Good luck in finding Ericc."

Santorray smiled, spit in his own hand, and shook the Nums little hand. "May Ovlan walk your path."

With that, they parted ways. Santorray climbed onto the rubble to start his dig, while Thorik led his group down the mountainside. The destroyed bridge was no longer an option to leave the area.

"Where is Vesik located?" Thorik asked Bryus.

"Govi Glade."

"That sounds nice."

Bryus nodded his head with a smile and twitch. "Yes, I wish that were true."

Chapter 41
Strategies

Draq flapped his red-tipped wings hard to crest the Haplorhini Mountain Range and enter the Kings Valley. It had been a long flight for the dragon with news of Santorray's quest.

Diving into the valley, he soared past the thousand-foot tall Mountain King statue, its head and hands lying in the lake near the King's feet. The statue and the mountain it was carved from stood in contrast to the rich greens of the surrounding trees and grass. The atmosphere was always spiritually uplifting.

Vapors from the warm mineral water of the lake filled Draq's lungs as he flew just feet above its surface on the way to the carved city of Kingsfoot. The water had special properties that rejuvenated and healed. Just being in its presence caused one to feel fresh, calm, and clear headed.

Passing the docks, Draq approached the terraced open garden area preceding the city's main entrance. A wide staircase connected each terrace from the base stone courtyard up to the carved city walls.

On the top terrace was a man sitting among the plants. His untidy mahogany hair flowed down past his shoulders and his once trimmed beard was now scruffy. The cloak he wore was weathered and half his face showed signs of a burn nearly healed.

Draq landed near the man, perching on the ledge of the terrace wall. "Darkmere and his son have witnessed Ericc's sacrifice. Surod has been destroyed, therefore the prophecy has ended."

The man sat in the dirt near the plant he was tending to. He was missing both feet and the fingers from one hand, but it did not prevent him from pulling the weeds and cutting off stressed branches. "Where is Ericc now?"

"He was not captured by Varacon. He has escaped."

"Has Santorray located him yet?" the man questioned, never turning from his duties.

"He is in pursuit."

"I see." He dusted the rich soil off his hands. "I believe it is time I got to know my son again. Have Santorray bring him here once he has found Ericc."

"Ambrosius, do think this is wise? You are not fully healed from Darkmere's attack. What if they are followed by his minions or the dark lord himself?"

"As powerful as this lake is, the waters are slow at bringing back my limbs, but we cannot wait any longer. The hunt will start over again if Ericc is found to be alive." Ambrosius stopped to ensure his work was complete as he recalled helping Fir Beltrow cover this very plant to protect it from a past harsh winter. "Besides, I have protected him long enough. It is time he stood at my side with pride instead of in hiding with fear and anger."

"He will not be as warm to the idea as you may hope."

"We have no choice. War is coming and we must prepare. Grab the wooden box next to my chair and bring it out to me."

"Yes, my master."

Draq had difficulty walking; his body simply wasn't designed for it with his arms built into his wings and his back legs designed to perch and attack. Regardless, he still had all of his parts, unlike his friend Ambrosius, so he ventured into the city and collected the box.

Upon returning, Draq found his master sitting on a bench near the city's entrance. "Here you are, my lord," he said, setting it in his lap. "Is it wise that we rest so much on the shoulders of a Num without him even knowing we are depending on him?"

Ambrosius opened up the wooden coffer to find a pile of papers with notes and maps drawn on them. Scanning through the sheets, he pulled one out. "He can't know. We must trust his judgment."

They watched as the paper in his hand began to show new markings. It was filling in notes before their very eyes as though an invisible scribe sat with them.

"When did you realize Thorik had the other coffer?" Draq asked.

"I noticed it just before we reached Weirfortus. But it wasn't until after my battle with Darkmere that I realized what it was."

Draq leaned over to view the new writings. "If Thorik ever found out that the journals he places in his wooden box are recorded in the coffer's twin, he would never trust you again."

"It's imperative that he doesn't find out."

"The Num trusts you and continues to mourn your death."
"Which is exactly why he must not find out the truth."

Chapter 42
Lucian's Return

Four Southwind soldiers marched down the corridor at a pace shy of a run. Their boots echoed in unison like the beat of drums preparing an audience for the arrival of the protagonist in a play. Their steps continued to increase in speed until they stopped abruptly at two large wooden doors.

They waited in silence for the doors to be opened from the inside. Once they did, the four soldiers advanced to the center of the large room and tossed their cargo onto the floor.

A groan came from within the large sack, which they had deposited. Moving slowly, a man from within kicked his way free and shed the cloth's confines. His hands and legs were tied with rope. He struggled to speak, for his tongue and lips had been severely burnt. His eyes had been damaged so extensively from a fire that he could only see shadows with one eye. Hearing was the only sense that still functioned properly.

"Welcome back, Lucian," the Matriarch said. "Did you kill Santorray?"

Lucian lowered his head. "He still lives," he slurred out with great pain in his throat.

"Ah." She rested on the back of her chair as she crossed her ankles. "And Santorray was able to burn your face with a troop of Southwind's finest at your side?"

"He had help. A Num named Thorik Dain helped him escape from the mines. It was this same Num that did this to me." He coughed several times as he tried to answer.

Amused, she asked him to elaborate, knowing the pain he received each time he talked. "Your squad could not fight a Blothrud and a Num?"

"We were attacked by an army of Del'Unday. Corrock is on the move again."

"What happened to Santorray and Thorik?"

He lifted himself up onto his knees. "Escaped."

"How could you let them escape?"

"They had help. Other Nums as well as Ericc."

"Ericc? You saw Ambrosius' son and didn't die trying to bring him back to me?"

"Santorray and Thorik are protecting him."

Stepping down from her throne, she exclaimed, "You fool. You've cost me my youth!" Grabbing one of the copper plates of food from her servant, she swung it hard, hitting him in the head and knocking him to the ground. "Ericc was my gift to present to Darkmere. I need Ericc!"

Furious, she pounded his head with the plate several more times before tossing it onto the ground.

Waiting for her to end the assault, Lucian kept his hands over his head to protect himself, while everyone else in the room waited for her tantrum to be over.

Snatching a lantern from the nearest column, she began pouring out the oil onto his legs. "It saddens me, for I ask for so little," she reasoned with herself. "I give simple orders and priorities so you can understand them. You just don't listen."

Lucian could smell the oil and began to rise to prevent her from lighting him on fire, but was stopped short as she stomped down hard onto his leg, breaking it with a loud snap.

With the oil now soaked into his pants, she lit his feet on fire. "Don't you dare move." She ordered.

Others in the chamber looked on, fearful of appearing as a sympathizer if they would turn their heads from the torture.

The flames lapped at his lower legs as he began to feel the singe from the heat. "Please, no. I promise I'll do whatever you want."

She was cold in her response. "I *want* you to stay still. Stop moving."

He continued to try to appease her. Perhaps she would put out the flames if he did as she asked. But the heat was unbearable and his skin was starting to catch on fire. The smell of burning flesh filled the hall as the flame engulfed his feet up to his knees.

Trembling to prevent any movement, he asked forgiveness. Not receiving it, he screamed and began trying to put the flames out with his hands.

"You just don't listen." She cracked the bent up metal plate against his head one more time. "You don't trust me enough to do as

I tell you. I take care of your family. Is your trust too much to ask in return?"

"I trust you!" he screamed, stiffening his body to prevent himself from moving.

"Do you?"

"Yes!"

"Are you sure?"

"Yes!"

"Then don't move and don't speak."

The fire spread up his thighs and waist. The smell became repulsive and the sight revolting. The man stayed straight as an arrow, trusting that the Matriarch would put out the flames any second. The pain had past the threshold of understanding as he shook and convulsed from the trauma.

The Matriarch glanced at her audience of guards, servants, and advisers. Many couldn't take the sight any longer and had closed their eyes or turned their heads. The smell of burning flesh added to the horrifying scene. She had proven her point as to what it meant to fail her.

"Put him out," she ordered and waited for her men to fetch buckets of water before finishing her sentence, "...on my command."

Lucian heard the words and continued to live the torture. His body started shutting down. He no longer could feel anything or smell his own flaming skin. Only his brain remained active as the Matriarch waited until his entire body was in a blaze.

But before his heart stopped, she had her men dowse Lucian's body.

"Remove him from here. String him up on the street to send others a message about not obeying my orders," she said calmly. "And clean up this filth."

Her men removed Lucian immediately while other servants began to clean up the mess left on the floor.

"Hire a bounty hunter and two assassins," she told her lead bodyguard. "I want Ericc captured, but I want Santorray and Thorik Dain killed."

Pronunciation Guide

CHARACTERS

Ambrosius: aeM-brO-zee-ahs
Asentar: as-en-Tar
Avanda: ah-Van-Dah
Bakalor: Bah-Kah-Lor
Bredgin: Brehd-gehn
Brimmelle: Brim-'ell
Bryus: brI-us
Civej: si-vehj
Darkmere: Dark-Meer
Deleth: deL-'eth
Draq: draK
Emilen: ehM-il-eN
Ericc: ehR-iK
Feshlan: FehSH-Lahn
Gluic: Glu-iK
Grewen: Gru-'en
Hessik: HehS-ehK
Irluk: uhR-luhK
Lucian: Loo-sE-ehn
Ovlan: ahV-lahN
Rummon: Rum-mahN
Santorray: sahn-ToR-rAY
Thorik: Thor-iK
Varacon: Vahr-ah-Kahn

LOCATIONS

Corrock: koR-RahK
Cuev'Laru Mountains: Koo-ehV Lah-Roo
Cucurrian River: Koo-kuR-ee-uhn
Doven: dO-ven
Kiri: kE-rE
Lu'Tythis: Loo-Tith-is
Pelonthal: peL-ahn-THahl
Rumaldo: Roo-mahL-dO
Trewek: trU-ek

Pronunciation Guide

SPECIES

Blothrud (AKA Ruds): BlahTH-Ruhd

> *7' to 9' tall; Bony hairless Dragon/Wolf-like head; Red muscular human torso and arms; Sharp spikes extend out across shoulder blades, back of arms, and back of hands; Red hair covered waist and over two thick strong wolf legs. Blothruds are typically the highest class of the Del'Undays.*

Del'Unday: DeL-OOn-Day

> *The Del'Unday are a collection of Altered Creatures who live in structured communities with rules and strong leadership.*

Fesh'Unday: FehSH-OOn-Day

> *The Fesh'Unday are all of the Altered Creatures that roam freely without societies.*

Gathler: GahTH-ler

> *6' to 8' tall; Hunched over giant sloth-like face and body; Gathlers are the spiritual leaders of the Ov'Undays.*

Human: Hyoo-muhn

> *5' to 6' tall; pale to dark complexion; weight varies from anorexic to obese. Most live within the Dovenar Kingdom.*

Krupes: KrooP

> *6' to 8' tall; Covered from head to toe in black armor, these thick and heavy bipedal creatures move slow but are difficult to defeat. Few have seen what they look like under their armor. Krupes are the soldiers of the Del'Unday.*

Mognin (AKA Mogs): MahG-Nen

> *10' to 12' tall; Mognins are the tallest of the Ov'Unday.*

Myth'Unday: Meeth-OOn-Day

> *The Myth'Unday are a collection of Creatures brought to life by altering nature's plants and insects.*

Ov'Unday: ahv-OOn-Day

> *The Ov'Unday are a collection of Altered Creatures who believe in living as equals in peaceful communities.*

Polenum (AKA Nums): Pol-uhn-um

> *4' to 5' tall; Human-like features; Very pale skin; Soul-markings cover their bodies in thin or thick lines as they mature. Exceptional Eyesight.*

37975086R00153

Made in the USA
Charleston, SC
28 January 2015